TRACIE PETERSON
AND
JUDITH MILLER

A TAPESTRY
OF HOPE

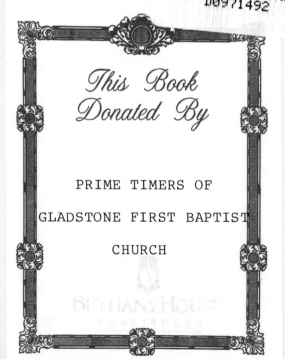

This Book
Donated By

PRIME TIMERS OF

GLADSTONE FIRST BAPTIST

CHURCH

BETHANYHOUSE
PUBLISHERS

A Tapestry of Hope
Copyright © 2004
Tracie Peterson and Judith Miller

Cover design by Dan Thornberg

Unless otherwise identified, Scripture quotations are from the King James Version of the Bible.

Published by Bethany House Publishers
11400 Hampshire Avenue South
Bloomington, Minnesota 55438
www.bethanyhouse.com

Bethany House Publishers is a Division of
Baker Book House Company, Grand Rapids, Michigan.

Printed in the United States of America

ISBN 0-7642-2894-3 (Trade Paper)
ISBN 0-7642-2910-9 (Large Print)

Library of Congress Cataloging-in-Publication Data

Peterson, Tracie.
    A tapestry of hope / by Tracie Peterson and Judith Miller.
        p.   cm. — (Lights of Lowell ; 1)
      ISBN 0-7642-2894-3 (pbk.) —ISBN 0-7642-2910-9 (large-print pbk.)
      1. Irish American women—Fiction. 2. Indentured servants—Fiction. 3. Textile industry—Fiction. 4. Lowell (Mass.)—Fiction. 5. Married women—Fiction.
I. McCoy-Miller, Judith. II. Title III. Series: Peterson, Tracie. Lights of Lowell ; 1.
    PS3566.E7717T37   2004
    813'.54—dc22   2004001022

To Ann Dunn—
my dear Proverbs 17:17 friend.
Thanks for your love and prayers.
Judy

Proverbs 17:17
A friend loves at all times. . . .

Special Thanks
To Retired Colonel and Mrs. Walt Hylander
of Rosewood Plantation, *Lorman, Mississippi,*
for their insight and hospitality.

TRACIE PETERSON is a popular speaker and bestselling author who has written over fifty books, both historical and contemporary fiction. Tracie and her family make their home in Montana.

Visit Tracie's Web site at: *www.traciepeterson.com*.

JUDITH MILLER is an award-winning author whose avid research and love for history are reflected in her novels, many of which have appeared on the CBA bestseller lists. Judy and her husband make their home in Topeka, Kansas.

Visit Judy's Web site at: *www.judithmccoymiller.com*.

CHAPTER · 1

May 1846, Lorman, Mississippi

THE TEMPERATURE was unseasonably hot, insufferably repressive. By all accounts, springtime had scarcely arrived in Mississippi, but nature's cruel trick was going unnoticed by no one, including the residents of The Willows plantation.

Jasmine Wainwright flattened herself against the bedroom wall, her right arm wedged against the red oak window frame. She wriggled in protest when a tickling bead of perspiration inched its way down her narrowed shoulders. Taking great care, she lifted the lace curtain between two fingers and peeked below. "I see a carriage arriving, Mammy. It must be Papa's houseguests. I'm tempted to pretend I have a headache and remain in my room. I know he plans to show me off like prize cotton from the season's first picking."

Mammy stood by Jasmine's dressing table with her arms folded across her ample bosom. "Um hum. Well, you don't know fer sure what your papa got in mind, but iffen you don't set yourself down, supper's gonna be over and dem visitors be gone afore I get a chance to fix your curls."

Jasmine glanced at the plump servant who had been her caregiver since birth and knew she could remain a few more moments before provoking Mammy. The old woman's gaze had not yet grown stern. "Just let me get a glimpse of them first. I'd like an idea of who will greet me when I descend the stairs. Oh, look, Mammy! One of them is nearly as old as Papa, but the other appears much younger—and more handsome."

"I thought you weren't lookin' fer no husband."

"I'm *not*! But Papa seems determined to marry me off." She pulled the curtain back a bit farther and continued spying on the two men. "The younger one has a kind face."

The familiar sound of Mammy slapping the hairbrush on her open palm captured Jasmine's attention. "Oh, all right. I only wanted one more look," she said while scurrying back to the dressing table. "The older man looks rather austere and rigid. Perhaps he's the younger man's father."

She plopped down and stared into the oval mirror as Mammy plunged her thick fingers in and out of Jasmine's heavy golden-brown hair, coaxing the strands into perfectly formed ringlets. Perspiration trickled down the sides of the black woman's face and dripped onto her bodice, leaving her cotton dress dotted with wet spots.

"Chile, I ain't never gonna get these curls fixed proper if you don't quit flutterin' that fan back and forth. Jest when I think I got one curl fixed all nice an' proper, you go whipping that fan around and stirring up a whirlwind. And quit that frowning. Them creases you's making in your forehead is gonna turn into wrinkles. You gonna look like your grandma afore you turn twenty if you don' stop making dem faces."

Jasmine giggled.

"Ain't funny, chile. When you's gone and got yourself all wrinkled and can't find no man to marry you, what you gonna do then? Come runnin' to Mammy, 'spectin' me to make you look young and purty?"

Jasmine met Mammy's stern gaze in the mirror's reflection. "I'm sorry," she said while grasping the servant's roughened hand and drawing it against her own soft, powdered cheek. "But since I don't want a man, I don't suppose it matters very much if I wrinkle my face," she added with another giggle.

8

"You bes' get that out o' your mind. 'Sides, I's hoping to see you bring some little babes into this house one day. Maybe I'll be takin' care o' them too."

Jasmine flushed at the remark. "Whatever would I do without you, Mammy?"

"Don't know, chile, but ain't no need to worry 'bout that. I ain't made plans to meet my Maker jes' yet. 'Course, He may have some different ideas. But if so, He ain't told your ole Mammy. And since I ain't never plannin' to be parted from you any other way, I's thinkin' we'll be together for a spell o' time." The servant gave a hearty chuckle, her ample figure jiggling up and down in tempo as she laughed. "We better hurry or you gonna be late to supper for sure. Then we both be in trouble. Anyways, that's as good as them curls is gonna get for now. This hot, damp weather makin' everything limp, including your hair."

Jasmine checked her appearance in the mirror one last time, patted the ringlets, and rose from the cushioned chair. "You won't get in trouble, Mammy. I'm here to protect you." She pulled the woman into a tight hug, her slender arms barely spanning the old servant's broad waist. "Besides, after all these years, you know Papa is all bluster and bristle. He'd never lay a hand on anyone."

"Um hum, you jes' go on thinkin' that, child."

Jasmine loosened her hold and leaned back. She looked deep into the old woman's eyes. "Whatever do you mean?"

"You never know. Your pappy might jes' decide you're still young enough to turn over his knee." The words were followed by another deep-throated laugh. "Now get on downstairs and be nice to your papa's visitors."

"You know they'll bore me. Papa's visitors always want to talk about business matters instead of entertaining topics."

"Well, hot as it is this evenin', you know your pappy's bound to be in bad humor. He don't like this heat—never has."

"He complains about the heat every summer. I don't under-stand why Papa doesn't move us north with Grandmother."

"How he gonna do that? Can't move this cotton plantation up there where it's cold. 'Sides, your papa stays here 'cause this here is his home. He wouldn't live nowhere else. Even if he could, can't nobody get your mama out o' this house anymore."

Jasmine's brown eyes momentarily clouded. "I convinced her to go to White Sulphur Springs two years ago."

The old servant's head bobbed up and down. "Um hum. And she convinced all of you to return home only three days after you got there. Your mama doin' some better this past year, though."

"It's her headaches," Jasmine commented.

"It's her fears," Mammy corrected. "I don' know—maybe that's what causes her headaches. But your mama's been full of fears ever since I knowed her. Yes, sir. Being afraid, that's her real problem. Don' know what she thinks is gonna happen outside this here house." The old woman shook her head back and forth. Her forehead creased and formed a deep V between her wide-set eyes. "Um, um, it's a terrible thing to be so afraid of life."

Jasmine knew her father wouldn't care for Mammy's forthrightness, especially in regard to the mistress of the plantation. But Jasmine wouldn't forbid Mammy to address the matter. At least Mammy was honest with her, saying the things that others thought but refused to confide.

Jasmine shook her head at the frustrating situation. "But she's been doing much better managing the household this past year. I've not been required to help her nearly so much."

Mammy patted Jasmine's narrow shoulder. "You's right, chile. She is doin' better." Mammy seemed to realize Jasmine needed encouragement. "'Sides, the Good Lord, He done give us His promise to never leave us or forsake us. He won't be desertin' us now."

Jasmine smiled. Kindness shone in the devoted servant's eyes as their gazes locked. "What about you, Mammy? Wouldn't you like to live somewhere besides Mississippi?"

"Don't reckon I need to be givin' much thought to such a notion. The Willows is where I been livin' most all my life, and it's where I'll die. Don't know why we're even talkin' 'bout such a thing, 'specially when you need to go get yourself downstairs. You's jes' tryin' to avoid going down to supper."

Jasmine flashed a smile that brightened her whole face. "You never know where God might take you, Mammy. You're always singing that song about meeting Jesus." Her words grew distant as she raced down the stairs with her blue silk gown swaying in quickstep rhythm while she descended the spiral staircase. However, one stern look from Madelaine Wainwright slowed Jasmine's pace.

All eyes were focused upon her as she entered the parlor. She looked at her father. His normal pleasant demeanor appeared to have escaped him this evening. He pulled on his fob and removed the gold watch from his vest pocket, giving the timepiece a fleeting look. "I was beginning to wonder if you were going to join us."

"I apologize for rushing down the stairs—and for my tardiness. I hurried only because I didn't want to further delay dinner."

Her lips curved into what she hoped was an apologetic smile before her gaze settled on one of her father's guests. He was grinning back at her.

"Jasmine, I'd like to introduce you to Bradley and Nolan Houston. They've come from Massachusetts."

The words brought a broad smile to her lips. "Massachusetts? Oh, but this is wonderful. Do you live in Lowell? My grandmother lives in Lowell. Perhaps you know her? Alice Wainwright?"

Malcolm Wainwright cleared his throat and moved to his daughter's side. "I believe we would like to go in for supper, Jasmine. You can interrogate our guests once they've had something to eat. You'll recall that we've been awaiting your arrival."

Jasmine's three brothers were all smirking at their father's riposte when Bradley Houston stepped forward and drew near to her side. He didn't appear quite so old as she had first thought when she spied him from the upstairs window, and when he smiled, the sternness temporarily disappeared from his expression. "Miss Wainwright, I'd be happy to await my supper every evening if it afforded me the opportunity to keep company with someone of your beauty and charm."

"Why, thank you, Mr. Houston. You are absolutely too kind." Jasmine grasped Bradley's arm, graced him with an endearing smile, and permitted him to escort her into the dining room. The moment he glanced in the other direction, Jasmine turned toward her three older brothers and, with a great deal of satisfaction, stuck out her tongue.

"You must be careful if you ever visit up north where the weather is cold, Miss Wainwright. You wouldn't want your lovely face to freeze in such a position," Nolan Houston whispered as he took his seat next to her at the table.

Jasmine looked up in surprise, then leaned slightly closer and grinned. "Thank you. I shall make note of your kind advice, sir."

Nolan laughed aloud at the reply.

Bradley furrowed his brow and turned his attention to Jasmine. "Pray tell, what advice has my brother given you?"

"Cold weather. I was merely explaining how easily one can freeze when the weather turns frigid," Nolan replied.

Jasmine gave a quick nod of agreement to Nolan's reply before whispering a brief thank-you to him. Although she knew her brothers would have enjoyed listening while she attempted to wiggle out of such inappropriate behavior, it appeared Nolan Houston had been amused rather than offended.

Malcolm Wainwright pulled a freshly pressed white handkerchief from his pocket and mopped the beads of perspiration from his forehead. "I could do with some frigid weather right now. This heat is stifling, and it's barely the end of May. I don't know how I'm going to make it through another summer in Mississippi. Once the cotton crop has been laid by, I'm hoping to convince Madelaine we should make a return visit to White Sulphur Springs in Virginia or perhaps journey to Niagara Falls."

Jasmine's mother flinched at the suggestion but nevertheless remained the epitome of genteel womanhood. "I don't think we need to weary our guests with such a topic just now," she said and smiled. "After all, they've known nothing but travel these past weeks. They must be anxious to settle in for a time."

"I wasn't asking them to make further journey, my dear,"

Jasmine's father stated evenly, the tension evident in his tone.

Jasmine listened with interest to her parents' exchanged remarks. Perhaps over the next two months she could influence her mother to travel east. Certainly such an excursion would do them all good.

A wisp from a large feather plume floated downward, interrupting her thoughts, and she glanced up at Tobias. The young slave was perched on his small swing secured to the ceiling above the dining table. Tobias gave her a toothy grin as he swung back and forth above them while brandishing his oversized plume to deflect any flies that might enter through the open windows and hover over the dining table.

"If you don't stop distracting Tobias, he's going to fall off that swing one of these days," Samuel said.

"And a fine mess that would make. I don't believe Father would be quick to forgive you if Tobias dropped into the middle of the dining table," David agreed.

Malcolm glanced back and forth between his two older sons. "Gentlemen, please forgive the behavior of my children. It appears as if we're having a jousting match rather than dinner conversation."

"I believe McKinley should be applauded for his behavior. He hasn't said a word all evening," Jasmine commented while giving her youngest brother a bright smile.

Her father shook his head. "I'm going to hire someone to teach all of you proper etiquette if this sparring doesn't cease immediately. Ring that bell, Madelaine, and let's get this meal underway."

The jingling bell signaled two servants into immediate action. They entered the room carrying heaping platters of ham, biscuits, and roasted potatoes. Jasmine daintily helped herself to a biscuit before turning her attention to Nolan. "I'm still anxious to discover where you live in Massachusetts and if you might possibly know my grandmother. She lives in Lowell," Jasmine eagerly explained.

"Although I've visited Lowell on several occasions, I continue to make my home in Boston. Were I ever to move, I believe it would be to Cambridge rather than Lowell. I have far more friends located in Boston and Cambridge," Nolan replied. "Bradley, however, has numerous contacts in Lowell. In fact, he recently relocated from Boston to Lowell in order to expand his business ventures."

"Truly, how interesting. I thought Boston was a much larger city than Lowell. How is it your business will expand by moving to a *smaller* city, Mr. Houston?" Samuel Wainwright inquired.

Bradley straightened in his chair, obviously pleased by the question. "I'm a member of a prestigious group of men known as the Boston Associates. Perhaps you've heard of them?"

Jasmine's father gave a brief nod. "I've heard some vague references to the group. Seems I've been told they're intent upon monopolizing the entire textile industry in this country."

Bradley shifted in his chair and faced Malcolm. "Actually, the Boston Associates *are* the textile industry in this country," Bradley said with authority. "There are others, of course, but they are inconsequential. However, the Associates are anxious to see this country achieve industrial independence from England rather than attempting to monopolize trade for themselves. By basing our own textile industry in America, we reap the benefit of creating jobs that utilize products raised in this country and are then sold both here and abroad. It also lessens our dependence upon England for manufactured goods. Additionally, it gives cotton producers an excellent market for their crop."

Malcolm finished chewing a piece of ham and then lifted his glass and took a drink of water. "We already have an excellent market for our cotton. The Wainwrights have exported their cotton to the same English mills for as long as I care to remember. Don't expect we'll be changing business partners at this juncture."

"I hope while I'm here you'll permit me to at least point out the possibilities for business growth and higher income by considering another market. Doubtless you want to receive the best price for your efforts. Am I correct?"

"I want a good return, but profit isn't my only consideration when forming a business alliance. Trust and reliability are key factors I insist upon from my business partners, and I give them the same in return. I owe loyalty to my English customers. They were understanding during the drought that hit us back in 1834. While many cotton growers determined it was best to leave this area and move west, my family was able to sustain with advances on future crops paid to us by our English buyers."

Samuel nodded his head in agreement. "There were many cotton growers who posted signs on their property reading 'GTT'—Gone to Texas."

"Then you were indeed fortunate to have aligned yourself with such loyal buyers. However, one must constantly be looking toward the future. I believe you will find the Boston Associates can meet your every expectation in areas of trust and loyalty, plus provide a higher profit margin," Bradley said.

Jasmine listened intently, although she was rather bored by the conversation. Her mother had always taught her that a woman's place was to be supportive of her menfolk. She should appear interested, but not in a mannish fashion that would lead to asking questions. But her brothers certainly could ask their questions, and they did so with an amazing like-mindedness to her own thoughts.

As if reading her mind, McKinley turned toward their father as a wry smile curved his lips. "Perhaps you don't concern yourself with the profit factor, Father, because you no longer worry over the accounts. I would like to see The Willows receive a higher price for its cotton. Certainly the cost of shipping cotton to Massachusetts would be somewhat less than shipping it to England. Isn't this true, Mr. Houston?"

"What difference? The buyer pays the shipping costs," David retorted.

McKinley tapped the side of his forehead with his index finger. "Ah, but if the shipping costs are less, we can demand a higher price for the cotton based upon that very issue. Could we not?"

"Exactly!" Bradley replied. "And the higher the volume you can deliver, the higher the price the Associates will offer."

Jasmine couldn't help but find herself caught up in the

moment. Bradley's enthusiasm was contagious. Samuel leaned forward and gazed down the table toward his father. "Perhaps we should talk to our uncles about the possibility of a joint venture in which we could *all* obtain the higher price."

Jasmine's father waved his hand back and forth as if shooing flies away from his plate. "Now hold on! You boys are moving much too quickly with this idea. Making business decisions is not something done over the course of only one evening. My brothers are cautious men—steeped in tradition and fiercely loyal, just as I am."

Samuel would not be put off. "But how many times have you admonished us to be considerate of change and the development of products that will improve our abilities? I'm merely suggesting that this might well be one of those times."

Jasmine could read in her father's expression that he was more than a little annoyed to find his son brazenly sharing information that had at one time passed for private family business issues. She bit her lip to keep from saying something that might further upset her father. She caught Bradley Houston's expression even as her father began to counter Samuel.

"We in the South have always prided ourselves on moving ahead—not in speed and haste, but rather in determined, well-planned movements. We aren't talking of popping pieces back and forth atop a checkerboard. Rather, we prefer something more like a game of chess, where each move will have consequence for the moves to come." Their father toyed with his glass before taking a long, steady drink. Jasmine thought it a nice touch, an emphasis of his previous words.

Putting down the glass, her father continued. "I could never risk the well-being of my family—my beloved wife and daughter, our home, and all of the people who live here—without a great deal of prayerful consideration."

Bradley nodded in agreement. "Nor without evaluating additional reports and information upon which to base your decision. However, I can assure you that the Associates would be pleased to count you among their suppliers. It would appear to even a casual observer that your home and grounds are evidence of how well you've managed your plantation—especially in light of the depression you suffered only twelve years ago."

"We haven't always lived so well, but this house was Madelaine's dream. Wasn't it, my dear?" Malcolm's gaze settled upon his wife.

"I will admit that after visiting several other plantations, I was somewhat obsessed with having a Greek Revival home in which to rear our children," she replied.

"And it reflects the charm of the two ladies who grace its interior," Bradley added.

"Why, thank you," Madelaine replied, a tinge of pink coloring her cheeks. "I was determined to find the exact pieces of rococo furniture to accentuate the beauty of our home. I had given up all hope of finding a reviving-game sofa that met my expectations when I discovered one of our slaves is an extremely talented woodcarver. He carved and fashioned the woodwork and frame, leaving only the upholstering to be completed."

"I find all of your furnishings exceptional," Bradley said, his gaze scanning the immediate area.

Madelaine appeared to bask in Bradley's flattering remarks. "I don't think my husband shares your enthusiasm for household furnishings, although he has been very generous in permitting me my fancy," she modestly replied.

"Ah, but your husband realizes that a finely furnished home increases his social standing. It's a visible sign of his wealth and status," Bradley said.

"I thought the South's most desirable social status was that of slaveholder, not of home or property owner," Nolan interjected.

"That's true," Malcolm responded with a modicum of pride. "And here at The Willows, I have nearly a hundred slaves. Why, some of my prime hands are worth fifteen hundred dollars, and I could easily get two thousand for that woodcarver Madelaine mentioned—not that I plan to sell him."

"Of course not," Nolan replied quietly.

Jasmine heard the reproach in Mr. Houston's tone. She eyed

him curiously. What was it he meant to interject? She suddenly felt uncomfortable, but she had no idea why. This was her own home, her family table where conversations of productivity and the land often took place, but Mr. Nolan Houston did not seem impressed or approving.

Bradley cleared his throat and appeared to frown at his brother. "How much land do you own?" he inquired, shifting his attention back to Malcolm.

"Two thousand acres—some planted with corn, but the vast majority is cotton. It's as much as we can handle unless I purchase additional slaves, and we're making a nice profit at this juncture. No need to be greedy."

Before Bradley could reply, Jasmine pushed aside her discomfort and flashed a charming smile in his direction. "I wonder if we might discuss something other than cotton and slaves." She looked to her father as if asking permission for such a transition. She saw her mother nod in agreement.

"Our women are of such a delicate nature," Jasmine's father began. "They are strong, don't get me wrong. But such matters are well beyond them, and I have come to realize that it wearies them if we remain upon such topics overlong."

Bradley wiped his mouth with one of the monogrammed linen napkins and gave Jasmine his full attention. "I'm sorry. I have monopolized the conversation, haven't I? What topic would be of interest to you?"

She straightened in her chair and met his gaze. "I'd like to return to my original question regarding my grandmother."

"Ah yes. I never did respond, did I? Well, I'm sorry to say I have not met your grandmother. However, it is because of your grandmother that I've come here."

"How so?" Jasmine asked.

"I'm told your grandmother visits frequently with the wife of Matthew Cheever. Mr. Cheever holds a position of importance with the mills in Lowell. During their conversations, your grandmother mentioned the fact that her family was involved in raising cotton. Since our mills are always in need of cotton, I decided a visit to The Willows might prove beneficial to all of us."

"I see." She twisted in her chair to face Nolan. "And *you*, Mr. Houston? What brings you to The Willows?"

"I'm a poet and writer, Miss Wainwright. I've accompanied my brother in the hope of capturing the tangible essence of the South in some of my writings. I find it difficult to adequately describe places or people in my writings without actual observation. Since I want my readers to authentically experience the words I write, I thought this visit would prove fruitful."

Bradley raised one brow and gave a sardonic grin. "Nolan is quite the romantic, much like all of his writer friends."

Jasmine's attention remained focused upon Nolan. "I keep a journal and find writing to be a liberating experience. Of course, my writings are merely musings over my daily routine, whereas your writing influences and impacts upon the lives of others."

"At least that's my hope. Of course, one must have a somewhat extensive following in order to effectuate the type of change you speak of," Nolan remarked.

"My brother tends to conceal the success he's accomplished with his writing. Many who attend his readings proclaim his writing excels that of his contemporaries." Bradley took a sip of his coffee before settling back in his chair, meeting Mr. Wainwright's stern expression. "Nolan makes an excellent traveling companion. Our observations are completely opposite. Obviously our interests differ greatly, but we are both hoping you will favor us with a tour of your plantation."

"And perhaps your brothers' and neighbors' plantations as well," Nolan added, looking overhead. "A genuine representation of Southern living is what I'm seeking."

Jasmine thought his words sincere enough in his interest, but there was something almost mocking in his tone. She followed his gaze up to the small wiry-haired boy swinging above the table. The child had fallen asleep, still clutching the feathered plume in his hand. For a moment, she actually wondered if this tiny event in their evening might well appear on the pages of some Nolan Houston work. She smiled to herself and lowered her gaze, only to realize Nolan was grinning at her.

CHAPTER · 2

THE NEXT MORNING Bradley and Nolan walked out the vast front door of the white frame mansion, passing through the Doric colonnade that stood sentry over the upper and lower galleries of the home. Mr. Wainwright and Samuel led the way, with Jasmine close on their heels.

"Please say I may go with you," she begged. "I promise I won't say a word."

"Absolutely not," Malcolm Wainwright replied. "Go back inside. Your mother needs assistance with her household duties."

Bradley watched the young woman's expression. There was a desire to defy but also a respect that kept her from making too much of a scene. He saw her lower her gaze, as if rethinking her plan, as her father continued to speak.

"We'll be stopping in the fields before we go on to visit your uncle Franklin's plantation," Wainwright said. "That's no place for proper young ladies to be seen."

Jasmine looped arms with her father, lifted her face, and batted her eyelashes. "Would it be so difficult to go directly to Uncle Franklin's? I haven't seen Lydia since the dance two weeks ago."

"I can make arrangements for you to go visiting next week. I've already determined our route for today. Besides, we'll be discussing business. You'll be bored."

"I would be pleased to escort you to your uncle's home tomorrow, if your father agrees," Bradley offered.

Jasmine brightened at the offer just as he'd hoped she might. "Perhaps all three of us can go. You could recite poetry for us, Mr. Houston," she said, turning her attention to Nolan.

Nolan exchanged a glance with his brother. "We'll see what occurs. I may be so overwhelmed with my memories of today's observations that I'll want to spend tomorrow committing my thoughts to paper."

"It would hardly be proper for you to gallivant across the land unescorted," Jasmine's father reminded the trio. "However, perhaps I can spare Samuel to accompany you. If not, then Mammy will surely enjoy the time away."

"Oh, Father, you are very generous," Jasmine declared, looking quite pleased.

Bradley's suggestion appeared to appease Jasmine more quickly than her father's vague proposal—a concept which gave him pause for momentary reflection. Apparently Southern women were no more difficult to handle than those he'd encountered in the North. Females were females, and controlling them was merely a matter of utilizing proper management skill, he determined. Pleased with his incisive observation, he settled into the carriage opposite Malcolm and Samuel Wainwright. The carriage pulled away from the mansion and down the circular driveway before turning onto the dusty road. They traveled a short distance with Wainwright giving a brief commentary on the flora and fauna along the way.

He carefully pointed out the Spanish moss that draped itself like a gray veil from the trees that dotted the landscape. "Northerners are always intrigued by our Spanish moss," he commented. "Jasmine calls it Southern lace, although I don't think most would share her romantic notion."

The older man became more energized as they neared the first sighting of his planted acreage. "I thought I'd begin by having you view the fields," Wainwright said, pointing toward the sprouting cotton crop. The fields were lined with slaves who were chopping at the young shoots.

Bradley leaned forward and peered from the carriage. "It appears they're hacking up your new crop."

"They know better than to ruin my crop," his host said before giving a hearty laugh. "The crop would be strangled if the sprouts were to remain this thick. The slaves use their hoes to thin out the plants and create a stand."

"Might we stop so that I may examine the plants more closely?" Bradley inquired.

Wainwright beamed at the request, obviously pleased by Bradley's interest. "Pull over," Malcolm ordered the driver, who immediately pulled the horses to a halt alongside the dusty road.

The foursome exited the carriage, and Wainwright led them out into the fields with a determined step. He stopped and waved his arm in an encompassing gesture. "All this land you see belongs to my family. We've been cultivating cotton on it for many years. There've been many a good year, and many a bad one to follow."

"I want to learn everything I can about the difficulties you endure to produce your crop," Bradley said. "Although we Northerners are well acquainted with what it takes to get cotton from bale to bolt, we have no idea about the seed-to-bale process. I realize that without cotton, our mills are useless. And, quite frankly, it's you cotton growers who are the true heroes in the industrialization process."

Wainwright's chest puffed in obvious delight. "It's good to hear someone finally acknowledge the South is needed in order to make the industrialization process a success in this country. I will be most happy to show you the trials and tribulations we are forced to endure yearly in raising our cotton. We are, of course, dependent upon the weather, which is an issue of great importance to growers—while of little consequence to mill owners who operate their business indoors."

Bradley pulled his hat down to block the sun, his gaze resting upon the dark-skinned men, women, and children in the fields. They moved up and down the rows like an army of ants, their backs bent forward from the waist as they swung their hoes and chopped at the growing crop in hypnotic rhythm. He wondered at the efficiency ratio in light of other factors such as sickness and expenses.

Nolan pointed toward the slaves. "And *these* people? Are they also heroes?"

The other men turned and looked at Nolan as though he were speaking a foreign language. Samuel seemed confused, while Mr. Wainwright appeared to at least try to understand why Nolan would suggest such a thing. He once again pointed toward the fields. "Heroes? No, sir, those slaves are my overhead, an enormous expense that is ignored by anyone not involved in operating a plantation. As I told you at supper last night, there are few slaves on this plantation that didn't cost me nearly a thousand dollars."

"Of course you breed them, and there's no expense as the years go by," Nolan remarked.

Wainwright tugged on his vest and stepped closer. "No expense? Who do you think feeds, clothes, and houses them? Who cares for them when they're sick? These slaves are a constant financial drain on our income, yet we can't operate without them. And I do take issue with your remark about breeding. I permit my slaves to marry and bear children. I don't breed them, and I don't separate them from their families by selling them off, though there are many slave owners who think me lenient, even disruptive to our way of life for my kindness. Until you've operated a plantation of this enormity, you can't begin to fathom the financial obligation of caring for over a hundred slaves."

"One of life's necessary evils?" Nolan asked. "At least when one engages in this peculiar little institution, eh?"

Their host actually sputtered "P-peculiar? Evil? There's nothing peculiar or evil about raising cotton."

Bradley grasped his brother's arm. "My brother didn't mean to offend you, Mr. Wainwright. We admire the abilities and strength of our Southern brothers, and we're thankful you've agreed to educate us on plantation life. Don't you agree, Nolan?"

Nolan looked up from his notebook, his brow creased. "Actually, as a writer and poet, my interest in the South is quite different from yours, Bradley. I'd prefer to move freely on the land rather than hear the facts and figures of cotton production. No offense, Mr. Wainwright."

Wainwright nodded in a stern but gracious manner. "I'll have my overseer bring you a horse if you like."

"That would be most agreeable. I'll ride about the countryside and return to the house later in the day."

"Strange man, your brother," Wainwright remarked a short time later when they had once again proceeded on their way.

Bradley glanced over his shoulder and watched as Nolan mounted the horse and began following the overseer into a field. "I find most writers and artists are much like Nolan. They're all dreamers, out of touch with the realities of life."

"I'm certain your father is pleased to at least have one son with a sound head on his shoulders," Wainwright said.

"I believe he was quite proud of me. Our parents are both deceased, which is one of the reasons I've taken Nolan under my wing. As the older son, I was expected to assume the reins of the family business and gladly did so. Nolan's artistic bent was accepted by my parents, even cultivated by my mother, who was overjoyed to have a poet in the family. An emphasis on culture in an age of industrialization, to be sure. However, as you are well aware, philosophies and thinking vary greatly from North to South. The country is a veritable selection of thoughts and opinions that may very well do more to see us divided and at each other's throats than any foreign enemy could hope to accomplish."

Wainwright eyed him quite seriously for a moment, and Bradley couldn't help but wonder if his comment would meet with affirmation or condemnation. Finally Wainwright nodded ever so slightly. "It is difficult to understand the heart of another man when sitting at your own table. I must at least credit your brother for wanting to know more."

Bradley smiled. "Then credit me as well, for I am here for no other purpose than to better understand how your family business operates and how my family business might benefit yours in the future."

The carriage continued onward, the fields spread along either side of the roadway covered with sprouting green plants for as far as the eye could see. "What is your family business?" Samuel inquired.

"My father was primarily in the shipping business. However, I've sold a portion of the business, which, as I told your father in my letter, I've recently invested in the textile industry. My investment is why I'm visiting the South. I believe a man must learn all aspects of a business in order to excel as a manager of his holdings."

"Absolutely. I couldn't agree more," the elder Wainwright replied. "And although we sell our cotton to England, we're pleased to help you in your endeavor. This is my brother Franklin's home."

The men stepped out of the carriage in front of a house that appeared to be a duplicate of Malcolm Wainwright's balconied Greek Revival home. "Who knows? One day I may be able to convince you to sell your cotton to me." Bradley concluded the statement with a confident smile and was pleased neither man issued a negative response.

Wainwright led them up the steps to the house and knocked at the front door. A tall black woman escorted them into the library, where Malcolm and Samuel made themselves comfortable. Bradley stood by the fireplace and immediately stepped forward when Franklin Wainwright entered the room. Malcolm rose from his chair. "Franklin, I'd like to introduce Bradley Houston from Massachusetts. Bradley, my brother Franklin Wainwright."

"Pleased to make your acquaintance, Mr. Wainwright," Bradley said while firmly grasping Franklin's hand.

"Thank you, Mr. Houston," Franklin replied before shaking hands with Malcolm and Samuel.

"Bring us something cool to drink," he ordered the servant before turning his attention back toward Bradley. "Malcolm told me you would be visiting, and I must say I am impressed and pleased that you've chosen to familiarize yourself with the production of cotton. Tell me, Mr. Houston, what do you think of our cotton kingdom thus far?"

Bradley took the glass of lemonade a young girl had just offered. "I'm impressed. Your brother has given me a brief over-view of the entire process, although it's difficult to imagine what these fields must look like when harvest time arrives."

"Likely they appear much like your New England countryside after a winter snow," Samuel submittted. "It's a virtual sea of white in every direction."

"Exactly," Franklin agreed. "You should return in the fall or early winter to see for yourself. It's truly a sight to behold."

"I may decide to do just that," Bradley replied. "And your acreage is comparable to Malcolm's?"

The two Mr. Wainwrights exchanged an expression that sug-gested Bradley had done something out of line. He revisited his words even as Franklin cleared his throat to answer.

"A gentleman seldom discusses the size of his property in com-parison to another. Perhaps in the North that type of thing is no longer considered intrusive, but in the South it is akin to my ask-ing you what your profit ledgers revealed from last year."

Bradley realized he was well out of his knowledge when it came to Southern manners and etiquette. "I do apologize. Please forgive me. I never meant to be offensive."

Franklin nodded, appearing appeased. He waved his hand and went on, much to Bradley's surprise, to answer his question. "I merely choose to apprise you of the matter. As for the Wainwright family, Malcolm owns slightly more land than either Harry or I. His inheritance was larger—oldest son," he said with a laugh.

"And a more frugal way of life that has afforded me the ability to continue purchasing additional acreage," Malcolm added.

"True. However, I believe Harry and I have outproduced you the last two years."

"But only because we haven't cleared and planted our addi-tional land." Samuel gave a hearty laugh and nudged his uncle. "Just wait and see what we do next year."

His uncle didn't appear in the leastwise offended that the

younger man had joined in to challenge his elder. Bradley's own father would have boxed his ears for such an intrusion.

A short time later the youngest Wainwright brother, Harry, arrived and joined them for the noonday meal. Bradley listened and watched the men, gleaning information in an unassuming, congenial manner throughout the afternoon. He liked the Wainwright men. They were ambitious but didn't appear overly greedy, determined to continue with their plantations, yet open to modernization and change—men he could possibly influence.

Bradley was in his room relaxing before supper when Nolan finally returned to The Willows. "I was beginning to grow concerned. I thought perhaps you'd lost your bearings and couldn't find your way back to the house."

"I apologize. I didn't mean to worry you, but you know how I am when caught up in a project. I become unaware of anything but what I'm working on at the moment."

Bradley finger-combed his thinning brown hair and patted it into place. "So your writing went well? I was somewhat concerned when we parted this morning. You appeared rather distressed, and I regretted letting you go off on your own. I think you would have found Malcolm's brothers to be quite entertaining."

"I'm certain they are fine men. However, I'm pleased Malcolm allowed me to see the countryside on my own. I spent most of the day with the slaves, watching them work, visiting their quarters, talking to them. Did you visit the slave quarters at any of the plantations?"

"No. Malcolm did give me a few additional facts and figures concerning the costs involved in caring for the slaves. He owns more than I anticipated, but of course, some are household help—and there are also the elderly and the children."

"But most of them work in the fields. It's a miserable existence—nearly indescribable."

Bradley jerked to attention. "Then there is no reason to make any attempt to illustrate anything other than the beauty of the countryside. After all, that's why you're here, to encapsulate the beauty of the South."

"Yes, of course, and that's exactly what I plan to do. Give Northerners a word picture of genteel Southern living."

"Good, good," Bradley replied earnestly. "In fact, I'm giving some consideration to returning in the fall or early winter when the crops are ready for harvest. Samuel tells me the entire country-side turns almost as white as New England after a winter snow. You may want to consider coming with me. The sight of all that ripe cotton would surely lend itself to poetic beauty."

Nolan sat down beside his brother. "If not poetry, I'm certain it would be worthy of at least a lengthy essay."

"Then you might come along?"

"Absolutely. I wouldn't consider remaining in Massachusetts if you return."

CHAPTER · 3

WEEKS LATER, Jasmine raced down the spiral staircase and bounded toward her father as he walked in the front door. "Papa, I need to talk with you."

"Honestly, Jasmine! You must cease running about the house like a child," Malcolm admonished as he continued through the foyer and into the parlor. "Good afternoon, Madelaine. I trust you've had a pleasant day."

Madelaine Wainwright sat on the velvet-upholstered settee while fanning herself with a vengeance. Her latest needlepoint project was lying on the couch beside her. "No mishaps of importance, thank you. And you?"

"Quite a few of the slaves are sick. I sent Luther to fetch the doctor. I don't want an outbreak of some kind right before picking time."

"It's only the end of June, dear. If there's sickness, they'll be fine by the harvest. You worry overmuch about their health. This heat is stifling, isn't it?"

"It's not too late to consider a trip to White Sulphur Springs," Malcolm suggested.

"You know I'm not able to travel, Malcolm," she replied.

"Besides, traveling to Virginia will not ensure or aid the health of our workers."

Jasmine remained near the doorway, pacing back and forth. "Do stop that pacing, Jasmine!" Her father turned toward her, beads of perspiration dotting his forehead.

His command brought her to an immediate halt. "I'm sorry, Father. I'll talk to you after supper."

"Oh, do come in and sit down. It's this unrelenting heat—it has me on edge. What do you want to discuss?"

Jasmine walked farther into the room and held up a folded sheet of paper. "I received this missive from Grandmother Wainwright. She asked that I come for a visit. You know how much I miss her, and I was thinking we could go to Massachusetts for a visit—where the weather is much cooler this time of year. An excellent solution to avoid the summer heat, don't you think?"

Malcolm alighted beside his wife on the yellow silk sofa. "I don't think a visit to Massachusetts is in the offing for any of us— at least not now. Didn't you hear your mother say she can't travel at present? Why don't you write and invite your grandmother to The Willows for a visit? That would at least alleviate your longing to see her."

"I invited her in my last letter. But she says she hasn't been feeling well enough to make such a tiring journey. That's why she requested we come visit her. Please take time and reconsider, Papa."

"What's this? Grandmother's ill?" McKinley, Jasmine's youngest brother, asked as he walked into the room and joined them. "I don't recall Grandmother ever ailing when she lived at The Willows. It must be something she's contracted by living in those crowded conditions in the North."

"What does she say is ailing her? Let me see the letter," Malcolm said. Wrinkles began to line his brow as he examined the contents of the missive.

"Nothing serious, I hope," Madelaine said, her gray eyes bright with concern.

Malcolm pulled out his handkerchief and swiped away the

perspiration that had formed across his forehead. "The letter is rather vague. She says she hasn't been feeling quite herself and finds it impossible to make the journey south. I do wish she'd been more explicit. She goes on to say that seeing Jasmine once again would fulfill her deepest desires."

By now Samuel and David had returned home and joined the family in the parlor. "Why is everyone looking so somber?" Samuel questioned, striding across the room to his usual perch. Jasmine noted Samuel and David were dressed almost identically in fawn-colored trousers, navy blue jackets, and knee boots. They'd apparently been riding.

"Did somebody die?" David chuckled as he scanned around the room.

Madelaine raised her hand to the neckline of her lavender and white striped dress and gasped. "Do you think *that's* why Mother Wainwright has asked to see Jasmine? Do you think she's—*dying*?"

David immediately moved to his mother's side. "What's this about Grandmother?"

"She's written Jasmine," their father announced. "She asks that Jasmine visit her in the North."

"I'm a dolt. Forgive me," David said, meeting Jasmine's steady gaze even as he patted his mother's hand. He quickly turned his full attention to their mother. "I shouldn't have said such a thing. Forgive me for upsetting you. Grandmother has always been fond of Jasmine and likely misses her very much."

"Yet she could be in dire circumstances and not want to worry us," their mother countered anxiously.

Jasmine watched as they all seemed to forget she was in the room. It was often that way. The men in her family were generally compelled to decide her fate regarding every issue of her life. Her mother accepted this graciously, with exception, of course, to traveling. Upon this issue, Jasmine's mother had made it very clear: There was to be no travel unless absolutely necessary. Perhaps Mammy was right. Fear of the unknown—or possibly the known—kept Jasmine's mother a homebound prisoner. Still, as easily as her mother accepted direction from her husband in most every other area, Jasmine was hard-pressed to be as congenial. As the only daughter in the family, she was generally doted upon and she tried not to abuse this privileged position. However, at times like this, she found it hard not to press to have her own way.

"It's difficult to determine the exact scenario from the meager contents of this letter," Jasmine's father was saying. "However, knowing my mother, I'm guessing supplying such scant information is her way of forcing me to heed to her beck and call. She's likely enjoying life to the fullest while suffering from occasional loneliness for Jasmine. I *knew* this would happen. I warned her when she returned north that she would miss being with family."

Jasmine could see her possibilities for a trip slip away with each turn of her father's reasoning. "She may truly be ill, Papa. Mr. Houston mentioned the fact that he hasn't seen her at any of the recent social functions he's attended in Lowell."

Malcolm turned toward Jasmine, his eyebrows arched into twin mountain peaks. "Mr. Houston? You're corresponding with him also?"

Her father's scrutiny caused her cheeks to grow even warmer. "I've merely replied to his letter. I didn't think you would disapprove. Before Mr. Houston departed The Willows, he begged me to reply if he should write to me. I finally agreed, although I had little interest in corresponding with him. I've received only one letter."

"It's not that I disapprove. I'm merely surprised. He didn't mention your grandmother's illness when he wrote me. What exactly did Bradley say? Bradley is the Mr. Houston you're referring to, is he not?"

"Yes, Papa. He merely said what I've already told you. He said he had made it a priority to make Grandmother's acquaintance upon his return home. In fact, he called on her only three days after returning to Lowell. He went on to mention that she hasn't been present at recent social functions."

"I don't think his comment is indicative of anything worrisome. They simply may not be invited to the same social events," Samuel concluded.

"But what if she *is* dying and you ignore her plea? How could you ever live with such a decision?" Madelaine argued, much to Jasmine's surprise.

"So you think I should immediately heed to her bidding?" Malcolm asked.

"I think you should give serious consideration to making the journey," Madelaine replied. "I could hardly live with myself if something were to happen and you missed being in her attendance because of my poor constitution."

Malcolm rose from the sofa and prowled about the room like a cat searching for the perfect place to curl and rest. "And who would run The Willows during such a long absence? Leaving at this time of year isn't wise. What if we couldn't return in time for the first picking? I've never been gone from the plantation during any part of picking season."

"Really, Malcolm! Only a few minutes ago you were attempting to persuade me to travel to White Sulphur Springs."

"That is not even close to the same thing. We could certainly return home from there before first picking. A journey to Massachusetts will take much longer. And it's already late June."

"What about the three of us?" Samuel asked. "Do we not assist in the management of the plantation? Surely we could tend to matters while you're gone."

"Absolutely," McKinley said while David nodded his agreement.

Madelaine graced her husband with a winsome smile. "You see, you have already resolved that issue. And if a problem of consequence should arise during your absence, your brothers would be close at hand to lend assistance. After all, with adjoining plantations—Harry on one side and Franklin on the other—there would be scant possibility of the boys needing any further support."

"Could it be that you would consider making the journey with us?" Malcolm inquired, a hint of expectation lacing his question.

"You know my affliction makes travel impossible. I'm merely

pointing out that I would not be averse to you and Jasmine making the journey. After all, there are few plantation owners who would find themselves in such excellent circumstances if they needed to be away for a substantial period of time. We both know that many of the plantation owners leave for the entire summer with no one other than an overseer in charge."

"Well, they can manage their businesses as they see fit, but I'll not leave my plantation to the hands of an overseer for months on end. Even with my sons and brothers to take charge, I've no intent on being gone for a *substantial* period of time. If I agree to travel north, I will make every effort to return prior to harvest. It's difficult enough to consider leaving the boys in charge at this time; much more so during picking season."

"I understand your concerns, Malcolm, but you will give the journey consideration, won't you? It causes me great distress to think of your mother alone and ailing."

"I'll give the matter thought. If you would agree to accompany us, I would be willing to make immediate preparations. You know I'd go to almost any length to get you away from The Willows for a short time. It distresses me that you continue to seek refuge within the walls of this house, my dear. It's not healthy."

Jasmine immediately took up her father's argument. "Oh, do say you'll come, Mother."

Madelaine dropped her gaze toward her lap and began picking at the lace edging on her linen handkerchief. "I couldn't possibly travel to Massachusetts. And I do go outdoors—every day. I love tending the flowers in my gardens. Truly, my desire to remain at The Willows is not harmful to my well-being in the least. Please don't make my unwillingness to accompany you a factor in your decision. And if you want to be back in time for harvest, you must leave immediately."

Malcolm nodded. "I'll ride over and talk to Harry and Franklin tomorrow. Hopefully they'll be able to shed some light on Mother's possible ailments—or at least add their thoughts as to the obvious ambiguity of her letter."

"And you'll ask if they'll assist with the plantation should you decide to journey to Massachusetts?"

"Yes, dear. I'll discuss that matter also, but Jasmine need not begin packing her trunks just yet," he warned.

"Of course not, Papa," Jasmine agreed. She was barely able to repress the delighted giggle bubbling in her throat. Though difficult to believe, it certainly appeared as if her father would relent. If Uncle Harry were reasonably convinced Papa should make the journey, there was no doubt Uncle Franklin would agree also.

Samuel folded his arms and took a serious stance. "Should you decide to go visit Grandmother, I hope you will give me the opportunity to actually manage the plantation. It truly isn't necessary for Uncle Harry or Uncle Franklin to spend time at The Willows. David and I can manage the slaves, and McKinley already maintains the books and accounts for you. Should there be any sort of trouble, you know I would immediately send for one of them."

"I'm sure you would, Samuel. However, I want to speak with my brothers before making a final decision about any of this," Malcolm replied.

"May I please be excused?" Jasmine inquired softly. "This heat has caused me to feel faint, and I'd like to go to my room and lie down." It wasn't exactly a lie, but truth be told, she wanted to think out her plans for the upcoming trip. Despite what her father said about not packing her trunks, Jasmine felt confident the journey would take place.

"By all means," her mother replied. "I'll send Tobias to fetch you when supper's ready."

Mammy was busy mending a cotton chemise when Jasmine reached her bedroom. "What you doin' back up here so soon, chile? You feelin' poorly?"

Jasmine twirled around the room and finally fell upon the bed. "Oh, Mammy, I think I'm going to get to go to Massachusetts and see Grandmother!" she exclaimed. Rising up to a sitting position, she clasped her hands together. "Won't that be *wonderful?*"

"Um hum. It surely would be fine. I knows how much yo' grandma loves you."

"And how much I love her," Jasmine added. "It's been so lonely since she left The Willows."

Mammy nodded her head up and down as she continued jabbing her needle in and out of the white fabric. "Now tell me, when your pappy gonna take you north?"

"Well, it's not absolutely positive yet, but he said he was going to talk to Uncle Franklin and Uncle Harry tomorrow. If they agree that it would be wise for Papa to go and check on Grandmother's health *and* say they'll help supervise the work here at The Willows, I think we will leave very soon."

The old woman smiled, and her white teeth shone like a fine row of ivory piano keys. "What your mama think 'bout all this?"

"She encouraged us to make the journey. All I did was show Papa the letter, and Mama immediately took up the case. It was *so* perfect, Mammy."

"Well, I surely will miss you, chile," Mammy replied.

"And I'll miss you too, but I'm certain it's going to be a grand adventure, Mammy."

CHAPTER · 4

BRADLEY CARRIED the letter into his library, seated himself, and carefully opened the missive, excited to read the contents. He had anxiously checked the mail each day, eager to see if Jasmine would reply. He had begun his letter to her while he and Nolan were still on board ship returning home from their visit to The Willows, but he waited to mail it. He knew the girl would want to hear word of her grandmother. He hoped to woo her in a slow yet deliberate fashion. She was young for him, a closer match in age for Nolan, but she would fit perfectly into his own plans. Besides, women were more easily controlled if they married at a young age—before they developed a mind of their own. The fact that Jasmine was beautiful had been a pleasant surprise, but he also realized her beauty might prove an additional challenge in winning her hand. With that thought at the forefront of his mind, he had also been corresponding with Malcolm Wainwright. Once he had Malcolm as an ally, achieving his plan to marry Jasmine should prove uncomplicated.

A knock sounded, and the front door opened as Bradley finished reading the letter. "Bradley?"

"Nolan! I wasn't expecting you in Lowell. What brings you here?"

"Nathan Appleton convinced Henry and Fanny to accompany him to Lowell for a meeting of the Associates this evening. Since Nathan plans to stay in Lowell for several days, Henry thought I should join them and we could take a canal boat and reminisce about the leisurely summers that have long since passed."

"Henry Longfellow remains the constant romantic. I can't imagine how Nathan, the ever-vigilant businessman, abides a son-in-law with no business acumen whatsoever," Bradley said.

"He seems quite fond of Henry—perhaps because his daughter is so obviously happy in her marriage to him. I thought we might have supper together before your meeting with the Associates."

"I'd like that. We'll have sufficient time to dine at the Merri-mack House if we leave now. I can go on to my meeting from there."

Once they were seated at a small table in the Merrimack House restaurant, Nolan said, "Nathan mentioned you're planning to buy the Hinch estate. Is that true?"

"Word does travel quickly, doesn't it? I've made an offer to Hinch's widow. She's anxious to rid herself of the place, and I'd like a home that has some acreage surrounding it. It's become more and more difficult to find such a place, and even though it's a short distance from Lowell, I believe it would serve my needs very well."

"Serve your needs? That place is *huge,* Bradley. Why would a man with only one servant want to live—" Nolan stopped mid-sentence and stared at his brother. "Are you planning to wed in the near future?"

Bradley cleared his throat and tugged at his collar. "It is my hope, but I don't know if my proposal will actually be accepted. I hesitate even to discuss the matter for fear she'll reject me and the whole of Massachusetts will know I've been turned away."

"You can confide in me, brother. Ever since Nathan made mention of the matter, I've been attempting to determine if a woman might well be involved, and if so, who the woman might be. I'm thinking she's likely someone I haven't met. I promise I'll not breathe a word to any of the local gossips," Nolan said with a genial laugh.

"Actually, you *have* met her. When the time is right, I'm planning to ask for the hand of Jasmine Wainwright."

Nolan's brows furrowed as he placed his coffee cup on the white china saucer. "You jest!"

"No. I found her appealing."

Nolan leaned back in his chair and gazed at his brother, his eyes narrowed to thin slits. "Was it Jasmine you found appealing or her father's cotton plantation?"

"You believe me to have an ulterior motive?"

"Have you ever done anything in your life without an ulterior motive?" Nolan asked wryly. "I observed your enthusiastic efforts to impress the Wainwright family. You utilized every available moment to your advantage, plying them with the benefits of selling their cotton to you rather than shipping their crops to England."

Bradley fingered his thinning hair and met his brother's accusations with an unwavering gaze. "A marriage that combines both love and business is a match most men long for, Nolan. At least those of us who aren't enmeshed in your world of poetry and literature and must actually perform productive work."

"Ah, Bradley, you know that power and control are your aspirations in life. You would never choose to live in the literary world. Competition and power are your aphrodisiacs, not music and poetry. However, I, too, was drawn to Jasmine. She seemed a sweet girl—sheltered from the outside by her family. How do you propose to win her hand? Better still, how do you plan to fit her into your ambitious world?"

"Truly you can be a bother," Bradley said, shaking his head. "How often does the average wife fit into the ambitions of her husband's world? Women are necessary for the procreation of the race. A man wants a son to carry his name—to take the helm of the empire he builds as a legacy."

"Have you talked with her father?"

"I've been communicating with both Jasmine and her father.

In fact, I had a letter from Jasmine today telling me that she and her father are coming to Lowell for a visit with her grandmother. From the content of her letter, I doubt it was mailed much before they sailed. I'm guessing they'll arrive any day. I plan to speak with her father while they're in Lowell. If things go well, the marriage could take place when we go south for the harvest."

Nolan shook his head back and forth. "I can't believe you've plotted out this entire scheme. Have you considered her youth and the fact that she'd prefer a marriage based upon affection? Doubtless, in the beginning, she'll mistake your attention for love and later be disappointed. Surely you can barter an arrangement for the cotton without compromising the future of a young girl."

"Just like your friends, you think there are idyllic solutions to all of life's situations. Well, dear brother, that occurs only in your make-believe world of poetry and prose. Should Malcolm agree to the marriage, and I think he will, rest assured that I will treat Jasmine well."

"You'll treat her well so long as she adheres to your parameters," Nolan said.

Bradley arched his eyebrows. "Rules are made to be followed. As you've pointed out, she's young and will need guidance in what is expected of a proper wife. However, I'm confident that her mother has probably already seen to much of her training. You have to understand that in the South, especially among genteel families such as the Wainwrights, daughters are brought into the world with no other purpose but to make a prosperous match. Marriage to me would prosper that family in more ways than I can illuminate for you at this moment. Once she realizes how this match will benefit her, Jasmine Wainwright will be happy and content." Bradley pulled his watch from his vest pocket and glanced at the time. "Though I'm completely enjoying our conversation, I really must be on my way. The meeting tonight is important and I dare not be tardy. The Associates are considering me as their primary buyer. I'll present my proposal for expansion this evening. We can discuss this matter further tomorrow and perhaps have supper at that time as well."

———

Bradley leaned against the stone fireplace and surveyed the room, hoping to exude an air of confidence. He nodded to James Morgan and Leonard Montrose when they entered the doorway and then shifted his full attention to Nathan Appleton and Matthew Cheever. His fingers tapped nervously along the highly polished wood of the mahogany mantel as he waited for the meeting to commence. There was little doubt the members of the Boston Associates would follow the lead of Appleton and Cheever this evening. Consequently, Bradley knew he must impress them above all the others.

Leonard Montrose approached, blocking Bradley's view of the two men. "For someone who's hoping for a prestigious appointment this evening, you're looking rather grim, Bradley."

Bradley repositioned himself alongside Leonard, now able to once again observe Nathan Appleton. "I'm not certain the matter will come to a vote tonight, but if it does, I hope I can count on your support."

"I'll go along with them." Leonard tipped his head toward Matthew and Nathan. "If they want you, so do the rest of us. It's the way of things around here these days. With Tracy Jackson ailing, Matthew and Nathan seem to carry most of the control. I trust them to know what's best for the Corporation."

Bradley took a deep draw on his cigar and blew a funnel of gray smoke toward the ceiling. "Then once I lay out my proposal, let's hope they think I'm what's best for the Associates."

Leonard took a sip of port and looked around the room. "Thought maybe Tracy would be here tonight, but perhaps he's unable to tolerate the late-night air. These business meetings always take longer than necessary," he mused.

Before Bradley could comment, Leonard waved to several men across the room. "Good luck on the proposal," he absently remarked as he sauntered off.

Bradley didn't reply. Instead, he watched Nathan and Matthew as they continued their private conversation. Perhaps they were discussing him. He had yet to achieve the level of acceptance into the Associates that he so desperately desired. There was no doubt it was his substantial investment in the mills that had swayed the Associates to permit him entrance into their ranks. Selling his father's shipping business had been risky, yet Bradley yearned for the esteem his alignment with these powerful men would surely produce.

"Prepared for your presentation?" James Morgan asked jovially. The man's bulbous nose was the color of a cardinal. Bradley hoped James hadn't imbibed too much—he needed all the support he could garner, and none of the Associates would pay heed to a man who was in his cups. Perhaps it was merely the heat.

"I'm anxious to begin," Bradley told him, "and it appears that will soon occur." He nodded toward Nathan and Matthew, who were moving to the front of the room.

Nathan seated himself nearby, but it was Matthew Cheever who took immediate control of the meeting. Bradley maneuvered through the crowd, angling for a better view of the proceedings. Upon Kirk Boott's death nine years ago, Matthew had easily transitioned into the older man's powerful position, and that conversion had been a matter of intense interest to Bradley. The entire process reinforced his own desire to eventually be elevated into a position of leadership among the Associates. He hoped he would make that first step tonight.

"Now, I know you're all aware that as our textile industry has grown, so has the need for cotton. We have discussed the possibility of appointing a liaison to expand our acquisition of cotton from the Southern plantations. Demand is high for all of the textile products we can produce. However, I think you would all agree that unless we can purchase sufficient raw cotton, there is no need for further expansion or development."

Matthew waited until the murmuring ceased and then motioned to Bradley. "Move on over here, Bradley. All of you know our good friend and loyal investor, Bradley Houston."

"Indeed, and we're pleased to have his allegiance," Leonard Montrose called out.

"And his *money,*" some unseen member added from the back of the room.

A smattering of laughter followed the latter remark. Matthew smiled and waited patiently until the noise diminished. "Bradley has indicated a strong desire to help the Corporation convince our Southern cotton growers to refrain from exporting their products to England and begin looking to the North as their primary buyer. This won't be an easy task. As we all know, most of the Southern plantation owners are comfortable with the English markets they've developed and see no reason to change their habits. We've convinced a few of the growers, but not nearly enough."

"We'll have to give them reason to make those changes," Bradley said.

"They should be loyal to their own country, if nothing else," James put in, "but I imagine additional money is what they'll ultimately insist upon. However, if anyone can convince them they owe allegiance to this country, it's Bradley Houston."

Bradley gave him a grateful nod and then looked at the remainder of the gathered men. "I hope the rest of you will agree."

Wilson Harper, one of the more recent members to join the Associates, stepped forward. "Is this a *paid* position? Seems to me there might be others who need a job more than you, Bradley."

"I've told Nathan and Matthew I'd be willing to accept the position on a commission basis. You'll pay for nothing unless I'm successful—which will equate to your success also. Now, I know there will be stumbling blocks. I've heard reports some Southerners resent the growth and industrialization taking place in the North while the South is relegated to raising the cotton."

Robert Woolsey, another new member of the group, leaned forward and set his eyes on Bradley. "Those plantation owners don't realize how easy they've got it. Their slaves do the work while they live a life of leisure."

"I don't think we can approach negotiations with that kind of attitude, Robert." Bradley continued, "Our Southern brothers have a significant investment, in both their land and slaves. I've recently traveled south to learn more about cotton production, and while we face difficulties and expenses with our mills, they, too, face adversity. They're dependent upon the elements, whereas we have few concerns in that regard, and I believe we'll need to be sympathetic to their situation if we're to develop good relations. The Southerners resent their reliance upon Northern factories for the majority of their purchases while they are forced to depend upon agriculture for their economic well-being. I believe that's why many of them continue to ship their cotton to overseas markets. They'd much prefer to develop their own textile mills and avoid the tariffs placed on our products. And while you decry the fact that they have slaves performing their labor, the Southerners would likely argue that the mill girls and Irish work for *us* while *we* lead lives of leisure."

Robert's face knit into a tight frown. "The difference is, we pay wages."

Bradley shifted in his chair. He didn't want to beleaguer the point, but Robert's condescending attitude annoyed him. "And the Southerners have constant costs associated with their slaves, including food, housing, clothing, and medical needs, all of which I believe the mill girls are charged for. Slaves do not pay for these amenities; they are provided for by the plantation owner. In order to attract additional Southern suppliers, we need to refrain from imposing our values and harsh judgments upon them. After all, they might just as easily judge you."

Matthew cleared his throat. "I'm sure we all agree that we need each other if the country is going to prosper. Right now we need to embrace, rather than alienate, the Southern growers. Far too many of them still prefer to sell their cotton to England for the very reasons Bradley has so eloquently stated. They see no reason to practice any extended allegiance to the North because as far as they're concerned, they are a country unto themselves. Consider the current state of affairs. We have complications with Mexico and the southern territories they claim. We have individual states that prefer being left to decide for themselves how their particular regions will be operated—and no taste for Northern interference."

"I don't understand their separatist mindset," Wilson Harper threw in.

"Exactly," Matthew said, looking around the room. "Who here understands that fierce drive to isolate and serve the desires and means of the state, rather than the country as a whole?"

Mutters filled the air, but no one offered a concise thought. Bradley smiled. "I understand it—probably better than most Americans. My years in the shipping industry, traveling with my father to various southern ports, learning to deal with the businessmen and their aspirations—all that has afforded me a better understanding of the Southern mind."

"Pray include us in this understanding," Woolsey requested in a sarcastic manner that suggested he disbelieved Bradley's ability.

Bradley toyed with his watch fob. "I am a businessman and I offer you a business proposition. The risk to yourselves and this Association is very limited." He very nearly suggested that if the Associates weren't interested in his abilities, there would no doubt be others who would, but he held his tongue.

Leonard Montrose lifted his cigar in the air, with the ash glowing orange as a breeze wafted through the open window. "Since Bradley has agreed to take this position on a commission basis, I see no reason not to move forward with his election tonight."

With only minor exception, the men exhibited their faith in Bradley. At the same time, they had been quick to express the necessity for results. If expansion were to continue at the rate the Associates desired, the growth of their cotton markets must keep pace. They were placing their confidence in him to find a supplier. And he would prove their confidence was well placed. No matter the cost, no matter the effort—he would exceed their wildest expectations.

CHAPTER · 5

Lowell, Massachusetts

ALICE WAINWRIGHT quickly thumbed through the mail that had been delivered by her servant on the hand-painted breakfast tray only moments earlier. Breakfast in the private sitting room adjoining her bedroom was one luxury Alice afforded herself each morning. Not that she was a spoiled or pampered woman. On the contrary, she considered herself rather self-sufficient. However, she coveted this quiet time when she could gaze out her bedroom window and reflect upon God's creation while planning her day, for she knew that once she descended the staircase, interruptions would greet her at every turn.

As was her custom, she seated herself in the small alcove overlooking the tidy flower garden below her bedroom window and picked up Jasmine's letter. She couldn't deny the surge of anticipation and delight she felt each time one of her granddaughter's frequent letters arrived. She momentarily held the envelope in her hands while contemplating what tidbits of information the contents might divulge. Jasmine's letters were always filled with the daily happenings at The Willows. Somehow the child could make the most mundane occurrences seem exciting. Her imagination seemed endless, and Alice had encouraged Jasmine's interest in writing. In fact, she'd given her granddaughter a thick leather-covered diary before moving to Lowell, suggesting Jasmine try her hand at journaling or poetry.

As she edged the blade of her silver letter opener under the envelope's seal, Alice wondered if Jasmine had been writing any poetry. She'd be certain to ask when next she wrote. Removing the pages from their snug paper cocoon, Alice lovingly pressed out the deep creases with her hand.

Page by page, she read the letter before leaning back in her steam-bent, cushioned chair and staring out at the flowering trees. She remained motionless for several minutes, enjoying the shades of pink and ivory that peeked through the green foliage. Then, with a quiet determination, she picked up the small gold bell beside her chair and gave one sharp ring.

Moments later, Martha hurried in as though she expected to see the room engulfed in flames. "Yes, ma'am? Is something wrong with your breakfast?"

Alice waved the letter back and forth like a flag at half-mast. "No, my breakfast is fine, thank you. It's this letter from my grand-daughter. She says she and my son Malcolm will be arriving—possibly within the next few days. There's much to do, Martha. The guest rooms will need airing and we'll need fresh linens for the beds—and food, we'll need to discuss menus. Let me see—perhaps I should begin a list."

"A list is a fine idea, Miss Alice, but at the moment you need to prepare for your visit to the Cheever home."

Alice glanced at the mantel clock. "You're absolutely correct. We'll begin preparations as soon as I return home. For now, you can take my breakfast tray, and if you would ask Martin to bring the carriage around, I'd be most appreciative."

Alice was hard-pressed to believe her good fortune. If she'd known Malcolm could be so easily convinced to come visiting, she would have hinted she was ailing long ago. She smiled into the mirror while adjusting the lavender feathers that were quivering above the wide brim of her champagne-colored bonnet.

She then descended the stairs, barely able to contain her delight. By this time next week Jasmine no doubt would be here.

They would have such fun exploring Lowell, and perhaps Malcolm would escort them to Boston. She hoped Jasmine would find the house to her liking. It was, after all, very different from The Willows. Instead of a sprawling, pillared mansion, Alice had purchased a house much like herself: sturdy and dependable. She enjoyed its every nuance, and the fact that the home was situated on a small plot of land within the town of Lowell had been an added bonus.

Tall and rigid, Martha stood at the front door, resembling a soldier guarding the castle gate as Alice approached. "We'll begin our list when I return, Martha," she instructed before leaving the house.

Outside, Martin offered his hand and assisted Alice into the leather-clad interior of her small carriage. Alice was sprightly for her seventy years, and they both realized she was capable of lifting herself into the cab without help. But, of course, civility required a woman of her social standing to exercise decorum in such matters. Once she was ensconced in the carriage, Alice's thoughts immediately returned to Jasmine's letter. What perfect timing! If there were no problems on their voyage, Malcolm and Jasmine should arrive in time for the Cheevers' summer social. Once Malcolm visited Lowell and accepted the fact that refined people did reside in Massachusetts, she hoped to convince him that Jasmine should remain with her there—at least for the remainder of the summer and early fall. The matriarch of the Wainwright family crossed her arms and leaned back in the carriage. At this moment, Alice Wainwright was the personification of smug satisfaction. She had a plan!

Lilly Cheever stood at her front door in a daffodil-yellow morning dress embroidered with tiny white flowers bordering the scalloped flounces.

"Yellow becomes you, my dear. You should wear it more often. I adore yellow but, alas, it causes me to appear sallow," Alice said. She followed Lilly into the parlor, admiring the younger woman's graceful carriage.

"It is always a pleasure to have you visit, Mrs. Wainwright. I was delighted when you agreed to help with the charity ball. There's never a shortage of requests for the funds we amass but always a shortage of workers for the actual event. Do sit down."

Alice chose one of the overstuffed blue-and-gold brocade chairs where she had an unobstructed view of the rose garden. "Personally, I enjoy keeping busy, preferably with those of you who are youthful—it keeps me young at heart."

Lilly laughed and settled into a matching chair opposite Alice and began pouring tea. "I wouldn't call myself youthful. My two children think of me as old and decrepit."

"Tut, tut. What do children know of old age? They think anyone a few years their senior is ancient. Why, I remember a time when I thought twenty and five to be positively doddering. Time has a way of altering your perspective."

Lilly's lips curved into a winsome smile as she nodded in agreement. "You're certainly correct on that account." She handed a cup of tea on a saucer to Alice.

"And speaking of young people, I received word earlier today that my son and granddaughter will be arriving in Lowell for a visit."

"That's wonderful news. Will they arrive in time for my summer social?"

Alice smiled. "Indeed, they will. In fact, when I opened Jasmine's letter and discovered she was coming to visit, your social was one of the first items that crossed my mind. It will be a perfect opportunity for her to meet a few people her own age. And I'm certain she'll enjoy Violet, even if she is a few years younger."

"Where does Jasmine attend finishing school?"

"Jasmine has received her entire education at home. Madelaine, that's my daughter-in-law, insisted on having a tutor rather than sending Jasmine to a finishing school. In my opinion, the isolation has stilted Jasmine's level of maturity. She's a dear girl, very sweet, but I fear she's rather naïve for a young lady of eighteen years. However, having her at home all those years permitted me the opportunity to develop a closer relationship with her while I was living at the plantation. I must admit I've missed her terribly. In fact, I'm hoping to convince my son to allow her to remain with me until the Christmas holidays, or at least until fall. I'd like Jasmine to experience life away from her mother and the confines of The Willows."

"The Willows?"

Alice nodded and took a sip of tea. "Yes, The Willows is a cotton plantation that has been in the Wainwright family for generations. But certainly not an enterprise that was ever near or dear to *my* heart. However, from all appearances, my sons and grandsons will follow in their ancestral footsteps. Having been reared in Massachusetts and not having lived in the South until after my marriage, I never really embraced plantation life. Of course, my sons thought me daft. When I decided to move back North after my beloved husband's death, my entire family opposed my decision. They thought me completely foolish." She leaned forward and lowered her voice to a whisper. "I'm certain my sons don't believe it, but I've been more content since my return to Massachusetts than any time since my husband's death."

Lilly patted Alice's hand. "I'm pleased to hear you're satisfied, and I'm looking forward to meeting Jasmine. Perhaps we can journey to Boston for a day of shopping while she's here. I'm certain Violet would enjoy the diversion. And Matthew has mentioned the possibility of spending some time near the ocean in August— perhaps Rhode Island. You might want to give that idea consideration."

"I have to admit I had similar ideas in mind. At least with thoughts of Boston and shopping," Alice said, smiling.

"I only wish Elinor were here," Lilly said absentmindedly.

"Elinor who? Have I met her?"

"She's Taylor Manning's younger sister. She's . . . well . . . I believe she's twenty-two. A smart woman, with a head for bookwork, believe it or not." Lilly smiled. "She's been married twice and unfortunately widowed twice. Poor girl. Taylor's wife, Bella, tells me she believes herself cursed with misfortune."

"She does seem quite young to have endured so much sorrow. Where is she now?"

"Philadelphia. Taylor and Bella have gone to fetch her home. Her husband died from a bout of yellow fever."

Alice nodded knowingly. "I had heard that many areas suffered horribly with the fever this year. Did Elinor take the sickness?"

"No, amazingly enough, she didn't. But it only served to deepen her sorrow."

"When she returns, she would probably benefit from spending time with others," Alice said. "Perhaps the shopping trip to Boston would be a bit taxing, but we could promise her time in her own interests."

"I think it would definitely do her good," Lilly said, finishing her tea. "When she lost her first husband at eighteen, I know she thought she would never love again. Poor man drowned in an accident at the mill," Lilly added, as though it were important.

"Then when she met Daniel Brighton at church, I know she was quite apprehensive about giving her heart. They seemed such a good match. He was the nephew of dear friends and had a good business in Philadelphia. He courted Elinor fervently, coming to Lowell whenever he could spare the time. I think he finally wore her down." Lilly smiled. "But don't take that to mean Elinor didn't love him. She did. I was so happy to see her find true love a second time . . . and now this."

"God alone knows why these things happen," Alice commented in a motherly tone. "We must trust that He knows better than we do."

Lilly nodded. "And that He has better things ahead for Elinor."

"Exactly!" Alice agreed. "Hopefully between the two of us, we can take Elinor under our wing and see her heart mended in time. Meanwhile, I do suppose we should turn our efforts toward planning the charity events for the upcoming year."

Laughing, Lilly rose to her feet. "This is probably why I suffer through with limited assistance from others. I am easily distracted. Come, I'll show you my list of tasks."

Jasmine swirled into her grandmother's bedroom and made an exaggerated pirouette. Her silk gown cascaded in a sea of pink ripples as she seated herself on the brocade fainting couch and waited for her grandmother's assessment.

"You look absolutely beautiful, my dear. However, I do believe my diamond-and-pearl necklace would add the perfect touch to your ensemble." Alice opened her jewelry case and lifted a velvet pouch from the depths of the box. With a practiced ease, she placed the necklace around Jasmine's neck and fastened the clasp. Alice stepped back to appraise the effect. "Stunning! There won't be another young lady who will compare."

Jasmine smiled in return, wishing the aura of self-confidence she'd exhibited for her grandmother moments earlier were genuine. "Will attendance be sizable, do you think?"

Alice stared into the mirror, her attention focused upon the cameo pin she was clipping to a wide ribbon she'd fastened around her neck only moments earlier. "I'm not certain. Do you like the cameo on this ribbon? Or shall I wear my topaz necklace?"

"The cameo." Jasmine blotted her face with a lace-edged handkerchief. "Will there be more guests than attend the balls at Hampton House or The Willows?"

"Why are you so curious about the number of guests?" Alice turned to face Jasmine. "Oh, child! You're white as a sheet. Are you ill?" Without a moment's hesitation, Alice moved to her granddaughter's side and placed a hand alongside her cheek. "No fever."

"I'm not ill, at least not in the way you're talking about."

"In what way, then?"

"Attending a party where I won't know anyone except you and Father makes me extremely uncomfortable. You won't leave my side, will you?"

Alice patted Jasmine's hand. "You might have difficulty dancing if I remain by your side throughout the evening. But I promise to stay with you as long as you need me if that will help conquer your anxiety."

Jasmine's lips curved into a timid smile as she nodded her agreement. "You think I'm acting like my mother, don't you?"

"Absolutely not! And don't you worry yourself with such thoughts. I want you to attend this party and enjoy yourself. There's an exciting world outside of The Willows, and I want you to experience a portion of it—beginning this evening." Alice wrapped a silk shawl around Jasmine's shoulders and pulled her into a warm embrace. "Now, set aside your fears, and let's be on our way. You're going to meet some fascinating people. By the end of the evening, you'll look back on this moment and wonder why you ever harbored the slightest concern."

Jasmine hoped she was right. She had the utmost respect for her grandmother's opinions. Still, this was possibly the most frightening event of her life. Jasmine followed her grandmother from the room, wondering what the evening might hold in store. So many of her friends back home had met their mates at just such events. Most had married within the last year.

Will I meet the man of my dreams? she pondered. *I've never concerned myself with such things before, but what if . . .*

Malcolm hurried forward to meet the women as they descended the staircase. "Look at the two of you! I'll be escorting the prettiest ladies to the party."

"Thank you, Papa," Jasmine said, her thoughts interrupted by her father's enthusiasm. She forced a smile. "Grandmother has loaned me her necklace. Isn't it beautiful?"

Jasmine's father nodded and glanced toward the tolling clock in the hallway. "Indeed, it is. We'd best be on our way, or I'd venture to say that we'll be more than fashionably late to the Cheevers'. I do wish I'd had time to inform Bradley Houston of our arrival. He knew we were making the journey, but he didn't know exactly when we planned to arrive. He wrote that he'd made a point of meeting you, Mother. What did you think of him?"

Alice donned her white lace stole and took hold of her son's arm. "He seemed nice enough, I suppose, but he was more interested in discussing cotton and textiles than any matters that were of interest to me. He probably believed my years of living at The

Willows made me an excellent partner with whom to discuss cotton markets. Little did he realize how I abhor the topic." She gave her son a fleeting apologetic look. "Now, his brother, Nolan, is another matter entirely. Nolan enjoys theatre, poetry, and literature and can discuss them all quite eloquently. He's a man after my heart. In fact, I shared one of Jasmine's poems with him. He confided she hadn't mentioned her literary abilities when he visited The Willows. Bradley didn't appear to show much interest, but Nolan was quite impressed. I wouldn't worry about business this evening. You'll have ample time for discussions of cotton and textiles later in the week if Mr. Houston isn't present tonight."

"Since it's obvious your health has greatly improved, Mother, I'm certain we won't be in Lowell for an extended period."

Jasmine stifled a protest. She might fear the events of the evening, but she longed to spend more time in her grandmother's company. Surely Papa wouldn't rush her back to The Willows without time for a good long visit.

A playful smile tugged at Alice's lips. "You're not hiding your agitation very well, Malcolm. Why don't we spend this evening enjoying each other's company and the fact that we have a lovely party to attend?"

Jasmine watched her father's expression soften. "I am enjoying your company, in spite of the false pretenses upon which you forced my arrival."

"Tut, tut. Tonight is for fun—not admonitions. I am determined to show my granddaughter, and perhaps my son, that the Northern states are just as fond of parties and revelry as is the South."

"Then let us go among your Northern neighbors," Jasmine's father said, smiling.

Jasmine relaxed a bit. Her father was clearly not nearly as annoyed with his mother as he let on. She followed her elders to the carriage, watching as her grandmother lovingly placed her gloved hand against her son's face. Jasmine couldn't hear what she said, but the look on her grandmother's face was one of pure love.

The exchange warmed Jasmine and made her forget her fears. At least momentarily.

By the time they arrived at the Cheevers', Jasmine's father appeared to relish the idea of a party, hurrying them out of the carriage and up to the porch with a swiftness that caused Jasmine's grandmother to tug on his sleeve.

"Do slow down, Malcolm. This isn't a footrace, and I'm an old woman."

Papa winked at Jasmine before turning back toward his mother. "Since when do you consider yourself old?"

"When such a comment suits my fancy, of course." She gave her son a smug grin and looped arms with Jasmine. "Come along, my dear. I'm going to introduce you to some of the most eligible bachelors to be found north of Mississippi."

Malcolm immediately sobered. "Don't get any ideas, Mother. As I said on our way here, with your improved health, we'll be returning to Mississippi very soon. I much prefer to be home in time for picking season."

"Don't discount my medical ailments so quickly, Malcolm. You assume because I'm able to navigate the streets of Lowell, I am completely well. However, my health hangs in the balance, changing from day to day, much like the weather."

"Or to suit your circumstances?" he inquired as they reached the front door.

Alice ignored his question, stepping forward to greet Lilly Cheever. "Lilly, Matthew. May I introduce my son Malcolm Wainwright and my dear granddaughter Jasmine?"

Matthew grasped Malcolm's hand in a warm handshake. "I believe Bradley Houston mentioned your name to me only this morning. He said he had visited your plantation and that you and your brothers have some of the finest cotton fields to be found in the South."

Malcolm nodded. "I'm pleased to hear he was so favorably impressed with our cotton. Bradley appears to be quite a shrewd businessman. In fact, we've corresponded since his departure."

"We're pleased to welcome you to our home. I believe Bradley is expected tonight, isn't he, my dear?"

Lilly nodded. "Yes. Actually, Bradley's already here, though Nolan hasn't yet arrived. He's coming from Cambridge with Henry Longfellow." She lowered her voice and leaned close as though she were sharing some privileged piece of information. "They've both agreed to read poetry for us later this evening."

Alice clapped her hands together in obvious delight. "How enchanting! I know we'll all enjoy hearing them," Alice said before stepping aside to permit the other guests entry.

The three Wainwrights walked down the hallway toward the drawing room, and Malcolm gave his mother a smug grin. "It sounds as though Mrs. Cheever's entertainment will provide me with ample opportunity to talk to Bradley Houston this evening."

"Listening to something other than the price of cotton would expand your mind," Alice gently chided.

When her father gave no retort, Jasmine looked upward and followed his gaze. Bradley Houston was wending his way through the crowd. He plainly stared at her as he approached where they now stood. He looked quite dashing dressed in gray and black. His rigid features gave him a hard but handsome appearance.

"I didn't know you had arrived in Lowell. I thought you would send word," he said. She couldn't discern if he was angry or merely surprised by her appearance. He took hold of her gloved hand and bent over it, refraining from touching his lips to the cloth. When he looked back up to meet her face, Jasmine thought his expression suggested that he expected some sort of explanation.

"There wasn't sufficient time, what with preparations for the evening and visiting with Grandmother," she replied. "I'm sorry."

"You're young." He straightened, his gaze boring past any facades of bravery Jasmine might have put in place. "You are forgiven. In time you'll learn where to direct your time and attention."

He then smiled with the warmth of a summer day. Yet something in his voice caused her to shiver.

CHAPTER · 6

JASMINE KNOCKED on her grandmother's bedroom door and then stepped inside when Alice bid her enter. "Good morning, Grandmother. I trust last evening's dinner at the Merrimack House didn't tire you overly much."

She smiled and motioned Jasmine forward. "On the contrary, I'm fine."

"I'm so glad. I thought perhaps the activities of the last week might have wearied you."

"You mustn't fret about me. I'm aging to be sure, but I'm still very capable. I've been meaning to ask if you enjoyed the Cheevers' party last week. We've scarcely had a chance to speak of it."

Jasmine considered that evening, and Bradley Houston immediately came to mind. "I'm not sure what to think about that night. I thought the party itself was lovely. Mrs. Cheever is very gracious. Mother would say she has the grace and manners of a perfect Southern lady. Although as I understand, she's very much of New England background."

"That she is. She was born and reared right here in Lowell," Grandmother replied. "But let us speak about you, my dear. What seems to trouble you about that evening?"

Jasmine shrugged. "I'm not sure I would say that the evening troubles me; rather, I'm not sure what it all meant."

Grandmother tilted her head to one side as if to study her for a moment. Jasmine felt silly for having even brought up the matter. "I suppose it was nothing," she murmured, looking away from her grandmother's prying gaze.

"Nonsense. You seemed completely perplexed. Tell me what this is about."

Jasmine turned, trying hard to put her thoughts into words. "Mr. Houston said several things to me—things that confused me."

"Did he try to take liberties with you, child?"

"Oh no," Jasmine assured. "It's just that he spoke to me in a very familiar way, as if he'd known me for a long time. It confused me."

"Did he speak of love?"

Jasmine grew warm around the lace of her collar. "No, not exactly. He spoke of obedience and helpfulness. He talked of my learning where best to direct my attention. I'm not at all certain what he wanted me to understand, but he seemed quite intent with his words."

"Well, child, you are of a marriageable age, and you're quite beautiful. The man probably fancies thoughts of you for his wife."

Jasmine shook her head. "Bradley Houston is too old for me, and he's a Northerner, after all. He would never understand our ways, and no doubt Papa would never consider him as a suitor for me."

"Yes, but what of you, Jasmine? Would you consider him?"

Jasmine couldn't give her grandmother an answer. Truth be told, she hadn't really considered anything so farfetched as a marriage proposal from Bradley Houston.

As if understanding Jasmine's bewilderment, her grandmother motioned to the chair. "Sharing these last few days with you has been wonderful. Sit down and have breakfast with me. Martha tells me your father is meeting with Mr. Houston again this morning, so perhaps the mysteries will be explained." She smiled with re-assurance. "But even better, we shall have the day to ourselves. I thought perhaps we might go to some of the shops and see about a small gift for your mother, something your father could take home that might cheer her."

"Perhaps a book of poetry," Jasmine suggested, pushing aside her troubled thoughts.

"An excellent idea. Nolan Houston is quite eloquent, is he not? His reading was impeccable the other night."

Jasmine placed a linen napkin across her lap. "It's a shame he doesn't have a published book of poems we could purchase for Mother. It would be great fun to give her a book written by someone she's actually entertained in her home, even if he didn't read any of his writings for us."

"I doubt your father would have encouraged him. And Bradley doesn't appear to lend much support either. I was rather horrified when the two of them got up and went outdoors during Mr. Longfellow's reading at the Cheevers', although I suppose I shouldn't have been. Your father told me he planned to utilize the time to discuss business. He's convinced my health doesn't require his presence in Lowell, and I'm certain he'll soon book passage for your return to The Willows. He thinks the first picking won't occur without him."

"Oh, Grandmother, do try to convince him we should remain awhile longer. We've only just arrived, and I don't think I could bear to leave you so quickly."

Grandmother Wainwright's face seemed to suddenly come alive with excitement. "What if I could convince him to allow you to remain until the end of November? I could then accompany you home and spend the holidays with all of the family." The animation in her tone confirmed she was quite delighted with her new idea.

Jasmine pulled her grandmother into a tight embrace. "What a *perfect* plan! Surely Papa will agree, especially if it means you'll be at The Willows for Christmas."

"I doubt he'll be quite as enthusiastic as you. He'll immediately worry about your mother's reaction to your absence. She'll be distraught when you don't come home and will surely take to her bed."

Jasmine pulled back, carefully contemplating her words before she spoke. "I do want to stay, Grandmother, but Mama's health is fragile at times. I wouldn't want to cause her distress. However, she was most supportive of our journey, even telling Father he had an obligation to come north and personally check on you. And she encouraged him to bring me along to see you."

Alice patted Jasmine on the cheek. "Then we'll leave it to your father and abide by his decision. In the meantime, let's get ready for our shopping trip. I saw some of the loveliest velvet at Paxton's Mercantile in town. I think it might make a very fetching Christmas gown."

Jasmine smiled and turned her attention back to the breakfast tea. "I'm certain to be impressed if it caught your attention." Jasmine pushed aside her anxieties and the pending question of whether her father would allow her to remain in Lowell and concentrated on the joy of the moment. Tomorrow would surely see her troubles smoothed over and her mind at peace.

Bradley stepped out of his carriage in front of the Merrimack House. He'd agreed to meet Malcolm Wainwright for breakfast and then escort him on a tour of the textile mills. Settling at his table with a steaming cup of coffee, Bradley contemplated the events of the past few days. He didn't believe Wainwright was ready to sign a contract, but he appeared somewhat receptive to the possibility of shifting his cotton sales away from the English markets. With a bit more time and persuasion, Bradley hoped to convince him such a decision would be beneficial for his entire family, as well as all of the Mississippi and Louisiana cotton growers. The Wainwright family was renowned in the South, and Malcolm Wainwright could be a strong ally.

The Associates were anxious for Bradley to move forward with a speed that defied developing the type of associations needed for long-term business relationships. Business was done much more quickly in the North, whereas Southern deals were struck over mint juleps and lazy summer afternoons.

Bradley had learned long ago that pushing a cause too strenuously often resulted in adverse outcomes—in all aspects of life. But nowhere was this truer than with Southern gentlemen, and Malcolm Wainwright seemed no exception to this rule. Bradley was willing to move at a more respectable pace if it meant accomplishing his goal in the end. After all, he didn't want to frighten off the patriarch of the Wainwright family before their business relationship had even commenced.

And then there was the matter of Jasmine. He would be extremely cautious in that regard. The girl was young and likely to object to any advances from him. What little he had tried to coax from her in conversation seemed completely void of depth and understanding. But he reminded himself that she had led a very sheltered life and that someone of his worldly knowledge was no doubt a threat to genteel sensibilities. Still, she had been quite spirited while associating with Nolan and his literary friends during the evening, which he found somewhat disquieting. Especially since she had been as frightened as a church mouse when he escorted her home from the Cheevers, careful to keep a safe distance between them and running into the house the moment he helped her out of the carriage.

You aren't a handsome man, Bradley chided himself between sips of coffee. He knew his features were considered by some to be quite stern, even imposing. He wasn't a very tall man, standing only five and eight, but his square jaw and penetrating gray eyes had managed to cower many an adversary. There was, as some said, a look of determination, even unto seeing the last man fall before giving up. Bradley rather liked that people considered this of him. It made them cautious in saying no to him. Of course, Malcolm Wainwright was not as naïve as some. He was the type of man, in fact, that was sure to smell a bad deal before it ever reached the table.

A shadow passed across the window in front of him, and Bradley glanced up to see Wainwright enter the building. "I didn't notice your carriage," Bradley remarked as the man seated himself.

"I walked. It's a lovely morning, and everything is close at hand here in Lowell. As a matter of fact, I find it rather refreshing that I can leave Mother's front door and walk downtown in such short order. The town is quite compactly organized."

"Indeed it is. In fact, that very concept is what the Associates envisioned when planning this community. I believe they were very successful in most aspects."

"I'm looking forward to touring the mills and seeing the remainder of the town. Of course, a man like myself could never live in these close surroundings, but I can certainly admire the thought and effort that was required for an endeavor such as this."

The men paused as a waiter placed a cup of coffee in front of Malcolm.

"Before you leave, I hope you'll have opportunity to meet with many of the gentlemen responsible for the achievement of their vision," Bradley commented. "Kirk Boott was the man who was originally in charge of managing construction of the mills, boardinghouses, and canals, and then the Associates determined he was the best man to remain in Lowell and direct the day-to-day operations as well. Until his death nine years ago, Kirk remained a viable leader, although he had begun grooming Matthew Cheever many years earlier. At the time of Kirk's death, Matthew was well positioned to take his mentor's place."

"Sounds as though Boott handpicked him, so it would be my guess he's well suited to the job. His interest in the Wainwright cotton is flattering. It's always encouraging to know that others value your work."

"I think you'd find that all of the Boston Associates value the commitment and hard work of cotton producers. While we realize the textile industry is dependent upon cotton, I doubt you'd find any one of us willing to assume the daily rigors or risks associated with planting and harvesting a huge cotton crop each year."

A satisfied smile spread across Wainwright's lips. He appeared pleased by Bradley's accolades, so Bradley determined to use the situation to best advantage. "If I might change the subject for a moment, I might say that I find Jasmine to be an engaging young woman." He paused as the waiter put a plate of food in front of each of them. "I'd like your permission to call upon her while you're visiting in Lowell."

Wainwright's eyes narrowed slightly at the request. "We won't be here long, and I specifically brought her to visit with her grand-mother. Don't misunderstand, Bradley. I have no objection to you as a suitor, although I always presumed my only daughter would marry one of our Southern boys. Still, it's a matter of timing. You do understand?"

"Yes, of course, but I had hoped you would remain in Lowell until the end of summer."

"My mother's health is much better than I had anticipated. Consequently, I'd like to return to the plantation before the first picking. Perhaps there will be another opportunity in the future that will prove mutually acceptable."

Bradley nodded in agreement and they made small talk as they finished their breakfast. Bradley placed his napkin on the table. "If you're still interested in a tour, I think we should be on our way."

By carriage, their trip to the Appleton Mill took only a matter of minutes, during which time Bradley pointed out the numerous mills and boardinghouses as they passed by.

Matthew Cheever stood near the front gate awaiting their arri-val. "Gentlemen. Good to see you," he greeted. "I'm anxious to show you at least one of our mills, Mr. Wainwright. Why don't we begin in the counting building," he said, leading the way toward the one-story brick structure. "The girls working in this area trim, fold, and prepare our cloth for shipment," he explained, pointing across the room. "We maintain the time cards, pay records, and accounts of the Corporation in our office adjacent to the counting room."

As they walked into the yard area, Bradley noticed Wainwright move toward the huge loads of baled cotton. "Appears you've got yourselves quite a bit of cotton to turn into cloth," he said with a smile.

"Absolutely. Once a bale is opened, the cotton is picked and cleaned on the large machinery over on that side of the room," Matthew said as they walked into a larger building. "From there it goes to those monstrous carding machines."

"That's quite a leap from the handheld carding tools we still use at the plantation. My wife has always enjoyed spinning her own yarn," Wainwright added.

"If you'd like to see our spinning and weaving machines, they're in these other buildings. We'll have to climb several flights of stairs," Matthew warned.

"I had best see it all so I can explain it to my brothers. And I'm sure my wife would be interested to hear about that carding machine too."

Matthew led them back across the mill yard and up the enclosed stairway until they stood in front of the door to the third floor. "We have drawing and spinning machines in separate areas on this floor. As you can already hear, it's very noisy. The long slivers from the carding machines are stretched until the cotton ropes are about two inches thick on the drawing machines. Those fragile ropes go to the roving machine, where they are drawn out and lengthened still further and given a slight twist," he explained before escorting them inside.

The men jumped aside as two young bobbin girls came scurrying through, pushing their carts of bobbins in opposite directions. Once the aisle cleared, they made their way slowly through the machinery before returning to the stairwell.

"An entire floor is given over to the weaving looms," Matthew said. "We'll go and see those if you're up to the noise."

Malcolm Wainwright gave an enthusiastic nod, and Bradley relaxed a modicum. The older man appeared to be impressed with what he had seen thus far. Once he actually realized the vastness of the Associates' holdings and the fact that this was but one mill among their myriad of brick buildings daily converting raw cotton into cloth, he surely would want to align himself with their empire.

"Have you traveled to England?" Bradley inquired after they bid Matthew good-bye and were traveling down a street that fronted the most advantageous view of the mills.

"No, I can't say that I have—although my father made two trips during his lifetime. I must admit, the sights of Lowell are not what he described having seen in England. He spoke harshly of both the working and living conditions. It appears that having farm girls work in the mills and constructing this paternalistic community around your business was a stroke of genius."

"Certainly not *my* stroke of genius. However, I take great pride in being associated with these men and their ability to take a giant step in the industrialization of this country. Do you think your brothers might be persuaded to come and see exactly what we're doing here in Lowell? That it might help convince them that the Wainwright cotton could be put to better use among Americans rather than Englishmen?"

"My brothers are reasonable men, and we've always been willing to support this country in her expansion so long as we didn't place our family's financial growth at risk in the process."

Bradley tightened his hand on the reins and carefully measured his words. "After seeing the amount of capital invested in this community, do you think you and your brothers might consider making Lowell the primary market for your cotton?"

Wainwright turned, his visage serious. "I couldn't speak for my brothers, but when I return home, I would be willing to tell them what I've seen here. They would be pleased to hear they could get a better price in Massachusetts than England, but that doesn't mean they'll want to cease doing business in England."

Bradley rubbed his forehead. "Then what will it take?"

"Guarantees. We've been doing business in England for many years. Accordingly, there's a level of trust and comfort in our relationship. Even though you can promise us higher prices *this* year, they may plummet by *next* season."

"That could happen in England also," Bradley argued.

"Not to the extent you might think. My father was able to barter an agreement whereby our prices could fall only by a given percentage if market prices dropped. We never experienced the huge losses suffered by other growers when prices deflated. With you, we have no guarantees and no trust."

Bradley was ill prepared for Wainwright's revelation and struggled briefly to gain his momentum. "I can't promise you percentage guarantees without the approval of the Associates any more than you can promise me all of the Wainwright cotton without your brothers' consent. But if you will give me percentage guidelines, I will speak to the Associates about such an arrangement on your behalf, just as you have agreed to speak to your brothers about changing their market to Lowell. Regarding the trust issue, I hadn't planned to discuss this with you so soon, but I now feel compelled to do so. As I mentioned earlier today, I hoped you would favor me with permission to call upon your daughter. My hope had been that one day you might consider me a suitable husband for Jasmine. I believe our marriage would seal the future with a level of trust and commitment that even your English associates cannot provide." Bradley cleared his throat, uncertain whether the words he would next offer would be impressive to the older man or completely irrelevant. "And lest you think me without feeling, I must say that I have been smitten with your daughter since our first meeting. She would not be without love and affection."

Wainwright leaned back against the carriage seat, rubbed his jowl several times, and then nodded his head up and down. "I believe this might work. We've not made any promises other than to do our best toward reaching a mutually satisfactory arrangement that will prove financially beneficial to all concerned."

"Except the English," Bradley said with a wry grin. "What of Jasmine? Do you think she will object? After all, she barely knows me."

"Most Southern women think they have a hand in choosing their marriage partners, but truth be known, few of them do. As I mentioned, it's all a question of timing, but perhaps these matters can be helped along. It might bode well for Jasmine to remain in Lowell when I return to Mississippi. I'll tell her I think her grandmother may still be ailing and also stress to her that a season in the North might better round out her education. Jasmine won't object to remaining with my mother. While she's in Lowell, you can call upon her, letting her believe this is a matter of romance. If I know my mother, she'll have Jasmine at every social event given in a twenty-mile radius.

"If our business arrangements are successful, you can move forward with the marriage, and Jasmine will be none the wiser. If our business arrangements go sour, you can cease calling upon her and declare you've lost interest due to her youth."

Bradley viewed Malcolm Wainwright with a new admiration. He had misjudged him—thought him weak where his only daughter was concerned. This man was much more cunning than even Bradley would have imagined. Definitely not a man to be taken lightly in business negotiations.

"Look, Grandmother. Papa and Mr. Houston are getting out of a carriage just up the street." Jasmine waved her closed parasol overhead until her father finally caught sight of them.

"What an unexpected pleasure," Bradley said as they approached, his gaze riveted upon Jasmine.

"Have you ladies been having any success with your shopping expedition?" Malcolm pleasantly inquired.

"As a matter of fact, we have. However, we were going to stop for a cup of tea. Would you gentlemen care to join us?" Alice asked.

"Of course," Bradley replied before Jasmine's father could object.

Bradley beamed her a smile that instantly set Jasmine's heart pounding. What was it about this man?

"I want to show you the wonderful gift I've found for Mother," Jasmine said as soon as they'd been seated. She carefully unwrapped the brown paper and pulled out a leather-bound volume. "Look! It's *Lays of My Home and Other Poems* by John Greenleaf Whittier. I decided Mother would adore the volume since she admires Mr. Whittier's writings. The bookstore had a copy of *Legends of New-England in Prose and Verse,* but I remembered you gave her that volume for Christmas several years ago. I think she will adore it, don't you?"

Her father took the book and leafed through the pages. "I'm certain she will be most pleased, especially since you chose it for her."

"Grandmother and I decided it was an absolute necessity to find Mother's gift today. We've been scouring the shops all morning, but our efforts were finally rewarded."

"Why the urgency to purchase your gift *today*?" Bradley asked. "The shops are open every day except Sunday."

"Papa is threatening to leave for Mississippi very soon, and I was afraid he would come home this afternoon with our passage secured on the next vessel leaving Boston."

"I've been giving that matter some additional thought, Jasmine, and perhaps I was a bit hasty in declaring the restoration of your grandmother's health. After all, I'm not a physician."

Jasmine gave a single clap of her hands. "We're going to extend our visit?"

"No. As you predicted, I'm going to sail on the next ship. You, however, are going to remain here in Lowell with your grandmother."

Jasmine and her grandmother exchanged looks of pure delight. "Truly? It's almost as though you were listening to our conversation this morning. Were you eavesdropping on us, Papa?" Jasmine teased in her lilting Southern drawl.

"No, but I'd be interested to hear what the two of you were planning."

"Grandmother suggested you might permit me to remain with her until the end of November, and then the two of us would travel to The Willows and she would stay with us throughout the holidays. Wouldn't that be grand fun? All of us together again?"

"Indeed. I think your grandmother has struck upon a very suitable plan—so long as her health permits the voyage."

Grandmother Wainwright gave her son a rather sheepish grin and took a sip of her tea. "I think my health will be much improved by the holidays."

"I'm pleased to hear that bit of news, Mother. I shared my plans with Mr. Houston earlier today and he has asked for exclusive permission to call upon Jasmine during her extended visit in Lowell. I have given my hearty consent."

Jasmine paled at her father's remark. Call upon her? The very idea brought back a rush of panicked and bewildered thoughts. Bradley Houston was no Southern gentleman. If he were to become serious-minded in matters of matrimony, he would never give any thought to living in Mississippi. What could her father possibly be thinking?

"My dear, are you quite all right?" her father asked.

Jasmine fanned herself with a lace handkerchief. "I'm sure I am. However, I am quite surprised by this turn of events. I must say, I never thought the journey north to be such adventure."

Bradley gave a deep, emotionless laugh at this, his beady gray-eyed gaze making her most uncomfortable. "You may find the North full of surprises and adventure, Miss Wainwright. And I will personally be honored to reveal them all to you in due time."

Stifling a shudder, Jasmine could only smile and look demurely to her shaking hands. Clenching the hanky between her fingers, Jasmine tried to imagine what the future might hold in the company of Bradley Houston. Somehow, the thoughts were not all that comforting—nor desirous. There was something about this man that made her uneasy—not at all like his brother, Nolan. Perhaps it was his more serious nature—his lack of genuine warmth and joy. Perhaps it was the fact that Bradley Houston seemed to be a man very much used to getting his own way. And this time, that might very well include taking Jasmine for his wife.

CHAPTER · 7

SUMMER LINGERED in the air, even as a decided chill announced the coming of autumn. The days had not been as pleasant for Jasmine as she had imagined them when she and her grandmother had planned for her extended visit in Lowell. Bradley Houston had made a positive nuisance of himself, and today was no exception.

Jasmine stiffened as Bradley pulled his chair closer and cupped her cheek in his palm. It seemed he was always touching her—something that would never have been tolerated at The Willows. Why, Samuel alone would have called out the first man to lay a finger to his beloved sister. But Samuel wasn't here to stand guard. Neither was McKinley or David or her father.

"Tell me, my dear, what is it that has been keeping you so busy of late? It seems that every time I send word I'd like to call upon you, your grandmother returns a message that you've already made plans or you're not available."

Grandmother padded into the room with the stillness of a soft breeze and placed a vase of flowers on the table beside him. "I prefer having her close at hand when I'm ailing, Bradley. It gives me comfort to have her read aloud or visit with me when I must take to my bed. Having Jasmine here to aid me during my times of illness is, after all, why my son had her remain in Lowell."

"Yes, I understand Mr. Wainwright's reasoning," Bradley replied cautiously. "But I've noticed her in town with Violet Cheever on several occasions and—"

"Taking care of some shopping for me," Jasmine's grandmother interrupted. "But I'm certain you find Matthew Cheever's daughter acceptable company for my granddaughter."

"Why, of course," Bradley said defensively. "I've merely been concerned."

"There's no need for worry, Mr. Houston. In the event there's a problem, rest assured I will immediately send word. However, it is heartening to know of your concern," the old woman decorously replied.

Bradley turned toward Alice Wainwright and placed his folded hands in his lap. He looked like a schoolboy preparing to recite his daily lessons. "I had hoped to escort Jasmine on a picnic after church tomorrow afternoon. With your permission, of course."

"I think a picnic would be very nice. In fact, the fresh air would likely do me good. Will you escort us to church also?" Jasmine's grandmother asked while fussing with the floral arrangement.

Jasmine held her breath, wondering what his reply might be. Bradley didn't seem the type overly concerned with spiritual matters. Then again, her own parents had been rather remiss in church attendance these past few years. It was, of course, due to Mama's affliction, but they were always faithful to at least read the Scriptures on Sunday morning.

Bradley hesitated only for a moment. "Yes, of course. I would be pleased to escort you to church."

"Why don't I have Martha pack our dinner? After church we can return to the house and pick up the basket. Oh, and I have a delightful idea. Why don't we invite the Cheever family to join us? Jasmine and I are going to visit with them later this afternoon, and I'll see if they're available. I know how much you enjoy Matthew's company. Yes! I think we'll have a grand time, don't you, Jasmine?"

Jasmine flashed a grateful smile at her grandmother. "Yes, and

I'm certain Violet will be pleased to join us. She told me only the other day she had been longing to go on a picnic."

Bradley stood and looked down at Jasmine. "Well, then, I suppose the picnic is arranged. Not exactly what I had planned. Nonetheless, I look forward to our time together. I hope you will make time for a walk with me. There are several things I would enjoy discussing with you."

Jasmine heard the determination in his voice and it took all of her resolve to keep from cringing. "Perhaps," she whispered, hoping it would be enough of an answer to satisfy him.

After Bradley made his departure, Jasmine sighed and leaned against the front door for a moment. "Thank you, Grandmother," she said as she walked back into the parlor. "I know Mr. Houston is likely a fine man, but his overbearing character disturbs me. Besides, I've written Papa that he is much too old for me. I'd prefer a gentleman caller who is more to my liking—and closer to my own age," she added.

"Don't discount the role your father has played in Mr. Houston's behavior. He gave Bradley exclusive permission to call upon you. There may be little you can do except begin looking for Bradley's finer qualities."

Jasmine plopped down on the settee beside her grandmother. "What do you mean? Surely you don't think Papa is arranging a marriage between Bradley Houston and me? Why, that's preposterous." She turned and looked deep into her grandmother's steely hazel eyes. "Isn't it?" Up until now, the entire matter of courting Bradley Houston had seemed simply a game, a sort of cat-and-mouse venture where Jasmine would find ways to escape being snatched up by Mr. Houston's sharp claws.

"No, Jasmine. In fact, the idea is quite believable. You seem to forget that you've reached a suitable age for marriage."

Jasmine detected the sad resignation in her grandmother's voice. What was she saying? Was she keeping something from Jasmine? "You truly believe Papa has chosen Bradley Houston as a possible husband for me?" She gasped the words, as though Mammy had just cinched her corset too tight. "I don't want to marry a man I don't love. I'd rather remain a spinster."

Alice chuckled and tucked a stray curl behind Jasmine's ear. "Sometimes we must accept the fact that we aren't the ones who make the choices affecting our lives. If your father chooses Bradley, you must accept him as your husband and work toward creating a happy home. This may come as a surprise to you, but I didn't love your grandfather when I married him. Our marriage was arranged. I thought I would never survive leaving Boston to live on a cotton plantation. Those first years at The Willows were very difficult. However, in time I learned to love your grandfather, I had my children, and we were very happy."

Jasmine grimaced and shook her head back and forth. "I could *never* learn to love Bradley Houston. We have nothing in common. Unlike Grandfather and Father, he's interested only in textile and cotton production. I don't believe he is educated enough to discuss anything intellectual or cultural."

"I, too, have noticed he expresses little interest in cultural topics, although I know he is well educated. Perhaps it will take some of your Southern charm to draw out his latent qualities. Even your father is difficult to dissuade from talk of business from time to time. However, once Bradley realizes a variety of conversational topics will serve him well both in private and in the business world, I'm certain he will make every effort to expand his realm of dialogue."

"Whether he does so or not will be of little consequence—I have no intention of changing my feelings toward Bradley Houston."

"I fear your mother's insistence upon sheltering you at home all these years has left you naïve concerning matters of marriage, my dear."

"You may be correct. However, I've always been able to somewhat influence Papa's decisions regarding my future. After all, he didn't force my introduction to society with a coming-out ball."

Alice gave her granddaughter a sidelong glance. "I believe your mother's fear of hosting such an event may have played a larger part in your father's decision than any argument you posed."

Jasmine moved to the marble-topped mahogany side table and idly rearranged the colorful zinnias her grandmother had placed in a vase only a short time ago. Unbidden, she looked into the gilded mirror across the room and met her grandmother's troubled gaze. Would her father force her to marry someone she didn't love? Could he do such a thing to her? Surely not.

That night Jasmine's sleep was restless, her dreams fraught with worrisome visions of her future. She saw herself as a bride, walking down the aisle to a masked man. She knew the man was Bradley Houston, but he refused to allow her to see his face. Once the ceremony was over and she was pronounced to be his wife, he lifted the mask, much as a bride would lift her veil. Beneath his coverings, Bradley's face contorted and turned monstrous.

Jasmine awoke screaming softly into her pillow. She sat up with a start, her heart pounding relentlessly.

What was it Grandmother had said earlier? *"I fear your mother's insistence upon sheltering you at home all these years has left you naïve concerning matters of marriage."* What did she mean? Was it something more than merely the thought that her father might marry her off to a man Jasmine didn't and couldn't love?

"Oh, I'm so frightened," she whispered to the darkened room. Jasmine thought momentarily of praying, but she had never been very good at such things. She always pictured God as a distant king upon His throne, a solemn-faced judge who tried each case with stoic indifference. Grandmother had other ideas, however. She spoke of God's tender compassion—His mercies.

"I pray you take mercy on me, dear God," Jasmine murmured, pulling her covers tight against her neck. "I pray you intercede on my behalf and remove this notion of marriage between me and Bradley Houston from my father's mind."

———

Bradley rested his back against a large elm and watched the unfolding scene. His plan for a quiet picnic with Jasmine had turned into an afternoon of frivolity attended by a myriad of people—some of whom he didn't even know. Bradley wasn't certain who had given Violet Cheever free rein to invite guests, but he suspected Jasmine may have had a hand in the situation. She'd been avoiding him since their arrival, and now that his brother had arrived with Henry and Fanny Longfellow, she was involved in an animated discussion about some literary nonsense. He motioned her to join him and grew increasingly irritated when she chose to ignore him. Unwilling to tolerate her behavior any longer, he stood and walked to her side.

He leaned down until his lips nearly touched her ear. "Please join me," he whispered forcefully.

His words were a command, not a request, yet she smiled demurely and said, "I prefer to remain here, thank you."

He grasped her elbow and squeezed more tightly than he'd intended. "I expect you to join me—now," he hissed.

"Please release my arm. You're hurting me," she said when they were a short distance away from the crowd.

"Perhaps you should have come when I motioned to you," he replied. "I invited you because *I* want the privilege of enjoying your company."

Jasmine sat down beside him. "You could come and join the rest of us. Perhaps I would take more pleasure in being with you if you would discuss something other than the textile mills."

"Ah, so you find me rather boring and would prefer to delve into the works of Shakespeare or Keats—perhaps Scott? You may be surprised to learn that I far outranked my brother while studying the classics in college. Merely because I do not stand around professing literary knowledge does not mean I have none. However, some of us have moved beyond such puffery, realizing what is truly important in life. And just look at Henry in his flowered waistcoat and yellow kid gloves. Wherever does he find those clothes?"

"There is more to life than work, and it appears there are many who find Mr. Longfellow—and his attire—quite interesting."

"I'm surprised Fanny isn't embarrassed to be seen with him in public. After all, her people are of some quality in Boston."

"She appears quite devoted to him," Jasmine replied, glancing toward the couple sitting side by side on a patchwork quilt. "I believe them to be very much in love—something I very much value."

"Well, I think he enjoys making a spectacle of himself. It's much easier than working for a living."

"You judge him rather harshly, Mr. Houston."

"When Longfellow married Fanny Appleton, Nathan gifted him with over one hundred thousand dollars worth of stock in the mills. Nathan's generosity has permitted Henry to enjoy the life of a wealthy man while he earns nothing more than a professor's salary at Harvard. For all intents and purposes, he lives off of his father-in-law rather than working to support himself."

"His writing is his work," she protested.

"It will never come to anything," Bradley asserted dryly. "He'll no doubt disappear into oblivion when his father-in-law's fortune and good intentions are gone."

"I think not," Jasmine declared. "Obviously Mr. Appleton can appreciate the fact that something other than textile production is of value to the world."

Bradley stroked his fingers down her arm softly. "There are one or two things I value more than textile production also."

Jasmine recoiled from his touch. "You forget yourself, sir," she said, her drawl quite pronounced.

Bradley shook his head. "I'm well aware of what I'm suggesting. I just wonder if you understand it as well."

CHAPTER · 8

ALICE TAPPED her fingers on the table beside her chair and contemplated the wisdom of her decision. If Malcolm should find out, he would be upset. No—he would be furious. She had given her consent to Jasmine in haste, and now she couldn't go back on her word. "And what of Bradley?" she muttered.

"Excuse me, ma'am?" Martha drew closer. "I didn't hear your question." The tall, stern-faced woman watched her employer with some interest.

"Oh, Martha, I didn't know you had come into the room. I'm talking to myself. I fear I've made a muddle of things," she confided.

Martha began arranging an armful of flowers from the garden. "I've never known you to possess anything but the soundest of judgments. How could you have possibly muddled any matter?"

"When Jasmine and I were at the library yesterday, we happened to see Lilly Cheever. She reminded me of the antislavery meeting that's taking place on Wednesday. Of course, Jasmine heard the conversation and immediately asked if she could attend."

Martha put her hand to her neck in surprise. "Oh, Mrs. Wainwright! You didn't agree?"

"Yes, I'm afraid I did."

"Whatever will her father think?"

Alice appreciated her housekeeper's frankness. They had always shared more of a friendship than a relationship of employee and employer. "That's my concern. I know Malcolm will be angry and likely never permit Jasmine to visit again. My only hope is that he won't find out. After all, it's only one meeting, and if I tell Jasmine never to discuss her attendance with anyone, perhaps Malcolm will remain unaware. Quite frankly, I'm more concerned with the possibility of someone mentioning her attendance to Bradley Houston. Should he find out, there is little doubt he'd tell Malcolm."

Martha trimmed the stems on several crimson roses before placing them in the vase. "I thought Mr. Houston was active in the antislavery movement."

"Nolan Houston is active, but I've never seen Bradley at any of the meetings or heard him profess his beliefs one way or the other. However, with his involvement in the textile mills, I think he would frown upon any active participation in the antislavery movement. And now that he's professed a romantic interest in Jasmine, I'm certain he won't want her exposed to the ever-growing antislavery sentiments."

"Have you considered telling the child you've reconsidered and believe your decision was ill-advised?"

"I could, but a part of me believes Jasmine needs to hear the truth about slavery. She's never given any thought to the fact that the Wainwrights actually own human beings."

Martha gave her mistress a shrewd grin while pushing a scarlet-red rose deep into the vase. "Well, if you change your mind, you could always be forced to remain at home due to a stomach ailment—or perhaps a headache."

Alice returned the smile. "I'll keep your suggestion in mind, but I'm thinking that if the need arises, I can always tell Malcolm and Bradley the truth: that hearing both sides of any issue is important to sound decision-making. Although I'm certain Bradley thinks a woman should embrace the same beliefs as her husband, *I* certainly don't adhere to such a viewpoint."

Martha nodded. "Whatever you think is best."

Bradley donned his black silk hat and checked his pocket watch one last time. Tardiness, he had decided many years ago, was a habit of ill-bred individuals who would never succeed in life. That resolve in mind, Bradley knew he would be on time for his meeting today, no matter the cost or inconvenience. His image with the Associates was of paramount importance, and today's meeting would likely prove decisive. He tucked Malcolm Wainwright's letter into his pocket, stepped up into his carriage, and arrived at Matthew Cheever's office within fifteen minutes. The number of carriages already present startled him, and he once again looked at his watch. The meeting wasn't due to begin for another ten minutes.

He hurried through the iron gate and across the mill yard toward Matthew's office. All of the other Associates who had been summoned to the meeting were already assembled in the room when he entered. All eyes turned in his direction. He hadn't felt this level of discomfort since his primary school days when the instructor would sometimes call upon him unexpectedly.

He took a brief moment to gain his composure before removing his hat. "Good day, gentlemen. Was the schedule for our meeting changed without my knowledge?"

"Welcome, Bradley," Matthew greeted. "No, the time wasn't changed. I asked the other members to come a half hour early."

Bradley waited, but Matthew offered no further explanation, which left him to wonder what the group might have wanted to discuss in his absence. "I trust I gave you sufficient time to conclude your conversation."

"Indeed," Nathan Appleton said. "What news can you share regarding our friends in the South? Are you making any headway with your negotiations?"

Bradley reached into his jacket and extracted Wainwright's recent letter. "As a matter of fact, I received this letter from Malcolm Wainwright only two days ago. He and his brothers are close to reaching an agreement with us. They sent a refusal to Mr.

Haggarty, their English buyer, with notice they'll negotiate terms no further. They requested Haggarty's signature on a refusal to contract. Once they receive the endorsed refusal, they will be prepared to contract with us. The tone of the letter is extremely positive."

"That's excellent news," Nathan commented. "I don't think I could be more pleased."

Bradley took a moment to bask in Appleton's accolades before continuing. "I believe the balance of the letter may prove you wrong on that account. There is even more good news," he said. "With my strong encouragement, Mr. Wainwright has taken it upon himself to tell other growers about our strong desire to do business with Southern plantation owners throughout Louisiana and Mississippi. There are a number of them who are looking favorably toward conducting business with us if it would prove more lucrative than continuing their current contracts with England. Of course, none of them would yield the amount of cotton that the Wainwrights' harvest will, but if we can gain control of the area one grower at a time, I'm certain we'll soon have all the cotton needed to keep our mills operating at maximum capacity. Perhaps it will even signal a time for expansion."

Nathan Appleton's tremendous enthusiasm was beyond expectations. He bounded from his chair and pumped Bradley's arm in an exaggerated handshake while encouraging the other members to offer their congratulations. "You see? I told you our earlier meeting was unnecessary. Bradley is worthy of the confidence Matthew and I placed in him."

Wilson Harper shifted in his chair. "I never said he wasn't worthy of our confidence. I said the reports thus far had not been favorable and I feared the Wainwrights would remain with the English markets. I'm pleased now that Bradley has been able to prove me wrong."

"That's good to hear," Bradley put in. He knew Harper had never been one of his strong supporters, which made his comment even more pleasurable.

"For planning purposes, does Mr. Wainwright say when we

may expect to have a signed contract in our hands? Or, for that matter, when do you expect to secure a signed contract with any of these men?" Wilson Harper asked with a sanctimonious grin curving his lips.

"I'll be returning to Mississippi in mid-November and expect we will already be receiving cotton from the Wainwrights by the time I sail. As for the other producers, I believe we'll have contracts from some of them in the very near future. Others may wait until the Wainwrights have actually begun doing business with us. However, we will benefit from their contracts even if they sign late in the year. Many of the producers are still harvesting in December and January."

"If you've secured an agreement with the Wainwrights, why do you find it necessary to return to Mississippi in November?" Wilson asked.

Several members turned their attention to Bradley, and he knew he must respond now. Otherwise, the powerful momentum he had gained during the meeting might be lost. "I'm going to escort Miss Wainwright back to The Willows, where we will be married during the Christmas holidays. I hope that news will put to rest any further concerns you might have, Mr. Harper."

There were several surprised gasps, followed by what seemed an interminable silence. Nathan was the first to speak. "Let me offer my hearty congratulations, Bradley. Miss Wainwright is a beautiful young woman, and I'm certain she'll make you a fine wife."

Eyes sharpened, Robert Woolsey gave Bradley a slow smile. "And seal his business transactions as well."

Bradley wasn't certain if Woolsey's remark was filled with scorn or jealousy, but he decided to let the retort pass when Matthew slapped Woolsey on the shoulder and said, "Sounds as though you're sorry you didn't have the wherewithal to win Miss Wainwright's hand for yourself."

Woolsey flushed. "No offense intended, Bradley. After all, your success swells all of our coffers. Accept my best wishes for your happiness with Miss Wainwright."

By the time the meeting ended, Bradley was receiving enthusiastic best wishes from every one of the men in attendance. He departed the meeting with a sense of elation he hadn't experienced since receiving his father's business assets, but by the time he arrived home his emotions were as mixed as when he'd been told Nolan would receive his mother's valuable paintings as his inheritance. Telling the assembled group of Associates that he planned to marry Jasmine Wainwright before advising Jasmine of his intentions and actually having the betrothal approved and announced by her father might prove to be a frivolous mistake. However, if luck remained with him, neither Malcolm Wainwright nor his daughter would ever become aware of his boastful—and premature—announcement.

CHAPTER · 9

ALICE SETTLED into the church pew with Jasmine at her side. Her granddaughter was busy looking over the crowd assembling in the old Pawtucket church, where antislavery meetings had been conducted for more than fifteen years. The church soon filled to capacity, and many of the attendees were forced to stand in the aisles or out in the churchyard.

There were two speakers, both freed slaves who spoke to the gathering of their work with Frederick Douglass and William Lloyd Garrison. When they finished their short speeches, it was Nolan Houston who called out from the back of the room and asked them to tell the crowd how they had gained freedom.

The slave who called himself George moved forward on the small stage. "It was de hand of God what moved in a mighty way to give us our freedom, for our master was cruel and so was his missus. We's got de scars to show for his mean streak. One day some Quakers come through Virginia, and dey stopped and asked if the master could spare a cool drink. Dem Quakers stayed and talked and talked to the master and his missus.

"Dey stayed for three days, talking and praying until they finally convinced our owner it was de right thing to emancipate his slaves. So de master and his missus, dey decided dey was gonna sell their place and move off to Ohio and earn dem a living by working with they own hands. Dey told us all we was free to go on our way. We thought it was a trick until de Quakers told us about de praying they'd been doin' for days. Even so, we 'spected de dogs to come huntin' us down. But dey never did. Don' know what happened to any of dem white folk. Ain't never see'd 'em since den. I ain't never looked back, but I'm mighty thankful for dem Quaker folk."

The two former slaves talked awhile longer, answering questions and removing their shirts to reveal the angry scars of abuse—scars that spoke louder than any words they might utter. The entire crowd seemed to groan in unison as the men told of iron shackles, bullpens, and stocks being used to punish slaves.

Jasmine nudged her grandmother. "I know all these people are abolitionists, but do they not realize there are many slaves who are well treated and happy?"

Alice arched her eyebrows. "And where would that be?"

Jasmine stared at her grandmother in disbelief. "Why, at *any* Wainwright plantation."

"Do you believe the slaves at The Willows are content with their lot in life, Jasmine?"

"Of course they are. They are well cared for. Happy. Content. They love us."

"You need not continue to defend your opinion. I'm not going to argue with you, dear, but why did you want to come to this meeting if you disagree with abolition?"

Jasmine fidgeted with her gloves. "I wanted to hear their views, but I didn't expect the speeches to be inflammatory. I think they should temper such talk by explaining there are slave owners who treat their people exceedingly well."

Alice smiled at her granddaughter but said nothing. She'd not enter into a disagreement that might cause Jasmine to discuss this gathering with her father at a later date. She sighed, knowing Jasmine had been sheltered from the realities of life on the plantation. Alice tried not to fret about the matter, but an uneasiness hung over her like a foreboding of tragedy to come. Now she was certain she'd made a mistake. She should have followed Martha's advice and remained at home.

The meeting broke up a short time later. Had Alice been there alone, she might have lingered to revisit some of the evening's discussion with her friends. Now all she wanted to do was depart before Jasmine managed to get drawn into some of the more heated arguments. With an authoritative, no-nonsense air, Alice moved Jasmine to the door.

"Why are we leaving so quickly, Grandmother? Is something wrong?" Jasmine questioned as they descended the stairs.

"The night air can cause us both to take sick," Alice replied, linking her arm with her granddaughter's. "Besides, Martha has promised to have fresh cinnamon scones ready for our evening tea. You haven't yet tasted her special recipe. They are quite delightful."

Jasmine seemed easily placated with this response. Alice almost felt sorry for the girl. Her innocence made it simpler for Alice to explain away their departure, but her ignorance of the truth was distressful.

They were but a short distance from the church when Alice noticed Nolan Houston walking toward them with a quizzical look on his face. "Good evening, ladies. I must say I was surprised to see you in attendance, Miss Wainwright. What brings a Southern belle to an antislavery meeting?"

"I was curious, anxious to expand my knowledge."

"And does my brother know you were in attendance this evening?" He flashed her a broad smile as if already knowing the answer.

Alice stepped forward and took Nolan's arm. "No, he doesn't, Nolan. And I would be most appreciative if you didn't mention seeing us. I fear I took it upon myself to bring Jasmine without seeking her father's approval. I beg your indulgence in this matter."

Nolan's smile faded. "Of course, Mrs. Wainwright. I would never betray your confidence."

Alice breathed a sigh of relief. The handsome young man seemed to easily understand her plight without forcing her to give further explanation. "Thank you. And if I may be of assistance to you in the future, you have only to ask."

He nodded. "I understand the delicacy of the situation." Turning his attention to Jasmine, he said, "I hope you found the meeting informative, Miss Wainwright."

"I thought the presentation rather one-sided. As I was telling my grandmother, there are many slaves who are happy and well cared for. In fact, we have such slaves on the Wainwright plantations."

"That's good to hear. For when I toured your plantation, I failed to ask the slaves I saw whether they were happy. Of course, most of them were out in the fields laboring in the relentless heat, but when I again visit The Willows, I'll make it a point to inquire."

Jasmine frowned at his seemingly flippant reply. "You need only ask Mammy. She'll tell you how happy she's been living with us."

Alice cleared her throat. "We really must be going home. We have a full day tomorrow. The Ladies' Society from the church is meeting at my house."

"Certainly," Nolan said graciously while tipping his hat.

Once they were settled in the carriage and Martin flicked the reins, Alice took Jasmine's hand in her own. "The meeting tonight is *not* something you should mention publicly, my dear, even with those who were in attendance. Caution is the best practice."

Jasmine arched her thin, perfectly shaped eyebrows. "So tomorrow I'm not to speak of having been at tonight's meeting? Is that what you want me to understand, Grandmother?"

"No need to take umbrage. I make this request of anyone I take to the meetings. Those who attend the antislavery meetings have an expectation their confidentiality will not be breached. I'm asking no more of you than I request from any of my other guests."

Jasmine bowed her head. "I'm sorry. I'm acting like a spoiled child after you were kind enough to take me to the meeting. My lips are sealed. You have my word."

"Thank you, dear. I knew I could count on you."

But even with her granddaughter's promise, Alice Wainwright could not settle her discomfort. She could hardly explain her situation to Jasmine. How could she hope for her granddaughter to understand that the very institution that put jewels around her throat and silks on her back was the very nightmare Alice had turned her back on when she returned to live in the North? No, there would be no easy way to explain the matter. To Jasmine, life on the plantation was leisurely afternoons reading and sewing—it was tender care by Mammy, who had raised the girl since infancy—it was a facade of a utopia that didn't exist.

But I won't be the one to open her eyes to the truth, Alice thought uncomfortably. *She'll see it for herself soon enough. She's an adult now, and while protected, Jasmine is no dolt. She'll learn the truth.*

"And the truth shall make you free," a voice whispered deep in her heart.

"But the truth is often very hard to take," she responded quietly.

Jasmine looked up and smiled. "What did you say, Grandmother?"

Alice shook her head and patted her granddaughter's hand. "Just the mutterings of an old woman. Nothing of import." But in her heart, Alice knew better. It was possibly the most important lesson Jasmine would ever learn.

———

Jasmine stood beside her grandmother while affably greeting their guests the next afternoon. The ladies flocked into the house in their plumed hats and silk carriage dresses as though they were attending the social event of the season rather than a meeting of the Ladies' Society.

Violet grasped Jasmine by the arm and pulled her away from the crowd. "Did you enjoy the meeting last night?"

Jasmine cocked her head and met Violet's intense gaze. "What meeting?"

"The antislavery meeting, silly. I saw you there with your grandmother."

"I have no idea what you're talking about," Jasmine insisted.

Violet placed her fingertips to her lips. "Oh, I understand. You're holding fast to the privacy rules. But it doesn't matter if you talk to me—after all, I was in attendance too. However, I must admit that I was quite surprised to see you at the meeting. What did you think after hearing those poor slaves talk about how they were mistreated? And those dreadful scars on their backs—did you *look* at them?"

Jasmine chewed on her lip and strengthened her resolve. She would keep her word. "Would you like a cup of punch? It's really quite good. I tasted it earlier."

Violet sighed and folded her arms across her chest. "Well, then, let's talk about your wedding. I'm surprised you've remained in Massachusetts. Is your mother making all the plans for your nuptials without you? I would much prefer to plan my own wedding when I get married."

Jasmine's soft laughter floated through the room. "Nuptials? I'm not getting married. Wherever did you get such a preposterous idea?"

"My father told us at breakfast this morning. If you don't believe me, ask my mother."

Jasmine clamped on to Violet's arm and pulled her out the stained-glass doors leading into the garden. "Exactly *what* did your father say?" Dread rushed over her like a cold, damp breeze.

Violet's gaze was riveted upon the fingers digging into her flesh. "You're hurting my arm."

Jasmine loosened her hold but didn't turn the girl free. "Tell me what your father said about marriage plans. I don't even have a suitor."

"Of course you do," Violet retorted, shaking free. "Bradley Houston! He's been your constant escort since you arrived in Lowell. Although, personally, I find his brother much more appealing. He has the loveliest eyes—don't you think?"

"Is *Bradley* who you're talking about?" Jasmine placed her hand on her chest and sighed in relief. "Bradley's not my beau. He escorts me as a matter of convenience and safety—at my father's request."

"Really?" the fourteen-year-old questioned. "Well, my father said that Mr. Houston would be escorting you back to Mississippi in mid-November and the two of you would be married during the Christmas holidays. Perhaps your father has requested more of Mr. Houston than you realize."

A flash of anger stabbed at her like a red-hot poker. "Mr. Houston has never asked me to marry him, and I'm certain he hasn't asked for my father's consent. In addition, my mother would have written me."

"I can't imagine he'd announce your wedding plans to all of his business associates if he didn't have your father's permission," Violet countered.

Jasmine was uncertain how to respond. She had more questions than answers, and right now she wanted only to awaken from this nightmare. The warm afternoon heat closed in like a suffocating shroud. "He made a public announcement?" She shook her head and looked around. "I must sit down. I feel as though I'm going to faint."

Violet helped her to the bench and then sat down beside her. "I'm sorry I was so unkind, but it never entered my mind you didn't know. I just thought you were being coy. When Father told us, I did express my surprise that you would agree to marry Mr. Houston since you've told me in the past you did not enjoy his company."

"His behavior makes me extremely uncomfortable," Jasmine confided. "Besides, he's too old for me. I'm but ten and eight and he's . . . well . . . he's much older."

"What will you do?"

"As soon as the meeting is over, I'll talk to Grandmother and see what she knows of these arrangements. If she, too, is uninformed, we'll need to talk with Bradley Houston. Until then, I'm going to pray this is all a misunderstanding."

So great was her sense of humiliation that she wanted to disappear from sight, and Violet's wan smile was doing nothing to help buoy her spirits. There was nothing to do but return to the parlor and act as though all was right with the world.

"I suppose we should join the others," Jasmine said, finally staying her nerves. "But please, Violet, say nothing about this."

"I promise I won't," the girl said, jumping to her feet. "I cannot vouch, however, for what my mother might say or do. She loves weddings and babies. I think she always longed to have more daughters to plan events for, but alas, she has to suffer with me. Of course, my brother, Michael, keeps her very busy. Mother often says that twelve-year-old boys are much more difficult to contain than fourteen-year-old girls."

Jasmine listened only half-heartedly to Violet's girlish chatter. Inside her head, a million questions were spilling over one another. How could Bradley Houston have made a public announcement of marriage? It was unheard of. The embarrassment he would face when she rejected him would be a hard matter to face among his peers. Why would he put this burden upon himself? Unless . . . Jasmine couldn't even bear to let the words form in her thoughts. It couldn't be true. Her father and mother would have said something.

"Oh, I'm so glad you've joined us," Lilly Cheever said as Jasmine and Violet came into the room. "I have someone I want you to meet."

Jasmine forced a smile, meeting the dark-eyed gaze of the woman. Lilly Cheever wasted little time pulling Jasmine along beside her.

"Elinor, this is the young woman I was telling you about. Jasmine Wainwright, I'd like you to meet Elinor Brighton. She's the younger sister of Taylor Manning. His wife, Bella, is that lovely woman speaking with your grandmother."

Jasmine met the face of Elinor Brighton and knew immediately that the woman was in no more mood to be at this gathering than was Jasmine. "I'm pleased to meet you," Jasmine said, struggling with her composure.

Elinor nodded. "As am I."

The brown-haired woman looked immediately past Jasmine as

though expecting someone to come through the door. Jasmine had heard from her grandmother that this woman had been recently widowed. In the South she wouldn't be allowed to join in a public gathering.

In the South a man would never speak out of turn about marrying a woman he hardly knew.

But we aren't in the South, Jasmine reminded herself.

———

Bradley had planned to take the train to Boston, but Alice Wainwright's message summoning him to her home had required him to postpone the journey. The old woman's note had been vague and somewhat terse, and he had momentarily considered ignoring her request. But caution prevailed—he dare not upset Malcolm Wainwright's mother at this juncture. Even though his meeting in Boston wasn't urgent, Bradley detested the interruption nonetheless.

After all, he'd made arrangements to meet with Mr. Sheppard first thing in the morning to go over the shipping business accounts, and now he'd had to send his apologies and ask to reschedule their appointment. Although Bradley had sold the majority of the family shipping business upon his father's death, he still retained ownership of two of the newer vessels and a moderate share of the stock. And while he didn't look after daily maritime operations, Bradley was an astute businessman who knew the wisdom of making an occasional visit to inspect Mr. Sheppard's books.

Attempting to squelch his irritation as he walked up the steps, Bradley took a deep breath and knocked on Alice Wainwright's front door. He nodded at Martha as he handed her his silk-banded hat. "I trust the ladies are expecting me," he commented brusquely.

Martha returned his aloof gaze, her chiseled features void of emotion. "They're in the parlor, sir."

Although he was none too happy about Mrs. Wainwright's request for him to make an immediate appearance, he was determined to maintain his composure. Losing his temper with the old woman would not be wise.

Bradley entered the elegant yet simple sitting room. To one side of the room Jasmine stood near a large floor-to-ceiling window. Her gown of pale pink hugged her figure, stirring Bradley's interest. She might well be the factor that clinched the deal in his business relationship with Malcolm Wainwright, but it certainly was beneficial that she was slender and beautiful.

He flashed her a smile just as she turned to meet his gaze. She said nothing and turned away quickly to take a seat, a frown lining her otherwise worried expression. Bradley turned to greet Mrs. Wainwright, who sat stock-still in a high-back padded chair.

"I'm pleased to see that you both appear to be in good health. The vagueness of your message left me wondering what mayhem might greet me when I arrived," he stated.

"Sit down, Bradley."

The chill in Mrs. Wainwright's words sent icy fingers racing down his spine. He glanced toward Jasmine, whose cold stare held the same chill as did her grandmother's words. Perhaps this matter was more serious than he had contemplated. Bradley startled when Mrs. Wainwright rang for Martha and then instructed her to bring tea. He wanted to forego the ritual. Instead, they sat quietly, saturated by an ominous silence that hovered over the room like a vaporous fog. Waiting. Staring first at some indistinguishable spot on the floor and then the ceiling. Listening as the mantel clock ticked off the minutes. Finally, when he thought he would surely break his resolve and speak out, Martha reappeared with their refreshments, and Mrs. Wainwright ceremoniously poured their afternoon repast.

The old woman took a sip of her tea, leaned back into the soft cushion of her chair, and met Bradley's stare. "I summoned you here because I have heard what I hope is only idle gossip."

His teacup hit the saucer with a loud clink, the amber liquid splashing over the edge of the cup and spilling onto the carpet. He ignored it. "You summoned me here to discuss gossip? Do you realize I cancelled a business meeting in Boston? I care little about the nonsensical chitchat of women who have too little to occupy their time or their minds, Mrs. Wainwright."

The silver-haired woman stiffened. "Your condescending tone will not serve you well today, Mr. Houston, for I have heard from a most reliable source you have announced in public that you plan to marry my granddaughter this winter. What say you, Mr. Houston? Idle gossip or truth?"

The blood drained from Bradley's face. How had word spread to the old woman so quickly? He'd been certain he would have time to correspond with Mr. Wainwright before she found out. Apparently members of the Associates gossiped as much as their wives. The very thought provoked him. There was nothing to do but own up to his words. If he lied, he'd surely be made the fool.

"What you've heard is a true expression of exactly what I *hope* will occur this winter. I admit my folly in speaking as though I've already received Mr. Wainwright's permission. I will tell you, however, that the marriage proposal is under consideration, and Mr. Wainwright has given tentative approval to our marriage."

"*Our* marriage? *My* marriage? To *you*?" Jasmine wagged her finger back and forth between them as she spoke. "Preposterous! I simply don't believe you. Papa has never said one word in his letters. Nor has my mother. And she would have written about wedding plans, wouldn't she, Grandmother?"

Mrs. Wainwright didn't answer. Bradley watched the shrewd look of awareness slowly creep into her countenance, and he knew she understood. He was careful not to smirk. After all, he didn't want to alienate her. He doubted Jasmine's father would be pleased by his social blunder, and Bradley certainly didn't want his business acumen judged by this one mistake.

"So, then, this is to be a *business* arrangement," Alice finally replied.

"If all goes according to plan."

Jasmine rushed to her grandmother's side. "Grandmother, what are you saying? Don't take his side against me in this."

Alice turned to face her granddaughter. "I'm not taking his side, my dear. I have no say-so in this matter. But you may trust I will make every attempt to dissuade your father. I doubt Malcolm will be pleased to hear of your conduct, Mr. Houston. There is little doubt in my mind that you've overstepped the boundaries of your gentlemen's agreement with my son."

The blood rushed to his head, throbbing in his temples like a pounding drum. He must remain calm or all would be lost. This wretched old woman could ruin everything. He longed to retaliate with venom-filled words, but instead he smiled graciously. "I hope I can convince you that this is more than a business arrangement, Mrs. Wainwright. I care deeply for Jasmine and I will do my utmost to make her happy."

Tears were now streaming down Jasmine's face. "If you want to make me happy, you'll tell my father you don't wish to marry me."

Her disgust at the possibility of their union was evident, causing Bradley's anger to grow. He was determined to hold his tongue, however. It would be to his benefit to show contrition for his actions, even sorrow at her rejection.

"I am sorry for having spoken out of line. I'm afraid the spirit of the moment was upon me and I erred in judgment. However, I believe that in time you will grow to love me. And once we have children, you'll be content with this union."

Jasmine shivered. "Children? I'll *never* have your children." Her look of repulsion deepened, offending Bradley in such a way that he put down his cup and saucer and got to his feet.

He knew he must leave or he would explode in anger. How dare Jasmine assess his plans with such distaste? She could do much worse than to marry a wealthy Northern businessman. He'd held his temper in check as long as humanly possible. "I think we are all distraught with this surprising turn of events. I'll come back tomorrow morning when all of us have had time to gain our composure and think rationally."

Before either of them could say anything further, Bradley turned and exited the room. "I'll see myself out," he said as he hurried into the entrance hall.

CHAPTER · *10*

BRADLEY BOUNDED into the room as though he hadn't a care in the world. Jasmine watched his animated behavior, amazed at the change in demeanor since his hasty departure only yesterday.

She had spent a restless night reliving the moment when Bradley had not only admitted to his loose tongue but also announced his plans to marry her as a means to further his business. Her heart ached at the very thought, and she felt she had aged overnight. Her girlish naïveté had altered in the wake of conversations with her grandmother. She could still hear the older woman say, *"Arranged marriages for the sake of bettering the family coffers are nothing new, Jasmine. It has been done this way for centuries."* But how could her beloved papa allow it to happen to his only daughter? *Wouldn't he want me to marry for love?*

"You're looking quite lovely, my dear," Bradley announced. The return of his confidence was apparent. "Perhaps reflection has caused you to feel more favorable toward the idea of matrimony."

"You appear to be feeling rather brash," Jasmine remarked dryly.

He glanced about the room and into the garden. "Indeed. Where is your grandmother?"

"She'll be down shortly. She spends the first few hours of the morning studying her Bible and praying."

"Asking forgiveness for her sinful nature, I suppose."

"What?" His rude remark caught her off guard. "My grandmother is an honest, gentle lady."

"Your grandmother is willing to bend the rules to suit herself when necessary."

Alice Wainwright descended the stairs wearing a green-and-gold print morning dress that accentuated the golden flecks in her hazel eyes. "If you care to defame me, please wait until I'm present, Mr. Houston."

He held out a letter that had been neatly addressed to Malcolm Wainwright. "I took the liberty of removing this from the tray in the entrance hall. After we've completed our conversation, I doubt you'll want to post your missive."

Jasmine's surprise at his boldness bordered on hysteria as she turned to her grandmother. "I cannot believe such behavior."

Her grandmother took the letter and placed it on the table beside her. "I'm certainly pleased I took ample time for prayer this morning, Mr. Houston, as you are already trying my patience. I must say, this is a side of you that I have not yet been burdened to witness."

Bradley seemed to enjoy watching her irritation rise. In fact, Jasmine thought he seemed quite pleased with himself.

"Before you say anything you might regret, let me advise you that when I left here yesterday, I stopped at the Merrimack House. There was quite a crowd, and I was seated near a table of people who were discussing the merits of abolition." Jasmine noticed her grandmother startle when he mentioned abolition.

"That's of little interest to us, Bradley. I thought you came to discuss the improper announcement of our impending marriage," Jasmine interjected.

"If you'll not interrupt, you will see how this all comes together, my dear. Just sit down and listen."

Bradley relished the moment as Jasmine appeared stunned by his command and immediately dropped onto the brocade-upholstered bustle chair. Watching as she followed his commands gave him a heady feeling of power.

"As I was saying, the people sitting adjacent to me were discussing abolition. In the course of their discussion, they mentioned an antislavery meeting that was held at the old Pawtucket church several days ago. Apparently there were a couple of former slaves who spoke about their life on a plantation. But then, you two already know what they talked about, don't you?"

"Excuse me? What *are* you talking about?" Jasmine asked.

"There's no need to feign ignorance. I know that both of you attended the meeting. I'm certain your son would be appalled to discover you took Jasmine to an antislavery meeting, aren't you, Mrs. Wainwright? After all, how would it look for a man of his status and reputation—an owner of over a hundred slaves—to have his daughter and mother notably involved with such a movement? Why, it might mean their neighbors would condemn the family. It could mean a great loss for everyone."

He paused, watching both women carefully. Jasmine paled considerably, but her grandmother held her head upright, waiting for him to continue.

"Not only that, but it could see the family fortune in ruin."

"Our family is very successful," Jasmine protested. "It would take more than something this trivial to ruin us."

Bradley raised a brow. "Trivial? You think this trivial?" He shook his head. "The Boston Associates are heavily dependent upon cotton for their mills. Your father and uncles are vast producers of this cotton. However, the Associates are not fools. They won't brook nonsense or a threat to their well-being. Your father and his brothers have already cut many of their ties with English markets. They are counting on the Associates to purchase their cotton crops. A single word from me could put an end to that."

"But what purpose would that serve?" Jasmine questioned, her voice breaking slightly. "How would it help your case?"

"It might not necessarily help my case, but it would devastate your family. If I choose to tell the Associates that your family is less than reliable—that there are problems with the dependency of the product—your father and uncles will sit with tons of cotton on the docks and no buyer. England won't have them now, not even if they agreed to take a huge loss of profit. No, my dear ladies, the Wainwright family has burned several bridges over these past few days. Wouldn't you say so, Mrs. Wainwright?"

Alice Wainwright remained silent, staring at the rose bushes in her flower garden, obviously unwilling to make a rushed admission.

Bradley rubbed his hands together in satisfaction. "Let me see, what were your words to me yesterday, Mrs. Wainwright—'idle gossip or truth'?"

Alice glared at him. "Truth. And now, Mr. Houston, what is it you want from me?"

Bradley gave her a self-satisfied grin. "I'd say this piece of information puts us on equal footing, Mrs. Wainwright. I'll not mention to your son the fact that you escorted Jasmine to an anti-slavery meeting if you'll refrain from divulging my overzealous declaration of our impending marriage. I won't suggest to the Associates that the Wainwright family is anything other than solid, and you, my dear Jasmine, will happily agree to our union. Think of it, my dear. You will be saving generations of Wainwrights from disgrace and financial ruin."

"This can't be our only recourse," Jasmine said, looking to her grandmother.

The old woman shifted in her chair and gave Jasmine a look of defeat. "I won't send the letter, Mr. Houston."

"And there will never be any mention of this to Mr. Wainwright from either of you. Is that agreed?"

Jasmine and her grandmother locked gazes and then nodded their heads. "Agreed," they stated in unison.

Bradley stood. "I believe you'll both begin to see the wisdom of this in time. For now, I simply require that you keep your unhappy thoughts to yourself." He gave a brief bow. "Now, you ladies finish your tea." He started to go, then turned and fixed his gaze on Jasmine.

"Oh yes, I nearly forgot. There's a social at the Harper home next Friday evening. I'll expect to escort you, Jasmine. Be ready at eight o'clock."

The two women sat in stunned silence after Bradley Houston departed. For Jasmine, it was the moment she realized that she had very little say over her life and future. Men would make choices for her, and she would be nothing more than a pawn in their game.

How could this be happening? What had started out as a lovely trip north to spend time with her grandmother had turned into a nightmare.

"Father will agree to this marriage, won't he?" she whispered.

Her grandmother shrugged. "It is very possible, but there is no way of knowing the full truth of the matter without discussing it with your father. And of course, we've just agreed not to do that."

"Surely Papa doesn't want to see me married to the likes of Bradley Houston? He's much older and not at all pleasant company. He's pompous and overly confident in his abilities."

"Some would say those are the perfect qualities for a leader—a man of great means. Bradley Houston is, unfortunately, the very kind of man your father would look for."

Jasmine shook her head, still unable to believe that her world was tumbling so chaotically out of order.

Jasmine examined herself in the mirror. Grandmother had insisted she wear her peach silk gown to the Harpers' party. Jasmine's preference was to remain at home or, in the alternative, wear her old green plaid. She had no desire to impress Bradley Houston with the lovely new gown. But her grandmother was already distraught, so she deferred.

Alice came into the bedroom as Jasmine was clasping her grandmother's pearl necklace around her neck. "You look absolutely beautiful. The color of your dress accentuates the blush of your cheeks."

"Thank you, Grandmother. I do wish you were going along

this evening. I dislike being alone with Bradley. He makes me uncomfortable."

"He's never acted in an ungentlemanly fashion, has he?"

"I consider his threat regarding our attendance at the antislavery meeting ungentlemanly. Especially since I merely wanted to expand my education. If I didn't fear the whole issue would cause harm to Father, I would have told him to leave the house and never return."

"I appreciate your willingness to join with me in accepting his terms, dear. This will all work out for the best, I'm sure."

A knock sounded at the front door, and Jasmine checked her reflection one last time. "There he is. I'd best go down."

Jasmine lifted the skirt of her gown ever so slightly before descending the stairs, followed by her grandmother. She could feel Bradley's gaze upon her as she approached, but she purposefully ignored him. Instead, she turned to Martha, who was holding her shawl, lace gloves, and beaded miser purse. Moving in slow motion, she pulled on one glove and then the other in leisurely fashion. She then took the purse from Martha and methodically reviewed its contents.

When her shawl had finally draped to her satisfaction, she turned around and faced Bradley. "I believe I'm ready to leave when you are, Mr. Houston."

If her actions annoyed him, he didn't reveal his dissatisfaction. Instead, he smiled and offered his arm. "We can leave immediately," he said.

She leaned down and kissed her grandmother's cheek before taking Bradley's arm.

"You look quite lovely this evening, Jasmine. Orange becomes you," Bradley emoted.

"Peach."

"Excuse me?"

"The color is peach, not orange."

"Oh, I see. In that case, peach becomes you, as does the style of the dress. I was pleased to see you had taken such pains to look your most beautiful tonight. I feared you might come down in sackcloth and ashes."

"That would have been my preference. However, Grand-mother insisted I dress appropriately."

He emitted a deep belly laugh that completely surprised her. "I realize your youth is responsible in large part for your audacity. However, you'll learn that I will tolerate only occasional impu-dence. Fortunately for you, this evening happens to be one of those instances." He helped her into the closed carriage, then with great audacity, sat close beside her.

Jasmine hugged her side of the carriage, desperate to avoid even the aroma of his cologne. "Since you are being so tolerant, I suppose I should move forward with great boldness. I've hesitated to ask previously, but I would like to know your age. I'm certain you won't mind sharing such private information with your future wife."

"I am pleased to hear you've accepted your role as my future wife, albeit I may have detected a caustic ring to the words. As for my age, I'm thirty-nine. Old enough to channel your zealous behavior in the proper direction, yet young enough to father your children."

"Mr. Houston!"

"If you ask cheeky questions, you should expect answers in kind."

"I expect nothing but the worst from you," she replied.

He appeared to consider this for a moment before continuing. "Jasmine, you can make this very easy or very difficult. I cannot deny I have goals and ambitions in taking you as my wife; how-ever, I am prepared to forget our rather rocky beginning and work toward a smooth path. You may find the aspect of our union to be completely abominable, but I assure you it will not change my mind on the matter. I intend to be your husband. The sooner you get used to the idea and accept it, the better for all concerned."

"Hardly that," Jasmine retorted. She tried hard to keep from allowing tears to come to her eyes. "I do not think it better to marry a man I do not love—cannot abide—rather than return to my father's house and remain a spinster. Does it not bother you in the least that I do not love you—that I will never love you?"

Bradley surprised her by laughing. "You are such a child. If only the choices were that simple. This has nothing to do with love."

"Exactly my point," Jasmine declared. She determined to ignore him rather than partake in his verbal sparring, and for the remainder of their carriage ride, she turned a deaf ear to his questions. But he seemed not to care, eventually growing silent himself. The carriage came to a halt in front of a gambrel-roofed frame home, banked by an abundance of birches and pines. It was, Jasmine decided, a cozy-appearing house that seemed to beckon visitors enter and stay for a while.

A servant took their wraps and then directed them toward Mr. and Mrs. Harper. Their hosts stood below the two steps leading into the drawing room, and after proper introductions had been made, Bradley escorted Jasmine into the large candlelit room. The rug had been rolled back and couples danced in the center of the room while others congregated in small groups around the perimeter, the muted light causing their shadows to flutter upon the walls. They appeared to go unnoticed until Josiah Baines called out Bradley's name and waved in their direction.

"Come join us. We've plenty of questions, don't we, Thomas?" Josiah said, drawing Thomas Clayborn into the conversation as Bradley and Jasmine neared the men.

"Ah, so this is the future Mrs. Bradley Houston, I take it," Josiah remarked. "I'm pleased to make your acquaintance, Miss Wainwright." He leaned toward Jasmine in a conspiratorial fashion. "We already know your name since the Boston Associates are quite impressed with your father's cotton empire."

"And because Bradley shared your wedding plans with us at our last meeting," Wilson Harper added as he joined the group. He slapped Bradley on the shoulder. "I can see why he was anxious to announce his betrothal."

Jasmine blushed at the remark, but her presence was soon forgotten as the men's conversation shifted to talk of the mills and reduced productivity. Her attention soon shifted to the laughing couples swirling around the room.

"Would you care to dance?"

She startled and turned at the voice, for her thoughts were distant. "Why, yes, Nolan. I would be pleased to dance with you." She began to walk toward the dance floor, and he touched her arm.

"Let me ask Bradley's permission. We don't want to offend him." He gave her a lopsided grin. "It would serve no useful purpose."

Jasmine nodded and waited. Bradley looked at her before returning his attention to Nolan. She waited, wondering if Bradley was denying the request, but Nolan returned, took her hand, and led her onto the dance floor.

"He didn't object?"

"Why should he? Bradley's hoping to impress the Associates, and he can't do that if he's on the dance floor. If you're otherwise occupied, he won't be required to leave his discussion."

Jasmine shrugged. "He won't leave his conversation on my account. Bradley knows I have no desire to dance with him."

Nolan moved back an arm's length and arched his eyebrows into twin peaks. "You told him that?"

"No. There was no need. He knows exactly how I feel about him."

"But he just now told me the two of you are to be wed."

"Since we will soon be related, I don't think your brother will mind if I share with you the actual reason *why* we will be married."

"It's really not my business, Miss Wainwright. As you likely noticed upon first meeting us at your plantation, both our age and our interests divide Bradley and me. We live, if you will, in different worlds. Bradley enjoys amassing wealth and influence. However, I find my pleasure in seeking the beauty of God's hand in nature and creativity. Of course, I attempt to find God's beauty in mankind also, but it becomes increasingly difficult," he said and then smiled at her.

She tilted her head to one side and looked into his eyes. "Your smile is filled with sadness."

"Perhaps because I feel so inadequate to make changes in the evils of mankind. My labors seem fruitless and my prayers continue to go unanswered."

"Mammy says no prayer goes unanswered," Jasmine said gently. "She says God responds to every request with either a 'yes,' a 'no,' or 'not right now.'"

Nolan nodded. "And I'm certain Mammy and the rest of the Negroes living down South are quite used to hearing God's 'not right now' response to their prayers."

"Well, I certainly hope God isn't going to deny my prayers regarding marriage to your brother. This wedding will be nothing more than a charade. The entire idea is nothing more than a proposed business arrangement. I've not yet discussed the bargain with my father, and consequently, I'm not privy to all of the details. In fact, my father hasn't even formally agreed to the marriage."

"Possibly you won't be forced into the marriage after all," he said uneasily.

"I fear all chance of such an escape has been ruined."

He led her from the dance floor and retrieved two cups of punch from a nearby table. They walked out the wide door leading into a small garden off the drawing room. The rosebushes were in full bloom, filling the summer night with an intoxicating fragrance.

"Will your father not listen to your protest? Surely he'll be offended that Bradley has announced your engagement without gaining his consent."

"I can't tell him what Bradley has done." She surprised herself by explaining the requirement exacted by Bradley after his discovery she'd attended the antislavery meeting.

Nolan rubbed his palm across his forehead as though he were trying to erase what Jasmine had told him. "I wish I could tell you I'm surprised by his deed, but I can't. My brother mentioned his intentions some time ago. However, I shall pray that having you in his life will soften and change him so that one day he will realize what is truly important."

"No doubt he had formulated his plans from the moment he set foot in our home. How is it that two brothers who were reared in the same household could be so dissimilar?"

Nolan glanced over his shoulder toward where his brother stood in the drawing room. "Bradley was fifteen years old when I was born. He was being groomed to take over my father's business. Quite frankly, another child was quite unexpected so late in my parents' lives. My father took little interest in a second son. After all, he had already set in motion the plan to ensure his shipping business would survive. Consequently, I spent much more time with my mother, who was an artist. From an early age, I would sit and read the book of Psalms to her while she created lovely pastoral settings with her oil paints."

"And were you jealous of Bradley and his close connection to your father and his business?"

Nolan smoothed down the lapel of his wool coat. "No. Quite the contrary. I thought my life wonderful—I still do. I never wanted to trade places with Bradley. When our father died, Bradley inherited the entire business. A year later our mother died. I inherited her paintings, as well as her small art collection, and the family home."

"Did you not feel a twinge of jealousy when Bradley inherited the business?"

Nolan laughed. "No. Bradley had worked for years with my father. He loved the business and deserved to receive it. Besides, I had always known Bradley would inherit the business, and I knew I would receive Mother's artwork. However, I would much prefer her company to her art collection. I still miss her."

"I can't imagine what it must have been like to lose both your parents in such a short period of time. Of course, you and Bradley had each other, but I do hope you had other family to help you through your time of loss."

"We have no other family in this country. Both of my parents emigrated from England at an early age. At the time of my mother's death, my grandparents were all deceased, except my maternal grandmother, who had returned to England several years earlier. Bradley wasn't around much. He was involved in negotiations to sell the business shortly after Mother's death."

"I don't understand why he would sell the family business, especially since it was profitable and he claimed to enjoy it."

"He had become acquainted with Nathan Appleton through the shipping business. Nathan was already heavily invested in the textile industry and was looking to expand his horizons by investing in a small shipping firm. It was through Nathan my brother learned about the Boston Associates and their powerful influence throughout New England. He became obsessed with the idea of becoming a member of their elite group."

"Couldn't he have entered into their numbers with his shipping firm?"

"Nathan was building his own shipping empire and didn't want the competition. Even though Bradley assured him there was more than enough business for both of them, Nathan rejected the idea. The Associates required a sizable cash investment, more than Bradley had available without selling a substantial portion of the business. He wanted a more powerful position in the business world more than he wanted to retain the business, although I'm not certain the shipping firm wouldn't have made him wealthier had he retained full interest in it."

Jasmine's head was swirling with all the information Nolan had conveyed during the past half hour. The glimpse into Bradley's life was even more unattractive than what she had conjured up in her own mind. It appeared his only goal in life was to achieve money and power.

"How did you and Bradley happen to visit The Willows?"

"He wanted to find cotton growers in the South who would be willing to consider changing their markets from England to Boston. Through contacts in the shipping business, Bradley gained access to manifests with names of growers who shipped large quantities of cotton to England. Your family was his first choice to visit. However, he truly didn't go to The Willows with marriage in mind. The availability of a prospective bride was an added bonus."

Jasmine pressed her fingertips to her temples. "And now I find myself unwittingly drawn into this quagmire. What little respect I might have had for Bradley has disappeared."

Engrossed in their conversation, they failed to hear the approaching footsteps. "People are going to begin gossiping if you two remain secluded out here much longer."

Even in the darkness Jasmine could detect the disapproval in his eyes. She wondered how long Bradley had been listening.

CHAPTER · *11*

JASMINE'S ENGAGEMENT to Bradley Houston was soon spoken of in all the social circles. Jasmine found it laborious to accept congratulations for a marriage she hoped might never take place, and she avoided discussing the event whenever possible. Her grandmother tried to encourage Jasmine at times when the thought of marriage to Bradley left her particularly discouraged. Still, there was nothing she could do about it. This was, as her grandmother told her in no uncertain terms, the way things were done.

Adjusting the lace collar on her pale yellow gown, Jasmine tried to think of another way to word her request in such a manner that her grandmother would yield. She'd been cajoling the Wainwright matriarch in the rose garden for well over half an hour, but there was no indication she would budge from her position.

Grandmother concentrated on her stitching as though the piece of embroidery required unremitting attention. "You will not change my mind upon this matter," she said as if reading Jasmine's mind. "I insist upon acquiring Bradley's permission. If you'll recall, the last time I hastily agreed to one of your requests, we suffered dire consequences."

Jasmine thought to stomp her foot but stopped short of the act. She knew such childlike behavior wouldn't serve her cause.

"There's nothing further Bradley can do to me—to us. He's already imposed himself on me with this ridiculous engagement."

Alice Wainwright looked up and shook her head. "You know better, Jasmine. There are many ways Bradley could punish us both. However, he's been civil and even kind. It was very generous of him to send us that gift of exotic fruit."

"I don't care how many gifts he sends. I have no desire to be his wife."

Grandmother caught her eye and was silent a moment before saying, "This truly isn't an issue about whether you want to marry him or not. Your father has arranged an advantageous union. It is your duty to put your family ahead of yourself. Women have done this for generations and will go on doing it for generations to come."

"Not if I can help it," Jasmine replied bitterly. "I would want my children to marry for love."

"But emotions are greatly overrated. There is much to be said for making a good marriage—knowing you and yours will be provided for, that you will always have shelter and food. It was thus with my father, and I learned to be happy, even grateful, that he had made such a choice on my behalf."

"Well, I'll never be grateful for Bradley Houston," Jasmine said, folding her arms against the ruching of her bodice. For several minutes she paced back and forth before trying to turn the conversation back to her original request.

"I can't see the harm in this outing. Besides, I truly want to go, Grandmother. You'll be with us, and we could ask Violet and Mrs. Cheever to attend."

"No need to extend an invitation until you've received Bradley's permission. You're now betrothed to him, Jasmine. It is improper to go on an outing with another man without Bradley's express permission."

"Nolan isn't another man; he's Bradley's brother. And I need no further reminders I am betrothed. That distasteful news constantly haunts me."

Grandmother looked over the top of her reading glasses with a raised brow. "I don't believe Bradley would appreciate your appraisal of the situation." Her expression softened into sympathetic concern. "My dear, you must try to accept your fate and make it work so that you'll be happy. I would not have chosen this man for you, but your father has."

Jasmine plopped down on a cushioned garden chair. "Yes, I know." There was resignation in her voice. The issue of her marriage to Bradley Houston was no longer something to be discussed or deliberated. Her father had agreed to their betrothal, and her mother was already making arrangements for the wedding. Perhaps that was why it seemed so important to insist on this one simple outing. "So there is nothing I can say that will convince you?" she finally asked.

"Nothing short of Bradley's consent." The old woman continued stitching. Jasmine wondered how she could possibly be so at ease. Without looking up, her grandmother asked, "Shall I send word to Bradley?"

Jasmine shook her head and folded her hands in her lap. "No need. I didn't expect you would relent. He should be here any moment."

Alice stopped stitching and gazed at her granddaughter. "Had I yielded, what would you have asked him when he appeared?"

Jasmine shrugged. "Something would have come to mind. However, I hadn't prepared. I was certain you wouldn't acquiesce."

Alice shook her head and pursed her lips. "I dare say—"

"Excuse me, ma'am. Mr. Bradley is here to call on Miss Jasmine," Martha said quietly.

Bradley came up behind Martha in long, determined strides and brushed past her. "I told her I didn't need to be announced, but she insisted. I'm in a bit of a rush, Jasmine. What is so important?" He gave a slight bow in the direction of each woman, then waited for an explanation.

Jasmine looked up in distaste. She didn't always abhor his presence, but his forceful nature irritated her. Even now, he was in a hurry to be somewhere else, tending to business far more important than the needs of his fiancée. Getting to her feet, Jasmine held his gaze. "I'd like to attend a gathering in Cambridge on Tuesday, and Grandmother insisted I obtain your permission before accepting the invitation."

He smiled in that self-satisfying way that Jasmine had come to hate. "I can't escort you on Tuesday. I have business that needs my attention."

He spoke slowly, enunciating each utterance as though she couldn't possibly understand anything more complex than a two-syllable word.

Jasmine barely held her temper. "I'm not asking you to escort me. Nolan is attending and has agreed to act as an escort for Grandmother and me. I understand Lilly and Violet Cheever will be attending also. Fanny Longfellow has invited all of us to be guests at her home."

Bradley sat down on one of the benches and gave a wry grin. "Henry and Fanny are hosting another one of those literary gatherings, aren't they?"

Jasmine came to stand directly in front of him. "I believe that's what Nolan said. I understand there will be various discussion groups. Nolan tells me that Nathaniel Hawthorne, Horace Greeley, and many others will all be in attendance." She couldn't contain her excitement.

"And I'm sure Henry Longfellow will be in his glory with his erudite cronies surrounding him. As much as I don't understand why you would want to make a tedious journey to hear pompous men profess their intellectual and philosophical beliefs, I don't suppose it will do you any great harm." He got to his feet. "Now, I really must get back to my business. You may walk me to the door, Jasmine."

She knew his words were a command, and under other circumstances she would have balked. However, he had granted her the permission she earnestly sought, so she submissively followed him to the entrance hall. After collecting his hat, Bradley turned and tenderly caressed her cheek. Instinctively, she moved back a step and hovered in the doorway.

Bradley's eyes narrowed into an icy stare. "You should be

favoring me with accolades. Instead, you withdraw from my touch. I'll remember your thankful nature the next time you seek my agreement."

The slamming door shuddered in the wake of his anger. She'd made a mistake, but permitting him to stroke her cheek had been insufferable. His very touch repulsed her.

Nolan offered an arm to Jasmine and Alice Wainwright and escorted them to the carriage, one of them on either side of him. "I must say I was surprised to hear of Bradley's accord. I expected him to recite the many arguments against your attendance. Did he not attempt to dissuade you at all?" Nolan asked. After helping the older woman into the carriage, he took Jasmine's hand and assisted her up.

"No. At first he thought I expected *him* to escort us, but once he realized his presence would not be required, he was most amenable to our attending."

Jasmine hadn't informed her grandmother of the encounter with Bradley prior to his departure, and telling Nolan about it would certainly be reckless. Although she believed she could trust Nolan, there was no need taking undue risk. She'd already alienated Bradley with her behavior.

"And what of Violet and Lilly Cheever? Have they decided to join us?"

"No. They had a conflict and send their regrets. I had tea with Violet yesterday and she said her father isn't fond of the transcendentalist views espoused by those who frequent the gatherings at the Longfellows' home. I'm afraid I appeared quite the fool as I didn't realize you adhered to such beliefs."

"I'm not a transcendentalist, and I certainly don't count myself among those who believe God is immanent in man and that individual intuition is the highest source of knowledge. That kind of thinking has led such believers to place an optimistic emphasis on individualism and self-reliance. I believe in God and His ultimate authority. My faith and trust are in God, not myself. However, I do occasionally enter into debate with them. For I believe if I'm going to associate with these men, I have an obligation to speak God's truth."

"Good for you, Nolan," Mrs. Wainwright said. "I'm glad you have the courage to express your beliefs."

"Thank you, ma'am. However, I must admit that many times I would prefer to remain silent. Doing battle with that group of learned men makes me realize how David must have felt when he confronted Goliath."

Jasmine's grandmother chuckled at his reply. "I'm sure you can hold your own with any of them."

"I'd like to think·so, but Bradley has always been much stronger in the skill of debate. He could certainly make some of them appear foolish if he had a mind to do so."

"Are his Christian beliefs well-founded enough that he would challenge such men?" Jasmine inquired. She'd seen no evidence that her future husband esteemed any faith except that which he placed in himself.

Nolan's gaze remained fixed upon the roadway. "He attends church regularly."

Jasmine gave him a sidelong glance. "Simply attending church doesn't mean he's a Christian. Is he truly a believer?"

"That's a question you'll need to ask Bradley. I don't feel qualified to answer for another man's salvation, even if he is my brother."

"If I were to ask Bradley if *you* were a Christian, how would *he* answer?" Jasmine persisted, now certain he was avoiding her question.

Nolan gave her a lopsided grin. "I'd like to think he would speak in the affirmative, but then, I hope that is true of anyone who knows me. Although I'm not always successful, my goal is to make Christianity my life pattern. I want other people to see Christ in me rather than merely hear me advocate some vague philosophy."

"And is that what your brother does? Practice religiosity?"

He chuckled and shook his head. "I never said such a thing.

You're putting words in my mouth, Miss Wainwright. If you truly want to find out who Bradley is and what he believes, you've merely to ask him. In fact, now that the two of you are betrothed, it would seem prudent for the two of you to discuss these matters."

Jasmine smelled the heavy scent of pines as the carriage moved into the countryside. "I haven't asked him because I fear his answers. Unfortunately, I know that no matter what he believes, I'll be forced to marry him. Remaining ignorant somehow seems easier."

"You must do what you believe best, but lack of preparation can sometimes prove fatal."

Jasmine leaned back and stared out the window of the coach, but the beauty of the passing countryside wouldn't erase the ominous warning in Nolan's earnest words.

───────

Nolan motioned Jasmine from the circle of older women gathered in one corner of the room. "Come meet a few of these people," he said, taking her by the arm.

They moved through the crowd, stopping in front of a wingbacked chair. "Jasmine, I'd like to introduce you to Horace Greeley," Nolan said. "And, of course, you know Fanny Longfellow."

Jasmine dipped in a small curtsy. "It is a genuine pleasure to meet you, Mr. Greeley," she said while attempting to hide her excitement.

"My pleasure," Horace replied. Before he could say anything further, Henry Longfellow grasped him by the elbow and pulled him off in another direction.

Jasmine turned her attention back to Mrs. Longfellow. "I do want to thank you, Mrs. Longfellow, for the gracious hospitality you've extended to Grandmother and me."

"It's my pleasure, Jasmine. And please, call me Fanny. Only Father refers to me as Frances and only *very* young children address me as Mrs. Longfellow. Now come sit with me and let's get better acquainted." She patted the cushion of a nearby chair.

Jasmine glanced toward Nolan. He said, "I'll leave you ladies to become better acquainted while I join Henry and the other men for some stimulating conversation."

"Isn't Nolan quite a wonderful man? I've attempted to play cupid on several occasions but to no avail. He always tells me my choices have not been women that adhere to his beliefs. Probably because most of the people whom Henry and I befriend have become transcendentalists. Poor Nolan finds himself quite outnumbered in these gatherings. Unfortunately, there are few Episcopalians, Baptists, or Methodists who care to discuss topics that interest the rest of us—including Nolan. However, I'm pleased to see he has found a young lady who meets his requirements."

A warm blush colored Jasmine's cheeks. "Nolan is my escort this evening. However, I am betrothed to his brother."

Fanny's eyebrows arched. "Bradley?"

"Yes. Do you know him?"

A vague smile played at the corner of Fanny's lips. "Don't think me impolite, but you'll soon come to learn that all of us who attend these gatherings speak quite frankly to one another. I know Bradley better than I care to, and I must say that you seem more suited to Nolan than to his brother—both in age and disposition. How did you and Bradley become acquainted?"

"Our marriage is a business arrangement between my father and Bradley. He is certainly not the man I would choose to wed."

Fanny nodded earnestly. "I thought not. Bradley has little in common with any of us, and he wouldn't abide Henry or me were it not for my father's position among the Boston Associates. I think Nolan is drawn to us as much because of our antislavery beliefs as our literary discussions. Bradley, however, aspires to be in the hierarchy of the Associates, but I'm certain you already know that. Now, do tell me about yourself. You have an odd accent. Where do you call home, Jasmine?"

"The Willows. It's a cotton plantation near Lorman, Mississippi."

"Oh? I may have misjudged you, Miss Wainwright. You may have more in common with Bradley than I thought."

"Whatever do you mean? Because I'm from the South you

believe me interested in power and money rather than kindness?"

"I'm certain your views on slavery would be vastly different from the views of everyone else in this room, but they would likely coincide with Bradley Houston's. Of course, when he's in our company he professes merely to tolerate slavery and, like many of his contemporaries, advocates no further expansion of the practice—an opportunistic attitude at best. Would you agree?"

"I realize there are few among you who will believe me, but there are slaves who are content and even happy with their owners. I believe generalities are an unfair way to judge people, especially when you've not investigated for yourself. Not all slaves are mistreated, and not all owners are ogres."

Fanny turned her attention to Nolan, who had returned to stand quietly behind Jasmine's chair. "Would you agree with Miss Wainwright's statement, Nolan?"

"Having investigated for myself, I can say with authority that I never found a slave who was happy to be held captive, but I can't speak as authoritatively about their owners. I didn't spend much time with them."

"Have your slaves expressed to you that they are happy with their lot in life, Miss Wainwright?" Fanny asked.

"I've never asked them," Jasmine admitted. "As I told Nolan, our slaves are treated very well. He visited our plantation with his brother earlier in the year, and I'm certain he can confirm that fact."

Nolan moved from behind the chair and offered his hand. "They're beginning a reading in the other room. You won't want to miss hearing Mr. Greeley."

Jasmine took his hand and nodded at Fanny. "A pleasure visiting with you. I look forward to further discussion while we're here."

"I'm glad you found our time together enjoyable," she replied with a wry grin.

"Thank you for saving me," Jasmine whispered to Nolan as they walked away. "I fear she intensely dislikes me. Perhaps Grandmother and I should plan to stay at an inn here in Cambridge."

Nolan laughed. "She may disagree with some of your beliefs, but you're much too sweet-tempered to dislike. And you would certainly affront Fanny by leaving to find accommodations elsewhere."

"I imagine my father would find your remark quite amusing, for he finds my temper quite disagreeable. And what have you been off discussing?"

"Unfortunately, several of our group got themselves caught up in talk of the war with Mexico. You've probably heard General Taylor and his men inflicted over a thousand casualties before moving south out of Palo Alto last May, while our navy has more recently seized Monterey and Los Angeles. Killing and mayhem based upon the concept of Manifest Destiny is an idea I certainly don't embrace."

"Our family and General Taylor's are quite close. Believe me when I say he is quite a gentle soul. Still, it sounds as though we both were drawn into uncomfortable discussions. Perhaps we should remain together."

With his eyes twinkling and a smile tugging at his lips, he said, "I certainly wouldn't object, but I believe Bradley might lodge a complaint."

CHAPTER · *12*

JASMINE SAT waiting in the parlor with her parasol firmly balanced against the deep-cushioned chair, her trunk packed and stationed beside the front door. Everything was in readiness for the future—everything except her heart. She tapped her foot and pulled at the lace edging on her handkerchief until she could no longer sit still. Jumping to her feet, she began pacing back and forth in front of the carved marble fireplace, her steps short and frantic. "I pray Bradley has changed his mind. And if he hasn't, then I pray something has happened to prevent him from making the journey."

Grandmother frowned her disapproval. "You need to resign yourself to this marriage, Jasmine. Bradley is not going to change his mind, and you'll be much happier once you accept the fact that you are going to be his wife. Gladly I must admit, I've seen changes in him over these past months. I honestly believe he has grown to care for you."

Jasmine knew her eyes revealed the unremitting resentment that festered in her heart. She saw it there every time she looked in the mirror. "I care little whether he's grown to care for me. I don't love him, and I don't want to be his wife. We are unsuited. I pray daily Bradley will decide against the marriage."

Before Alice could reply, a knock sounded at the front door.

"Perhaps Nolan has come to tell us Bradley was struck down by a runaway carriage and died a quick and painless death," Jasmine said in a sardonic manner. She hated her own cynicism but felt there was no reason to change it. It wouldn't win her freedom from this farce of a marriage.

"Jasmine Wainwright! What shameful things you are saying. You need to ask God's forgiveness for having such thoughts about your future husband."

"Did I hear someone mention a future husband?" Bradley asked as he took long strides into the parlor.

Grandmother quickly interceded. "Jasmine had just mentioned that you were in her prayers each day."

"Surely you know I don't put much stock in prayer—hard work and determination benefit a man more."

Jasmine looked at her grandmother with her eyebrows arched. The older woman immediately turned away, obviously unwilling to acknowledge what Jasmine already knew: Bradley Houston placed his faith in himself—not in God.

"I've had your man load the trunks, and we should be on our way," Nolan called out from the foyer. "If we don't hurry, the train will leave for Boston and we'll miss our voyage." He came into the room and immediately went to Jasmine's grandmother. "May I escort you to the carriage?"

"Certainly." She took up a wool cloak and Nolan quickly moved to help her don it. "There's a chill in the air," she said as if explaining her actions as they walked out of the room.

"There certainly is a chill," Bradley said dryly as Jasmine moved to take up her own cloak and parasol. "I do hope you will warm to the idea of this trip and of the celebration to come," he continued as Jasmine swung the voluminous cloak around her shoulders. "Surely you are anxious to see your family."

"Being reunited with my family and Mammy are of utmost importance to me. If my future included plans to remain with them, you would hear pure delight in my voice." She walked from the room, not even bothering to look back.

Bradley lengthened his stride and came alongside her as they approached the carriage. He leaned down close to her ear. "Perhaps if you could show more enthusiasm toward our marriage, I would be willing to make arrangements for Mammy's return with us."

So that's how Bradley viewed their future marriage, Jasmine realized—as a bartering system. If she behaved in a fashion he found acceptable, he would reward her efforts. There was little doubt he planned to train her like a pet. Be good, follow orders, and you'll get the scraps from the table. She didn't reply. After all, she didn't need Bradley Houston making arrangements for Mammy's future . . . or anything else, for that matter.

The carriage came to a halt on Merrimack Street, where the four passengers disembarked. Nolan took charge of their trunks and baggage while Bradley escorted Alice and Jasmine into the train station. Excitement filled the air. Passengers scurried about, anxious to ensure their tickets and baggage were in proper order; small children clung to their mothers' skirts, obviously frightened by the huge iron monster billowing and puffing like a giant demon; and the remainder sat waiting, their anticipation reaching new heights when the conductor finally called for them to board.

The four of them were alone in the finely appointed coach belonging to the Boston Associates. Jasmine sat down near the center of one of the supple leather-cushioned seats. Her hope had been to sit alone, but Bradley immediately wedged himself into the narrow space beside her. She scooted close to the window and turned her attention away from him. The train jerked and hissed into motion, and Jasmine leaned back and stared at the passing countryside, contemplating her future with this man sitting next to her.

After several curt responses, she was relieved when Bradley finally turned his attention to her grandmother and Nolan. The three of them conversed continually until they arrived in Boston an hour later. Jasmine longed to shout she would go no farther until she was released from this contemptuous engagement. Instead, she boarded the private carriage awaiting them at the station and rode in silence to the docks, where Captain Harmon greeted them. The jovial bewhiskered captain personally escorted the entourage onboard the *Mary Benjamin,* one of the few vessels remaining in Bradley's trimmed-down shipping business. The captain's dutiful attention left little doubt he understood the primary reason for sailing down the coast to New Orleans. The important cargo on this ship was his four passengers, not the partial shipment of goods loaded on board earlier in the day.

"I believe I'd like to retire to my cabin," Jasmine said.

Bradley offered his arm but instead of leading her to the cabin, held tightly to her hand and moved toward the ship's railing. "I think we should remain at the rail. It's always exhilarating to watch as a ship sets sail. Rather romantic—slowly moving away from land on the rising waves, watching the city finally grow dim on the horizon."

Jasmine knew he was toying with her, attempting to play the role of a besotted lover. Had it been anyone but Bradley, she would have found the effort amusing. But everything he did served only to annoy her. If it meant she must stand arm in arm with Bradley, she didn't want to watch Boston disappear from sight. In fact, she didn't want to be in Bradley's company at all. Hurling herself into the depths of the sea seemed a much more appealing alternative.

Alice Wainwright came alongside her granddaughter and patted Jasmine's shoulder. "Jasmine didn't sleep well last night, Bradley. I fear she may become ill if she doesn't get her proper rest. Perhaps if she could lie down and take a short nap, the voyage would go more smoothly."

"I don't see how remaining on deck for an hour is going to cause her enough distress to ruin the remainder of our voyage. I can bring a chair for her."

"Sitting in a chair isn't the same as actually resting. Jasmine is prone to excruciating headaches when she doesn't sleep well."

Jasmine stood sandwiched between the two of them, listening while they discussed her until she could abide no more. She pulled away from Bradley. "Why don't you two remain at the rail and watch the city 'grow dim on the horizon' as Bradley suggested? I, on the other hand, will go to my cabin and rest." She hurried off across the deck, motioning to a deckhand who had carried their trunks on board. "Take me to the cabin where you placed the large black trunk with engraved hasps."

She expected to hear Bradley's footsteps and feel his fingers clutch her arm. Instead, he let her escape to the safety of her cabin, where she bolted the door and fell upon the bed. Her tears flowed freely. How could she possibly survive a loveless marriage? There must be a way to convince her father this plan was doomed for failure.

Surely Papa will listen to reason. He loves me and wouldn't want me unhappy. If I simply tell him the truth, then things could be different, she reasoned. For the first time Jasmine gathered hope from her thoughts. She sat up and dried her eyes.

"I haven't told Papa of my feelings. We haven't discussed the marriage," she murmured. "He has always spoiled me. . . . Perhaps I can convince him to give me my way just one more time."

The thought intrigued her. If her father understood the misery she felt, he might very well relent and break his agreement with Bradley. After all, surely her father would rather see his only daughter happy than expand the family fortune.

Wouldn't he?

———————

"I just need you to keep Bradley occupied while I speak to my father," Jasmine told Nolan. "If you can draw Bradley's interest long enough for me to talk in private, perhaps I can convince my father to reconsider this entire situation."

Nolan seemed less than convinced. He rubbed his chin and looked past Jasmine. She turned and followed his gaze to where Bradley reprimanded the stevedores who were handling their luggage. "I suppose I could seek a delay by suggesting the need to stop by the bank. That would keep us here overnight, but Bradley would never allow you to journey to The Willows by yourself."

Jasmine returned her gaze to Nolan. "Leave that to me. You suggest the delay to Bradley, and I'll speak to my grandmother. Perhaps I can convince her to request a delay as well. She could explain how much the trip has tired her and that she'd like to rest before we continue to The Willows."

"That would seem very reasonable. It's a good day's journey from this point to the plantation," Nolan said thoughtfully. "Bradley surely can't protest an older woman's request for rest, while he might very well deny the delay for something as insignificant as bank business."

"I'll speak to my grandmother," Jasmine told him. "Can you manage to keep Bradley away from us for a few minutes?"

Nolan nodded solemnly. "I'll do what I can. I just hope you know what you're doing."

Jasmine drew a deep breath. "I hope so too."

She went quickly to her grandmother as Nolan ambled down the dock. "Grandmother," Jasmine said, rather breathlessly, "we need to talk."

Alice Wainwright looked up from where she sat patiently waiting for the next portion of their journey.

"Whatever is wrong?"

Jasmine sat down. "I need to talk to Papa without Bradley anywhere around. I've had an idea, and I need your help."

Her grandmother raised her brows. "What are you saying?"

"I'd like you to ask Bradley to delay our trip to The Willows. Just ask him to allow us to spend the night here—tell him the journey has taxed you overmuch."

"Well, that would be no lie," Alice Wainwright admitted. "But, Jasmine, I don't know what you hope to gain with this delay."

Jasmine squared her shoulders. "I'd rather not divulge my plan, otherwise you might face Bradley's wrath. The less you know, the better."

"This isn't like you," Jasmine's grandmother stated in a worried tone.

"I'm afraid," Jasmine said, feeling somewhat strengthened by her own revelation, "that I'm not the same girl I used to be." She patted her grandmother's hand. "Truly, this is very important. I hope it might even mean changing Papa's mind regarding the wedding."

"I cannot do something that would place you in harm's way."

"I won't be in harm's way. This is where I grew up. I know most everyone here in Lorman and in the surrounding country-side. You mustn't worry. I'll be as safe here as in Mammy's arms. Just trust me on this—please."

It took some convincing, but Bradley finally relented and the foursome checked into the nearest hotel. Jasmine and her grand-mother pleaded to be left to rest for the remainder of the day, while Nolan suggested that Bradley could use the time to speak to other cotton growers in the area.

Jasmine waited until her grandmother went into the adjoining room for an afternoon nap before hastily exchanging her traveling suit for a riding habit. She would borrow a horse from the Bor-dens. Dr. Borden was a good friend of the family and had tended most every Wainwright member for one illness or another. He and his wife were also much more liberal in their beliefs than some of their Southern contemporaries. They wouldn't think anything amiss or in the leastwise troubling when Jasmine made her request known.

Jasmine knew she would have to hurry if she were to make it home before dark, however. Her father would not be at all sym-pathetic to her cause if he thought she'd risked her well-being by traveling in the darkness—unescorted. *He won't approve of this,* she knew in her heart. But on the other hand, once he saw what she was willing to do in order to plead her case, Jasmine felt confident her father would at least delay the wedding, if not cancel it al-together.

Dr. Borden was gone on rounds when Jasmine arrived at the house, but his wife, Virginia, was more than happy to accommo-date her.

"You will hurry back for a long visit, won't you?" Virginia

questioned as the groomsman came forward with a fast-looking bay.

Jasmine touched the horse's dark mane, stroking him gently as a means of introduction. "I will do my best to see that we have a nice long talk very soon." Jasmine allowed the groom to help her into the sidesaddle. "Thank you again for the loan," she said. Then without further ceremony, she yanked the reins to the right and quickly headed out.

Her biggest fear was the possibility of running into Bradley as he moved among the folk of Lorman seeking yet someone else to devour. Jasmine thought momentarily that perhaps it wasn't fair to equate her fiancé with the devil, but it didn't overly bother her conscience.

The road home was in good condition, much to Jasmine's relief. The old sights and sounds of her beloved Southern home reached out to embrace her, welcoming her back to that which she loved. Urging the horse to a canter, Jasmine passed from town into the rural areas, where cotton fields were dotted with dark-skinned workers. She slowed the horse momentarily and watched with interest as she remembered the words of the abolitionist speakers back in Lowell. She saw no signs of rough treatment, no proof that these slaves were unhappy or ill-treated.

Picking up her pace again, Jasmine smiled to herself. Surely the things spoken of in Lowell were extreme circumstances and not the normal events of Southern life.

The hours passed as Jasmine urged the horse to his limits. The sun had long since set and the skies were pitch black when Jasmine rounded the final bend for home. Her skin tingled from the exertion of the ride, as well as the overwhelming knowledge that her father would be greatly displeased with her actions. Still, she had seen no other recourse. She had to be allowed to speak her mind and explain her feelings on the matter.

A groomsman approached as Jasmine brought the bay to a stop at the porch stairs. "Miz Jasmine?" the man asked in disbelief. "Is dat you?"

"It is indeed," she replied, happy to be home at last. "I need to speak to my father. Is he here?"

"Shore 'nuf. He was over to Master Franks, but he comed home nearly half an hour back."

Jasmine smoothed her dirty habit and bounded up the steps in an unladylike fashion. She didn't bother to knock but rather pushed back the ornate oak door and stepped into the sanctuary that had been her home for eighteen years.

"Hello?" she called out as she moved through the foyer and into the front sitting room. The room was empty. Jasmine sighed. She knew in her heart that she'd most likely find her father in his study, but she had hoped that she might encounter him first in the presence of others. That way, she presumed, the shock would be less and his anger would abate more quickly.

Giving up on that hope, however, she made her way to her father's office and took a deep breath before knocking loudly on the door.

"Come in."

Jasmine opened the door and peeked in. "Hello, Papa."

"Jasmine!" Her father got to his feet from behind his austere mahogany desk. "I didn't realize you were arriving tonight. We'd had no word and had intended to send someone to check on you tomorrow." He came forward and embraced her.

Jasmine enjoyed the moment, knowing that once her father learned the truth there'd be no pleasantries. "I missed you so much. I just couldn't wait another moment." She pulled away and eyed her father seriously. With any luck at all, she'd get their conversation started before he realized the situation for what it was.

"We must talk, Papa. I'm not at all happy about this marriage."

He looked at her oddly. "But Bradley assured me . . . well . . . that is to say, he implied you were content with the arrangement."

"But I am not. I do not love Bradley Houston. I have no intention of ever loving him. Please reconsider this marriage, Papa. I am most desperate to be freed from this responsibility."

Her father backed away as if she'd struck him. "I'm afraid I don't know what to say."

Jasmine nodded and tried her best to sound sympathetic. "I

know arrangements have been made and that people are counting on those arrangements. But, Papa, I long to marry for love—not because it suits the family business. Would you deny your only daughter this one request?"

"Have you discussed this with Bradley?"

Jasmine wondered how best to answer. "He knows of my feelings, if that's what you're asking. But, Papa, I'd rather all of this conversation stay between you and me. I would rather not worry Mama, and I certainly don't wish to anger my brothers or bring any further shame down on the family. I wanted to write you and discuss the matter sooner, but then before I realized what was happening, we were on our way back here. That's why I had to come to you alone—why I had to talk to you before Bradley or Grandmother or anyone else."

"Truly we cannot continue to discuss it now," her father said. "It's very poor manners that we should leave them alone. Where are they? Did you at least situate them with refreshments?" Her father began to pull on his jacket.

Jasmine looked down. "They are in Lorman."

Her father stopped even as he was buttoning up the coat. "What did you say?"

"I said they remained behind in Lorman. I rode out alone. No one knows I'm gone." Jasmine watched her father's face contort. "Before you get angry, please hear me, Papa." She went to him, tugging on his arm like a little child. "I had to talk to you about this marriage without Bradley hanging on my every word. I cannot marry him. He's abominable to me."

Her father stared in disbelief. "You risked your life—your reputation—to ride all the way from Lorman unescorted, for this?"

"I thought if we had some time to talk, for me to explain how I feel . . ."

He jerked away from her and began to pace. "Jasmine, this has nothing to do with feelings. This is a business arrangement that will benefit generations of Wainwrights to come. It will see our family secure, as well as the families of your uncles and cousins. How dare you come here as a spoiled and frightened child and declare that the entire arrangement be dissolved in order to suit your feelings?"

Jasmine felt as though she'd been slapped. Her father had always been gentle and protective of her. This was the first time she'd ever faced his wrath.

"I only pray that Mr. Houston doesn't change his mind. If that were to happen, this family would face extreme consequences."

Jasmine shook her head, forcing back the tears that threatened to spill. "But, Papa—"

He held up his hand. "No. No more. I won't hear another word." He came to stand directly in front of her. "You are too young to understand the importance of this matter, and because of that, I can and will overlook your foolhardy behavior of this evening. I am uncertain as to how we will explain the matter to Mr. Houston or whether he'll be as sympathetic, but you will not speak of this again."

Jasmine felt the truth tighten around her neck like a noose. "So it doesn't matter to you that I not only do not love Mr. Houston, but I cannot bear to be in his presence?"

"Time will change that," her father assured. "Few women can honestly say they marry for such luxuries as love and attraction. This is a good match. It benefits the greater good of our family."

Jasmine saw the determination in her father's eyes and in that moment felt herself age a decade. "So my heart is to be sacrificed for the greater good, is that it?" How foolish she had been to imagine that her desires were important to anyone other than herself. Somehow she had been confident that she could come home, speak to her father in private, and persuade him to put an end to her engagement. She realized her foolishness.

"You may not understand my decision at this moment, but in time you will."

Jasmine shook her head. "I understand that I am nothing more to you than a possession to be bartered. I might as well be one of your slaves, up on the block, sold to the highest bidder."

Jasmine hadn't expected the hard slap across her face. From the look of her father's expression, the move took him by surprise as well. It was the first time he had ever struck her. Jasmine touched her gloved hand to her cheek, staring in disbelief at the man she thought she knew so well.

Embarrassed, her father went back to his desk. Toying with some papers there, he said, "We will speak of this no more. Your wedding will take place as planned. One day you will understand, but until that time, I demand that you keep your childish notions to yourself. I cannot have you ruining this arrangement for nothing more serious than little-girl fears. This is an excellent arrangement. You will never want for anything, and despite your feelings, Bradley assures me that he has come to love you quite ardently. Your love for him will come in time. You'll see."

Jasmine stared at her father for several minutes, then backed away as if it were impossible to grasp the meaning of his words. For the first time in her life, she felt very much alone.

————

Jasmine sat alone in the music room when Bradley approached her. "I believe we should talk," he said rather dryly. He closed the door behind him and, to Jasmine's surprise, slid the lock into place. "I'd rather we not be disturbed."

Jasmine trembled at Bradley's tone. No doubt he meant to berate her for her actions. "I presume you wish to discuss last night."

"Among other things," he said, pushing out his coat tails before taking a seat. "Your actions were imprudent—dangerous."

"I thought you would see it that way," Jasmine replied, trying hard to show no fear. "I do not regret my choice, however. I was very homesick."

Bradley nodded. "I'm sure you were. But you could have met with grave harm. It was inconsiderate of you to risk your life in such a manner."

"I didn't know you cared," she said sarcastically. "Unless, of course, you're speaking merely out of concern for your business arrangement."

"You do me injustice," Bradley said softly.

Jasmine hated his calm, determined manner more than the times when he was forceful and mean-tempered. "You are the one forcing me to marry you. I'd say that's a bigger injustice."

"You feel that way now because you're young. In a few years, you'll see this as a completely different matter. You'll have children and a new home . . . you will be happy."

"Or else?"

Bradley's expression altered and a hint of anger tinged his voice. "Why do you insist on making this difficult?"

Jasmine got to her feet and began to pace. Her burgundy gown swirled around her heels as she turned abruptly. "If you were the one being forced against your will to marry someone you don't love, perhaps then you would understand my difficulty."

"I am sorry that you cannot conjure up some kind of affection for me. I have tried to win your heart. I've tried to show you that I am worthy of your love—that I will make a good provider and protector. Still you refuse to yield any ground to me whatsoever."

Jasmine looked at him hard. "You speak as though it's some kind of war—a battle for territory. I speak of the heart and a desire to be in love with the man whom I marry. Why is that to be considered such a terrible fault on my part?"

Bradley got up and came to her. To Jasmine's surprise he didn't sound in the leastwise angry. "It's not a fault, my dear. It's simply unrealistic. Do you honestly mean to tell me that your friends have married purely for love—that their feelings were considered first and foremost?"

Jasmine thought of her three closest friends. One had been matched to a man nearly twenty years her senior because his land holdings adjoined her family's property. Another friend had been pledged to her cousin since birth, while the third was also a victim of an arranged marriage to a local politician.

"I can see you realize the truth of my words." He reached out and took hold of her. "I'm not asking you to lie and say you love me. I know that you do not. I am, however, demanding the respect I am due. If you want to be happy in this union, you will respect me and honor my wishes."

Jasmine knew there was little to be gained by agitating Bradley. She would marry him no matter her desires. "Very well. I will do as I am bid."

Bradley seemed surprised by her response. He stared at her for several moments before saying, "But?"

Jasmine shook her head. "But nothing. I have no say in this. My father has arranged for the marriage. My husband doesn't care that I feel nothing for him. My life has been decided for me and I am resigned to acquiesce." The girlish dreams of her childhood faded into oblivion with the realization that nothing she longed for would ever be realized.

Bradley stepped back, dropping his hold. Jasmine thought he almost looked shocked—perhaps stunned by her declaration. But why? Why should he find this surprising? Then again, maybe it bothered him to realize that she was resigned to their union—not happy but no longer angry, merely reconciled. What a horrible revelation. Especially for one with Bradley's passion for life.

Composing himself once again, Bradley asked, "And you will no longer put your life at risk for foolish notions?"

"It wouldn't really serve any purpose, would it?" Jasmine said softly.

————

A tear trickled down Jasmine's cheek as Mammy arranged the Honiton lace wedding veil onto her soft, honey-brown curls before carefully fastening it into place. She circled Jasmine, straightening the lace to accentuate the turkey-tail edging and delicate florets. "You jes' as well quit that boo-hooin'. You know them tears ain't gonna change nothing 'cept to make your face all splotchy."

Jasmine took the handkerchief Mammy offered and blotted her cheeks. "None of this is fair." She was trying so hard to remain calm and resigned to her lot, but as the moment of her nuptials came closer, Jasmine found it more difficult. It was as if her heart were rising up in one last charge of emotion—one last moment of hope before her feelings were forever buried deep within.

"Lots of things in life ain't fair—don't mean they gonna change. 'Sides, you gonna have Miss Alice livin' nearby, and that's a blessin'. She'll make sure you okay."

"Having Grandmother close at hand didn't stop this wedding," Jasmine curtly replied before patting Mammy's hand. "I'm still hoping to take you with me, Mammy. Father hasn't given me his final answer."

"I don' know iffen I'd be likin' it up north. People says it's mighty cold up der. 'Course, it might not be so bad, but I'd still miss da other slaves. Best you don' be pushin' at your pappy to send me along, or Mr. Bradley be gettin' mad."

"If Bradley said he had no objection to your coming, you wouldn't be unhappy or complain, would you?"

"Complainin' don' do no more good than dem tears you was crying a few minutes ago. Jes' a waste of time and words. Now stand up and let me see you afore I go and tend to your mama." The old slave pressed a palm to her forehead and wiped away the beads of perspiration. "I'll likely never get your mama dressed. Last night she tol' me she was takin' to her bed and never gettin' back out." Mammy moved her finger in a circular motion, and Jasmine slowly turned around for inspection. "You look mighty fine. Now sit down while I go and check on your mama and Miss Alice."

The bedroom door opened and Alice Wainwright stepped inside. Her attire was impeccable. A sapphire blue ruching bordered her silk gown and perfectly matched the beaded reticule she carried. "You take care of Madelaine. I'm ready," she announced. Her face was painstakingly powdered and rouged. A strand of iridescent pearls dangled from one finger. "For you, my dear. A wedding gift. Actually, I have another gift awaiting you in Lowell, but the pearls must suffice for now."

"They are beautiful, Grandmother. Thank you so much."

Alice ran her fingers over the lace veil. "Not so beautiful as this wedding veil. When Bradley told me his mother's veil could not be equaled, I questioned his words. But I've never seen such beautiful lace—or such a beautiful bride."

"I wanted to wear *my* mother's veil. I didn't force him to wear clothing that belonged to a member of my family, so why should I be forced to wear *his* mother's veil?"

"Bradley's mother is dead. This is one way he can include her in his marriage. If the veil were unsightly, I would understand your feelings. However, it is stunning. You should be honored and delighted to wear it, Jasmine."

Jasmine sat quietly while her grandmother reached under the veil and arranged the pearls around her neck.

"You don't appear pleased. Perhaps I should have purchased an emerald. Would you have preferred an emerald? Or perhaps a diamond?"

"No, Grandmother, the pearls are perfect. Your gift is too generous, especially under these circumstances."

"What do you mean, *these* circumstances?"

"You know this wedding is a farce. I don't love Bradley Houston, and even though he seems to have convinced you and Father he cares for me, I believe he loves only his money. A man doesn't barter for a wife and then avow he loves her."

"Now, now, my dear. I've told you, it's best you begin to think of your marriage in positive terms. When you wanted a chance to speak to your father on the matter, I completely understood. However, you gave it your very best and the time for questioning the event is past. In time, I'm certain you'll learn to care for Bradley. Perhaps you'll never love him, but these arranged marriages are not so bad as they sometimes seem at first."

"Easy enough for you to say. You're not the one being bartered off to seal a business relationship. And that's all I am, you know: a commodity they're using for their own purpose. Why is it my brothers are permitted to choose any young woman they desire, while I am forced into a loveless marriage?"

"You know your statements aren't completely true, my dear. Your brothers will also be expected to make marriages that benefit the family. And even though you don't want to believe it, I think Bradley is quite smitten with you. He keeps you in his sights like a man who is totally besotted."

"Or a man intent upon keeping his prey within striking distance. I want a marriage like you had, one that is based upon love instead of financial gain."

Alice's lips curved into a wry grin. "As I told you before, Jasmine, my marriage to your grandfather was arranged. Some would say it was almost barbaric. We met only once before our marriage, and our parents monitored the entire conversation during that meeting."

"But you appeared to be blissfully happy. Was it all a charade?"

"Of course not! I *was* happy—though not at first, I admit. In those first months, I was too frightened to be anything but gloomy and depressed. However, as time passed, your grandfather and I fell deeply in love. We became devoted to each other. Ironically, years later, your grandfather confided that he, too, had been terrified when we married. So you see, you may be misjudging Bradley."

"Bradley isn't afraid of anything. He's a consummate businessman who is used to having his own way."

"He may excel in business, my dear, but affairs of the heart tend to intimidate even the most stalwart of men."

Jasmine wanted to hear no defense of Bradley Houston. "Still, my marriage is different. Bradley schemed with Father to arrange our marriage, while Grandfather was innocent of such behavior. I'd truly like to believe you're correct, but I've found nothing to like in either Bradley's beliefs or his behavior. I know you consider Father a good judge of character, but he's missed the mark this time. Unfortunately, I'll be the one to pay for his mistake."

Alice cupped Jasmine's quivering chin in her hand. "Have faith, Jasmine. Faith that even if your father has made a mistake, your heavenly Father will sustain you. Your mother is distraught over this entire turn of events and blames me. And I suppose she's right. If you hadn't come north to visit me . . ."

Her grandmother's voice trailed off into a deafening silence. Jasmine reached up and took her grandmother's hand tenderly in her own. "Don't blame yourself, Grandmother. I don't regret coming to visit you. We had a wonderful time together. My father could have denied Bradley's request. If Mother wishes to place blame, she has only to look at her husband—he's the one holding the ultimate power."

"I do regret the role I've played in creating your unhappiness, but now there's nothing we can do to change things except maintain our faith. We best go and see how your mother is faring. It will soon be time for the nuptials to begin."

The two women walked hand in hand down the hallway. Jasmine could hear her mother's soulful weeping mingled with Mammy's soothing voice as they neared the bedroom door. She glanced at her grandmother.

Alice gave her a reassuring smile. "Your mother will be fine. She doesn't think so right now, but she will. If only she would release herself from her self-imposed confinement here at the plantation, her life would be more enjoyable."

"I think it's too late for her to change her ways, Grandmother. She's become so emotionally frail, I fear that one day she won't rebound from her depression. Her condition seems to worsen as she grows older."

"I'll speak to your father. Perhaps if he encouraged her to invite some of the ladies for tea or to attend a few social functions, it would help. And with both of us living in Lowell, we'll work toward having her come and visit us."

Jasmine brightened. "Yes, that's a wonderful idea. If need be, I'll come back and escort her. We just will not permit her to refuse our invitation."

Alice pulled Jasmine into an embrace. "Exactly! Now chin up and take courage in the Lord. You are not facing this alone. Remember what the first chapter of Joshua says: 'Have I not commanded thee? Be strong and of a good courage; be not afraid, neither be thou dismayed: for the Lord thy God is with thee whithersoever thou goest.'"

The words touched Jasmine deeply. *I am not alone . . . God is with me.* "I'm not alone," she whispered.

Bradley Houston straightened his cravat, tucked his watch into the pocket of his vest, and walked to the gallery. He surveyed the willow-lined road that led in and out of the Wainwright plantation, certain fate had delivered him to this point in his life. He was destined for greatness—he knew it. Indeed, these past months had been heady. His new position with the Boston Associates, coupled with his engagement to a beautiful Southern belle, had placed him in an enviable situation. His ability to align himself as the only buyer of Wainwright cotton was hailed as a major coup by the Boston Associates. They'd promised a bonus with each delivery of raw cotton that exceeded projections, which was something he was anxious to discuss with his future father-in-law.

"Ah, Bradley, there you are."

He turned to see Malcolm Wainwright walking toward him and reached forward to grasp his future father-in-law's hand in a hearty handshake. "Not much longer until I'm a married man," Bradley said victoriously.

Malcolm patted him on the shoulder and gave a deep chuckle. "I trust you're not reconsidering your decision."

"That thought hasn't once crossed my mind, Mr. Wainwright."

"I believe it's time you called me Malcolm," the older man declared.

Bradley smiled. "If that's your wish, Malcolm. I was anxious to meet with you before we leave for the church."

"Sounds serious."

"I met with Matthew Cheever and Nathan Appleton the day before departing Lowell. As you know, they are pleased with your agreement to supply the mills with your cotton crop. They wanted me to inform you that they were delighted when you convinced your brother Franklin to market his cotton with us as well. Should you convince your other brother, Harry, to join us, they will reward you. In fact, they said that any shipments above what was previously agreed upon will entitle you to a substantial bonus."

"That's quite generous, isn't it?"

"Indeed. I thought you would be in high spirits. Their offer gives you ample reason to move your production to maximum levels."

"We're already at maximum production."

"You can't tell me that a heavy hand on the whip won't cause those slaves to increase your production."

"I've found the whip to be a hindrance—except for runaways. It creates resentment."

"Perhaps you might find some innovative measures that could be taken. Isn't Samuel in charge of production? Surely he could think of some method to increase production."

Wainwright's lips tightened and his brows furrowed into wiry lines of disapproval. "Samuel does a fine job on production."

Bradley knew he'd overstepped his bounds by inadvertently insulting Malcolm's eldest son. He pulled out his watch and clicked open the silver casing. "I suppose we should be leaving soon. I'm certain Jasmine won't forgive me if we're late."

Malcolm's eyebrows arched. "Then she's finally content with the marital arrangement?"

The question startled Bradley. "Has she expressed dissatisfaction regarding the marriage since our arrival in Mississippi?"

"Yes, of course. I've listened to a myriad of complaints, but women have no idea what they want or need when they're young, especially those like Jasmine, who have led protected and sheltered lives," Wainwright replied. He gave his future son-in-law a shrewd wink. "I'm certain she'll come around."

Bradley's face flushed with the humiliation of knowing Jasmine had continued to express dissatisfaction over their marriage to her father. Although Bradley had exerted time and energy on their relationship, it was apparent Jasmine had not intended to yield, even with their wedding close at hand. It seemed as if his kindness and indulgence would pass without reward. If she continued down this path, his attempts to win her over would cease. When Jasmine had cajoled and wept, he had begrudgingly conceded to a church wedding, although he would have much preferred the ceremony be held at The Willows. But he would no longer tolerate her childish behavior. He had neither the time nor the need to cater to her whims once she was his wife.

"Here's our carriage now."

Bradley hoisted himself up alongside Malcolm and glanced back toward the doorway. "Your sons aren't riding with us to the church?"

"No, I sent them on ahead to escort the women." He directed the servant to move on and turned his attention back to Bradley.

"That bonus you mentioned earlier. Was there an exact figure agreed upon?"

Bradley hesitated a moment. "Five percent above the regular price. How does that sound?" He watched Malcolm's reaction closely.

"Considering the fact that they've already agreed to pay me more than I can receive in the English markets, the additional five percent seems fair. Of course, I don't foresee much excess, at least not this year."

Bradley didn't exhibit his jubilation. Wainwright had imparted a subtle message in his reply: it was obvious his future father-in-law would take advantage of the bonus next year. This tidbit helped remove the sting of embarrassment from his future wife's complaints regarding their marriage. He would train her in short order that there would be repercussions for such inappropriate behavior.

C H A P T E R · *13*

March 1847

JASMINE SAT opposite Bradley at the breakfast table, her gaze fixed upon the pristine white china plate. She traced her finger around the gold edging while contemplating the most effective way to approach her husband. She peeked at him from under hooded eyelids to see if he was looking in her direction. But Bradley's attention was focused upon serving himself hearty portions of scrambled eggs, sausage, biscuits, and gravy.

She continued to secretly watch him, her emotions muddled with uncertainty. Bradley's behavior remained perplexing. One day he was kind and generous, while the next he was angry and overbearing. Throughout the past three months she had attempted to be a good wife, hoping her grandmother was correct—that in time she would learn to love Bradley. But thus far she had not developed any feelings of love. Sometimes she intensely disliked him; sometimes she merely tolerated him; yet, on some occasions, when he was kind, she took pleasure in his company. However, she was never certain of his mood, and this morning was no exception.

While spreading one last spoonful of jam onto his biscuit, Bradley glanced in her direction. "I'm certain you'll be pleased to know I have business in Boston. I'll be leaving tomorrow and will be gone for several days. Please have one of the servants see to my baggage."

"Of course. Business for the mills or with your shipping business?"

He dipped his fork into the sausage and gravy before looking up from his plate. "How unusual. You sound genuinely interested." Sarcasm dripped from his voice like the gravy dribbling off his fork.

"I do take interest in your work, Bradley. I've tried my very best to assist in every way possible. In fact, I'm hosting a group of your Associates' wives this afternoon, just as I have on several previous occasions. I'm doing my best to become acquainted and entertain on your behalf. However, it seems as if you inevitably find fault with all my efforts."

"Your tea parties seem to garner me little aid. I asked you to entertain these women and learn about the mills. Thus far they've shared nothing but recipes and needlepoint designs. Tell them you have an interest in hearing what goes on in the mills so that you may intelligently converse with your husband about his work."

"When I broached the subject of the mills at our previous socials, the ladies quickly turned the conversation to other topics. Since I want to represent myself as a suitable hostess, I granted them the courtesy of discussing issues they found of interest. However, I will do as you suggest. I'm sure it will prove successful, and when you return this evening, I'll have much to tell you."

He stared across the table as though memorizing her features. "We'll see."

She twirled a ringlet of hair around her index finger and smiled. "If I am successful, will it please you very much?"

"Yes, it will please me."

"Enough that I might ask a special favor?"

He motioned to the servant and pointed to his coffee cup. "You are always free to ask, my dear."

"But will you grant my request?"

"We'll wait and see how successful you are—and just what it is you want."

She pushed her food around her plate for several moments. "Would you like me to tell you now?"

He pushed away from the table, wiped his mouth, and placed the linen napkin on his plate. "No. It can wait until I return this evening."

He moved to where she sat, pecked her on the cheek, and left the house. She sighed. Her hopes now rested on the success of the women who would visit this afternoon, and success she would have. If necessary, she would break the rules of etiquette.

"Mammy," she called out while scurrying up the stairs. "Please pack Master Bradley's bags—he'll be gone for several days." She thought for a moment and added, "Better pack for a week. He'll be leaving for Boston in the morning. Take special care that everything is in order. I want to keep him very happy."

The old slave's ample body filled the bedroom doorway. "Keepin' dat man happy is harder than tryin' to shoot a rabbit dat keep poppin' in and out of its hole."

Jasmine giggled at the remark. "Well, difficult or not, we must try. I'm hoping he will agree to a visit from Mother. I plan to ask him tonight."

A broad toothy grin lit up Mammy's face. "Miss Madelaine gonna come see us? Oh, dat be very nice. I be sure to pack extra careful so Massa Bradley say he gonna let her come. You think your mama gonna be willin' to make dat boat ride?"

"No. I would have to go and get her. I thought Grandmother and I could travel to The Willows, remain a few weeks, and then return with Mother. If Bradley doesn't want her to stay with us, she can stay with Grandmother for a portion of her visit. I'm hoping Father will come and visit and then accompany her home."

Mammy placed her hands on her broad hips, her elbows sticking out like plump chicken wings. "Um, um. Don' know if Massa Bradley gonna agree to all dat."

"I'm hoping that he'll be in an extraordinarily good mood this evening. The ladies are coming for tea, and if I do as he's told me, I'm certain things will go according to plan."

"Ain' nothing gone accordin' to no plan since you been in dis house," Mammy muttered.

Jasmine ignored the comment. "I'm going downstairs to make certain things are on schedule in the kitchen. I want everything to be perfect this afternoon."

The cook and her helper were hard at work; Sarah, the maid, was ensuring the house was in proper order; and Mammy was busy packing Bradley's bag. Jasmine took her Bible into the small sitting room and spent the remainder of her morning reading. Grandmother always took such comfort from her quiet time with God that Jasmine had tried hard to emulate the practice. She had to admit there was a certain amount of comfort, although some of what she read confused her.

After lunch, Jasmine carefully dressed for the gathering, all the while contemplating the proper way to maneuver the afternoon of tea and conversation.

"You gots to sit still iffen I'm gonna finish your hair," Mammy said as she struggled to twist a handful of golden hair into a stylish coiffure.

"I just want everything to be perfect," Jasmine protested. She wiggled on the chair, trying to reach the pearls her grandmother had given her. "If things go well this afternoon, we shouldn't have any trouble convincing Bradley."

Mammy *harrumph*ed, obviously unconvinced. She pinned the last of Jasmine's hair in place, then took up the pearls to secure them around her young mistress's neck. No sooner were the pearls secured than Jasmine jumped to her feet to survey her image in the mirror.

She loved the powder blue color of the gown and turned quickly to watch the skirt fall into place. "Do you think this gown smart enough?" she asked Mammy.

"I think it be fine."

Jasmine nodded. "It needs to be perfect."

One by one, the ladies arrived, all impeccably attired and obviously looking forward to an afternoon away from home. A buzz of conversation filled the room until Lilly Cheever raised her voice just a bit and gained their attention. "Ladies, I don't know if you've been advised, but Tracy Jackson's health continues to decline. Matthew has been most concerned about his health. I told Matthew I would be certain to inform you and ask that you pray for Tracy and his wife. This is a very trying time for them, and I know they would be most appreciative. And you all know how Tracy is: he wants to be in the midst of all that's happening with the Associates, which makes it doubly hard for him to follow the doctor's orders and remain abed."

Nettie Harper nodded in agreement. "Especially with all the problems in the mills right now. Wilson has been most difficult to live with over the past few months. It seems as if there is one problem after another to deal with."

"What kinds of problems?" Jasmine asked. All of them looked at her as though she had lost her senses. "My husband is gone much of the time, what with purchasing cotton and overseeing shipments and deliveries. He doesn't have opportunity to keep abreast of the inner workings of the mills."

"Well, of course, my dear. I tend to forget there's more to the operation than the mills and canals," Nettie said. "After all, we can't operate without cotton, can we?"

Rose Montrose patted Jasmine's hand. "Absolutely. Your husband's position is extremely important. Because of his hard work, I'm sure our husbands are relieved of many headaches. In fact, Leonard has told me your husband is a very shrewd businessman."

"Indeed," Wilma Morgan agreed. "James mentioned just the other day that your husband had been very successful in contracting with several plantation owners since he became chief buyer. I know from what he's told me that those additional suppliers have eased many concerns."

"Coming from the South, I know little of the mills and would be most interested in learning more. As you know, Bradley and I have been married only a few months. I long to talk with him about matters that are of interest to him."

"Well, of course you do," Rose Montrose put in. "I think that's an admirable attribute. Currently Leonard expresses dismay over the workers. Since they've begun using more Irish women in the mills, he says there appears to be more discontent."

"Really? Does your husband believe the problems are because the Yankee and Irish girls dislike working together?" Lilly Cheever asked.

"Well, the Irish girls obviously don't believe the Yankee girls should be paid higher wages for the same work," Rose replied. "And, of course, there are the ongoing complaints about the speedup and premium methods, but if the companies are to retain a profit margin, they must be innovative."

"What is that? A premium and a speedup?" Jasmine inquired.

"It's merely a method of keeping the mills operating at top production in order to make the best profits," Rose said.

"Not quite," Lilly Cheever corrected. "The speedup method is exactly what it implies. The machines are set to operate at a faster production level, which means the workers are forced to work at a higher rate of speed all day. However, the machinery is dangerous, and speeding up the machines heightens the likelihood of accidents. There are already many accidents in the mills, and I'm certain the additional speed worries all of the girls. The premium method means the girls are paid according to how much they produce rather than the hourly wage that they've always been promised."

"I forgot you were once a mill girl, Lilly. Your sympathy for the workers certainly seems to outweigh your loyalty to the Associates," Wilma Morgan observed.

"This isn't a matter of loyalty, Wilma. It is a matter of right and wrong. I believe the Associates made certain promises to the workers, and if they are going to change those promises, they need to go about it in a proper manner rather than merely forcing their new methodology on the workers without any concern for their welfare.

"I know what it's like to work in those mills. Speeding up the machinery is not safe, and I don't agree with the premium method. The workers have always been hired for hourly wages, and those have decreased rather than increased. It's little wonder there's strife among the workers. And the attitude that wages should be adjusted because of where you were born doesn't sit well with me. Who has control over her place of birth? Only God, I believe. Does an Irish girl not work as hard as a Yankee girl?"

"The Yankee girls have been in the mills longer and have more experience," Rose defended.

"Some, but not all. I don't disagree with paying higher wages to the more experienced girls, but I do disagree with paying different wages to employees with equal experience," Nettie remarked. "My husband says the girls complain more about having the windows nailed down than about the nationality of the girl standing at the next loom." She looked at Jasmine and said, "They nail down the windows to keep the rooms humid. That way, the threads don't break as easily. The girls, of course, would prefer to have the windows open. In fact, they say the steam and lint fibers are making them ill."

"You mark my words: unless these issues are addressed, the girls will begin talking of another strike," Lilly advised. "And I don't think our husbands want to see that occur."

"Nor do I. There would truly be no living with my husband if a strike became imminent," Nettie Harper put in.

Wilma Morgan turned her attention back to Jasmine. "And what do you and yours think of the growing antislavery movement?"

The women stared in her direction, obviously awaiting a response. The room was silent—like a cold winter night after a fresh snow. "I attended an antislavery meeting at the Pawtucket church before my marriage to Bradley. Two former slaves spoke at that meeting. I was as shocked at their revelations as anyone else in attendance. But you must remember that not all slave owners are cruel and treacherous. My father is certainly not that kind of man."

"Surely you realize that we who live in the North abhor the very idea of slavery," Wilma submitted.

"Yes, I've been told. But those of you who live in the North need the cotton the South supplies. Who will raise your cotton if there are no slaves?"

"You could free them and pay a fair wage for their labor," Rose argued.

"And if the price of cotton rises and you must finally pay the mill workers higher wages in order to keep them from striking, your profits decrease. Will you remain staunchly against slavery when that occurs?"

"Of course we will," Rose insisted. "It's only because you've been indoctrinated with these beliefs that you can rationalize these matters in your own mind. One human owning another is wrong."

"Perhaps you are correct, Mrs. Montrose. I'm no more an authority on slavery than on the issues between the Irish and Yankees. There appears to be injustice at every turn, doesn't there?" Jasmine replied. "May I pour you some more tea?"

Rose covered the cup with her hand. "No, not right now."

Lilly Cheever picked up her teacup. "I would like some more tea, please. You know, given our differing opinions, I think we should each pray and see how God directs us. I'm sure there are more than enough injustices in this world that need correction, and there are too few willing to be used in God's service. If we each seek where we can best serve, I believe we'll find our perfect place to do God's will without causing divisiveness among our little group. We want to remain friends and still serve our fellow man. If there is conflict among us, we'll be of no use to God or others."

"You're right," Rose agreed. "I apologize, Jasmine. I spoke out of turn. And while we're praying, let's pray that there's not another strike and the conflicts in the mills are settled in an amicable manner."

"I do wish the girls hadn't formed that labor group. I think it has only made matters worse," Wilma said.

"If someone would have taken their complaints seriously when they were seeking a ten-hour workday, I doubt whether they would have thought a union necessary," Lilly observed. "Establishing the Labor Reform Association seemed the only answer at the time. That's why I believe all of these issues should be a matter of prayer."

The ladies nodded in agreement as Rose picked up her reticule and dug deep inside. "I almost forgot—I have a recipe I want to share with the rest of you."

A smile tugged at Jasmine's lips. If Rose discussed recipes and sewing designs for the remainder of the afternoon, Jasmine would be fine. Surely she had garnered enough information to satisfy Bradley. He should be in excellent humor after hearing the details of today's discussion.

Bradley gazed out the carriage window and spied Jasmine standing by the open front door. He had been gone a full week, and she was obviously anxious to see him. At least, he surmised, she was anxious to hear his decision. She had been completely deflated when he announced he would wait until his return from Boston to answer her request.

Granted, she had gathered a good deal of information regarding the mills and had done exactly as he'd instructed. However, he hadn't been prepared for her question. He had thought she wanted merely to purchase some fancy bauble or new dress fabric; he hadn't anticipated she would request permission for her mother to make a lengthy visit in their home. Having Madelaine Wainwright in the house would not be comfortable. He would need to be on guard with everything he said and did in his own house, which he found foreign and distasteful. Jasmine's suggestion that her mother spend a portion of her time with Grandmother Wainwright made the idea somewhat palatable but not enough so that he wanted to render an immediate decision.

After his meetings in Boston, he was glad he had waited. He silently congratulated himself on his choice as he walked up the front steps of the house and greeted his wife. "How pleasant to have you dutifully waiting to greet your husband."

She smiled and turned her cheek to receive his kiss. "Let me take your bag."

"No. I'll take it upstairs. Why don't you join me and we can talk."

Her excitement was evident as she hurried up the stairs while chattering about events that had transpired throughout the past week. She watched as he placed his baggage in his room, obviously fearful to ask if he'd arrived at a decision yet. They were playing a game of cat and mouse, and he enjoyed watching her attempt to bait him. However, if he was going to complete his accounting work before supper, he must cut short this diversion.

"I've decided your mother's visit is acceptable. However . . ."

Before he could say anything further, she flung herself into his arms. "Oh, thank you, Bradley. Thank you, thank you, thank you." She turned her face to kiss him.

He met her lips with a passionate kiss before taking her by the arms and holding her a short distance away from him. "You didn't permit me to complete my statement. Your mother may come to visit. You and your grandmother will go to fetch her, and she will spend half her time in our home and half her time in your grandmother's home. Is that acceptable?"

"Oh yes! Completely acceptable." Her face was alight with pleasure.

"There is one other condition. One that will likely displease you."

Her smile began to fade. "And what is that?"

"You must take Mammy with you."

Her smile once again brightened. "Is that all? Why would I be unhappy to have Mammy join me?"

"You misunderstand what I'm telling you, Jasmine. Mammy will *not* return to Lowell with you. She must remain at The Willows."

The happiness evaporated from her face like a morning fog rising off the lake. "Why? What have I done that you're punishing me?"

"This has nothing to do with punishing you. I've been berated all week because we have a slave in our household. Slavery is a topic frowned upon by the Associates—at least as it pertains to the *Northern* states."

"What does *that* mean? The prestigious Boston Associates find slavery acceptable so long as it remains in the South?"

"Exactly. It's the general consensus that slavery may continue in states where it is already in effect; however, they do not believe it should spread to other states. Nor do they believe anyone living in the North should own slaves, especially one of their members."

"You don't own Mammy. She belongs to my father."

"It doesn't matter, Jasmine. Another person owns her. She's a slave. I'll find you another maid to take her place—someone to help with your hair and other personal needs."

He stepped toward her, but she quickly turned and pulled away from his embrace. "What the Boston Associates want is more important than your wife's comfort? You tell me you want a child. Well, I can't imagine having a baby without Mammy here in Lowell to help me."

He clenched his jaw and fought to keep his anger in check. "Is that a threat? Are you telling me you'll refuse me my marital rights over the loss of that old slave?"

She obviously knew she'd overstepped her bounds. He could see her resistance had now been replaced by fear.

"I'm saying I don't want her to leave me."

"There is no choice. She must go." He walked toward the bedroom door. "I must get to my bookwork or I'll not complete it before supper." He stopped and turned as he reached the doorway. "I saw Nolan while I was in Boston. He will escort you and your grandmother."

"Why? We don't need an escort to make our journey to Mississippi."

"Nolan was particularly fond of The Willows. He thought this trip an excellent opportunity for another visit. Besides, my dear, it will give me comfort knowing there is a man along to look after you should any difficult circumstances arise—and it assures me of your return to Lowell," he added. "You sail at week's end. I'll send word to your grandmother so that she may prepare for the voyage."

CHAPTER · *14*

The Willows, Lorman, Mississippi

"NOLAN, WAIT!" Her voice was a raspy whisper in the night air, and she prayed he would hear. He slowed but then picked up his pace. "Nolan!" He stopped. "Nolan! It's Jasmine. Wait for me."

The tall shadow of a figure remained still, waiting, poised—as if ready to take flight and hide under cover of darkness. She ran hard, with her chest heaving, lungs begging for air as she forced herself onward. A piece of dead wood rose up to greet her. Without warning, she sprawled pell-mell into Nolan's arms. They fell to the ground, his arms cradling her while she gasped for breath. Several minutes passed before her ragged breathing returned to a steady cadence.

"What are you doing out here?"

He was still holding her close; she could hear the beat of his heart, and the sound was reassuring, comforting. She remained very still, not wanting to move away from the warmth of his chest. "I heard you ask one of the kitchen servants if you could deliver food to the quarters for her tonight," she said. "I also heard her agree."

He shifted and pulled himself to his feet, then gazed down at her. "Your plan was to follow me to the slave quarters?"

"Yes," she said as she stood and brushed debris from her skirt.

"Why?"

"For many reasons. Some of them date back to conversations with you and with Mrs. Longfellow at Cambridge, as well as that first antislavery meeting I attended before my marriage to Bradley," she explained. "Since then, there have been discussions that made me realize I didn't truly know anything about the slaves here. I've never been to their quarters, never talked to any of them except the ones who work in the big house. In fact, I've seen the other slaves only from a distance. Father never permitted me to go near the field slaves or anyplace where they work. So I decided it was time I found out for myself what it is like to be a slave at The Willows."

"If Bradley or your father finds out, there will be a terrible row. I fear there's already too much dissension between you and Bradley. You need to work toward smoothing the troubles in your relationship. Going to the slave quarters will only make matters worse."

"Bradley will never find out unless you tell him when we return to Massachusetts. Father is going over his accounts and will soon go to bed, and I've sworn Mammy to secrecy. I've already kissed both my mother and grandmother good-night. By the time we return, everyone in the house will be asleep, save Mammy. She promised she would be waiting to let us in the door."

"You've thought of everything, haven't you?"

"I hope so," she whispered.

He didn't argue further. Instead, he grabbed her by the hand and pulled her along. With only the sliver of a moon and a smattering of stars to provide light, they neared the quarters. Nolan yanked her to a halt. "We'll need to circle around or we'll pass the overseer's house. He has dogs that will catch our scent. If that happens, we'll be spotted. There will be no escaping those hounds. Stay close and don't talk."

For the first time since deciding to follow Nolan to the quarters, a fleeting tremble shuddered through her body. As a child she'd watched from the gallery when the overseer brought the baying hounds to the big house for her papa's review. She'd seen those hounds straining at their leashes with foam dripping from their jowls and hunger in their eyes. They were a fearsome sight and one she didn't want to personally encounter.

She did as she was told, following Nolan in a wide circle and then inward, where her gaze settled upon four long rows of dilapidated wooden cabins that lined either side of two narrow dirt roads. "This is it? This is where the slaves live?" she whispered in hushed wonder. The sight held her spellbound. "But we have over a hundred slaves. Surely there are other quarters."

Nolan was already on his feet, carefully moving forward when he turned and waved her onward. "Come on," he hissed into the balmy darkness.

She crouched low and followed him in a zigzagging pattern toward one of the cabins. "How do you know where you're going?" she asked.

"I was in the quarters more than one time on my first visit to The Willows with Bradley. Once your father granted me permission to explore the property, I came out here at least once a day, at varying times. I also came back to visit with the slaves when I was here for your wedding in December."

"If the overseer knows you, then why are we hiding?"

He stopped and looked down at her, the whites of his eyes barely visible in the thin sickle of moonlight. "Because I'm smuggling in food from the main house. And even if I could slip these provisions past the overseer, it would be difficult to hide *you*. There's little doubt in my mind that Mr. Sloan's first priority would be your safe return home. I don't think you want him waking the household to announce he's rescued you from the slave quarters."

"No, of course not. I wasn't thinking clearly. Please lead the way."

They inched forward until they were in front of a sagging door hanging on worn leather hinges. The plank swayed on its hinges as Nolan tapped. "Carter! It's Nolan Houston from Massachusetts."

The door opened a crack, and Carter peeked out at them. His

eyes grew wide and shone like ebony marbles set in bolls of snowy cotton. "Yes, suh?"

"I brought you some food from Tempie. She's worried you and the children aren't getting enough to eat."

"We's doin' fine." His voice was unconvincing, his gaze veering off toward Jasmine as he spoke. "You tell Tempie we's doin' good and we hopin' to see her come Sunday. We don' need no extra food. Massa feed us jes' fine."

Jasmine was certain her presence was contributing to the slave's standoffish behavior. She touched his hand and he jumped back as though he'd been scalded. "I'm not going to tell anyone that Tempie sent food. Please take it. You can trust me."

Carter's gaze swerved toward Nolan and then he nodded toward Jasmine.

"She won't tell," Nolan said.

"'Den I guess we'll be takin' dat food you brung." He reached out and took the cloth-wrapped bundle and was soon surrounded by a throng of smaller black faces and a rush of grabbing hands.

Only meager slices of moonlight sifted through the chinked log walls, but Jasmine's eyes had now adapted to the darkness, and she viewed the unsightly conditions within. There was a small fireplace at the end of the room, and a few cots had been fashioned from saplings. A shabby hand-hewn table sat near the fireplace along with two worn stools. And, although she couldn't be certain, she determined there were likely twelve or thirteen people living in this cramped cabin.

Her gaze settled on Carter and she pointed toward the end of the room. "You cook in that fireplace?"

His white teeth gleamed in the darkness. "No, ma'am. Dis ole slave don' know how ta cook," he said and then gave a hearty laugh. "I leaves da cookin' fer da womenfolk. But dey do mos' da cookin' outdoors 'cause dat chimney gets too hot. When dat happen, it catches on fire and we hafta push dat chimney away from da house. And dat ain' no good time."

Jasmine frowned, not understanding how a chimney would

catch on fire. "How do you keep warm in the winter if you can't use the fireplace?"

"Oh, we lights da wood in der, but sometimes we haftta get up in da middle o' da night and push da chimney away from da house. Dat chimney can catch fire purty easy 'cause it be made o' sticks and clay and moss—ain' like dem brick chimneys in da big house," he explained.

Even though the room was warm, Jasmine shivered. "So you must wear warmer clothes and pile under heavy blankets at night when the weather turns cold?"

Carter slowly wagged his head back and forth. "You don' understan' much 'bout life here in the quartah, ma'am, and best it stay dat way," he said before turning toward Nolan. "You need ta get her outta here afore the massa finds out. But I do thank ya fer bringin' da food."

"They don't receive ample food or clothing, do they? Does my father know this?"

Carter turned, his eyes alight with fear. "Don' say nothin' to your pappy, girl. Iffen you do dat, the overseer gonna think us'n been complainin' and he whup us fer sho'."

"Whip you? Surely not," Jasmine replied in disbelief.

It took only a fleeting glance around the room to observe young and old alike in tattered clothes and bare feet. The truth slowly sank in. She realized something substantial needed to be done. "I want to try and help if you're not getting enough food—or clothing."

"Can't nobody help us 'less you got some way o' convincin' your pappy to set us free."

Jasmine met Nolan's gaze. He didn't smirk. His eyes weren't filled with recrimination. He didn't say a word. His body appeared weighed down by the overwhelming helplessness that surrounded them.

"Surely there must be something we can do," she whispered to Nolan.

"If you want to help Carter and these others, do what he's asked. Say nothing. If you want to see an end to all of this suffering, work against slavery now that you're married and living away from this place. Time will tell if the sights you've seen tonight will fade from your memory or if they will burn more vividly each day and spur you onward to greater good."

CHAPTER · 15

ALICE DIPPED a linen cloth into a basin of cool water, wrung out the excess, and placed it across her granddaughter's forehead. "Jasmine, I am concerned. You are much too pale, and your inability to hold down any food over the past few days worries me. Never in your life have I seen you in this condition while at sea. I hope you haven't taken yellow fever."

Jasmine gave her grandmother a bleak smile. "I'm sure it's nothing so dramatic. I can't imagine why I'm ill. The waters have been calm throughout our voyage."

"At first I thought the illness was caused by something you'd eaten. But you've eaten the same meals as the rest of us. As far as I can determine, no one else appears to be suffering from this malady. Try a sip of water," Alice fussed. "You need to have some liquid in your body. I'll see if the ship's cook has some broth you might be able to tolerate."

The mention of broth caused Jasmine to think of food, but the thought of eating caused her to once again begin retching. When the unwelcome gagging finally ceased, she fell back upon the damp, flattened pillow, her forehead beaded with perspiration. Her stomach and ribs ached from previous days filled with sporadic heaving followed by constant painful headaches.

"I suppose this is a fitting conclusion to our trip. The entire journey has been nothing but one disaster after another."

"Now, now, no need to exaggerate, my dear. You'll only upset yourself and feel worse. Moreover, we had many relaxing days visiting with your dear mother."

"If you recall, Mother was supposed to return with us. That was the entire reason we made this voyage. As for visiting with her, I don't think she even knew we were there most of the time. I fear she's completely escaped into a world of her own making and hasn't any idea what's going on around her." Jasmine shifted and turned on her side, resting her head on one arm. "It breaks my heart to see her in this condition. I wish I were close at hand to help care for her, but I doubt there's any chance Bradley would consider moving south."

Her grandmother's waning smile confirmed what Jasmine already knew. Bradley would never consider leaving his position with the Boston Associates.

"If we look at the positive outcomes of our journey, I think you'd have to agree it was a good thing Mammy returned with us and is remaining at The Willows."

Jasmine gave a weak nod. "That's true. Leaving Mother didn't seem quite so terrible with Mammy there to care for her. But being without both of them is a greater personal loss to me. The house will seem quite empty with only the hired help. Mammy had become my confidante—I trusted her." She swallowed hard, not wanting to once again begin the violent retching. The wave of nausea momentarily passed and she squeezed Alice's vein-lined hand. "At least Bradley should be pleased."

"Whatever do you mean?"

Jasmine knew she shouldn't speak objectionably about her husband to her grandmother. And since her marriage to Bradley, she'd attempted to refrain from doing so. But she wondered if her reticence to criticize Bradley's behavior caused her grandmother to believe he had evolved into a genuine saint rather than remaining the difficult, demanding man Jasmine had married. "I had to bargain with Bradley in order to gain his permission for Mother's visit."

Alice grew wide-eyed at the remark. "In what way? Or dare I ask?"

"Mother's visit was contingent upon Mammy's permanent return to The Willows."

"I wondered why you weren't overly upset about Mammy leaving. But I thought perhaps she had asked to return because she missed the warmer climate."

"There's no doubt Mammy prefers the South, but she would have remained in Lowell had it not been for Bradley's edict that she leave. Apparently he received severe criticism from many of the Boston Associates because a slave was living in his household." She wrinkled her nose and pursed her lips together. "And, of course, we must manage our households as ordained by the Boston Associates."

"You shouldn't be surprised by their disdain. You know slavery is abhorred by most in the North, Jasmine."

"And I now see the merits of abolition also. However, the Northerners speak from both sides of their mouth. They speak against slavery except as it relates to making them wealthy; then they turn their heads the other way. It's pure hypocrisy. The slaves are necessary to produce cotton, and the cotton is necessary to operate their mills. I don't see any of them refusing to buy cotton from Southern plantations. In fact, that's precisely why Bradley was hired—to convince Southern growers to sell up north instead of shipping their crops to England."

"You have a valid argument, child. Of that, there is no doubt. This very issue has been argued at antislavery meetings. However, you must remember that Bradley's position hinges upon doing what his superiors request. And having Mammy with your mother is for the best." Alice gave her a bright smile and plumped Jasmine's flattened pillow. "I know you and Bradley are eventually going to look back upon these early days of your marriage with amusement. You'll wonder how you ever thought it impossible to love him," she said in an obvious attempt to buoy Jasmine's spirits.

Jasmine glanced up at her grandmother. "Bradley is *not* the man you think he's become, Grandmother, and I doubt I will ever grow to love him. I try to be a good wife and I will continue to do so. However, his distasteful actions make it difficult to like him, much less consider feelings of love."

"Don't let this particular matter divide you. There are many Northerners who decry slavery when what they actually believe is slavery should not spread into other states. I think this one issue may eventually split the antislavery movement—at least politically. I pray it doesn't fracture the movement so badly that we lose our impetus. I'm for complete abolition, but if we can't have abolition, I don't want to see any more proslavery states coming into the Union."

"My disagreement with Bradley wasn't over the slavery issue. Bradley insisted that I give Mammy up, and he also insisted that Mother spend half her visit with you. As for Mammy, I said we could request her papers from Father and free her. We could hire her as a servant like the other maids. But he denied my request."

"You've not been married long. He likely requested your mother spend time with me because he wants more time alone with you. And even if you freed Mammy, folks know she came to your household as a slave and would always think of her in that capacity. It has all worked out for the best, Jasmine. Your mother needs Mammy, and Mammy is much happier at The Willows. Think about how pleased she was to see the other slaves when we arrived at the house. Overall, I think we had a good visit."

Jasmine dipped her fingers in the cup of water and moistened her lips. "Have you ever been to the slave quarters, Grandmother?"

"Only once. I never went again." Alice peered at her for a long moment. "Have you, Jasmine?"

"Yes. I had to go and see for myself what it was like. You know that I have declared the Wainwright slaves are well treated. However, I decided if I was going to continue making such statements, I needed to assure I was speaking the truth."

"And what did you find?"

"I find I have spoken falsely. I saw and heard things that made me weep." She paused and looked toward the wall. "Does Papa advocate whipping the slaves?"

Her grandmother said nothing for a moment, so Jasmine looked back and saw her expression take on a look of discomfort. "He believes in discipline."

"And discipline is meted out at the end of a whip, correct?"

"I suppose you could say that. Although your father generally leaves such matters to the overseers."

"I suppose that assuages his conscience," Jasmine said, shaking her head. "And no doubt the overseers rid themselves of guilt by saying they are only following orders."

"You are probably right."

"But what good does it do me to be right, when such injustice is going on? I thought our slaves were happy and well kept. I thought things were different because we were good, honest people."

"But in learning otherwise, what can you do?" her grandmother asked softly.

"I learned slavery should be abolished. I can work toward that end."

Alice leaned forward and placed a soft kiss on her cheek. "Then this journey was not a disaster—this journey was designed by God."

"And this illness? Is it a part of the design also?"

"With God, who can tell? You try to rest. I'm going to finish one more row on my needlepoint, and then I'll see about that—"

Jasmine put a finger to her lips. "Don't mention food, Grandmother. My stomach has finally settled."

Alice smiled. "Try to sleep. We'll soon be home."

CHAPTER · 16

County Kerry, Ireland

KIARA O'NEILL grasped her legs tight and pulled them to her chest, her gaze fastened upon the young boy lying before her. She leaned forward, resting her dimpled chin upon bent knees while she listened to her brother's labored breathing. Padraig turned onto his side and curled his body into a half-moon. Instinctively, she reached out and brushed the shock of black curls away from his damp forehead. The fever must be breaking. She drew closer to his side. His thin body was drenched in perspiration. As if she held a fine wool coverlet, Kiara wrapped a filthy piece of blanket tightly around the boy and then mopped his face with the hem of her ragged skirt.

Through the open door of the hovel, a thin shaft of golden light could be seen on the horizon. "Ya ain't answered many o' me prayers, God, but I'm takin' this as a sign that ya'll be savin' Paddy from the grave. And I'll be tellin' ya I think it's the least ya could do under the circumstances."

"Who ya talkin' to, girl?"

Kiara startled and turned. Mrs. Brennan was peering in the door of the cottage with a misshapen basket hooked on one arm. "I'm talkin' to God. Nobody else around here to listen to me complaints."

Mrs. Brennan jumped away from the door as though struck by a bolt of lightning. "Ya best keep that sass to yarself. I doubt the Almighty needs ya tellin' Him what He should or shouldn't be doin'."

Kiara gave a snort and wheeled around to face the woman. "Outside o' killing Padraig, there's not much else He can do to hurt me."

"He could take *yar* life too if ya're not careful."

"And I'd be considerin' that a blessin', so I doubt He'll favor me with such a decision."

"Ya're not the only one sufferin', Kiara O'Neill. All of us have endured loss."

"Right you are—and the Almighty could'a saved the potato crop instead of sending this awful curse upon us. Does na seem it would be so difficult for Him to look upon us with a bit o' favor. We already got the hatred of the English to contend with . . . seems as though that ought to be enough for one group of people. Unless, o' course, He's planning to rid the world of us Irish. Then it would seem He's doing a mighty fine job."

"That smart mouth is gonna be your downfall, lass. If I told yar mother once, I told her a hundred times, ya—"

"Well, me ma and me pa are dead along with all me brothers and sisters, exceptin' for Padraig. So whatever ya told me ma is of little consequence now. All I'm carin' about right now is keepin' this lad alive, and if I'm to do that, I'm gonna need food for 'im."

"Well, ya'll not find anyone around here to help ya, and that's a fact. I been to every hovel this side of Dingle, and there's not a potato or a cup of buttermilk to be shared. We're all goin' to starve to death if we don't soon find some help. Ya may have pulled the lad back from the brink only to watch 'im die of hunger."

Her eyes burning with an undeniable fury, Kiara jumped up from Paddy's side, and in one giant stride she was in front of the woman. "Don't ya be placin' yar wicked curse upon me brother." Kiara's command hissed out from between her clenched teeth and caused Mrs. Brennan to back out of the doorway. The sun cast a bluish sheen on Kiara's greasy black mane as she leapt after the woman. "My brother'll not starve so long as I'm drawin' breath."

The woman held out her arm to stave off the attack and met Kiara's intent scowl with her own steely glare. "Stop it, lass. I'm not yar enemy, just a starvin' neighbor hopin' to live another day."

The words sliced through the hazy morning mist and pierced Kiara's heart. The hunger and worry must be driving her barmy. She'd heard of such happenings—men and women unable to deal with the ongoing starvation and suffering of their families going completely mad. Only last week, Mr. MacGowan tied his entire family to himself before jumping off a nearby cliff. All of them had been crushed on the rocks below. Death had finally released them from their agonizing hunger, and the seawater below had washed over their bodies, sanitizing them of the dirt and grime of Ireland.

Kiara stepped back and shook her head as if to release her mind from some powerful stranglehold. "I'll be askin' yar forgiveness, Mrs. Brennan. It's these last weeks of watching me da die and then me ma and now Paddy getting so sick. And then burying them."

"Now, now, child, don't go thinkin' on those last weeks. It ain't healthy."

"I go to sleep at night thinking about me ma and pa laying in that cold ground without so much as a warm blanket around them."

"At least ya protected the boy, and he did na realize the cruel grave they went to," Mrs. Brennan said.

Kiara glanced toward Padraig's emaciated form. "I'm prayin' no one tells him. If he knew the undertaker slid ma's and pa's bodies out o' those coffins into a dark dirt grave, well, he'd likely try to dig them up with 'is fingers."

Mrs. Brennan's head bobbed up and down in agreement. "'Twould be terrible for 'im to find out, but if he does, ya'll just have to explain it's the way of things. Ain't enough wood to build coffins for all them what's dying in these parts. How ya plannin' to make do, Kiara?"

"I'm thinkin' of goin' to Lord Palmerston and askin' him if there might be a bit o' work at his fancy estate. Maybe workin' in the house or even the gardens. And Paddy's good with horses."

Mrs. Brennan gave her a weary smile. "Ya do that, lass, and I'll be prayin' he'll give ya some work. Ya might show him a bit o' your lace. You got a real talent with the thread. He might be willin' to put ya to work makin' lace for his lady friends."

"I do na think he'd hire someone to sit and make lace. Besides, I pinned me last bit o' lace to Ma's dress afore they buried her. 'Twas the least I could do. She deserved so much more than a scrap of fancywork."

The older woman glanced in the door toward Padraig. "Appears the boy's beginnin' to stir."

Kiara turned toward her brother and then looked back at Mrs. Brennan. "Would ya consider lookin' in on him while I'm gone on the morrow?"

"That I will, and may God be with ya, Kiara O'Neill."

"And with yarself, Mrs. Brennan," Kiara whispered as she sat down beside her brother's straw pallet. "Are ya feelin' a mite better, Paddy?"

The boy gave a faint nod of his head. "How are we gonna make do, Kiara?" His voice was no more than a raspy whisper.

"Don't ya be worryin' yar head. I'm gonna take care of ya, Paddy, just you wait and see. I'll be gone for a bit tomorrow, but Mrs. Brennan will stop by to check on ya, and I'll make sure there's a tin o' water nearby. I wish I could promise ya a biscuit or cup o' buttermilk, but I can't."

"I'll be fine."

The day wore on in a slow, monotonous mixture of hunger and fear. As night approached, Padraig slipped into a fitful sleep with Kiara steadfastly holding his hand. Throughout the remainder of the night, the boy wavered between a deep sleep and restlessness that kept Kiara awake and vigilant. When Paddy was quiet, she worried he had quit breathing; when he was restless, she feared his fever was returning. When morning finally arrived, her eyes were heavy and she longed for sleep. But there would be no rest this day, of that she was certain.

"I'm goin' down to the creek and get ya some drinkin' water

and wash me face a bit. Once I bring ya yar drink, I'll be headin' off for a while. I'll be back before nightfall."

"Where are ya goin', Kiara?"

"Never ya mind, but I'm hopin' to be bringin' some good news when I return."

She trekked through the countryside, her body weakened by hunger and threatening to faint on the road. The sight of starving families along the way, their mouths green from the grass and weeds that were now their daily fare, confirmed her decision to seek help from Lord Palmerston. Although she'd never seen the man, she had once passed by his manor with her ma.

It was her ma who had observed Lord Palmerston many years ago when he was riding through the countryside with his companions and their ladies. Her ma had said he was a wee bit more handsome than most Englishmen, but her da had laughed at that remark, saying there wasn't an Englishman alive who could turn the head of an Irish lass. He said Irish women were accustomed to men who would protect them rather than hide in the shadows. Kiara wasn't sure what had caused her da to believe Englishmen such cowards. However, *spineless* was the kindest word she'd ever heard him use when he referred to the men from across the sea. Although her da may have thought Lord Palmerston lily-livered, Kiara was thankful their landlord hadn't begun evicting his tenants like so many of the other propertied Englishmen.

Her strength seemed to swell as the manor house came into sight. She quickened her steps to keep pace with her racing heartbeat and hurried onward, turning when she reached the road leading to the mansion and circling in front of the house. Carriages lined the circular drive, providing an assurance the wealthy visitors were not required to walk far before entering the grand front doors, Kiara decided. She spied a cobblestone path leading to the rear of the huge stone edifice and, keenly aware she would never be permitted entry through the front doors, continued around the manse. The sound of laughter and chattering voices carried toward her on a warm afternoon breeze.

She had barely turned the corner of the house when a man

grasped her arm, then quickly turned her loose. With an air of obvious irritation, he began to rapidly swipe his hand back and forth across his buff-colored breeches. "You are filthy! Where did you come from?"

Kiara jumped back, flattening herself against the outer wall of the cold stone manor house. Her eyes were wide with fear. "I came from across the hills—that way." She pointed to the east, but her focus remained upon the angry man who was questioning her. "I'm in search of Lord Palmerston. Is he close at hand?"

"He may be. Why would the likes of you be asking?"

The sound of merriment filtered across the green expanse, and she guardedly looked toward the guests gathered in the yard. The men were playing some form of game while the women appeared to be cheering them on and laughing.

"Well, girl? Why are you asking for Lord Palmerston?"

"I'm in need of aid. Me and me brother, we're starvin' to death." Her voice trembled in rhythm with her shaking hands.

The man looked at her as though she spoke some foreign tongue. "Benton! You've got a girl here who fancies your attention."

The group of visitors turned toward them and began strolling in their direction. In the front was a tall man in a stylish russet waistcoat and matching trousers, with a woman flanking him on either side like two lovely bookends.

When the tall man finally stood directly in front of Kiara, he extended his walking stick and poked it under her chin. He lifted the cane, forcing her head upward to meet his piercing stare. "Why have you come to my home?" His tone matched the disgust etched upon his face.

Instinctively, Kiara took one step backward, and his walking stick dropped away from her chin. "I'm one of yar tenants, and we're starvin' to death. Surely ya know the famine has claimed the lives of many. Are ya not concerned about the welfare of yar people?"

His appearance quickly changed from disgust to anger, his eyes burning like hot embers as he moved forward and closed the short

distance between them. "Don't you speak to me in that tone. Who
do you think you are to question my behavior? As for starving
tenants, if you'd learn to cultivate your crops in a reasonable fashion instead of insisting upon that ridiculous lazy-bed method
you've all adopted, there would be potatoes in your bellies. Head-
strong, incompetent people inhabit this country. You refuse to
change your ways, so of course you'll all starve to death."

"And ya'll be lendin' us no assistance?"

One of the beautiful bookends tugged at his sleeve. "I think
you should find some way to help the girl," she cooed.

The other woman fluttered her lashes and grasped his arm
more tightly. "Yes, Benton, let's help her. Devising a plan to help
this girl will be much more entertaining than playing bocce. Don't
you think so?" She turned toward the other guests and waved
enthusiastically, apparently hoping to solicit support from the
crowd. Their immediate shouts of agreement caused her lips to
curve upward into a charming smile. "Help the girl!" she shouted.

"Help the girl! Help the girl! Help the girl!" The chant grew
louder and louder until Lord Palmerston finally brandished his
cane aloft.

"Enough! Why do you care what happens to this poor excuse
for a human being?"

"We've never done such a thing before—it will be entertaining. Come along, girl. Stand over there, and we'll circle around
and decide what's to become of you," Sir Lyndon Wilkie ordered.
He prodded Kiara along with his cane until he had her positioned
in the center of the grassy lawn, where they'd been playing their
game.

Linen- and lace-covered tables lined the edge of the bocce
field, and Kiara's attention was riveted upon the servants, who
were now arranging food and drink for Lord Palmerston's guests.
She watched as visitors ambled by the tables, viewing and discussing the culinary delights before carefully selecting each item. Plates
full, they seated themselves on the blankets and small rugs that had
been strategically placed on the lawn. She watched the guests feed-
ing pieces of mutton and pork to the dogs wandering the grounds

until she could no longer contain her anger.

Pointing to a woman holding a piece of meat over a sleek greyhound, she called out, "There are people dyin' of hunger while ya feed those dogs the finest cuts o' meat."

"Those starving people aren't here, but the dog is," the woman replied. "Perhaps you would like something to eat?" She walked toward Kiara, carrying a hunk of dark bread and a small slab of cheese. "Shall I give you this?"

Had it not been for Paddy, she would have refused the haughty woman. Instead, she grabbed the food, bit off a chunk of the bread, and tucked the remainder into her skirt.

"I've heard tell people can go mad when deprived of food. This girl has a wild look in her eyes."

Lord Palmerston stepped forward. "Sit down, Winifred. The girl is frightened, stupid, and starving, but she's not insane. You were one of those chanting to help her. Have you had a change of heart?"

"No, I suppose not." She turned on her heel and walked back to her blanket.

Lord Palmerston remained beside Kiara. "Now, what would you have me do with the girl? You were all anxious to have her act as your entertainment. What say you?"

"Let's give her a new life. Let's send her to England," one of the women called out.

Another man jumped up from his blanket. "England is already swarming with starving, typhus-infested Irish immigrants. She'd be no better off in Liverpool than she is here. Let's think of some other country we can send her to."

"Yes! In fact, what about sending her to the Colonies? Let her go across the sea and start a completely new life," Mathias New-house suggested.

"Don't you have distant relatives who absconded to America, Palmerston? You could send her as an indentured servant to your relatives."

"Hear! Hear! Send the girl to America!" several men shouted as they raised their glasses in a jubilant toast.

Lord Palmerston paced back and forth in front of Kiara several times and then nodded in agreement. "America it is. Now can we get back to our game of bocce?"

Kiara jumped in front of Lord Palmerston. "I can't go to America, sir. I have a young brother, and both me parents have died from the famine. I canna leave Padraig. I *won't* leave 'im."

"What's the problem, Palmerston?" Mathias Newhouse asked. A large number of the guests were striding toward them. "The girl wanting some additional money?"

"She has a brother and simply won't leave without him."

"Well, send him too—that's easy enough. It's not as though you can't afford passage for the two of them. It's the most expedient way of returning to your game of bocce, isn't it?"

Lord Palmerston grunted before looking down at Kiara. "I'll send the two of you, but you'll sign papers for five years of indentured service to my second cousin. Come back tomorrow with your brother, and I'll make the arrangements. You've ruined my afternoon of entertainment with your antics, so you'd best not fail to appear or I'll send my man looking for you, and he'll snip off your ears when he finds you. Do you understand, lass?"

Her lips twisted into a disgusted wrinkle. She'd bite off his fingers before he'd have a chance to snip at her ears! But she and Paddy would appear on the morrow, for if they remained in Ireland, they'd surely starve to death. She had no desire to leave her homeland or the graves of her parents—the very thought weighed heavy on her heart. Yet she knew there was nothing to do but agree. "Yes, sir. And if I might get a bit more food to take with for me neighbors, I'd be grateful."

"Take some food—take all of the food, just be on your way."

One of the women grasped Lord Palmerston's arm. "Now, wasn't that an enjoyable diversion? And look at the good your wealth has accomplished. You've saved two sad souls today. Surely that will buy you a place of honor with God." They all laughed at this.

Kiara took a cloth one of the servants gave her, along with instructions to return it the next day. She circled the table, placing food into the fabric while listening to the group of partygoers, who were congratulating one another on the good they'd done this day. Their words rang in her ears, a mockery of the devastation that abounded throughout the countryside. She longed to confront each one of them and say what selfish dolts she thought them, but she dared not. She took the bundle of food and hurried toward home, anxious to share a small portion of their abundance with Paddy and their neighbors. Anxious, too, to see what joy the small feast would bring this night and yet knowing for some, it would merely prolong life for a few more miserable days.

CHAPTER · 17

LORD PALMERSTON'S servants scrubbed and outfitted Kiara and Padraig for their journey, and when all was in readiness, they were summoned to the front hallway. Lord Palmerston stared down upon them as though they were outlandish creatures that should be banished as quickly as possible.

"This is a letter of reference for my cousin, along with the money for your passage to America and enough for transportation from Boston to Lowell, where my relatives reside. You and your brother will be indentured to my cousin for five years in order to settle up your debt to me. Don't consider any attempt to besmirch these arrangements, or I shall arrange for your brother's demise and force you to watch while he dies a slow and painful death. And don't think I won't find you, girl. I have eyes and ears everywhere, including on the docks and aboard the ship you'll sail on. See that you don't repay my generosity with deceit. My driver will take you to the docks and remain until you board the ship. Do you understand?"

Kiara nodded.

"Speak up, girl. I want to hear more than your brains rattling in your head. Give me a verbal affirmation."

"Aye, I understand. When we arrive in this place called Lowell, will there be someone meetin' us? I do na know how to locate yar relative."

Lord Palmerston looked heavenward and shook his head. "No wonder you people are starving to death. I doubt there's one of you that has the sense of a church mouse."

"We're not starvin' because we're stupid; we're starvin' because our potatoes 'ave the blight. A problem no Englishman has been able to solve, I might add."

"You've a smart mouth on you, girl. Hearken my words, your sassy remarks will cause you nothing but trouble. Now listen carefully—my cousin's name is clearly marked on the outside of the letter I gave you." He snatched the missive away from her and tapped his finger atop the penned words. "You will be indentured to Mr. Bradley Houston, who is a man of importance in Lowell, just as I am in County Kerry. If you asked any of your neighbors how to find Lord Palmerston, could they direct you to this estate?"

She nodded but immediately remembered his earlier admonition and said, "Aye. I'll do as ya've instructed."

"And as for the potato problem, Miss O'Neill, if the Irish had taken the advice of the English years ago and learned to plant properly, their potatoes *wouldn't* be rotting in the ground."

Kiara was certain he was testing her, anxious to see if she'd argue with him. Well, she'd not give him the satisfaction. She knew that from the early days of the blight, the English had argued the lazy-bed method of planting had caused the potato famine. Yet they had no answer why this traditional Irish way of farming had always yielded large, disease-free crops in the past. Arguing would serve no purpose. None of it mattered anymore. Her ma and pa were rotting in the ground, just like the potato crop, and she and Paddy would likely never set foot on Irish soil again.

Lord Palmerston turned to his servant. "Take them to Dingle and wait until they've boarded. In fact, wait until their ship actually sails. Given the opportunity, I'm not certain the girl won't disembark or even jump overboard and swim for shore with my coins in her pocket. I can't trust the likes of her to keep her word."

Once again Kiara remained silent. She wanted to tell him

about the "likes of her"—Irish men, women, and children starving to death while the wealthy English played games on the lawn and wasted food that could be used to save their lives. Yes, indeed, the "likes of her" might just steal his money or food to save a fellow Irishman because the pompous English landlords cared nothing about saving their tenants from certain death.

They'd traveled only a short distance when Paddy snuggled closer and rested his head on Kiara's shoulder. "We'll likely never be settin' foot in such a lovely place as Lord Palmerston's estate again. It was right nice, wasn't it? And all that food. Do ya think the estate in America will be so nice?"

"I don't know, Paddy, but we'll be havin' five long years to find out."

"Ya're sad to be leavin' Ireland, aren't ya?"

Kiara took a deep breath and forced herself to smile. "Leavin' is the right thing to do—the only thing to do. We'll die if we stay in Ireland."

"And our new landlord might be a nice man who will treat us well."

"He's not goin' to be a landlord, Paddy, and we'll not be farmin' our own patch of ground. We'll be servants forced to do whatever work we're assigned."

Paddy gazed up at her, his deep brown eyes wistful. "But we'll not be hungry, will we?"

She pulled him near and ruffled his freshly washed and trimmed black curls. "No, Paddy, we'll not be hungry. There's no potato blight in America. Now take a good long look at the countryside so ya can remember the beauty of yar homeland. One day ya'll have children of yar own, and I want ya to be able to tell them of the beauty of the Emerald Isle."

Paddy rested his chin atop one arm along the edge of the carriage window, doing as his sister bade. He traveled in that position, with his thin body swaying with each pitch of the carriage, until they neared their destination. With an excited bounce, he turned toward his sister. "I love the smell of the ocean. We must be gettin' close."

Kiara clenched her fists, fighting to keep any emotion from her voice. "Aye, that we are."

When the carriage jerked to a stop, the driver jumped down, unloaded their baggage, and opened the carriage door. "Come along. We'll go and pay for your passage and see how soon the ferry will be sailing."

"Do ya think it will sail today?" Paddy asked the driver. "There's more people here than I've seen in all me life. Would they all be sailin' for America? Do ya think they'll all fit on one ship? It'll be mighty crowded if we all try to get on one ship, won't it?"

The coachman gave Paddy a look of exasperation as he hoisted the trunk. "Lord Palmerston said the ship sails today, and since ya can see it anchored out there, I'm sure ya'll soon be taking the ferry. I don't have answers to the rest of yar questions. The two of ya get the rest of yar belongings."

Kiara picked up the satchels and hurried Paddy along. "But what if there's no space available?" Kiara inquired. "Will you stay with us here in Dingle?"

"Don't ya be gettin' any ideas, lassie. If that should happen, I'll return ya to Lord Palmerston and await his biddin'. Now come along with ya."

Kiara and Paddy followed, careful to stay close behind the coachman. With a determined stride, he led them through the multitude of gathered passengers and into one of the shipping company offices.

"I need steerage for two children on the ship that's sailin' for America today," the coachman told the agent.

"Steerage is full. If you wanna pay extra, there's a cabin still available. Ya're late gettin' here. That ship sailed from England, and there's only toppin' off space available. And those two pay full fare, for they're way past the age of being considered children. 'Tis extra for the ferry."

"But there's no other way to get to the ship. Is that not included in their passage?"

"If it was included, would I be tellin' ya it's extra? I told ya, if ya're wantin' to board a ship to America today, the ferry will be leaving in an hour."

The coachman didn't argue. He pulled out a leather pouch, counted out six pounds for each of them, and listened to the instructions the man barked in their direction. They stepped aside, and the man began his speech to the people who had been standing in line behind them.

Kiara tugged on the coachman's sleeve. "Did you hear what he told them? I thought he said we were gettin' the last cabin."

"He sells passage on more than one ship. Come along now. Ya have to go through the medical inspection before ya can board the ferry." He pointed them toward the line outside another building along the wharf. "Just follow along, and I'll be waitin' when ya come out."

The two of them did as instructed, winding through the building and into a wooden cubicle, where they walked by a doctor who asked if they were ill and motioned them on when Kiara replied they were not. A man at the end of the table signed a paper saying they'd passed inspection.

"Ya weren't gone very long," the coachman remarked when they reappeared.

"That doctor did na even check us," Paddy told him. "He jus' asked if we was sick and told us we were fit to sail. He said we should hurry; the ferry leaves in less than an hour."

The coachman bade them farewell as a crewman relieved them of their trunk. Once the passengers were loaded onto the ferry and they had moved away from the shore, the coachman waved, tipped his hat, and strode off toward the carriage. Kiara felt an odd sense of loss watching the man leave. Perhaps because he was their last connection with their homeland.

Once aboard the ship, Kiara waited at the rail until a crewman loaded their trunk. "I'll stow this fer ya, and ya can claim it when we arrive. Ya can take yar smaller baggage with ya." He led them down a dark companionway to a long, gloomy space beneath the main deck. The hold was already teeming with noisy passengers. "Ya get two spaces," he said, pointing to a six-foot wooden square built into the ship's timbers along one side of the hold.

"Wait! We're entitled to a cabin. Our coachman was told the steerage was full. We paid six pounds and we should be havin' a cabin."

The crewman gave a laughing snort. "They tell that same story to ever'one. The only cabin on this ship is the captain's. There's only steerage for passengers. Like I told ya earlier, ya each get a space." He held his hands about a foot and a half apart.

He turned to walk away, but Kiara grasped his muscled arm with her slender fingers. "Wait! Ya mean that's all the space we'll be gettin' to sleep on?"

The sailor gave an affirmative nod. "That space is yar home until we arrive in America. Once we've set sail, ya can come on deck for a bit o' air," he said, then quickly took his leave.

"Psst. You! Come over here."

Kiara looked toward the corner, where an auburn-haired girl was motioning her forward. The girl continued waving her arm in wild circular motions until Kiara and Paddy began walking in her direction. She bobbled her head up and down as though her frantic movements would encourage them onward as they zigzagged through the mass of passengers.

"Do ya have bunk space yet?" the girl asked.

Kiara wagged her head back and forth. "No. We were supposed to 'ave a cabin, but they lied to us. Six pounds apiece they charged for passage."

"They lie to ever'one. Come on, ya can share this space with me. Throw that baggage on the floor over there and join me on this stick o' wood we'll call a bed until we arrive in America. Ya can put your satchels on here. That way no one else will take yar space."

Kiara did as the girl instructed. "I'm Kiara O'Neill, and this is my brother, Paddy."

"Bridgett Farrell. Pleased ta meet ya. Do ya have family in America?"

"No. We have only each other. Our ma and pa died this year—the famine."

The girl looked sympathetic. "Mine too. I got me an aunt, some cousins, and a granna livin' in America. I'm gonna join them and get me a job in the mills. Granna says there's work to be had if I come. Me cousins work for the Corporation, and they saved up the money for me passage. Where do ya plan to make yar home? In Boston?"

"No. We're goin' to a town called Lowell."

Bridgett slapped her leg and smiled. "That's where I'm gonna be livin'. Are ya gonna work in the mills too?"

"I don' know nothin' about no mills. We're gonna be servants on an estate. We indentured ourselves fer five years to pay fer our passage." The complexity of her decision weighed heavily once she had spoken the words to Bridgett. Actually speaking the words of what she had done caused the full force of her decision to crash in upon her. "I think I'll go up and watch as we sail."

Bridgett nodded. "Ya go ahead now. Me and Paddy will stay with the belongin's and save our space."

When the ship finally heaved and swayed out into the Atlantic a short time later, Kiara stood at the rail and watched her beautiful Ireland fade out of sight. All that she held dear was left behind save Paddy. She'd never again see the beauty of her homeland, visit with the friends and neighbors whom she held dear, or put a sprig of heather on her ma's grave. But even if she'd made the wrong decision, there was no turning back now. She shivered against a sudden gust of wind and pulled the warm woolen shawl tightly around her shoulders. "Selfish lass," she murmured into the breeze. "Ya should be thankful the good Lord saw fit to save ya from a certain death instead of feelin' sorry for yarself. If ya hadn't agreed, ya would na even have this shawl to keep yar body warm."

After what seemed an eternity on board the ship, Kiara was more than a little grateful to see the shores of Boston in the distance. So many times she'd been certain they would never make it. Sickness had sent many a stiff, unwashed body overboard to a watery grave, and while it had reduced the number of people on board, it left everyone wondering if they'd be next.

Kiara had entertained Paddy with stories she'd learned as a child—telling him of the fairies and their craftiness, of superstitions that had guided the lives of their people. It had eased the hours of boredom and gave them both a sense of home, which they desperately missed.

"Our people saw that the sun, moon, and stars all went west to die away so that they could be reborn and rise another day," she'd told Paddy at the beginning of their trip. Now, standing at the end of their journey, she wondered if it might be true for people as well. Her journey west had been a small death—an end to the girl she'd once been—a dying to the people she'd loved and known all of her life. Would she be reborn to rise again?

"Just look at it all, Kiara!" Paddy exclaimed. "Fer sure it's a grand city."

"Stay close at hand, Paddy. There's bound to be pushin' and shovin', what with everyone wantin' to get on dry land again. I don't want to lose sight of ya among all the others."

The boy danced from foot to foot. "Isn't it excitin', Kiara? We've finally arrived at our new homeland."

Kiara smiled down at her brother, thankful he hadn't succumbed to the dysentery contracted by so many of the passengers during their voyage. His health had actually improved on the journey, and she had begun to relax as they drew closer to Boston. However, just when she had thought there were no other concerns, medical inspectors boarded the ship, and she watched with increasing trepidation as they denied entry to passengers who showed the slightest sign of illness. What if they were refused entry after the long and dreadful voyage? She pulled Paddy into her embrace and issued up a silent prayer the inspectors would find nothing wrong with them.

There was little control as the crowd carried them forward. Kiara heard Bridgett's voice and strained to see around the hefty woman in front of her. She smiled at the sight of her new friend, who was jumping and waving from among an assemblage of passengers. Bridgett had pushed ahead, and her group had already passed through the medical inspection. "Meet me on the dock," she called out.

"Aye," Kiara hollered back.

"Over here! Hurry along now, and let loose of the boy so I can check him. Hand him over, for you'll not step foot off this ship until he's been examined," the medical inspector commanded as he tugged at her arm.

Begrudgingly, she loosened her grip and continued praying while they both endured the examination. "You'll do," he said, pointing them toward the passengers waiting to disembark.

Kiara flashed the inspector a smile and grasped Paddy's hand. Now that they were in America, where he would have proper nourishment and fresh air, he could flourish and grow into a strong young man. He would be reborn—they both would. "Move into that line," she said. "Once we're on the wharf, we need to be findin' Bridgett and then locate our trunk. It will likely take a while, but perhaps we can find a place to sit."

"Or walk around and explore."

"I'll be wantin' to remain near the ship. The coachman told me we should stay close at hand while they're unloadin'."

"Why?" Paddy asked, his sparkling brown eyes filled with wonderment.

"Because thieves come to the docks, and they steal cargo and trunks that are left unattended. At least that's what he told me. I do na want to take a chance on losin' the belongings Lord Palmerston's servants packed for us. And Ma's teacup is in there too. I would rather die than be losin' Ma's teacup."

"You *would*?"

Kiara tousled her brother's hair and laughed. "I'm supposin' that's an exaggeration, but I would be very sad to lose our only keepsake."

"Then we'll be stayin' close by the docks and watch carefully for our trunk. Look! There's Bridgett, and she's already come across her trunk."

The coachman had been correct. A variety of unseemly-looking men wandered the quay, watching with interest while the cargo was unloaded. Occasionally one of the thieves would skulk forward, hoist a trunk, and scurry off without notice. Once the passengers realized what was happening, they began giving chase, sometimes with success but generally not, leaving tearful families lamenting the loss of all their worldly goods.

"There it is!" Paddy pointed toward their baggage and rushed from her side.

Kiara caught sight of Bridgett, who was now moving in their direction. It appeared as if she'd convinced a young man to carry her trunk. Both Bridgett and Kiara reached Paddy at the same time. He had planted himself atop the hump-backed trunk and his lips were curved in a smile of pure delight. His enthusiasm was contagious, and Kiara leaned over and pulled him into an approving hug.

"Ya've a good eye, Padraig O'Neill," Kiara said.

Bridgett nodded toward a building across from the dock. "There's a lady over there what tol' me where we can buy our tickets to Lowell at the train station. I don't think it's far off."

"If it's not far, perhaps we can just drag the trunks along with us."

"What if the woman gave me improper directions? We could be draggin' those trunks until our arms are so weary we can pull them no further. Do ya not think it would be safe for Paddy to stay with the trunks while we go and make arrangements for the rest of our journey?"

Kiara studied the boy, uncertain whether she should leave him alone.

Paddy's shoulders squared and he raised himself up straight and tall. "You and Bridgett can count on me. I'll protect the trunks with me life."

"I'm more concerned about you than any old trunks," she said, giving him a quick peck on the cheek. She knew his young ego would be crushed if she insisted he go with them, so she cautioned him to be careful and hurried off with Bridgett. The train station was exactly where the woman had promised. The ticket master explained that if the train arrived on schedule, it would be leaving for Lowell in an hour.

The two girls nodded in agreement. They purchased the tickets and then followed the man's directions to find a small shop, where they purchased biscuits and cheese enough to tide them over until their arrival in Lowell. Paddy was still sitting astride the trunk when they returned, with his short legs draped down on either side. The boy looked almost as if he were riding one of Mr. Connelly's horses back in Ireland. Kiara smiled and waved. "I've paid for our train tickets and got us some biscuits and cheese," she announced. "We need to get our trunks to the train station. Jump down and let's get movin'."

"Can I have a biscuit? Me stomach's growlin'."

"Fer sure ya can, but after we get ourselves to the station. We can't go missin' our train to Lowell."

Paddy nodded. He was such a good-spirited little man, Kiara thought. He understood the need to see to the work first and he never complained. Together they pulled the trunk up and dragged it along behind. Kiara thought it unnaturally heavy, but then again, she was unnaturally tired. She had fretted over most every mile across the ocean—worrying that Paddy would take sick, fearing someone might steal him away and harm him, stewing over whether they'd have enough to eat.

Kiara was blessed when the baggageman came forward to take the trunk from them at the station. Bridgett handed her trunk over as well, then tossed the man a penny. Kiara regretted her inability to offer him the same, but she had no choice. She'd not been given money to waste.

Paddy hurried to find a seat and motioned Kiara to a place by the window. He positioned himself nose against the glass, anxious to be started. Kiara smiled and handed him a piece of cheese and a biscuit. "And here's yar lunch, little man."

He immediately devoured it, wolfing down the simple fare as though he hadn't eaten in weeks. It was good to see him with a hearty appetite and feeling well.

"Do ya think there will be someone who can help us find Mr.

Houston's estate when we get to Lowell?" Kiara asked Bridgett. Her stomach had suddenly begun to tighten into a knot, clamping down upon the biscuit and cheese she had eaten in sharp, jabbing pains.

"Don' ya be frettin'. Me granna promised they'd be watchin' for me arrival. They can help ya. Of that I have no doubt."

The train lurched forward, then stopped, then lurched again. The jerky motion caused Kiara to let out a squeal. Her stomach did a funny flip-flop.

"'Tis nothin' amiss," Bridgett told her. "I've been on a train before. It's always like this. Soon we'll sail along as smooth as ya please. Why don't ya have a rest? We'll be there before ya know it."

Bridgett's words helped calm Kiara's fears, and the stabbing pain eased enough for the rocking motion of the train to lull her to sleep. When the train hissed and belched to a stop, Kiara jolted awake with a start.

"We're in Lowell already?" Her fear returned tenfold. She could barely swallow.

Bridgett pressed her nose against the train window and peered out onto the platform, her eyes scanning the crowd gathered there.

"Do ya see your granna?" Paddy asked.

"No, but they'll be here. Come on, we need ta be gettin' off," Bridgett said.

As soon as they were inside the station, Bridgett marched up to the ticket counter and talked to the ticket master. She was there only a few minutes. "He says there should be a wagon outside ya can hire to take you and the luggage wherever ya need to go. He did na know my granna. Says he's not acquainted with the Irish. Kinda insultin', he was. Come on. I'll go outside with ya and see if we can get ya on yar way. Don' ya be fergettin' to come and see me. My granna says most all the Irish live in the Acre. Ya be rememberin' that so ya can come visit."

Kiara agreed as they walked toward the wagon parked in front of the station. "Can ya take us to the estate of a Mr. Bradley Houston?"

The driver looked down from his perch and fixed his gaze on Paddy. "If you got money, I can get you there."

Paddy looked up at the driver with obvious admiration. The man shoved his hat farther back on his head and gave Paddy a grin. "Get on up here, boy," he said. He jumped down from the wagon, and while he loaded their trunk and satchels in back, Kiara bid Bridgett farewell. Kiara turned in her seat, waving at Bridgett until she could no longer see the girl. She barely knew her, yet she felt as though she'd lost yet another member of her family.

The drive to the Houston residence was nearly fifteen minutes by coach, and Kiara was thankful they'd not been forced to walk the distance. The driver tipped his hat, and Kiara walked to the front door while Paddy remained with their luggage. She had barely lifted her hand to knock when the front door flew open and a dour-looking woman pointed them to the rear of the house.

"Not so different from Ireland, is it, Paddy? The likes of us will always be shoved out of sight."

Paddy was busy examining their new home. "It's not such a big house, is it? Not like Lord Palmerston's at all. Do ya think this is the right place?" the boy asked.

"We'll know soon enough," Kiara replied. The same austere woman was waiting for them when they arrived at the rear door. "Good day, ma'am. I'm Kiara O'Neill and this here's me brother, Padraig. We've come from Ireland to work for Mr. Houston. Here's our letter of introduction."

The woman took the letter and motioned them into the kitchen. "Wait here." She stopped short and turned back to face them, her features softening. "Have you eaten? I hear tell there's many a passenger that starves to death on those coffin ships coming from Ireland."

"Aye. We got some biscuits and cheese in Boston," Kiara said.

"But I'm still hungry," Paddy added.

"I'll have the cook bring you some food. Was Mr. Houston expecting you? He didn't say a word."

Kiara shrugged. "Lord Palmerston said he wrote to your master."

Moments later a man with a receding hairline and pale skin walked into the room. Kiara couldn't decide if it was his thin lips or long forehead that gave him an unkind appearance. His gaze settled upon her as he held her letter between his finger and thumb and waved it aloft.

"I must admit that even though I received my cousin's letter, I never expected you to actually arrive in Lowell," he said.

"And why is that? Were ya thinkin' we'd die at sea?"

His laugh was cruel. "No. I was thinking that if you had any sense at all, you'd have remained in Boston and started your life anew. After all, how would I have found you? I had never seen either of you and had no idea what you looked like."

"I gave me word—ya may na think I have good sense, Mr. Houston, but na everybody is a liar. Some of us protect our honor no matter what the cost."

"You'll have five years to prove that to me. I can make good use of you here in the house, but what am I to do with this spindly boy?" Mr. Houston asked while giving Paddy a look of disdain. "He's of little use to me. Perhaps I can sell his papers to someone who could make better use of him."

Kiara lunged forward and, without thinking, grasped the man's arm. "No! Me brother must stay with me."

Bradley's focus moved to his arm, where Kiara's fingers were digging deep into his flesh. "Turn loose of me, girl." He waited until she removed her hold. "Now that I understand how important your brother is to you, I suppose I can find something to keep him busy. What might you recommend?"

Kiara gave him a winsome smile. "Paddy's very good with animals, especially horses. Would ya be ownin' any horses?"

Bradley rubbed his narrow jaw. "As a matter of fact, I do. I suppose he could help muck out the stables and curry the horses. Do you think you could do that satisfactorily, boy?"

Paddy cocked his head and gave Mr. Houston a bright smile. "Aye. I'll work very hard carin' for yar animals, sir."

The man's leering gaze returned to Kiara. "I'm sure you and your sister are going to make me very happy."

CHAPTER · *18*

WHEN THE CARRIAGE rounded the driveway, Jasmine was genuinely pleased to be home. Not that she longed to see Bradley—
quite the contrary. Although her stomach had settled during the
final day on board the ship, she remained pallid and frail, and arriving home was somewhat comforting. Concerned over her continuing infirmity, Nolan had insisted upon escorting the two women
on the final leg of their journey from Boston to Lowell. He had
been resolute in his decision, stating he would leave for Boston the
following day. Alice had argued briefly, but Jasmine hadn't had
strength to resist and was exceedingly thankful for the capable care
he had provided.

A dark-haired girl was sweeping the gallery when their carriage came to a halt in front of the house. Cupping one hand over
her eyes as she stepped down from the coach, Jasmine blinked
against the sun until the young woman came into focus. She was
certain she'd never before seen her.

"I'll be comin' right down to help ya," the girl called out as
she hurried back through the gallery doors.

Before Nolan and the two women had time to enter the front
door, the girl came bursting outdoors as though shot from a cannon.

"I'm sorry I was na here waitin' for ya, ma'am," she apologized with a deep curtsy.

Jasmine stared wide-eyed at the young woman. "Who are you?"

"Kiara O'Neill, from the beautiful Emerald Isle. Me and my brother, Paddy, are indentured to ya."

"Indentured? How is that possible?"

Nolan grasped her elbow and urged her forward. "Let's go inside where you can sit. You're much too weak to be standing out here having a lengthy discussion."

"Aye, ya're lookin' mighty pale, missus." Kiara hoisted both satchels and scurried ahead of them. "I'll just be takin' these to yar room, missus, and then I'll be back down to get ya a cup o' tea."

Before Jasmine could assent or object, the girl was running up the stairs with a satchel in each hand, her black mane flying wildly while Alice and Jasmine watched from the hallway.

"I want to get you settled before I leave for home," Alice said.

Kiara looked over the railing at the threesome standing below. "Do na worry yarself about the missus. I'll be givin' her good care, ma'am. I'll be back afore ya can count me out of yar sight."

The remark brought a smile to Jasmine's lips. "Take your time, Kiara. My grandmother will remain with me for a little longer."

Nolan rubbed his hands together and glanced toward the door. "If you two ladies will be all right for a short time, I want to see to the horses. One of them appeared to be developing a limp. I don't want to take him farther if he's injured or has a stone lodged in a hoof."

Sarah, the older pinch-faced maid who had faithfully cared for the house since Jasmine's marriage to Bradley, hurried into the parlor. "Mrs. Houston! How good to have you home. Mr. Houston said you'd be arriving today, but I was out back and didn't realize you'd arrived. Did Kiara or Paddy get your baggage?"

Kiara came bounding down the steps and skidded to a halt in the parlor doorway. "Yes, ma'am, I got their bags, 'ceptin' for the trunk. I'll have Paddy help me take it upstairs when he gets back from exercising the horse. I told the missus I'd get her a cup o' tea, and then I'll be unpackin' 'er bags." The words tumbled out in one rushing breath.

Jasmine took in the black-haired beauty. "Sit down, Kiara, and tell me how you've come to be with us."

Kiara looked toward Sarah. The maid nodded, and Kiara perched on the edge of the straight-backed chair opposite her mistress. "Yar husband owns me and Paddy, missus. We're indentured to him."

"I don't understand. How did all of this occur?"

With a haunting sadness in her eyes, Kiara carefully explained how she had come to Lowell and would be required to spend the next five years indentured to her husband.

Jasmine's mind was reeling with the information. "Bradley agreed to this?"

"Yar husband said I would be workin' as yar personal maid when ya returned from visitin' yar ma and pa. Me brother, Paddy, is workin' in the stable, helpin' with the horses. He's a good boy. I've no doubt ya'll be likin' him fine."

The girl's words sounded genuine, yet doubt was knocking at Jasmine's heart like an unwanted visitor in the night. The entire tale was maudlin. Parents dying and being dumped out of their coffins into the ground without a proper burial, a voyage in a lice- and dysentery-infested ship with only inches of space to sleep, papers of indentureship requiring five years of one's life to pay for the journey. However, the facts might be true, for she knew of the terrible famine in Ireland. Hadn't their ladies' group been collecting funds for relief before she had sailed for New Orleans?

The sound of the front door closing was quickly followed by Nolan's footsteps in the hallway. "The horse is fine. Appears the little Irish fellow knows his way around horseflesh quite well. He removed a small stone from one of the hooves in short order."

Kiara beamed a look of appreciation in Nolan's direction. "He's a hard worker, Paddy is. And he loves animals, especially the horses. Happy he is to be workin' with them."

Jasmine patted the settee cushion beside her. "Come sit down, Nolan."

He made no move toward the couch. "Your grandmother and I should be leaving soon."

"Oh, do sit a moment. I promise not to keep you long. I've something to ask you."

He laughed and moved toward the settee. "Considering our time aboard ship and at The Willows, we've been together for nearly three months. I can't imagine there's anything you haven't asked me."

"Had I known anything about the possibility of English relatives, I would have already inquired. Tell me, Nolan, does your family have relatives in England? Kiara says an Englishman owning vast holdings in Ireland was her family's landlord. She went to him seeking assistance after the death of her parents. It seems that after some urging and perhaps a wager of sorts with his wealthy visitors, this fellow paid for Kiara and her brother to come to America in exchange for five years of servitude. Supposedly, he then assigned the papers to Bradley. Have you ever heard of anything so indecorous?"

"In answer to your first question, we do have some distant relatives in England. My mother's uncle was some sort of nobility, I believe. I'm not certain. Bradley maintained some contact with their children or children's children. They'd be cousins once removed or some such thing, and I must admit I never had much interest in any of them. However, Bradley was rather awestruck upon learning we were related to nobility. He began corresponding and may have visited once when he was in England, but I didn't realize he was still in contact with any of them. I believe their name was Plamerson or Planster. . . ."

"Palmerston. Lord Palmerston," Kiara interjected.

"Yes! That's it. Palmerston," Nolan agreed. "Now, in answer to your second question, Jasmine, owning indentured servants is quite common in England, as it was in this country for many years—still is, to some extent, although it's been replaced in large part by slavery."

"So if Bradley has received papers on this girl and her brother, he could return their papers and let them go on their way?"

"Yes, of course. And I would like to think that's exactly what he'll do."

"Obviously the thought hasn't occurred to him yet, since he immediately put them to work. He refused to allow me to keep Mammy because the Associates look down on slavery. Why in the world would he keep indentured servants? It's akin to the same thing."

"Not in the eyes of society," Nolan replied. "The indentured man or woman can work off their servitude, and generally they've already benefited from their employers. Just as this woman and her brother have no doubt advanced their station in life by receiving free passage across the ocean and a new life in America."

"Aye," Kiara said. "It saved our lives, and while I'll be missin' me homeland, I know we'd be dead by now had we stayed."

Jasmine shook her head. "Still, this surprises me greatly, and I intend to speak to Bradley about dissolving this arrangement."

Nolan tugged at the stiff collar wrapped tightly around his broad neck. "You might suggest the possibility, but I'd wait until he broaches the topic. He's generally more flexible when the discussion is his idea. At least that's been my experience in the past."

"Thank you, Nolan. I'll remember your suggestion."

"And now, Mrs. Wainwright, if you're quite ready, I believe I should escort you home."

"Fine. And I insist you spend the night before beginning your journey to Boston."

Nolan gave her a broad smile. "It's not so far to Boston and there's another train leaving soon, I'm sure. If need be, I can always remain at an inn for the night."

Alice thumped the tip of her parasol on the floor. "I insist! I'll not take no for an answer."

Jasmine giggled at her grandmother's antics, her new servant problem forgotten for the moment. "I believe you've no choice in the matter."

"Indeed. You may tell my brother I'll be spending the night

with your grandmother if he wants to visit with me before I leave for Boston."

"I'll do that. Thank you again for agreeing to escort us on our journey, Nolan. I don't know what we would have done without you. You proved yourself a capable guardian and an excellent instructor. I enjoyed our discussions."

"And just what enthralling topics did you and my brother find to talk about?"

Jasmine startled at the sound of Bradley's voice. She turned, praying that after a three-month absence the sight of him might well stir something inside her. It didn't. His pale skin, intense stare, and tendency to always look as though he were sneering did nothing to endear her. "I didn't hear you come in the house."

"Probably because I came through the back of the house. I wanted to check on the stable boy." His gaze shifted to Kiara. "And what, pray tell, are you doing? Are you sitting in the parlor, playing the part of the lady and expecting tea?"

"There's no need for your derision, Bradley. I invited her to sit and tell me how she came to be living here."

"Well, I'm here now and can answer your questions. Get off to your chores," he commanded.

Kiara jumped out of the chair and fled from the room while Bradley drew close to Jasmine and placed a kiss upon her cheek. "I'm pleased to see your ship returned as scheduled. That means the voyage was uneventful. Always glad to hear my ships have made a safe journey. I trust they also loaded the vessel with cargo for the return?"

"I didn't inquire. However, the captain sent you a parcel," Nolan replied. "I placed it on the desk in your library."

"And Father sent you a letter also," Jasmine added. "It's in my luggage."

"And your mother? Is she upstairs resting?"

"No. She's ill and was unable to make the voyage. Perhaps later in the year."

"Ah, well, that's a shame, isn't it?"

His words rang false, but Jasmine concealed her irritation.

"And this young Irish lass and her brother—I understand you've taken them in as indentured servants."

Nolan aimed a look of warning in her direction and stepped forward before Bradley could reply. "We really must be on our way, but in the event your wife decides she doesn't want to worry you with concerns about herself, you should know that she was quite ill on our return voyage."

"Really? Were the waters rough?"

"Actually the seas were quite calm," Nolan answered.

"That's odd. My Jasmine has always been quite the sailor, haven't you, my dear?"

Jasmine gave him a waxen smile and nodded. "Must have been something I ate. I've been feeling better these last few days."

"And here I thought you must have been quite well. I thought you appeared a bit thicker about the waist when I came in the room."

Alice immediately shot a look at her granddaughter's waistline and then lifted her eyes, meeting Jasmine's gaze. "Could we have a moment alone before I depart?" she inquired. "Perhaps you and Nolan should locate the parcel the captain sent along."

Nolan's brow furrowed momentarily. "I explained it's on the . . . Yes, of course. Let's go into your library, Bradley," Nolan suggested, leading his brother into the other room.

Alice quickly settled herself next to Jasmine and took the girl's hand in her own. "Tell me, dear, have you given any thought to the fact that you may be expecting a child?"

Jasmine hesitated and thought about the probability—one she'd contemplated on the return voyage. Distressing as the concept might be, she knew her grandmother was likely correct. "Yes, it's possible. But Bradley is a poor husband, and he will make an even worse father. I know Bradley Houston." She was aware that verbalizing her fears would not change anything, but her grandmother was now well aware of her opinion.

"A child may be exactly what the two of you need to draw you closer. I'm going to send Dr. Hartzfeld to see you tomorrow."

"If you think that's best, I won't argue." Her tone was dismal as she slumped and rested her back against the settee.

———

Jasmine was despondent when the doctor departed the next day. He had obtained her consent to tell Alice upon his return to town, for she knew her grandmother would give the poor doctor no peace until he revealed his findings. The old woman would be pleased to hear the news, but Jasmine was in no mood to celebrate.

"I saw Dr. Hartzfeld as he was leaving," Bradley said as he strode into the parlor. "I must say, I was surprised he'd come to call. I thought you were feeling better. However, he says you have some news to share with me."

Jasmine picked up her stitching and briefly contemplated telling her husband she had a terminal illness with only several months to live. The thought was enticing, but she quickly discarded the idea. Bradley would find little humor in her antics when she was finally forced to reveal the truth.

"I'm expecting a child in November," she whispered.

He hurried to her side and knelt down beside her. "Truly?" His voice radiated a joy she'd never before heard and his eyes actually shone with delight.

"Yes, truly."

He jumped up and sat across from her. Leaning forward, he rested his elbows atop his knees and drew near. Grasping her hand, he yelped and then pulled back.

"Did you not see the needle?" she asked. "Here, use this." She pulled a handkerchief from her pocket and dangled it in midair.

He hastily wrapped the cloth around his finger while keeping his gaze affixed on her eyes. "Not even a jab from your sewing needle can diminish the happiness I'm feeling at this moment."

She looked down at her stitching, unwilling to share his excitement, and when Kiara entered the room with a tea tray, she issued a silent prayer of thanks. "You may put it here, Kiara."

"Would you like me to pour, ma'am?"

Jasmine smiled at the lilting sound of the girl's voice. "Yes, that would—"

"No. We'd like to be alone. Go on back to the kitchen," Bradley ordered.

With marked nervousness, the girl skittered off without a backward glance.

"Do you take pleasure in treating others unkindly?" Jasmine asked.

"I didn't treat her unkindly. I told her to leave the room because I didn't want to share this moment with a serving girl."

"Don't you mean with a slave?"

"She's not a slave. I don't own her."

"You own her for five years. She can't leave this place without fear of being sought after by the police. Aside from being five years rather than a lifetime, how is that different from slavery? Your cousin bought five years of that girl's life just as my father buys slaves for a lifetime. And Kiara tells me that in Ireland and England, indentured servants usually are owned for a lifetime because their owners claim costs for their room and board that exceed their ability to pay off the cost of their contract."

"Well, it was kind of the girl to share that information. Perhaps I should begin keeping a tally of costs for her room and board. I may be able to retain the two of them longer than I anticipated."

Jasmine silently berated herself. Why hadn't she listened to Nolan's advice? Instead of picking a fight, she should have used this moment to her advantage. Perhaps she still could. "When Dr. Hartzfeld told me the news, I realized you had been correct in sending Mammy back to The Willows. I didn't notice how much she had aged until we returned to Mississippi. And now, with my confinement, I'm going to need more assistance than usual. I doubt she would have been able to provide the help I'll need."

Bradley's mood lightened at Jasmine's rare and unexpected praise. "You see? I actually do know what is best for you. Kiara is young and energetic. She'll be able to provide all the help you need."

"And if she does well, perhaps we should reward her efforts."

"Of course," he obligingly replied. "Once you've finished your tea, I think you should lie down and rest."

"No need. I'm feeling fine."

"I thought you just agreed that your husband knows what is best for you. I must get back to work, but I'll instruct Kiara to accompany you upstairs for a nap. I don't want anything happening that would adversely affect the baby. You need to take proper care of yourself. When I return home this evening, I don't want to hear that you've failed to follow my advice." Although he was smiling, there was a warning edge to his voice. He expected to be obeyed.

Bradley hastened back to his office with the packet of information from Captain Harmon and the letter from his father-in-law tucked into a leather pouch attached to his saddle. He had planned to ride the chestnut mare today, but the Irish boy was busy currying the animal when Bradley arrived at the stable, so he'd taken the black gelding. Bradley was pleased the boy appeared to have a genuine fondness for the mare. The horse was a beauty and he wanted the animal to receive only the finest care. Bradley had paid much more than he could afford to spend on a horse, but he'd been unable to negotiate a lesser price.

Jasmine's news that he would soon become a father caused Bradley to remain in a state of euphoria throughout most of the afternoon. But as the day wore on, his thoughts returned to the satchel. He decided to examine Malcolm Wainwright's letter and the packet from Captain Harmon before leaving his office. Captain Harmon's information consisted of his usual logs and reports, and after skimming the material, Bradley set it aside to open the other letter.

He carefully read the missive, his euphoria now replaced by an unrelenting irritation. In the letter Malcolm expressed disappointment in his son-in-law. He had gone so far as to set out each payment received, those that had arrived late, and those that remained due. The letter made it abundantly clear that Malcolm had expected to receive a payment when Jasmine visited The Willows.

Bradley paced across his office as he began reading the letter aloud, his irritation growing as he put voice to Malcolm's words.

"'Not only did you fail to send a payment with Jasmine when she came to visit us, I have yet to receive the three payments due to the Wainwrights. You are aware I did not wish to enter into an arrangement for installment payments, but because you are my son-in-law, I agreed to do so.'"

Bradley's thoughts traveled back to the conversation he'd had with Malcolm. It had taken a great deal of persuasion to convince the older man that such business dealings were a common practice with the Associates. He had carefully explained the Corporation preferred conducting their business on the installment method in order to maintain a greater cash flow. As a businessman himself, Malcolm could understand the difficulty that would be involved if the Associates were required to pay all of the cotton growers simultaneously. Consequently, he had yielded to Bradley's request. However, Malcolm's letter was filled with undeniable disillusionment and anger.

Bradley returned to his desk and pulled out a piece of stationery. No doubt he would need to send funds, but not until he received another payment from the Associates. He quickly penned a letter to Malcolm explaining he would be traveling to Boston for a meeting of the Associates next month and the funds would be forwarded to Mississippi at that time.

CHAPTER · *19*

JASMINE'S ATTENTION waned as Bradley droned on with his list of innumerable instructions she was to follow in his absence. He painstakingly advised he would be traveling to Boston the next day to complete business matters for both the Associates and his shipping enterprise. Jasmine cared little why he was going. However, the length of his stay was of paramount interest. In her estimation, the longer he was gone, the better. Since her return from Mississippi, Bradley's moods had alternated between overbearing attentiveness and brooding irritability, with no apparent logic. Once he finished his tiresome oratory, he advised his wife he would be out of town for a minimum of a week, perhaps longer, depending on the progress of his business matters. Although she dared not reveal her feelings, Jasmine was secretly delighted.

She had noticed the servants, particularly Kiara, gave her husband a wide berth when he was in the house. Obviously, Jasmine wasn't the only recipient of his ill humor. Likely the entire household was going to take pleasure in his departure.

He handed Jasmine the list of duties he'd earlier enumerated, along with a similar list for each of the servants, kissed her farewell, and finally took his leave. As the sound of his carriage grew distant, she leaned against the door and relaxed against the hard, cool wood. She knew she would not miss her husband.

I cannot love him. There is nothing worthy of love. Jasmine sighed and closed her eyes. How very different her life was from the dreams she'd once had, little-girl dreams of living in the South with her own plantation house to run and a loving husband to take pride in her efforts. She touched a hand to her stomach and thought of the child that grew there. She didn't want Bradley's children, but this baby was also her own. She couldn't very well disregard that fact.

I can hardly punish the child because I do not love his or her father.

She put aside her disparaging thoughts and entered the parlor, where Kiara was carefully dusting the furniture she had dusted only the day before.

"Excuse me boldness, but will the master be gone for very long, ma'am?"

"At least a week." Jasmine eyed the busy girl. She couldn't be much older than sixteen—maybe seventeen. "Sit down and let's visit."

"Excuse me? You're wantin' me to sit and visit in the parlor?" The girl looked appalled at the idea.

"I thought we were becoming friends. I visit with you when you're helping me dress or fixing my hair."

"That's different than sittin' in the parlor like I'm company. I don't think Mr. Bradley would be likin' to see such a thing."

"Well, he's gone to Boston so we need not worry. I'm in charge now and I want you to sit and visit."

"Yes, ma'am," she said, perching on the edge of her chair like a bird poised to take flight. "What is it ya're wantin' to hear from me?"

"You remember I told you my mother was ill and couldn't return to Lowell with me?"

"Aye."

"I've been thinking about how much I miss my mother. My longing to be with her has made me realize how difficult life must be for you and Paddy. It's difficult to imagine all you two have suffered."

"We've suffered no more than most of the Irish. And when I'm missin' me mother the most, I try to remember all the good times instead of dwellin' on when the famine struck us down." Kiara stared out the window as though she were in a trance that carried her back to the grassy hills and valleys of her homeland. "We always worked hard, but our house was filled with love and plenty of laughter. Even when food got scarce, we made do for a while with sellin' lace. But when times got really bad, me da fell into a state o' sadness, the likes of which I ain't never seen before—and hope I never see again. He took the few coins me ma had saved back for thread and spent them on ale."

"Your mother made lace to help support you?"

Kiara looked at Jasmine as though she were a stranger. Obviously the Irish girl's thoughts remained focused upon Ireland and memories of a happier time. "Aye, both of us. She taught me how to make the lace. Lots of the women learned so as to help feed their families. The nuns at the convent taught some of the girls in our village, and they taught others. They sold the lace for us—to the wealthy English landowners. Their ladies are very fond of Irish lace."

"I'd like to see some of your handiwork, Kiara. Do you have some of your lace you can show me?"

"No, I had but a wee piece left, and I pinned it on me mother's dress when we buried her. I thought it only fittin' since we could na give her a proper burial."

"What a lovely idea. I'm sure she would have been pleased."

Kiara pointed toward Jasmine's sewing basket. "Do ya know how to make lace, ma'am?"

"No, but I'd be delighted to have you show me. We could go into town and purchase the necessary supplies, if you like. I don't want to place another burden upon you."

"Making even a small piece o' lace takes many hours, ma'am. Some find it tedious to finish only an inch or two after hours and hours of work. But I love keepin' me hands busy with the thread. Watching as a piece of thread turns into a delicate piece o' lace is truly a thing of beauty."

"Then we must get you some thread. I have a meeting tomorrow afternoon, but we could go into town after supper tonight."

"The shops are open for business in the evenin', ma'am?"

"Yes, to accommodate the girls working in the mills. The shop owners know they must remain open if they're going to attract business from the mill workers. Grandmother told me the shopkeepers have maintained evening hours since the very first stores opened in Lowell."

"I never heard o' such a thing, but if you're wantin' to go, I'd be 'appy to go along."

"Good! Then it's agreed."

Kiara cleared her throat and her expression grew tense. Jasmine wondered at the look but had no time to ask before Kiara questioned her. "Ma'am, forgive me bein' so bold, but I'm wonderin' if we could buy a wee bit of material for some aprons. I've only got the one dress and I'm washin' it out every night, but—"

"You've only got one dress?" Jasmine asked in disbelief. "Why didn't you say so sooner?"

"I've never had more than one dress at a time, ma'am. I can make do just fine with it, especially if I have an apron or two. Lord Palmerston's lady servant said she did na have time to sew me or Paddy any clothes afore we left Ireland. She did na pack any material in our trunk either, although she had plenty in her sewin' room—tightfisted, she was. Fact is, she packed us a trunk, but most of the contents were for yar husband . . . not clothes for me and Paddy."

"Well, I cannot allow you to make do with that. We'll buy materials for you and for Paddy. Do you sew?"

"Aye. I can do very fine work, if I do say so meself," Kiara replied.

"Very well. Make a list of what you'll need in order to create two—no, three—work dresses. Better yet, let's buy serviceable material for three work dresses and two gowns of better quality for special occasions."

"Oh, but for sure I couldn't be lettin' ya do that, ma'am. An apron or two will be just fine."

"Nonsense. You're my personal maid—you mustn't look dowdy," Jasmine insisted, trying her best to sound authoritative.

"Oh, I hadn't thought of it that way," Kiara said, touching the top of her frayed collar.

"Don't fret. This will be fun. We'll go and purchase everything you need. Then, tomorrow you'll spend the day sewing instead of worrying about household duties. We'll get materials for Paddy as well, so make a list of what you'll need to make the boy at least three shirts and two pairs of trousers."

"For sure I don't know what to say," Kiara murmured.

Jasmine smiled. "Say nothing at all."

Kiara jumped up from her chair, obviously anxious to hasten back to her duties. But before she could escape, Jasmine grasped the girl's hand. "Are you happy here, Kiara? I know you'd be happier in Ireland if you could have stayed, but are you reasonably comfortable here with us?"

She hesitated briefly. "I'm very fond of you, ma'am, and this is a lovely house. Sure and it's finer than anyplace I ever hoped to live in. And Paddy's happy workin' with the horses."

"And Master Bradley?" Jasmine inquired.

Kiara's eyes grew as cloudy as the fog-layered moors of Ireland. "He can be a bit frightenin' at times, ma'am, but I'll not be sayin' a single bad word about yar husband. I'm just thankful the two of us are alive and together. Now, I best be gettin' back to me chores. Cook will be needin' me soon."

Jasmine nodded. She wouldn't force Kiara to talk about Bradley—she didn't need to. The girl's fears were evident.

─────────

"They've quite a selection of thread, ma'am. A bit thicker than I like, but we can make do even if it's not quite so fine."

"Let's take a look over here," Jasmine suggested while leading the way through the emporium, which was beginning to hum with activity. Mill girls, anxious to see the new merchandise advertised in the newspaper, swarmed into the store in groups of five and six, their chatter carrying throughout the store, while several were overcome with fits of coughing.

"Mrs. Paxton, did you get your shipment of Dr. Horatio's Spice of Life?" one of the girls inquired.

"Yes, indeed. We received a full shipment this morning, and I've already placed another order. It seems all of you girls are beginning to use Dr. Horatio's rejuvenating spirits. Before long, I won't be able to keep up with the demand."

"You should try it, Mrs. Paxton. It helps my cough and boosts my energy. Ask any of the girls who have used it. Why, it's not only given me more energy, I've found it makes my life more pleasant."

"What she says is true," another girl agreed. "Before I would leave the weaving room feeling completely exhausted, what with the hot, damp rooms and not being able to open the windows for a bit of fresh air. Then I began taking Spice of Life, and within a day or two, I was feeling like a new person—full of energy, not coughing nearly so much, and enjoying myself again."

Jasmine approached the counter where the girls were standing and picked up a bottle of the cathartic. "Forgive me for interrupting, but did I overhear you say you've found remedial success with this product?"

"Absolutely! Why, the medicinal value of Dr. Horatio's spirits is unsurpassed. Those of us working in the mills have found it extremely beneficial. Of course, we're required to work in conditions that you aren't likely to endure. Employment in those mills can drain the very life out of you, but after only a few doses of Dr. Horatio's, I feel wonderful again."

Jasmine held on to the bottle. "Thank you for taking time to explain the benefits of the product. I believe I may purchase a bottle," Jasmine remarked as she watched the girl purchase four bottles of the remedy before leaving the store.

"Are ya feelin' poorly, missus, that ya think ya need that mixture?" Kiara inquired.

"I've just not been able to regain my strength. Perhaps this will help."

Kiara shook her head. "I'm guessin' there's nothin' but a dose of whiskey and water, along with a bit o' flavorin' and perhaps a few herbs in that bottle, missus. Ya're feelin' tired because of yar condition. It's just the growin' babe sappin' yar energy."

"I've talked to other ladies, and they've been able to maintain their normal routine without this constant weariness. I think Dr. Horatio's mixture might be worth a try. Besides, were the contents merely whiskey, I doubt whether these girls would be having such impressive results. The fact that Mrs. Paxton can't keep it in stock is evidence of its benefit."

"Mr. McCorkey could na keep enough ale in the pub on payday either, but that did na mean the ale was helpin' them what was drinkin' it." Kiara held the bottle at arm's length and examined the label, which was emblazoned with the picture of a distinguished-looking bearded man. "I'm thinkin' your Dr. Horatio's elixir is no different than Mr. McCorkey's ale."

Jasmine took back the bottle. "And I'm certain Mrs. Paxton wouldn't sell alcoholic spirits. I know for a fact that she's an upstanding member of the Lowell Temperance Union and extremely opposed to the use of intoxicants." Jasmine moved closer to Kiara and lowered her voice. "My grandmother told me that Mrs. Paxton's father was an alcoholic and very mean to her. Furthermore, Mrs. Paxton blames his early death upon his drinking habits. Under the circumstances, I don't think you'd find her willing to sell alcoholic substances."

Kiara handed a bobbin of thread to Jasmine without further comment regarding Dr. Horatio's Spice of Life. "I believe this thread will do nicely."

Jasmine nodded her agreement, ignored Kiara's disapproving look, and added two bottles of elixir to the pile of lace-making supplies. "Now let's go look over the materials for your new dresses." Kiara followed Jasmine across the store.

"Why, Mrs. Brighton," Jasmine exclaimed as she turned a corner. "I've not had a chance to speak with you since returning to Lowell."

Elinor Brighton smiled in greeting, but her eyes remained filled with grief. "Yes, it has been quite some time. How are you?"

"I'm doing well, thank you for asking." Jasmine turned to Kiara. "This is Kiara O'Neill. She's working for us now."

Kiara curtsied. "Pleased to meet ya, ma'am."

"Thank you."

"Kiara makes lace," Jasmine said, anxious for something else to say. "We've come for supplies."

"I learned to tat a bit when I was a girl," Elinor told them. "I'm sure I've forgotten much of what I learned for lack of practice."

"No doubt it would come back to ya, ma'am."

Elinor seemed to consider the statement. "Yes, you are probably right." She sighed and looked once again to Jasmine. "I must be on my way. I do bid you have a good day, Mrs. Houston."

"And you, Mrs. Brighton."

Jasmine waited until Elinor had exited the store before turning to Kiara. "There is a sad soul to be sure. She has lost two husbands in a short span of time, and she has not even one child to offer her comfort in their passing."

"Poor thing. She's quite a beauty, even in her sorrow," Kiara said softly.

"Yes, she is," Jasmine agreed, thinking how tragic that Elinor should so pine for her dead husband while Jasmine could barely endure the sight of Bradley.

"There'll be no comfort for her," Kiara said, shaking her head. "Me ma was that way when Da passed on. He took her broken heart to the grave, same as Mrs. Brighton's husband has done for her."

Jasmine felt strangely sad to know that such a thing would never be her fate with Bradley. Bradley would never break her heart—because she'd never give it to him in the first place.

Over the past three days, Bradley had diligently worked on the accounts in his Boston shipping office and was thankful the Associates were assembling for dinner this evening before commencement of the series of meetings scheduled over the next few days.

He was in desperate need of a diversion from the tiresome columns of numbers. Not that his time hadn't been well spent. The accounts of Bradley's oceangoing business now reflected the company's profits and losses over the past six months—at least in the manner in which he desired to have them appear. There remained a number of documents that required his attention, but he would attend to those after his meetings with the Associates had concluded.

He slipped into his waistcoat and checked his appearance in the mirror. Passable, he decided, for a dinner meeting in the hostelry. He walked down the wide staircase of the newly constructed hotel, thankful both the dinner and meeting would be held in the dining room of the facility.

He waved a greeting to Matthew Cheever and James Morgan, who were entering the door as he reached the foyer. "Gentlemen, good to see you. I trust your journey from Lowell was pleasant."

"We looked for you on the train," Matthew said. "You must have come in earlier this morning."

"I arrived several days ago—business with my shipping company that needed attention," he explained. "We might as well go into the dining room and see if any of the others have arrived. Personally, I could use a glass of port."

Bradley gave James a gentle poke in the side as they entered the dining room. "Looks like quite a few of our members were anxious for a glass of port."

"Either that or anxious to solicit one another's votes on impending issues," James said.

"Speaking of concerns, I'm hoping you'll join with me when Robert Woolsey begins pushing for more railroads."

"I didn't realize Robert was going to become a strong proponent for additional rail lines."

"It only stands to reason. He and Tracy Jackson were the strongest proponents of the railroad from the very start. Now, with Tracy's death, he'll likely propose increased railroad usage as some sort of memorial for him. I'm certain he'll think such a concept will garner sympathy votes. Of course, you and I know the only reason he'll be pushing the railroad is because he's so heavily invested."

James peered over the top of his wire-rimmed spectacles. "We're all a bit self-serving, aren't we, Bradley? Besides, with Nathan now partial owner of a shipping line, I'm sure he'll be swaying the members in a direction that will please you."

"Perhaps, but I've grown to believe some of the men have begun to vote in opposition to Nathan for that very reason—they believe his holdings surpass the rest of them, and they've grown jealous of his powerful position."

"You could be correct, although I've not heard such talk. If you'll excuse me, I want to have a word with Leonard."

Bradley watched James walk off and then surveyed the room in an attempt to decide which group of men might be won over to his position. Matthew Cheever was with a small conclave that might possibly shed some light on the evening's agenda. He wended his way through the crowd, stopping to shake hands and exchange civilities with several men along the way. He was only an arm's length away from Matthew when they were summoned to dinner.

Unfortunately, he found himself lodged between two lesser-distinguished Associates. However, instead of becoming disheartened, he used the time advantageously, quickly assessing their views and lobbying their support. By the time the meeting began, he was convinced they would support anything he proposed throughout the meeting. And after several hours of heated argument regarding railroads and seagoing vessels, Bradley was certain he would need their votes.

Bradley's evening of diversion was hastily turning into a nightmare. Feeling he could take no more of the avid support for rail usage, he jumped up from his chair and waved his arm high in the air.

Matthew Cheever gave him a look of exasperation. "I believe we've all heard your opinion on this issue, Bradley. I'd like to move forward and call for a vote."

"Before you do, I believe there are a few matters the members should hear."

"Very well." Matthew motioned for him to come to the front and take the floor.

"As many of you are aware, I have been diligently working to provide our mills with ample cotton to continue production at a steady pace. Much of that cotton comes from the Wainwright plantations; those contracts were implemented with the under-standing that the cotton would be shipped on vessels belonging to me or other members of the Boston Associates at a reduced rate. I redirect your attention to this fact because I'm assured that if my wife's family should be required to pay higher prices for shipping their goods, they would consider their contracts invalid and likely return to the English marketplace."

Murmurs of dissension could be heard throughout the room. "Sounds like you're using the family cotton as a bartering tool!" one of the men near the back of the room called out.

Bradley rested his hands upon the table and leaned forward toward the crowd with his jaw tightly clenched. "I'm merely tell-ing you the facts."

Matthew stood and called for silence while motioning the men to be seated. "There's no need to resort to mayhem. We'll resolve nothing by shouting angry accusations. Bradley wanted us to make an informed decision based upon facts that weren't previously known to us. He ought not be the recipient of your anger merely because he's related to the Wainwrights."

"Thank you, Matthew, for your support," Bradley said.

"I didn't mean to imply my support, Bradley. I'm merely offer-ing an explanation."

But apparently his words, along with Nathan's long-winded speech about the cost of additional railroads when ships were already available, had a positive effect upon the men. When the vote was finally taken, the tally was in favor of transporting by ship whenever possible.

Several days later, as Bradley sat in the office of his shipping business, a pleasurable smile crossed his lips. Things had gone very well for him during this journey. He leaned back in his chair thinking of the dark-haired Irish girl at home—thoughts he knew he ought not be having.

"I'll be back later this afternoon," he told the clerk sitting near the door.

He hailed a carriage near the docks and instructed the driver to stop in the business district. After passing several shops, he entered a store specializing in ladies' apparel. When he left the store a short time later, he carried a carefully wrapped blue silk robe under his arm.

"Perhaps she'll be less inclined to move away from me when she sees what I can offer her in return for her affections," Bradley murmured to himself.

CHAPTER · *20*

KIARA PULLED Paddy close, her fingers digging into the flesh of his arm. "Ya're hurting me, Kiara." He squirmed, trying to gain his freedom.

"Do ya not realize the consequences of what happened today, Padraig?"

"Aye, but 'twas a mistake, and the horse has only a small cut on his leg. I do na think the master will even notice. Besides, it may be healed before his return."

"Ya best be hopin' that horse is good as the day Master Bradley left this house or that he does na come near the barn. I do na want him gettin' so angry he sells yar papers. I could na bear to have ya taken away from me."

"What else can I say? I did na want the horse to run off and I know I should have made certain the stall was closed. I truly thought it was, Kiara. Ya know I love those horses, and I do na want anything bad to 'appen to them."

"And I do na want anything bad happenin' to *you*, so you best be checkin' those gates two times instead of one," she warned.

"I'll go out and put some more liniment on his leg and make sure he's doing all right. Do na worry so much, Kiara."

She watched her brother run out the door with his flat cap

219

pulled low over his eyes and his legs flying helter-skelter like a young colt let loose in the pasture. The thought of a future without Paddy was unbearable. Without warning, unbidden tears coursed down her cheeks, and she gave way to the insurmountable sadness that daily filled her. The show of strength she exhibited for her brother's sake crumpled in her solitude, and she wept bitter tears.

"Is it so terrible living here that you are reduced to this level of grief?" Jasmine asked.

Kiara lifted her head and attempted a smile. "I do na mean to seem ungrateful. I'm thankful for yar goodness to me. But I do na know what will happen to Paddy should Master Bradley discover his fancy horse escaped and was running wild for two days—and if that cut does na heal, I fear Master Bradley will sell Paddy's papers of servitude to someone else. I could na live without me brother." The words caused her tears to flow once again.

"You know I would never permit such a thing to happen. If my husband even suggests such a notion, I will vehemently protest his action."

"Thank you, missus. But we both know that if Master Bradley makes up his mind, there's nothing anyone can do that will stop him."

"But I would try," Jasmine vowed. "We'll hope he never finds out about the incident."

Kiara wiped her nose and attempted to cease the hiccuping that had laid claim and was jolting her body with merciless spasms.

"Why don't you and Paddy take some time and go visit your friend Bridgett? I'm sure she'd be delighted to see you, and on a Sunday afternoon she'll not be working. Visiting Bridgett will take your mind off your sorrows."

Kiara brightened at the suggestion. She'd seen Bridgett only once since her arrival, and then it had been for only a short time. Bridgett had managed to find the Houston home and had walked from the Acre to see Kiara and Paddy. That had been only two weeks after they arrived in Lowell. She'd made the visit and told Kiara she'd be starting work at the mills the next day and wouldn't have much time for visiting. Kiara wondered how she liked her new job.

"That would be ever so nice. I'd like to go visitin'."

"Good! We'll take a carriage, and I'll visit with Grandmother while you and Paddy go to the Acre. You can come to Grandmother's when you've finished your visit, and we'll return home. How does that sound?"

Kiara beamed. "That would be grand, ma'am. I'll go out to the barn and fetch Paddy. He'll be needin' to scrub up a wee bit."

"If you'd tell Charles to bring the carriage around once he's hitched the horses, that will save us some time."

"Yes, ma'am," Kiara called over her shoulder as she raced out of the house.

Kiara and Paddy jumped down from the carriage when they neared the Acre. "Just follow that street and ask anyone you see if they know your friend," Charles instructed. "All the residents of the Acre know each other."

Kiara took Paddy by the hand and led him through the row of run-down shanties, stopping the first person who looked in her direction. "I'm lookin' for Bridgett Farrell. She lives with her cousin, Rogan Sheehan, and her granna Murphy."

The woman pointed down the street. "Turn right at the end of the street. Third door on the left."

"Thank ya, soul, and God go with ya," Kiara said, hurrying off toward their destination. "Oh, Paddy, I do hope Bridgett's home. We're not likely to soon get this chance again."

Paddy grinned and danced down the street ahead of her, twirling about to face Kiara. "She'll be there. I can feel it in me bones." He turned the corner and ran to the door, knocking several times. Kiara had reached his side when Bridgett opened the door.

"I can na believe me Irish eyes. Kiara O'Neill, get yarself in here and meet me granna Murphy and set a spell. My cousin's gone out to enjoy his Sunday afternoon, but I stayed home with Granna. She has a touch of the gout and needs a bit o' help. I'll put on the kettle, and ya can tell me for sure about life in yar big mansion, and I'll tell ya about life in the Acre and workin' in the mills. Michael O'Donnell lives next door, Paddy. He's about yar age. Get over and meet him. Tell him Bridgett sent ya."

Once Paddy had gone and Bridgett finished brewing a pot of tea, she sat down with Kiara. "Are ya happy and are they treatin' ya well at yar big house?"

"The missus is very kind. She's not much older than me. She lived far away from here on a big farm of some kind until she married the master. She misses her home and family just like I miss Ireland, so we've lots in common."

Granna Murphy appeared to be asleep on the small cot across the room, but Kiara leaned close to Bridgett just in case she might not be sleeping soundly. She didn't want the old woman to hear what she was going to say. "Master Bradley's another kettle o' fish. I do na like the way he looks at me, Bridgett. He frightens me."

Bridgett's eyes widened and filled with concern. "Ya think he might be one who would try and force ya to his bed?"

The sound of Paddy and some other boys playing in the street drifted into the house, causing Kiara to feel even more self-conscious. "That I do. He has evil in his eyes when he looks in my direction. And his wife is a beauty. He has no reason to be lookin' elsewhere. She's gonna give him a wee babe. Ya'd think he'd be content."

"Maybe that's why he's lookin' yar direction. Sometimes when a woman is expectin', she doesn't want her husband a botherin' with 'er."

Kiara shook her head. "I do na think that's it. He's looked at me that way since the first time he laid eyes on me."

"Just keep yar distance whenever ya can, and tell him ya'll tell his wife if he's tryin' to lay a hand on ya," Bridgett whispered.

"I can na tell him that. He'll sell me papers, and then I'd be separated from Paddy."

"It's a bad spot yar in, fer sure, but it was good o' him to let ya come visit me."

"He's gone to Boston. The missus brought us in her carriage

and then went to visit her grandmother across town."

"In her carriage, no less? Well, ain't ya the fancy one?" Bridgett said with a giggle. "I don't believe I've ever had visitors before who came in a carriage."

"What are ya hearin' from Ireland? Is there any relief?" Kiara felt desperate for news. She had no one to write to—no one to give her a word of the homeland.

"The famine is only gettin' worse. Folks dyin' every day from lack of food. It's lucky we are to be here, Kiara. But the Yankee girls in the mills are complainin' about the terrible conditions. They don't know what we've come from, or they'd be thankin' the good Lord for the privilege of the pay they receive every week."

"I heard some of the ladies who come to have tea with the missus talkin' about troubles in the mills. Do they truly keep those windows nailed down so ya can't get a breath of fresh air?"

Bridgett nodded. "Aye. But still 'tis better than starvin' to death in Ireland. They don't quit their jobs 'cause they know there's Irish lasses what would take their place the same day. They don't pay the Irish workers as much as the Yankees, which I do na think is fair, but there's nothin' we can do. If we want to keep our jobs, we keep our mouths shut."

"That hardly seems—" Kiara paused in midsentence.

A blinding shaft of sunlight shone through the door as it opened. Kiara looked toward the entry, where a tall figure stood surrounded by a halo of light. The sun danced across his curly black hair and dappled the mass of locks with streaks of midnight blue.

"Who 'ave we here?" he asked, stepping aside and pushing the door closed behind him.

Kiara took in the man's deep blue eyes and could not help but notice his finely chiseled features and muscular build.

"This is me friend Kiara O'Neill. She's the one what sailed with me from Ireland," Bridgett explained. "And that's her brother, Padraig, outside playing with Michael O'Donnell." Bridgett turned her attention back to Kiara. "This is my cousin, Rogan

Sheehan. He's the one that saved his money to bring me over here." Bridgett's gaze was filled with grateful pride as she gave Rogan a winsome smile.

Rogan motioned her to hush. "'Twas nothin' special, lass. Quit yer makin' such a fuss. How's Granna doin'?" he asked, looking toward the cot.

"She's been sleeping all afternoon. I let her sleep when she can. At least she's not feelin' the pain when she's having a lie-down."

The three of them visited while the old woman slept, Rogan regaling them with stories of his life since arriving in America, his friendly voice and easy laughter delighting Kiara. He was the kind of man who made her feel very special—although he'd done nothing more than smile and talk.

Kiara glanced toward the window where the sun was beginning a slow descent. "I did na realize it was gettin' so late. I best be on my way so the missus does na worry."

"I wish ya did na have to go," Bridgett said.

"I must na be late, or the missus might na be so generous about lettin' me come again. Besides, it may take me a bit to find the house. I do na know my way about the town."

"In that case, I'll be pleased to take ya and yar brother wherever ya're needin' ta go," Rogan said. "There's no place in Lowell I can na find."

"That's kind of ya, but I do na want to be a bother."

He gave her a jaunty smile and walked to the door. "Ya could na be a bother if ya tried, lass."

Kiara blushed at his flattering remark. Secretly, she was pleased he had offered to spend a little more time in her company.

———

Bradley stormed through the front door with his jaw clenched and his lips set in a tight, thin line. "Where is he?"

Jasmine hurried from the parlor at the sound of her husband's shout. "Bradley! Whatever is wrong? When did you return from Boston?"

"Only a short time ago. Where is Paddy?" His tone remained

strident. He stood before her while slapping his leather riding whip into his palm. "Tell me where he is."

"I thought he was in the barn. I've not seen him."

"Where's his sister? He's likely with her."

"She's in the kitchen helping Sarah and Cook. Supper's nearly ready. I don't think Paddy's in the house."

He strode past her, now slapping the riding whip against his thigh. "Where's the boy?" he barked.

Sarah emerged, her hands quivering at the sight of her employer. "I sent him to town to pick up necessities from the mercantile. He should return shortly. In fact, he's coming now," she said, pointing out the window.

Bradley rushed out the door. His whip came down across Paddy's back full force, scattering the contents of Sarah's basket of goods in all directions. He continued the flogging while screaming and cursing at Padraig until Kiara could take no more. She raced into the yard and attempted to grasp Bradley's arm, but to no avail.

"You can't even properly care for my horse after all I've done for you, you worthless good-for-nothing!" he yelled. "I'm gone for a week and come home to find my prize animal with a gash on his leg. I think I'll sell your papers so you'll find out what it's like to *really* work for a living. I'll send you down south to live on the Wainwright plantation, where you can spend your time in the hot sun picking cotton and hoeing weeds. You'll spend all your time out in those fields wishing you were back caring for my horses. They'll lay the lash to your backside until it's raw, and if you dare try to run away, they'll slice the back of your ankle so you'll never walk right again."

"Ya don't even know what happened and—" Padraig stopped short with his argument. " 'Tis sorry I am. Ya're right. The horse's injury is all me fault. I promise if ya'll just give me one more chance, I'll do better and ya won't have to be worryin' about such a thing ever happenin' again."

The boy's abrupt change of heart surprised Bradley, and he hesitated a moment before replying. "I'll give it some thought and let you know what I decide." Turning abruptly, he caught sight of

Kiara motioning to her brother. She'd obviously signaled the boy to cease his argument. The fear in her eyes reinforced what he already knew: Kiara's greatest fear was separation from her brother.

"Pick up these things and get back in the house and tend to your duties, girl. You've no business out here. And you get back to the barn. There's muck that needs to be shoveled," he snarled at Padraig.

Bradley watched the brother and sister exchange looks before hastening off to do his bidding. He followed Kiara at a distance, enjoying the sway of her hips as she preceded him into the house. There was a degree of satisfaction in knowing the power he possessed over her.

Jasmine was pacing in the hallway when Bradley returned to the parlor. "Come and sit down. I don't want you to tire yourself. How have you fared during my absence? No problems with illness, I trust?"

She seated herself on the brocade-covered sewing rocker and picked up her needlepoint. "I've been well," she replied in a soft voice.

"Good! We don't want any problems with the babe. I want you to continue taking excellent care of yourself. I want a healthy son."

"What about a healthy daughter?"

He frowned at the question. "Is your question an attempt to snuff out the pleasure I derive from anticipating the birth of a *son*?"

She looked up from her stitching. "No, but I do want you to accept the possibility of a daughter. It is my hope that you would not be overly disappointed by the birth of a healthy daughter."

"There's no need to dwell on such a thought. I'll deal with the issue of a daughter only if and when I'm forced to do so. Shall we go in for supper?"

Jasmine remained quiet throughout supper, obviously angered by his earlier remarks. Irked by her behavior, he excused himself after the meal and retreated to his library. He remained there until the house was dark. Once he was certain Jasmine and the others had retired for the night, he removed the package from his satchel, made his way to the back stairway, and climbed to the third-floor attic room. Without knocking, he shoved his way into the room where Kiara lay on the bed. The sight of him caused her to bolt upright. Ripping away the paper, he tossed the silk robe onto her bed.

"It's a gift—for you. Put it on. I want to see how you look in it," he commanded.

Kiara lifted the robe between her finger and thumb as though it were infected with impurity. Her voice trembled. "I . . . do . . . na want your gift. T-take it to yar wife—she's the one ya should be givin' such a thing as this."

Bradley removed his jacket, taking pleasure in the fear that filled her eyes. He yanked at his shirt, pulling it free.

"Do na go any farther. Ya may own my papers, but that does na give ya rights to any more than me labor."

Bradley smirked. "Then you may consider this a part of your labor, because one thing is certain—I'll have my way with you."

"Ya best not be tryin', or I'll scratch yar eyes out."

"Only if you want to bid your brother farewell. I'm sure the lad will find life on a cotton plantation much less to his liking than caring for the horses with his sister close at hand."

Recognition shone in her eyes. "So that's how it's to be."

Bradley continued removing his clothes as she cowered on the bed, pulling the coverlet up around her neck. "Yes, my sweet Kiara. If you want to keep your brother with you, you'll do as I say and keep your mouth shut." He grasped her cheeks, squeezing them between his thumb and fingers as he pulled her forward and forced his lips upon hers. She cringed but did not fight. Her surrender pleased him. Explaining scratches or other evidence of a scuffle to his wife could prove problematic.

A short time later, he left her bed. "I really should thank your brother for his irresponsible behavior. How else could I be assured of a future filled with pleasurable nights?" He smiled down at her form. Her body was curled into a quivering mass, with the covers pulled over her head.

CHAPTER · *21*

A KNOCK SOUNDED at the front door, and Jasmine watched Kiara bound out of the parlor at breakneck speed.

"Good afternoon, my dear," Alice greeted as she entered the parlor a moment later. "I decided if I was ever going to have a nice long chat with you, I'd have to come to your house since you don't seem to find time to come to mine. The only trouble is that I cannot stay long, so our chat will have to be brief."

Jasmine opened her arms to receive her grandmother's embrace. "I promise I'll come see you next Sunday afternoon. Bradley will be in Boston. Perhaps you'd like to come along, Kiara," she said to the girl as she gathered her lace-making supplies. "You could go and visit Bridgett. You could even send a note to let her know your plans."

Kiara brightened. "That would be very nice. I'll be leavin' the two of ya alone for yar visit. I've some chores that need attention."

"I was going to show Grandmother your lace."

"I've not enough done to be showin' to anyone," she said. "But thank ya for the thought," she added before leaving the room.

Jasmine wagged her head back and forth. "I don't know what's come over her. She's become so moody of late. For the life of me,

I can't determine what's amiss. I've asked on numerous occasions, but she merely says there's nothing wrong."

"Strange," Alice remarked. "Perhaps it's just your imagination. Has Bradley mentioned the fact that she's been irritable?"

"I doubt that he'd be any kind of judge of another person's level of irritability. There's been no making him happy of late either. Seems he's constantly finding something that makes him temperamental. Between the two of them, I don't know which is the more changeable. Kiara is sad and withdrawn, while Bradley is angry and explosive."

"Seems strange you'd see such dramatic changes in *both* of them. You do understand that women in your condition become temperamental, don't you? Perhaps it's you that's experiencing changes rather than them."

"I don't think Bradley's shouting vituperations could be considered a change in *my* behavior, Grandmother."

Alice's features knit into a tight frown. "Something must have occurred to cause such radical changes. You can think of nothing?"

"There was an incident a while back when Bradley was in Boston. Paddy had failed to latch one of the stalls and Bradley's prize horse ran off. By the time Bradley returned, the horse was safely back in the stable, but it did have a cut on its leg. Bradley thrashed Paddy with his horsewhip."

"I'm sure Kiara must have been distraught over the whipping."

Jasmine bobbed her head in agreement. "Yes, but I thought she'd gotten over the incident. Paddy's the one who suffered the flogging, and he seems to have forgotten the entire matter."

"It seems improbable Bradley's change in behavior would be connected to that episode. I had hoped to hear you were happier in your marriage."

"I've accepted my station in life, Grandmother. I am pleased I will have a child to love. And, if it's a boy, Bradley will be pleased."

"He'll be every bit as happy should you bear him a daughter. Men always say they want sons, but they love their daughters as well."

"Either way, I think children will make a difference for both of us, and I certainly cannot say I've always felt that way. At first I simply did not want Bradley's children, but then I realized I was being completely selfish. This baby didn't ask to be the son or daughter of such a ruthless man."

"Children are a wonderful gift, Jasmine, but strengthening your relationship with God might prove of greater benefit right now. Drawing closer to God might also help your marriage. Bradley doesn't seem like such a poor husband. He may well be gruff and unreasonable at times, but all men are." She smiled as if she'd shared a great secret. "Why not use this time before the child comes to deepen your beliefs so that when difficult times come, you can lean upon the Lord, knowing He'll see you through? Spending time with the Lord each morning is the best part of my day—and the most beneficial."

"I hope I've already seen my difficult times, Grandmother. Along with marrying a man I do not love, I'm deeply disappointed in my father, I'm constantly worrying over Mother's mental condition, and I've had to give up Mammy. Added to this now it appears as if I've lost Kiara's friendship. I've prayed about all of these matters, Grandmother, but to no avail. I'm beginning to think God has designated me as his female Job."

Alice gave a hearty chuckle. "Oh, my dear, I hardly think your difficulties are any match for Job's, for along with your difficulties, you're also enjoying some wonderful events in your life. Why don't you try what I've suggested for a month and see if it helps?"

"I'll try," Jasmine agreed. "Have you seen Lilly and Violet recently? I had hoped to see them at the tea last week but was ill that afternoon and unable to attend. Bradley was in a complete rage when he discovered I hadn't attended. He feels it's absolutely essential that I be present for every gathering of the wives."

"I'm sure he wants to become more widely accepted here in Lowell and feels you can accomplish much on his behalf, especially among the Associates' wives. Incidentally, Lilly invited me for tea last Wednesday, and we had a nice visit."

"Did she mention anything about the mills or the Associates?

Bradley seems to enjoy hearing any tidbits I glean regarding the business. Perhaps it would cheer him this evening if I could give him a report of some recent occurrences."

Alice closed her eyes and leaned her head against the back of the divan for a moment. Suddenly her eyelids snapped open and her eyes sparkled with excitement. "As a matter of fact, she did mention the mill girls. I think she feels a deep affinity for those working girls, since she once worked in the mills. Apparently many of the girls have been sickly and not keeping a good pace with their work."

"Yes. I heard the same thing when I was shopping last week. Apparently many of the girls were unable to work due to sickness. The supervisors feared they had contracted some unknown ailment and it was being passed among them. The Associates were concerned production was going to decrease if the girls couldn't report for work."

"That's exactly what Lilly told me. It appears the girls have had a recent boost in energy and are back on their regular work schedules with production at an all-time high. Lilly related the girls have begun taking Dr. Horatio's Spice of Life elixir and credit the tonic to their renewed vigor. She said the supervisors even plan to suggest the Associates purchase the tonic and have all of the girls begin taking it on a daily basis."

"I purchased some of that very tonic at Paxton's. I was going to try it, but when we got home from town, Kiara put my purchases away and I've not seen the bottles since. I completely forgot about the tonic. I'll have to look for it. This information should please Bradley."

"I do hope it helps. Now I really must be going home, but don't forget your promise to visit on Sunday. I'll be expecting you."

Jasmine walked alongside her grandmother into the hallway and embraced her. "Thank you for coming, Grandmother. I look forward to seeing you again on Sunday."

Alice patted her cheek. "And don't forget your promise to meet with the Lord each morning before you begin your day."

Jasmine smiled. "I remember."

She stood in the doorway until her grandmother's carriage had pulled away before returning to the parlor. With renewed enthusiasm, she picked up her stitching. She was almost anxious for Bradley's return, pleased she would have news to share with him that might create a renewed sense of unity between them.

As usual, Bradley's mood was sour when he returned home, and although she greeted him with a kiss, he stalked off toward the kitchen. She didn't see him again until supper was served.

"I have some news to share with you," she said.

He gave her a cursory glance. "What news would *you* have?"

She related the information in her most animated voice, hoping to elicit a positive response from him. Instead, he slammed his fork onto the table and locked her expectant gaze in an icy glare.

"You see how much information is to be gained by mingling with these women? We are constantly excluded by the socially elite here in Lowell, while your grandmother receives invitations to so many functions she's unable to attend them all. It's obvious you don't know how to carry on a proper conversation with women who are accustomed to an industrialized city and can intelligently discuss the manufacturing business. If you were a proper wife, you'd know how to converse about something other than the latest English fashions. I want you to begin entertaining these women, become more like them, and listen and learn from them so that my stature will be enhanced with the Associates. Your lack of sophistication is a detriment to my future and the cause of our ostracism from important social functions."

"You forget I capably hosted a tea for you and discussed many issues concerning the mills. If you'll recall, there were many words of praise for your efforts on behalf of the Corporation during that gathering. I related all that information to you, along with talk of the speedup of the looms. Have you forgotten?"

Bradley scowled, and it only served to make his appearance even less appealing to Jasmine. "You believe acting as my hostess on one occasion is what I expect of you? You think gathering information at a single meeting is all that I need from you? If so, you're even more of a detriment than I imagined."

"I thought you would be pleased," she whispered. She folded her hands and lowered her gaze.

"I would be pleased if you would attend these functions yourself rather than relying upon bits and pieces randomly gathered by your grandmother."

Jasmine swallowed hard. She didn't want to cry. "I'll invite the ladies for tea next week. I promise."

Bradley grunted and pushed away from the table. "You look as though you're not taking proper care of yourself. You're pale and appear sickly. Are you attempting to injure my unborn son in an effort to cause me distress?"

Jasmine looked up in disbelief. "How could you think I would do such a thing? I want this child even more than you do."

He didn't answer. Instead, he stomped out of the room without another word. She remained in the parlor all evening until she finally accepted the fact that he was not going to join her.

I don't understand any of this, she thought. *Even when I think I'm doing the proper thing—the pleasing thing—he destroys it before my very eyes. Destroys me.* Jasmine looked at her needlework and realized she'd hopelessly knotted the thread. She tried diligently to free the tangles, murmuring a prayer as she did.

"Father, I don't know what to do. I'm not even sure that my prayers are being heard. Something is very wrong here, and I don't know how to make it right. Please help me."

The threads refused to budge. Exasperated, Jasmine set aside her handiwork. "I might as well go to bed," she muttered, wondering what had become of her husband.

Gathering her skirts, she went upstairs to prepare for bed. As she walked past her dressing table, she caught sight of herself in the mirror. Bradley was right. There were circles under her eyes, and her complexion was pasty. She searched through the drawers in the large dresser until she felt the smooth glass bottles filled with Dr. Horatio's Spice of Life elixir. Kiara had hidden the remedy beneath her undergarments in the bottom drawer. Since Kiara was the one to lay out Jasmine's clothing, she probably presumed that Jasmine would never dig through the drawers for any reason.

Jasmine pulled out one of the bottles and unstopped the cork. Taking a long drink, she started at the taste. She frowned and looked at the bottle. Kiara had suggested it was most likely nothing more than herbs and whiskey. Jasmine had once tasted brandy at Christmas and she had to admit the flavor was somewhat similar. Especially the way it burned her throat.

"I can bear the bitter taste," she told herself, "if it will give me the energy I need." She slipped into her nightgown, climbed into bed, and pulled the covers up to her chin. Unable to sleep, she tossed and turned, waiting to hear Bradley enter the door to his adjoining room. But, as was becoming his habit, it was late into the night before Jasmine heard his door unlatch.

———

When Bradley departed the next morning without bidding her farewell, Jasmine assumed he was still angry. However, she was pleased to find Kiara's mood had improved when she went downstairs later that morning. And by the time Sunday arrived, Kiara actually seemed her old self.

Jasmine pulled on her kid gloves as they neared the front door. "I hope you don't mind leaving early this morning. I'd like to surprise Grandmother and attend church with her since Bradley is in Boston."

"Yar husband will na be unhappy with yar decision to attend the Methodist church?"

"Bradley attends the Episcopal church because that's where he believes it's best to be seen, not because he has deep beliefs in the church—or in God, for that matter. He ought not take issue if I miss one Sunday."

"We should arrive in time for Paddy and me to attend St. Patrick's with Bridgett. At least I'm hopin' we will. It will be good to be goin' to church again."

"You could ride to town with us on Sundays and attend every

week if you like. I had no idea you wanted to attend church, Kiara. I'll speak to Bradley upon his return."

"No. Please do na speak to your husband. Things is fine just as they are."

Jasmine thought she detected fear in the girl's eyes, yet why would her suggestion cause misgivings? "I'll do as you ask, but should you change your mind, please let me know."

"That I will, ma'am, and I'll be thankin' ya for abidin' by me wishes."

Once Kiara and Paddy had been delivered, the carriage driver followed Jasmine's directions to the Methodist church on Suffolk Street. Their timing would be just right.

Hurrying from the carriage, Jasmine climbed the steps to the open door. She stood in the rear of the church and scanned the heads of the worshipers, seeking her grandmother's perfectly coifed cotton-white hair. Her eyes sparkled with delight when she finally located the familiar sight. By the time she reached her grandmother's side, a bright smile was tugging at her lips.

"May I join you?" she whispered.

Alice embraced her before scooting down the pew. "I'm *so* pleased you're here," Alice whispered in return.

Jasmine's fingers clenched around the hard oak wood of the church pew as Reverend Wells announced he would preach from the book of Job. "There is much we can learn from Job's trials and tribulations. Job was a man who had everything men seek: he had good health; a good wife; children, both sons and daughters; an abundance of land and animals. And he was wealthy. Most importantly, Job loved the Lord. Because of his love for God, do you wonder how he managed to maintain that trust? I honestly doubt we can even imagine the depth of Job's suffering," the preacher said.

Jasmine gave her grandmother a sidelong glance before returning her full attention to the preacher. She listened intently, wondering if God had designed this message especially with her in mind.

"When difficulties enter our lives, we are quick to shake a finger toward the heavens and ask why God has permitted something tragic to occur in our lives. We wonder why we should be plagued by suffering or pain when God can prevent such occurrences. Surely these events should be suffered by someone who doesn't love the Lord, instead of us."

"Exactly my thoughts," Jasmine whispered to her grandmother.

Alice placed a gloved finger to her pursed lips and issued a soft shushing sound in Jasmine's direction.

"We must remember that God can and often does prevent misery and disaster from entering our lives. But at those times when God does not intervene and troubles befall us, He will use those circumstances to His glory if we will only trust Him. Just as Job's friends forgot, we also tend to forget that God's character and nature is love. Out of our need we come to Him; we seek His face and unburden our hearts.

"Near the end of Job's suffering, he admits to the Lord that he, Job, spoke of things he did not understand, things too wonderful for him to know. He tells God, 'I have heard of thee by the hearing of the ear: but now mine eye seeth thee.' Just think of the excitement and pleasure Job experienced! Although God had not prevented Satan from causing Job pain and suffering, Job grew even closer to Him. And what can we learn from this?"

Jasmine glanced heavenward. "To enjoy our misery?" she whispered.

The preacher looked out over the congregation. "If we will soften our hearts, there is much to learn. God is waiting, anxious to draw closer."

Alice tapped Jasmine on the arm and tipped her head ever so slightly toward the preacher.

"God can use our trials to allow us to see Him and to know His character. In the midst of difficulties, we often forget the equation of time. We often think of 'poor Job'—but I would submit that Job was blessed. The Scriptures clearly point to the fact that Job was blessed in his early life, but in the latter portion of his life his blessings were *doubled*. Yes, God permitted Job to suffer, but

Job reaped many benefits, the greatest of which was a closer relationship with God. When trials come, my children, remember the blessings that follow as we, too, spend time with our Lord."

———————

They were seated at her grandmother's table beginning their noonday meal when Jasmine commented how much she had been enjoying her time with God each morning. "I must admit the sermon this morning appeared to have been intended specifically for me. For a moment I wondered if you had divulged my difficulties to Reverend Wells," she said with a giggle, then quickly sobered. "I wish I could report that I see evidence of matters easing between Bradley and me."

"It's only been a few days, dear. Why not wait until the end of the month before admitting defeat."

"I know you're right, but it's quite difficult. When I related your information about the mill girls to Bradley, instead of being pleased, he chastised me because I hadn't personally attended the tea. He became very angry and stormed from the room after accusing me of attempting to hurt our unborn child by not properly caring for myself. His temper frightens me at times."

Alice nodded as she forked a piece of chicken onto her plate. "Since our talk the other day, I've given some thought to our discussion. It has occurred to me that Bradley is under a great deal of stress with all of the expectations placed upon him in his new position: the acquisition of new Southern cotton producers and his responsibility for coordinating shipments—and then there's his own shipping business to deal with also. I'm wondering if it has all become too much for him."

"You may be correct. I hadn't given thought to the fact that he's had to deal with many new situations since our marriage."

"I'm thinking that I could write a letter to your father and suggest he have someone else coordinate the cotton shipments and even work toward developing new connections among other growers. Possibly one of your brothers. If your father agrees, Bradley would have more free time to devote to his other duties with the Associates, and he could spend more time at home."

Jasmine could well imagine the workload that awaited Bradley each day. And while she couldn't bring herself to admit love for her husband, she did feel compassion for his needs. "I believe such a plan may very well be what Bradley needs to help him relax and deal with matters in a less agitated state. I've agreed to hostess a tea next week, and I'll do all within my power to attend any of the upcoming events organized by the Associates' wives. Perhaps you could also help me by taking me along to some of your public engagements. That way my introduction into proper Lowell society will be accomplished more quickly."

Alice nodded. "I believe we've developed a workable plan. With prayer and hard work, we may be able to smooth the troubled waters you've experienced these last few months."

Jasmine felt as though a weight had been lifted from her shoulders. "Thank you, Grandmother. I can't tell you how much better I feel. And Kiara seems happier also." She lifted her handbag and removed a small piece of lace. "Look what I've brought along to show you," she said, holding the piece of lace in the palm of her hand. "Kiara fashioned this as an insert for the neckline of my plum silk gown. Have you ever seen such exquisite work?"

Alice carefully examined the intricate pattern, turning it in all directions. "This compares with the finest European laces. Are you certain she made this?"

"Indeed. We went into Lowell and purchased the supplies. During Bradley's absences, she sits with me and works on the lace while I'm doing my needlepoint. It's slow and painstaking to create even this small piece, yet she seems to thoroughly enjoy the task."

"There's every reason to believe she could earn enough to support herself once her servitude has been completed. She should create as much as possible while she's living with you. She can sell it and save her money for the future. The lace will sell itself, and cost will be no object. The affluent women will beg to purchase it. When she has a piece she's prepared to sell, let me show it to some of my friends. I'll have more orders than she can supply."

"I'm certain your news will boost her spirits. I love having both Kiara and Paddy with us, but I know she would be much happier living in the Acre with Bridgett and the other Irish immigrants. She has more in common with them. Not long ago I mentioned Kiara's unhappiness to Bradley and suggested he tear up their papers and give both of them their freedom. That, however, was a terrible mistake." Jasmine shivered. "His angry outburst was dreadful."

"One thing you must learn, my dear," her grandmother said carefully. "No man likes to be dictated to by his wife. You must learn more subtle ways of persuasion. Make him think it's his idea—or someone else of import. The less you try to impose or insist upon your own will, the happier you'll be."

Jasmine now fully recognized the truth of her grandmother's words. Nolan, too, had tried to caution her to do this very thing. Apparently it was advice that merited consideration.

———

To Jasmine's surprise, her first guest of the day was none other than Elinor Brighton. The young woman stood on the threshold looking much displaced—almost startled to find herself in such a position.

"Good day, Mrs. Brighton. I'm so glad you could come," Jasmine said from the foyer where she stood ready to greet her guests.

"I hadn't thought to come until the last possible moment. I'm sorry that I could send no word."

"Nonsense," Jasmine declared. "We have more than enough food and plenty of room. You are very welcome here." She again thought of the sorrow Mrs. Brighton had been forced to endure. Still, the woman appeared quite capable and strong.

"I haven't yet had a chance to offer my condolences. I am sorry for your loss. I pray God gives you strength to endure your sorrows."

Elinor stiffened and her expression grew almost ugly. "God has long since forgotten my existence—at least I hope He has, lest He suffer any more horrors upon me."

The bitter words so startled Jasmine that she actually took a step backward. "I . . . well, that is . . ."

"Jasmine, don't you look lovely," her grandmother declared as she entered the house.

Jasmine looked to the older woman's smiling face and then back to Elinor, whose countenance had once again taken on a look of serenity. For a moment Jasmine almost wondered if she'd imagined the entire episode, but a remnant of hardness around Elinor's eyes left Jasmine little doubt that the widow had spoken her harsh declaration.

Jasmine's guests began to arrive in groups of two or three, and suddenly there was no more time to consider Elinor Brighton and her feelings toward God. Jasmine did her best to greet each woman with a personal statement.

"Mrs. Harper, I heard that your sister visited last week. I pray you found her in good health."

"Mrs. Donohue, it's so good of you to come. I trust you and Liam have been well?"

Daughtie answered affirmatively and made room for the Cheevers.

"Mrs. Cheever, Violet, I'm so pleased to see you. I was so relieved to hear that little Matthew wasn't injured overmuch when he fell from the tree."

"He suffered no injury from the tree—rather his father's swift deliverance of discipline was perhaps more harsh to his backside than the ground upon which he fell," Lilly Cheever exclaimed.

Violet giggled and added, "Papa has been after Matthew forever to stay out of the trees. Matthew is an absolute reprobate, however. He never listens unless a good spanking accompanies the instruction." Jasmine tried not to cringe at the thought. She could easily recall Bradley's beating of Paddy and wanted no part of the memory. She could only pray that Mr. Cheever had not used a horsewhip in his endeavors to direct his son.

Jasmine sighed with relief as the parlor filled with even more women than had attended her previous tea. Had the turnout been poor, she knew Bradley would fault her.

Fortunately, it wasn't long before Nettie Harper spoke up. "Wilson has developed distressing stomach ailments over the past month. He says there's a new labor movement that has joined both the men and women in an unholy union against the textile industry. Those are *his* words, not mine," she quickly added.

Mary Johnson, one of the supervisors' wives, nodded in agreement. "Michael mentioned the same thing. I'd never tell my husband, but I secretly admire those women who aren't afraid to sign their names to articles being published in *The Voice*."

"What kind of articles?" Jasmine asked.

"Rather than merely publishing flowery poetry and articles filled with words of praise for their subservient role as they've previously done in *The Offering,* these girls are now stating they believe the female workers should be treated as equals to the men," Nettie explained.

"Well, I for one don't believe that's what the Bible teaches," Wilma Morgan said.

Janet Nash, wife of a supervisor at the locomotive shop, perked to attention. "I've not read in the Bible where it says men and women are to receive dissimilar pay. I believe it says a laborer is worthy of his hire. I interpret that to mean exactly what it says: a laborer should be paid a fair wage. The verse makes no mention of whether the laborer is a man or woman. If the workers are performing identical duties, they should be paid an identical wage. However, I don't believe the girls in the mills should receive the same pay as mechanics and engineers working on the locomotives being built in the Corporation's machine shops. Their work is specialized and requires training."

Mary Johnson fidgeted with her handkerchief, folding it first one direction and then the other. "Have you visited the mills, Janet? Those jobs require training. And there are workers constantly suffering injuries. If it's not a finger being snapped like a twig in one of those monstrous machines, a metal-tipped shuttle is flying across the room with the speed of an arrow and every bit as dangerous, or a girl is scalped when her hair is caught—"

"Do stop this gruesome talk," Rose Montrose interrupted.

"We could argue this issue until next week and still reach no conclusions."

"We're not arguing, Rose. We're exercising our brains by discussing an intellectual issue," Mary asserted. "I've recently read articles by acclaimed doctors who maintain we don't use our minds nearly enough."

Daughtie Donohue walked around one end of the settee and sat down beside Alice Wainwright. "And what of the Irish? They're now working in the mills. None of them, whether man or woman, is paid the equivalent wage of a Yankee mill girl. Are those who are writing articles for *The Voice* making mention of that fact? Are they arguing for the Irish to receive an equal wage, or do they find lesser pay acceptable for those born in Ireland while unacceptable only for themselves?"

Wilma puckered her lips into a bow of tiny creases. "I should have known you'd find reason to sympathize with the Irish, Daughtie. It seems you're determined to address their plight at every turn."

"I'm sorry if you've grown impatient with my pleas, but somebody needs to speak on behalf of the downtrodden, Wilma. I don't limit myself to the Irish. I'd be pleased to address the plight of the Negroes. Even their freedmen aren't permitted the smallest advantage, yet they count themselves blessed because they've broken loose from the shackles of slavery."

"We've taken up collections for those suffering from the famine. The people of Lowell contributed over four hundred dollars for the Irish." Wilma gave a satisfied nod while primly folding her hands and placing them in her lap.

Daughtie tilted her head to one side and smiled. "And I applaud that effort. But what of the Irish living right here in Lowell? And what of the slaves held against their will down South? There is much to be done, Wilma. While that collection of money is admirable, it doesn't begin to address issues that need resolution in the South and right here in Lowell."

"I know we need to do more to help the slaves," Mary chimed in. "I read an article in the Boston newspaper just last week that addressed the issue of Northerners taking a more active role in assisting runaways. While I find the concept frightening, I must admit it is also quite exciting to think of helping someone begin a new life."

"Of course, there may be those among us who don't hold with our views," Rose remarked while turning her attention toward Jasmine. "I believe you and your husband have a slave living right here in your home, don't you?"

Jasmine didn't miss the look of condemnation leveled at her from several directions around the room. She picked at the ivory silk threads embroidered into a spray of meandering flowers that decorated her dress of peach silk. "No, although I will admit she was with us for a time. Mammy was more of a surrogate mother than a slave. I don't say that to lessen the impropriety of owning slaves but rather to explain she was always well cared for. I would have preferred to free her, but *I* do not own her. She is my father's slave. Only *he* has the legal authority to set her free. However, I want all of you to know that I am opposed to slavery. I saw first-hand the poor—no, the outrageous living conditions—in the slave quarters. I had no idea." She shook her head sadly.

"I honestly grew up thinking our slaves were happy," she continued. "I saw no reason to believe otherwise. Mammy was always cheerful and loving. The slaves who worked in the house seemed content, well fed, and always had a smile. I never imagined that they maintained their positive outlooks because it was required of them rather than because of true happiness."

She looked up and met the faces of her accusers. "I saw what my father wanted me to see, and I never questioned whether it was false or true. But now I know the truth—I've seen for myself and I am deeply ashamed to have been a part of such things. I've attended a number of antislavery meetings, as some of you know, and I want to help in any way possible. My grandmother can vouch for the fact that I have embraced the concept of freedom for all men and women."

"Indeed I can," Alice put in. "Jasmine realizes the immorality and impropriety of the issue. Only last week she mentioned the possibility of forming a society to aid runaway slaves, didn't you, dear?"

Jasmine bobbed her head in agreement. "There are enough ladies present right now that we could make a list of those interested in forming such a group."

"Excellent idea! However, I think we should take care, as there are those who would betray confidences. We don't ever want to place a runaway in harm's way," Daughtie said. "Once we have a list of names, we can meet. I may know someone who can assist us with the formation of our group and let us know how we may be of help."

"I agree," Mary remarked. "There are many Northerners, especially those associated with the mills, who speak out against slavery. But in reality, what they're against is the expansion of slavery into additional states. The mills are dependent upon cotton, and cotton can't be grown without slaves."

"I only partially agree with what you've said, Mary," Daughtie replied. "I think cotton *can* be produced without slavery, but there's little doubt it will cut into the profits of the owners of both the plantations and the mills. However, I'm not certain there are many in either group willing to accept a decrease in their own pockets. I believe all of you should be sensitive to your husbands' directives concerning involvement in the antislavery movement. I would only request you prayerfully consider what role you should play in this issue and then follow your heart."

Elinor Brighton got to her feet. "Prayer will do you little good. It has been my experience that a person does better for himself by taking matters into his own hands."

Lilly Cheever came forward. "Elinor, you speak out of your pain. My heart is burdened for you, but I cannot allow you to misguide our sisters. Prayer is a vital tool, ladies. We must each one remember that. There is great power in prayer. I have no doubt in my heart that God has brought us all together in this place for this very purpose and reason.

"Many of you know me and some are less familiar, but when the mills came to this place, I fought hard against them. I was mortified that our beautiful farmlands were being stripped away to make room for horrible brick buildings. It was only through yielding my heart to God that I found any peace at all. Change is not always good, but neither is it always bad. Sometimes we must learn to live in the midst of what we hate with thoughts toward making it better."

"That is well said," Jasmine's grandmother declared. "I can assure you after making my home in the South for more years than I care to remember that working against slavery is a good thing. However, it will come at a price. Whether it be increases in prices for your lovely gowns or reductions in your husbands' salaries—sacrifices will be made. You mustn't rush into this endeavor simply because it sounds noble. This will not be an easy matter. I would admonish each of you to devote yourselves to prayer before we move forward."

Lilly nodded. "I agree."

Jasmine sank back into her chair, wondering if she'd opened Pandora's box without realizing it. Suddenly she felt afraid. What if Bradley learned that she'd instigated an antislavery society? While he may well agree with the premise, she knew he had no problem accepting the institution of slavery when it meant he would make a profit.

When the women had finally departed, Alice sat down to relax for a few moments before taking her leave. "Your social went exceptionally well, Jasmine. The ladies appeared to enjoy themselves, and the conversation was quite stimulating, don't you agree? You'll have much to discuss with Bradley."

"I don't think I'll mention the antislavery issue."

Alice wagged her head back and forth. "I see no need. Except for attending a meeting or donating funds, you'll be unable to assume involvement until after the baby is born."

"I liked Lilly's friend Mrs. Donohue. She isn't afraid to speak her mind, is she?"

Alice laughed. "No. Daughtie cares little what others think. She's a brave woman. Lilly tells me she was reared by the Shakers up in Canterbury and came to Lowell full of courage and conviction—and that has never changed. In fact, she's married to an Irishman. She cared little that many people shunned her because of her choice. Of course, most of them have now accepted her; Lilly Cheever and Bella Manning saw to that. But Lilly tells me there were some rough years."

"I must say that I admire her veracity," Jasmine said.

"As do I. And now I'd best be on my way. I meant to tell you earlier—I did post the letter to your father regarding my concerns about Bradley."

Jasmine gave her grandmother a kiss on the cheek. "Thank you, Grandmother. It's a blessing having you close at hand."

"Tut, tut, dear. That's what grandmothers are for."

CHAPTER · 22

KIARA HURRIED off toward town, pleased to be away from the Houston household, if only for a short time. There were no visible locks or bars on the doors, but the home had become her prison just the same. Although Mrs. Houston had readily agreed she could go into town for lace-making supplies, Kiara knew she must be back before suppertime. If Mr. Houston became aware of her treks into Lowell by herself, there was no doubt the mistress would suffer his wrath. Neither of them mentioned the possibility, but they both realized they would be punished for not seeking his permission. They also knew he would not grant his consent if they asked.

She'd sent word to Bridgett she'd be in town, but likely Bridgett would be at work in the mills. However, even a few minutes with her friend would be a pleasure.

Quickening her pace, she hurried into Paxton's and handed the woman the note Mrs. Houston had given her. "I'll be needin' some lace-makin' supplies," Kiara said.

Mrs. Paxton led her to the back of the store, where Kiara had first purchased supplies when she and Jasmine had come to town. "I believe I'll take this thread," she said, pointing toward a bobbin.

"Anything else?"

"No. That's all I'll be needin'."

"You can wait up front. I need to mark my ledger."

Kiara did as she was told, and a short time later, Mrs. Paxton handed over the thread along with another package securely wrapped in brown paper. "Take this to your mistress," she instructed.

"Yes, ma'am, and thank ya for yar help."

She darted out the door and glanced about. Bridgett was nowhere to be seen, but then, it was only five o'clock—too early for the end-of-day bell to be ringing.

"Kiara O'Neill! What are ya doin' in town, lass?"

Rogan Sheehan came alongside her and tipped his cap. "How're ya doin', lass? I asked Bridgett just the other day when we might be seein' ya again."

"I'm doin' as well as can be expected, I suppose. I'd rather be livin' in the Acre with my own people, but me mistress is nice enough. I don't know when I can come visitin' again. The missus lets me come whenever her 'usband is out of town. He's not kindly about grantin' favors to me or Paddy."

Rogan nodded. "Know that ya're welcome whenever ya can come. And bring Paddy with ya. He's a fine lad."

"Thank ya. Tell Bridgett I said 'ello and I'm thinkin' of her."

"That I will, lass."

"I best be hurryin' back before the master gets home."

He tugged at his cap once again and gave her a wide smile. "Ya been a bright spot in me day, lass. Take care o' yarself."

She waved and rushed off, wondering if Rogan Sheehan would think she was such a fine lass if he knew how she was forced to spend her nights. If only she could think of another place where she might hide from Bradley Houston. She'd avoided him for well over a week by hiding each night in the opening beneath the stairs. The space was small and cramped, and she knew it was only a matter of time until he discovered where she was hiding. She knew he was looking; she heard him prowling the house every night after the others were abed. He skulked about like a beast seeking its prey.

"Perhaps I could ask Sarah," she murmured.

The housekeeper had a small corner area off the kitchen with little room for anything more than her narrow bed and a small chest. But Kiara needed only a sliver of space on the floor, and she knew Bradley would never pull aside the curtain and check in the housekeeper's quarters. She wondered if the austere old woman might take pity upon her or instead rush to Bradley and report the Irish girl was making terrible accusations against him. When she delivered the package to the mistress, she would inquire if Mr. Houston would be returning to Boston soon.

Paddy came running around the side of the house as she neared the driveway. "Where ya been, Kiara?"

"Off to take care o' some business fer the missus. I've got no time fer talkin', Paddy. I got to get this package delivered."

"What's wrong with ya, Kiara? Ya're never havin' time fer me anymore. Ya're actin' angry, like I've done somethin' bad. I do na know what's made ya so unhappy with me."

Kiara tousled his black curls and kissed his cheek. "I'm not angry with you, Paddy. There's problems that go on in the house that make life difficult for me. I wish there was some way we could get out o' this place. I wish I could be workin' in the mills and live in the Acre like Bridgett."

"I'm sorry ya're so sad, Kiara. I wish ya liked it here. Except fer missin' Ma and Pa, this is the best place on earth as fer as I'm concerned."

His words tugged at her heart. "I know, Paddy, and I'm thankful fer that. Now get on with ya. I've got to take this to the missus."

He dashed off but then turned around. He hurried back and grabbed her around the waist, giving her a tight squeeze. "I love ya, Kiara."

She held him close for a moment. "And I love ya right back, Paddy O'Neill." He ran off toward the barn, and Kiara hurried into the house with her parcels.

"I've brought ya a package from Mrs. Paxton. She said ya were expectin' it." Kiara handed the parcel to her mistress and hesitated for a moment.

Jasmine held the parcel close but made no move to unwrap it. "Was there something else you needed?"

"I was wonderin' if Mr. Bradley would be goin' to Boston sometime soon?"

Jasmine appeared surprised by the question. "I don't believe he'll be going until sometime next week. Why do you ask?"

"I was thinkin' maybe I could go to visit Bridgett on Sunday if he was goin' ta be in Boston."

"Oh, I see. I think your visit will have to wait until the following Sunday. However, if Bradley should be called out of town before then, I'll be certain to let you go visiting."

"That's fine. Thank ya, ma'am."

She walked out of the room filled with a sense of despair. Spending any more time in that cramped space beneath the stairway would be unbearable. She'd have to take a chance and talk to Sarah.

After helping wash up the supper dishes, Kiara had just begun to make her way down the hallway when a hand clamped around her wrist and pulled her into the parlor and onward into Bradley's library.

He stood with his back against the closed door, his jaw flexing, his teeth clenched in anger. He pulled her against his chest, holding her tight against his body, his arm wrapped around her back. She struggled to free herself, but he grabbed her hair and yanked until her face was turned upward. He forced his mouth on hers, crushing her lips and twisting her arm until she thought it would snap in two. Her scalp ached with pain, and she wondered if he would pull every hair from her head before he was through with her.

"Where have you been hiding? I've been to your room every night, and you've been gone." His grasp on her hair tightened. "Now you listen well, girl. You be in your room when I come to you at night or your brother will be sailing for New Orleans next week to make a new life for himself on a cotton plantation. Do you understand me?"

Fear coursed through her body like a wellspring. "Yes," she whispered.

"You foolish girl. Did you think you could hide from me for the next five years?"

"Bradley? Are you in the library?"

Bradley pushed Kiara away. "I'll join you in a few minutes," he called out, his body still resting against the door. "I'll leave this door slightly ajar when I leave the room. Watch until it's safe for you to exit the other way without being seen. And remember, if anything goes amiss and Jasmine discovers our affection for each other, your brother will be gone and you'll never see him again."

Kiara stared at him in disbelief. "*Our* affection? I detest you."

He chucked her under the chin and gave a husky laugh. "I think Jasmine would believe *me* if I told her you've been attempting to steal my affections. It would be quite easy to convince her you've tried to bargain for your freedom by plying me with your favors."

Kiara remained silent until he departed the room. "Ya're the devil himself," she murmured as she watched him leave the room with his head held high.

Bradley entered the parlor with a sense of jubilation. He had Kiara in his clutches, and there was no way for her to escape. He walked to where his wife was seated, leaned down, and placed a dutiful kiss upon her cheek. "And what did you accomplish today?" he asked.

Jasmine smiled up at him. "You'll be pleased to hear that I went to visit with Lilly Cheever today. She mentioned there's a meeting of the Associates tomorrow."

"Did you think I would not already know there is a meeting, or did you believe me too senile to remember?"

She cowered at his remark. "No, but I was alarmed when she told me there is great concern because many of the mill girls are desperately ill and several have even died. She said the doctors fear there's some sort of epidemic being spread among them."

"Why are you so concerned?" he absently inquired.

"I've seen the horrible results of an epidemic. We fight malaria and suffer dire consequences almost every year in Mississippi."

Bradley glanced over his shoulder in an attempt to see if Kiara had made her way out of the library. There was work that needed his attention and he certainly didn't want to sit in the parlor with his wife for the remainder of the evening. The door remained slightly ajar and he could not make out if she had exited the room.

Following his gaze, Jasmine leaned forward and peered toward the library. "Is something amiss? You keep looking toward the other room."

"Nothing's amiss. You need not concern yourself with my every movement."

She appeared taken aback by his abrupt reply. "I understand the conditions in the mills grow poorer every day," she relayed. "I've been told the windows are nailed shut, and with the steam and humidity in the mills, the fiber-filled air becomes deadly for the girls to breathe. I wonder if the girls are becoming ill because their bodies can no longer tolerate the conditions inside the mills."

Bradley was relieved to note the library door was now open. He wanted nothing more than to escape his wife's company and complete his accounting tasks prior to tomorrow's meeting.

He rubbed the back of his neck and glowered in her direction. "Why are you meddling in matters about which you know nothing? You need to keep out of issues relating to my business."

"What? But I thought you asked me to mingle with the wives and collect information for you. I'm merely doing as you asked. It seems nothing I do can please you."

"I have no time for your childish behavior, Jasmine. I have work to complete." He stormed from the room, knowing she'd not follow after him.

He worked well into the night, transferring and calculating figures, and when he'd finally completed his report for tomorrow's meeting, he was exhausted. He climbed the stairs while giving momentary thought to Kiara. Tomorrow, he decided. He needed his rest if he was to be at his best in the morning. Besides, let her worry when and if he might enter her room.

The little tramp deserves to be sleepless after the way she's led me on a chase.

Bradley arrived at the Cheever home the next morning promptly at nine o'clock. As had been Kirk Boott's custom before him, Matthew Cheever refrained from conducting meetings within the confines of the mills. Too many people could overhear and misinterpret conversations that had never been intended for their ears. Bradley would have preferred they meet in Boston since he had other business that needed his attention in the city. However, Matthew wanted the mill supervisors present at the gathering, and traveling to Boston for a meeting was out of the question for them.

There would be no period of socializing; it was apparent this meeting would be strictly relegated to business. "As most of you know, we've a problem with illness spreading throughout the mills," Matthew began. "Several girls have died, and there's fear of other deaths. The doctors have been unable to find a cause for the epidemic. There appears to be no connection other than the fact that those contracting the illness have been, almost exclusively, girls working in the mills."

"Do the girls who have become ill live in the boardinghouses?" Leonard Montrose inquired.

Matthew shook his head. "Some live in the boardinghouses; some live elsewhere in town; some live in the Acre."

"Any chance it could be the water?" Andrew Smith, one of the supervisors, suggested.

"If it were the water, the rest of us would be ill too. It seems there must be some common thread, but for the life of me, I've been unable to make the connection."

Bradley waved and Matthew nodded for him to speak. "I was hoping we'd have time to discuss expanding several Southern markets."

"Let's stick to the topic at hand," Matthew replied. "We need to focus our attention upon discovering the cause of this illness and hopefully finding a cure."

"Perhaps we should interview the girls and ascertain all of the details related to their illness. We could then compare notes and see if we can discover the common thread Matthew spoke of," Wilson Harper remarked.

"I've located several good prospects in Mississippi as well as in Louisiana who are willing to talk contracts on their cotton," Bradley interjected.

"In light of the fact that we're attempting to solve the mystery of the illnesses and deaths of these mill girls, Bradley, I find your self-serving attitude abrasive," Leonard said.

Bradley scoffed at the remark. "Really? Well, I don't think any of you fine gentlemen were overly concerned about the girls and their illness until production slowed and your profits began to drop. Now that we're experiencing diminished profits, you've donned the cloak of kindness and wave your sword of self-righteousness in my direction. Your behavior emulates my own, whether you care to admit it or not."

"We'll resolve nothing by arguing," Matthew asserted. "Wilson, will you head up a committee to interview the ill workers?"

Wilson nodded his agreement.

"I think we need to be mindful of the fact that some of these girls have little in the way of savings," Matthew continued. "Many, both Yankee and Irish, help support their families with their earnings. Some have no families here in Lowell to help care for them, and certainly few have money to pay for funerals. I think it would behoove us to pay for medical care for the girls and, when necessary, funeral expenses."

A murmur of discontent filtered across the room. "I'm all for trying to find the cause of this illness, but I don't see why you think the Corporation should be saddled with yet another expense when production profits are already down," Leonard objected.

"The better their care, the quicker they'll return to their jobs and the sooner profits will rise," Matthew replied.

"There are more and more Irish arriving every day. All of them are looking for work, and they'll work for lower wages. I say we'd be better off to replace the sick girls with Irish immigrants," Wilson countered.

One of the supervisors stood and asked to be recognized. "No disrespect, gentlemen, but it takes time to train these girls. You can't expect a girl who has never worked in the mills to produce at the level of those who've been working there for months or even years. Production will continue to falter using such a method. I bring this to your attention because I know you'll be looking to the supervisors for answers when you've filled all the positions yet there's no increase in production."

"Exactly my point," Matthew agreed. "Medical care and funeral expenses will be money well spent in goodwill and the return of trained employees."

The men continued their bickering, and it was abundantly obvious to Bradley there would be little time for discussion of his cotton if this matter was not resolved. "I suggest we agree to medical and funeral care but require the girls to sign a covenant agreeing to return to work for a specified period of time or they'll be obligated to repay the costs. The funeral expenses can be a matter of goodwill. We can hope there will be no more deaths, but if so, perhaps you can work out some arrangement with Mr. Morrison at the funeral home, Matthew. Some type of discount for the Corporation if the number of funerals exceeds three or four in the next several months."

"A bit morbid in nature, but I think you've struck upon a good idea," Leonard replied.

In quick order the men reached a consensus. "Now, about my cotton producers," Bradley said, knowing his solution had gained him power for the moment.

———

Kiara heard Bradley's footsteps on the stairs and, like a lamb to the slaughter, knew she must submit to his will. He held her brother's future in his hands, and she could not risk separation from him. Even if she could bear five years apart from him, it would be impossible for Paddy to withstand the rigors of working on a cotton plantation. He would surely die. So she lay quietly, listening for the door to open, awaiting Bradley's arrival like a dreaded curse.

Oh, God, forgive me, she prayed as the door handle turned. *Just keep him from takin' Paddy away. I can bear anything . . . anything but that.*

"I see you have finally taken me seriously," Bradley said, slurring his words badly. No doubt he'd been into his drink this night.

"May God 'ave mercy on yar black soul," Kiara said, scooting up against the wall. "May ya rot in hell for yar sins."

He laughed even as he removed his jacket and began unbuttoning his waistcoat. "I'm already in hell," he replied. "There's nothing more God can do to me. But there's plenty more *I* can do. Especially—" he cast aside his waistcoat, then sat down on the single rickety chair and pulled at his boots—"especially to you." He grinned wickedly, his eyes narrowing.

When he finally left her room, Kiara was buried deep under the covers. Just as she had listened to him make his ascent to her room, she now heard his heavy footsteps descend the staircase. Bitter tears spilled down her cheeks and her body quaked in heaving sobs as she raised a defiant fist from beneath the covers and cried toward heaven: "Why don't ya just kill me if ya care nothin' about what's happenin' in this place? Or must I do that fer meself also? Is that what ya're wantin' from me, God—that I just kill meself and be done with it?" Memories of her mother's admonition that even thinking such thoughts could send her to hell, gave Kiara pause.

Her tears and anger slowly ebbed into the pool of darkness that permeated the room, and for the first time she contemplated death at her own hand. It would be so simple. There were many ways she could attend to the task. Yet when all was said and done, she knew such a feat would prove impossible, for that would leave Paddy alone in the world to fend for himself. And that was a consequence she'd not force him to bear. Nor did she wish to bear further consequences—not in this life or the next.

"My life is over," she whispered into the shroud of blackness. "There's no man who would ever be wantin' the likes of me now—especially a man such as Rogan, with his dreams for a future on a beautiful farm out West."

CHAPTER · 23

KIARA WATCHED in delight from the upstairs window as Bradley handed his satchel to the driver and stepped up into the carriage. Finally he would be gone, and she could go and visit Bridgett on Sunday—and perhaps see Rogan. The thought caused an unexpected smile to tug at her lips. Though she feared there'd be no future for them, Kiara took a moment's pleasure in imagining it just the same. She might as well allow herself to dream—after all, there wasn't anything else she could hope for. As soon as the carriage pulled away from the house, she hurried to Jasmine's room and knocked on the door.

"Are ya ready fer me to fix yar hair, ma'am?"

"Yes, come in."

Kiara carefully brushed and twisted her mistress's hair into the parted and curled fashion Jasmine particularly liked. "I was wonderin' if I could plan on visitin' Bridgett on Sunday."

"Oh, I'm afraid not, Kiara. Bradley will be gone only until Thursday. His plans changed. I'm so sorry. I know I had promised you could go and visit Bridgett."

"I understand. Ya've no control over such things, ma'am."

Jasmine brightened and took Kiara's hand in her own. "I know! You can go tomorrow afternoon."

"Bridgett will be at work, ma'am. I suppose I could visit with Bridgett's granna, though. If I can na see Bridgett, 'twould be nice to see Granna. Yes, I'll go and see her. Thank ya fer yar kindness."

After bidding Paddy farewell, Kiara hurried off toward the Acre the next afternoon. She knew the boy longed to come with her, but the horses would need his care, and he dared not leave them unattended.

Jasmine had asked her to stop at Mrs. Paxton's on her way home to pick up a package. She'd even given her coins for more thread since Mrs. Wainwright had already sold a lace-edged hand-kerchief to one of her socialite friends in Boston, who was now anxious for more. Kiara had carefully tucked away the money and continued diligently working on the lace during her free moments. It was only after seeing the amount of money people were willing to pay for her lace that Kiara began to think of a plan. If she could save her coins, she'd take Paddy and run from this place, servitude papers or not—she'd take her chances with the law. She'd not be able to stay in the Acre, of that she was certain, for the Acre would be the first place Mr. Houston would come looking for her. Living in the Acre with Bridgett and Granna Murphy close at hand was Kiara's desire, but with many Irish immigrants living in Boston, she could surely become acquainted with some of them. Besides, relocating to a larger city would reduce her chances of being discovered.

Kiara arrived in the Acre well before the final bell would toll at the mills. She knocked on the door, expecting to be greeted by Granna Murphy. Instead, Rogan Sheehan welcomed her with a big grin and a hearty greeting. "Come on in, lass. Granna's busy preparin' supper. How is it ya managed to make yar way to the Acre on a weekday?"

Kiara explained Bradley's change in plans. "I knew Bridgett would still be at the mills, but I thought 'twould be nice to visit with Granna, and I'm hopin' I might have a few minutes with Bridgett before I must leave."

Rogan folded his arms across his broad chest, his dark blue eyes alight with an uninhibited cheerfulness. "What a disappointment this has turned out ta be. Here I thought ya were comin' ta see me, and now I find 'tis only the womenfolk ya're wantin' to visit."

She giggled at his response. "I'm happy to see anyone with a bit o' Irish blood."

"Then ya come to the right place," Granna Murphy said while wiping her hands on a worn cotton apron. "Come over here and give me a hug."

Kiara hurried into the old woman's arms, delighting in the warmth of the embrace. "It's good to see you, Granna. I told Rogan I had hoped to come on Sunday, but it appears that won't be happenin'."

"We'll be thankful fer what little time ya get with us. Come on into the kitchen. Ya can be stayin' for supper and visit with Bridgett, and we'll have us a fine time, Sunday or not."

"I do na know if I can stay. I'm supposed to pick up a package for the missus, and I told Paddy I'd spend time with him when I came home. I wanted to leave before his chores were done, so he could na come along."

Rogan sat down on one of the wooden chairs and pushed back until he was balancing the chair on the two back legs. "Once ya think Paddy's had enough time to finish with his chores, we can go back through town and get yar supplies and then go to the house and get him. Do ya think the missus would let ya come back if ya told her I'd walk ya back home?"

Kiara's heart pounded with excitement. "I think she'd agree."

"Then it's settled. After a spell we'll go and get Paddy, and by the time we return, Bridgett will be home and supper will be ready."

"But first sit a spell and visit with me," Granna said, pointing to a chair.

Kiara sat down and pulled a piece of lace from her small tapestry bag. "I hope you do na mind if I work on my lace while we talk."

Granna's eyes danced with mischief. "Ya're an industrious

young lass. Would ya be makin' yarself a weddin' veil?"

"Ah, don' ya be givin' the lass ideas afore I get a chance to win her heart," Rogan teased.

Granna waved her arm as if to shoo him out of the room. "Go on with ya, Rogan. Ya're na lookin' for a wife."

"I'm always lookin' for a lass ta marry me, Granna. I just have na found the right one."

"And likely never will," the old woman replied. "Quit yar teasin' and let me visit with the lass." Granna turned her attention back to Kiara. "That's a pretty pattern ya're making, and fine work ya do." She lifted one edge of the lace and examined it.

Kiara smiled, basking in the compliment of the old Irish woman. "The missus asked me to make lace cuffs for her mum for her birthday. I'm wantin' them to be special. Do ya think she'll like the wild roses I've formed into the lace?"

"Sure and she'll be likin' it, lass. 'Tis a bit of beauty ya're creating. Bridgett used to like to make the lace too, but since she's begun workin' in the mills, there's nothin' much she's wantin' to do when she gets home but sleep. They're workin' long hours, and short of help they are in the mills."

"If I could be spendin' me time workin' in the mills, I'd na be complainin' about anything."

"Ah, lass, ya do na know what ya're saying. Ya have the freedom to move about and go outside when ya're wantin' to; ya can work in a fine house and not a lint-filled room with the windows nailed down—ya should na be thinkin' ya're unhappy in such a fine place."

Kiara could not share the thoughts flashing through her mind—thoughts of the five years she'd have to suffer at the hands of Bradley Houston—so she offered no rebuttal to Granna's argument.

"Aye, and now with all the girls fallin' ill, I worry that our Bridgett will get the sickness. She's worn herself down with all the extra looms she must tend, and she dare na miss a day or there's the devil to pay."

"I heard a bit o' talk about sickness in the mills when some ladies came for tea, but I was helpin' in the kitchen and did na think it was more than a few girls suffering from a stomach ailment or the sniffles. So there's more to the tale?"

"Aye, and I'm wishin' I could be tellin' ya what's causin' the illness, but it seems ta be striking workers in all of the mills. There's been three or four die, all but one of 'em Irish lasses."

Kiara gasped and covered her mouth with her open palm. "That's terrible news, Granna. It's an ill wind that's blowin' over the Irish. Seems we can na escape the cold hand of death."

"Aye, 'tis true. We're a people created fer sufferin' and that's a fact."

Rogan jumped up from his chair and ran his fingers through the thick dark fringe of curls that covered his forehead. "I'll na be listenin' ta such sorrowful talk. 'Tis a fine day, and we should be countin' our blessings instead of sittin' here and mopin' about. I'm gonna go and see if Michael O'Donnell and Timothy Clary will gather up some fiddle players, and we'll have us a time of singin' and dancin' out in the street after supper." He started toward the door and called over his shoulder, "I'll be back to fetch ya in a short time, lass."

"I think the lad's got an eye fer ya," Granna Murphy confided when Rogan had cleared the doorway.

"But ya said he's a lad with a wanderin' eye."

Granna looked up from the pot of stew she was stirring, her lips curving into a sly smile. "Aye, but when the right lass comes along, he'll settle."

"He'll likely find the right lass afore I've completed my five years of servitude, so we best quit our talkin' about 'im."

"Ya might consider visitin' the church more often and gettin' down on yar knees, lass. The Lord knows what's happenin' in yar life, and He's watchin' over ya."

"He was na watchin' over my ma or my pa when they died. And if He cared about me at all, I would na be livin' where I am. I do na think a prayer or two is gonna get the Lord on my side."

"I know ya're unhappy, lass, but do na be blamin' yar troubles on the Lord. It's the devil roamin' around causin' us misery at every turn. And ya can be sure the devil's likin' it a heap if he can keep ya from prayin'."

Rogan burst through the door, waving a fiddle in the air. "I've taken Timothy Clary's fiddle hostage and told him he'll na get it returned unless he fiddles fer us tonight."

"Ya're a rascal if ever I saw one," Granna scolded.

"Aye, that I am. Are ya ready to fetch yar supplies, lass?"

Kiara nodded and hurried to join him. She kept up with his long-legged stride, taking two steps to his one, and listened to his easy monologue regarding his life in Lowell and the Acre.

"So if it's such a fine job ya have with Liam Donohue, why are ya sittin' about at home today?" she finally asked.

He gave her a lopsided grin and her stomach flip-flopped. "Ya're full of sassy questions, ain't ya, lass? Well, I'll have ya ta know that I been workin' from dawn to late into the night for nigh unto a month now completin' a fine piece o' work, and Liam saw fit to repay me with a few days to enjoy meself. We begin work Monday on another job that will keep me mighty busy too."

"I've heard that name before," she said, thinking for a moment. "I'm thinkin' his wife was at the tea. Would that be possible? Though I do na think she was Irish."

"Aye, she's a Yank—but a fine one fer sure. I been told some of the fine folks do na like her since she married an Irishman. Liam says she has a deep faith and believes what the Bible says. He says she lives her beliefs and does na concern herself with what other people think."

"Good for her." She opened the door of Paxton's and started inside. "Aren't you coming?"

"Most of these shop owners do na like Irish inside. They don't mind when it's a lass who works for a Yank, but they'd rather the rest of us stay away. I'd rather spend my coins in the Acre anyway. Ya go on and make yar purchases, and I'll be waitin' right here when ya come out."

Kiara pulled out the note and handed it to Mrs. Paxton. "I'll go and get my thread while you fill the order," she told the store-keeper.

Mrs. Paxton was wrapping several bottles in heavy brown paper when Kiara returned with the thread. "Is that medicine you're wrapping for the missus?" she asked.

Mrs. Paxton peered over the top of her glasses and down her pointy nose. "If your mistress wanted you to know what was in the package, she would have told you instead of sending me a sealed note."

Ignoring the acerbic remark, Kiara dug into her pocket and placed several coins on the counter. "Here's fer the thread." She took up the parcel and thread and headed for the door. *Just because I'm Irish is no reason to go bein' all uppity.* She would have loved to have spoken the words aloud.

"Let me carry that fer ya," Rogan offered.

The kindness of his gesture delighted her. As she handed him the package, sadness came creeping in without warning, replacing her joy. Determinedly, she pushed it away. At least for this brief time, she would take pleasure in her life. There was no hope that she and Rogan could have a life together. He was a fine God-fearing man, and he would expect a woman of virtue and purity. She could offer him neither. Tears came to her eyes, but she swiped at them quickly and stepped up her pace. There was to be a fine Irish supper and a night of music and dance. She would have the rest of her life to regret Rogan Sheehan, but tonight she would cherish their time together.

CHAPTER · 24

KIARA LOOKED heavenward at the sound of a loud thud above her head, then raced out of the kitchen, shooting her question at Sarah. "Do ya think the missus has taken a fall?" She took the stairs two at a time and skidded to a halt in front of the closed door. She tapped lightly but didn't wait for an answer before shoving open the door.

"Missus! Oh, Mrs. Houston!" She dropped to her knees beside Jasmine, who lay in a heap alongside the bed. "Speak ta me—are ya all right?"

"Kiara, help me into bed," Jasmine said in a strangled voice.

Sarah came in the door and stopped short at the sight. "What's happened?"

"I do na know. She was on the floor when I came in. Help me get her into bed."

As gently as they could, the two of them lifted Jasmine up into bed. "She feels as though she's taken a fever." Kiara poured water into the basin sitting on the commode and dipped a cloth into the cool water. Gently placing the compress upon Jasmine's forehead, she glanced toward Sarah. "Could ya hand me that bottle on the chest, please?" She covered Jasmine with a thick quilted cover before taking the bottle from Sarah.

"Just as I thought. Dr. Horatio's Spice of Life." The bottle was nearly empty. She took a deep whiff of the contents and ran her finger around the rim of the bottle before taking a taste. "Have ya been drinkin' this?" She held the bottle in Jasmine's view.

Her eyelids fluttered. "It gives me strength," she whispered. The words had barely escaped her lips before she emitted a low guttural groan and drew her body into a tight knot. "I'm having terrible pains. I'm afraid the baby's going to come."

"Don't ya even be thinkin' such a thing. It's only September! It's much too early for the babe to be comin'."

Jasmine wet her dry lips. "It can't live if it's born this soon, can it?"

"I'll na be tellin' ya a lie, missus. There's no way it would live, so you best be stayin' put in that bed. I'm goin' downstairs and try and mix up some herbs that might be o' help. How much of this have ya been drinkin'?"

"I take a couple of spoonfuls every few hours."

"Is this all ya have left?"

"No. There's more in the drawer."

Kiara opened the bottom dresser drawer. It was filled with Spice of Life glass bottles—all empty, except for one. "How did ya get all of . . ." She hesitated a moment, suddenly realizing what she had been carrying home in the paper-wrapped packages. "Is *this* what I've been bringin' to ya every time I went to Paxton's and bought my thread?"

Jasmine nodded. "I knew you disapproved, but without the medicine, I didn't have enough energy to meet Bradley's expectations for a proper wife."

Kiara seethed at the comment. *Bradley!* Self-centered, egotistical Bradley. Mrs. Houston had played the perfect wife, entertaining at weekly teas and attending all the fashionable parties in an attempt to please him. It now seemed that losing his heir might be the price for meeting those demands.

She raced upstairs to the attic room and hurriedly clawed through one of her worn satchels until the feel of slick, cool glass greeted her fingertips. Grasping the tiny bottles in her palm, she flew down the three flights of stairs and hurried into the kitchen. She silently prayed the few herbal compounds she'd brought from Ireland would provide a panacea to counteract the effects of the elixir. Taking great care, she measured and mixed the herbs and was preparing to add warm water to a tonic she hoped would aid her mistress when Bradley caught her around the waist.

"You weren't in your room last night."

"Paddy was na feelin' well, and I went to look in on him."

"You're lying. You were hiding from me. You think I won't keep my word and get rid of the boy. I don't need to wait for a journey to Boston to send him away. I could take him to work in the mills tomorrow. There's not a supervisor who wouldn't take him off my hands and put him to work on one of those monstrous carding machines. Of course, he'd likely end up losing an arm, but since you obviously care little about what happens to him, that wouldn't bother you."

"Get away from me! Your wife is ill and I'm fixin' medicine to help her. Instead of thinkin' of yarself, ya should be worryin' over her."

He drew back his arm in a wide arc. She flinched, expecting to feel the powerful whack of his hand. Unexpectedly, his arm remained extended in the half-moon position. "What's wrong with Jasmine?" He glared down at her as though the announcement of his wife's illness had just registered in his mind.

"I'm fearin' the babe may be comin' before its time. You best be ridin' for the doctor. I do na think I'm equipped to be of much help."

He turned on his heel and ran toward the barn. Kiara prayed Paddy would be quick to saddle the horse, for she knew he'd feel the sting of Bradley's whip should he tarry. Bradley's words of warning had not been forgotten; she dared not hide again tonight. An involuntary shudder raced through her body at the mere thought of Paddy working in the mills. Having her brother spend long days around the carding machines would be fearsome enough, but with the mysterious illness now plaguing the mill workers, she didn't want Paddy anywhere near the factories. She completed mixing the potion, corked the bottles, and hurried back upstairs.

Sarah was hovering over Jasmine, her face creased in a worried frown. "I was beginning to think you were never coming back," Sarah said. She moved around the bed and edged toward the door. "I'm better in the kitchen than the sickroom, Kiara. I'll go down and make some gruel if you think it would help."

"Go ahead with ya, Sarah. I'll look after her. I'm no stranger to a sickbed. You can make the gruel. I doubt she'll eat anything today, but ya never know."

Sarah skittered out the door without a look back. Hiding in the kitchen would have been Kiara's preference too, but she knew Jasmine needed her help. She had grown fond of the young woman who had shown her nothing but kindness since the day she arrived. Why a beautiful young woman with a kind heart would marry the devil incarnate was beyond Kiara's imagination. Yet she knew Jasmine desired this baby with all her heart, so she would do everything in her power to help her.

Cradling Jasmine in one arm, she lifted her upper body. "Drink this, ma'am. It will help stop the crampin'." Jasmine swallowed the potion and sank back against Kiara's arm. "I want ya ta stay layin' on your back, and I'm gonna prop your legs on some pillows until we can get the bed raised up with some bricks. I'll have yar husband help me when he returns. He's gone to fetch the doctor."

Jasmine's eyes were glazed with pain. "Bradley knows?"

"He came into the kitchen when I was mixin' the herbs. I asked 'im to go for the doctor."

"Does he know I've been drinking the elixir?"

"I did na say anything except you were crampin' and the baby might be comin'."

"Promise you won't tell him. If anything happens to the baby, he'll think I've done this intentionally in order to cause him pain. I'll never be able to convince him I was only trying to be a good wife."

The fear in Jasmine's eyes spoke volumes to Kiara. Apparently,

Bradley Houston didn't pick and choose: he meted out his cruelty to all who crossed his path—even his own wife. Jasmine held Kiara's hand, her fingers trembling in a weak grip. "I'll not be tellin' him. Now lay back and rest."

Kiara sat by Jasmine's side, watching as the herbal remedy began to ease the cramping. Within a few hours, Jasmine's restlessness subsided, and she slipped into a deep, peaceful sleep. Kiara pulled the rocking chair close to Jasmine's bed and remained nearby, wondering why Bradley hadn't returned with the doctor hours ago. It should have taken no more than a half hour to saddle his horse and ride into Lowell. She feared the pains would begin anew before the doctor arrived. When she'd nearly given up hope, she heard the sound of approaching horses through the open window.

Dr. Hartzfeld entered the room with the confidence of a man determined to perform the job set before him. "I see she's sleeping," he said, nearing the bed.

"For at least an hour now. What took Mr. Houston so long? I thought you'd be here long before now." Her voice was filled with recrimination.

"I was delivering a baby—breech birth. I couldn't leave one woman's bedside and run to another. There were two lives in danger."

"Aye. And there's two lives in danger here too. The mistress wants nothin' to go amiss with the babe," Kiara said.

Dr. Hartzfeld pulled back the coverlet and began to examine Jasmine.

"Why don't you go downstairs and give Mr. Houston a report. He feared they both might be dead, and he didn't want to come up. Tell him I'm checking his wife and I'll talk to him once I've finished my examination."

Kiara did as requested, distancing herself from Bradley while she relayed the information. Without waiting for possible questions, she ran back upstairs, explaining she was needed to assist the doctor. She hurried into the room, closing the door behind her.

"You've done some fine medical work," Dr. Hartzfeld

complimented. "Do you know if she took a fall or what might have brought on the early labor pains?"

"Do I have yar promise ya'll not breathe a word to Mr. Houston?"

The doctor gave her a sidelong glance. "So long as there's been no foul play."

"Nothin' such so bad as that," she said, motioning the doctor to join her across the room. "Have ya heard tell of Dr. Horatio's Spice of Life?" she asked, retrieving an empty bottle from Jasmine's dresser and handing it to Dr. Hartzfeld.

"These tonics come and go. Many people take them."

"Aye, but I think this one contains somethin' more than the usual whiskey and water. I tasted a bit of it, and I think it contains a poison herb. I used a concoction I knew helped counteract the effects, and it seems to be workin' on the missus."

The doctor's face twisted into a scowl. "And how would *you* know about poison herbs?"

Kiara met his gaze with dogged confidence. "There was them that mixed up evil brews in Ireland, sayin' it would rid ya of the devil. O' course, it did na work because them that took it needed health-givin' herbs, not poison. Mrs. Houston's been takin' this tonic for several months, hopin' it would give her energy. I think the poison has been buildin' up inside her."

The doctor stroked his graying beard. "Possible, possible," he muttered.

Encouraged by his remark, Kiara continued. "While I waited fer ya to get here, I was thinkin' that maybe this tonic is what's makin' the girls in the mills sick. I've heard they take it to give them enough energy to keep up with their work. I even heard talk the Corporation was furnishin' it for them so they'd work faster. 'Course, I do na know if that's true. But I'm thinkin' if the tonic could make me mistress sick enough to take to her bed, it surely could be the cause of them girls getting' sick and dyin'."

Dr. Hartzfeld slapped his hand on his knee. "I believe you just may have happened onto something. I'll go and talk to the mill supervisors and see if they can ascertain how many of the sick girls have been taking the elixir. Possibly the families or friends of the girls who died will know if they were using the tonic. Excellent deductions, girl."

"And what of me mistress?"

"Hard to tell. If I were a gambling man," he speculated, "I'd have to bet against the baby making it, but if she'll remain in bed and take care of herself, there may be a chance. She'll need constant care."

"I can care for her."

"I'll tell Bradley of her need to remain bedfast and mention your willingness to care for Mrs. Houston. You'd be the best choice with your abilities. You've no doubt saved her life today." Dr. Hartzfeld strode to the bedroom window and looked down. "Mrs. Wainwright is here. Bradley stopped to tell her of Jasmine's difficulty as we were leaving town. I'm not surprised to see her. She was distraught when she heard the news. I'd best go downstairs and talk with them."

Kiara remained behind to watch over her mistress, and before long she could hear Dr. Hartzfeld explaining Jasmine's condition. Soon after, the three of them entered the bedroom, and Alice Wainwright rushed to her granddaughter's bedside.

"I've explained your willingness to care for Mrs. Houston," Dr. Hartzfeld said.

"And we are most grateful," Alice added. "I think it would be best if we placed a cot in the room for Kiara. That would permit her to be with Jasmine around the clock. After all, we don't want her alone for a minute, do we?" She looked toward Bradley.

"Jasmine certainly needs care, but I don't know that she needs Kiara sleeping in here at night," he replied. "If she looks in on her several times throughout the night, that should be sufficient."

"Foolishness and stuff, Bradley! That makes no sense. Kiara would get no rest popping up and down throughout the night, and Jasmine might begin cramping at any time. A cot in this room for Kiara is the only way to proceed."

Bradley nodded. "You're right. I'll see to it immediately."

Kiara glanced heavenward. Perhaps God had seen her plight, heard her prayers, and was having mercy after all.

CHAPTER · 25

SLOWLY, AS THE weeks passed and October gave way to November, Jasmine regained her strength. The combination of removing Bradley's stressful social requirements from her schedule, along with eliminating Dr. Horatio's Spice of Life from her daily regimen, was working wonders. And the time with Jasmine was a blessed relief for Kiara.

The women spent hours talking, with Jasmine stitching her needlepoint while Kiara fashioned her lace into delicate three-dimensional pendants of butterflies, grape clusters, and nodding daffodils that she attached to black velvet ribbons to be worn instead of jewels around the neck. Captivated by the creations, Alice Wainwright had worn one of the designs to the Governor's Ball, which had been held in Boston several weeks previous. She had returned from Boston, delighted to tell Kiara that Sophia Dallas, the vice-president's wife, was in attendance and had been so impressed with her skill she requested five sets of lace cuffs. Kiara had been hard at work on the project, though truth be known, she made more money creating the small pendants. And money was what she needed if she was to accomplish her goal and get out of Bradley Houston's clutches.

There was little doubt that once the babe arrived, she'd be

relegated back to the attic to do his evil bidding. However, by then she hoped to have enough money to take Paddy and run off to Boston. Her greatest blessing was in knowing that she had not conceived by Bradley. It would have been impossible to explain a pregnancy, and no doubt Bradley would have forced her to do something awful to rid herself of the child. She could never imagine thanking God for making her barren, but at this moment that was exactly the praise she offered.

Once I've saved enough money, Paddy and I will head to Boston. No one knows us there and our own people will be more than willing to protect us.

"You're very quiet this morning," Jasmine said, giving her a cheerful smile.

Kiara smiled in return but said nothing. Her thoughts were on the future, but she could not share those ideas with her mistress.

"Bradley was required to make a trip to Boston this morning. He came in to bid me farewell while you were dressing in the other room. He was in an agitated state when he departed, although it seems he's unhappy most of the time. I'm certain much of his unpleasant temperament has to do with my confinement. Likely he'll be fine once the baby comes."

"There's somethin' I've been wantin' to ask ya, ma'am, but if ya do na want to answer, just tell me."

Jasmine grinned at Kiara. They'd become as close as sisters since the doctor had ordered Jasmine to remain abed. "I've told you everything about my life, Kiara. Surely you know there's nothing you can't ask me. We're friends."

"Ya've told me about how ya were forced to marry Mr. Houston, but I'm wonderin' how ya manage to live with a man who is so . . ."

"Sour?"

"That was na exactly the word I was searchin' fer, but it'll do."

Jasmine stabbed her needle into the fabric and met Kiara's gaze. "Even before I married Bradley, I was angry at being forced into a loveless marriage. Then as time passed and I could not please him, I thought God had turned His back on me."

"Sure and I know that feelin'."

"Do you remember the Sunday when Bradley was out of town and I told you I wanted to go early and attend church with Grandmother?"

"Aye. The driver took me and Paddy to St. Patrick's that mornin'."

Jasmine nodded her head. "That morning the preacher's sermon was on several verses from the book of Job. It was as though the sermon had been written just for me. I had become angry with God, blaming Him for my circumstances, but ever since I heard that sermon, I've attempted to apply the principles to my life. I've grown closer to God, even though my marriage has not improved."

"What was it that preacher told ya that made such a difference?" Kiara asked, leaning forward.

"He said our suffering and pain does not come from God because God's character and nature is love. Our woes come from Satan, but God sometimes uses our trials so we will seek Him because He desires a closer relationship with us. He explained that through all of Job's suffering, he continued to trust God. Because of Job's trust and faithfulness, God greatly blessed the remainder of Job's life.

"I'm trusting that God has a plan to bless my life and that I will be happy. Who knows? Perhaps this baby will bring us together and we will find happiness as a family."

Kiara gave her a sidelong look. "Perhaps. And for your sake, I hope that's true. But I do na see why people must suffer so much when God could cause it to come to an end."

"I know. None of us want to go through difficulties, but living with Bradley has made me a stronger person, yet more dependent upon God."

"Ya're stronger, but ya're weaker? That does na make much sense."

"I know my words sound like a contradiction, but being dependent on God is a strength, not a weakness. It's through trusting Him we finally become spiritual warriors, able to withstand the difficulties that come our way."

"I'm na lookin' to be a warrior, ma'am. I'd settle on just lettin' someone else take a few of the arrows that've been directed me way."

Jasmine's lips curved into a sympathetic smile. "Grandmother challenged me to begin reading my Bible every morning and spending time with God before I begin my day. Of course, now that I've been abed so long, it hasn't been difficult. Would you like to read with me in the mornings?"

Kiara looked down at the floor. "I'm na so good at readin'."

"I could read aloud if you like."

"Aye. That would be fine. Ya can read to me about Job, and I can hear firsthand what kind of blessin's he got for all that sufferin'."

"Job it is. We'll begin tomorrow morning. Kiara, I know you're unhappy here, but having you with me during this time has brought me great joy. I want you to know that if I could grant you and Paddy your freedom, I would do so."

"Thank ya fer thinkin' kindly of Paddy and me. 'Twould be a miracle for certain if we could go and live in the Acre."

"After all our talks regarding my desire to help free slaves in the future, you know I don't believe in slavery. And I don't see a great deal of difference between slavery and servitude. I'm going to try to find some way to convince Bradley to release you from your papers. It may take some imagination, but surely I can think of something."

"Don't do nothin' that would cause his wrath. I'd never fergive myself if somethin' happened because ya were arguing for me freedom."

Jasmine angled her gaze at Kiara. "I know Bradley has a foul temper and he's struck Paddy on occasion. Has he ever hit you?"

Kiara shook her head. "Are ya going to keep on with the antislavery meetin's after the babe's born?" she asked.

Jasmine's eyes brightened. "Yes. As much as I can, but I can't let Bradley know, and with the baby, it will be more difficult."

Pleased her mistress appeared oblivious to the change in topic,

Kiara picked up a bobbin of thread from her bag. "I'd be proud to help ya if there's any way I can be of assistance. Even if it's just watchin' after the wee babe while ya're busy helpin' with the run-aways."

"Thank you, Kiara. You've become the dearest friend I could ever hope for. Now let me see that new design you're working on."

Kiara held up the piece of lace and wondered what Mrs. Houston would think if she discovered what had happened in the attic room. Would Jasmine believe Bradley had come to her against her will? Or would she believe her husband's lies? Perhaps if Kiara would trust like Job, her mistress would never learn the truth.

Jasmine examined Kiara's workmanship, her fingers tracing the delicate petals of the lace rose. "It's lovely," she said, extending the piece toward Kiara.

Suddenly she leaned forward with a gasp and emitted a shrill cry. "I think the baby is coming! My water has broken." Her eyes reflected the odd combination of fear, pain, and elation that expectant mothers experience when birth is imminent.

"I'll send Paddy fer the doctor and be back before ya have a chance to miss me."

Her sturdy leather shoes barely touched the floor as she raced down the steps and ran outside to the barn. While Paddy saddled the horse, she gave him detailed instructions. "If the doctor is busy, do na wait for him. Tell him of our need and then come back and tell me so I'll na be sittin' here thinkin' somethin' has happened to ya. I'll go ahead and deliver the babe myself if ya can na bring the doctor."

"Aye," the boy replied. He swung himself up into the saddle and was off and down the driveway before Kiara reentered the house.

Sarah met her at the back door, her eyes wide with fear. "The mistress is calling for you. She's begun her labor. I went up there, but you know how I am with sickness."

Kiara nodded as the two of them walked toward the stairway. "I know, Sarah, but this is a babe bein' born, not a sickness. If you can na bear to be upstairs, at least stay where you can hear me should I need to call fer yar help."

Sarah's complexion turned the shade of day-old ashes. "I'll be down here praying—both for the mistress and for you."

Kiara grinned. "Ya might want to add a prayer fer yarself—that I'll not be needin' yar help."

Sarah dropped into a chair in the foyer, her body slumped into an abject heap. "Paddy's gone for the doctor?"

"Yes. He should return soon. And there's yet another prayer fer ya. Pray the doctor is na busy with another patient."

When Kiara returned upstairs, she carried string, scissors, clean sheets, and blankets. By then, Jasmine was writhing in pain. "I think it's close to time."

"It's much too soon. Ya've only just begun yar pains. Can ya roll on yar side, and I'll change the bed and get ya more comfortable. Sure and I'm glad we put that oilcloth on the bed last week," she said in a soothing voice.

Jasmine cooperated with Kiara's ministrations, and by the time the bedding had been changed, Dr. Hartzfeld was entering the room. He carried his black leather medical bag in one hand and his top hat in the other. "I was surprised to see Paddy," he said. "I thought it would be at least another week or two before the baby came. Let's check and see how you're progressing."

Two hours later, Jasmine's baby boy fought his way into the world and, with a lusty cry, announced his arrival. "He's a big, healthy boy," Dr. Hartzfeld announced. "Too bad Bradley isn't here to see his son."

"He should be home within a day or two," Jasmine replied while glancing down at the cherub-cheeked infant. "Hello, Spencer," she cooed while running her fingertips through the baby's downy-soft brown hair.

"Spencer? Is that the name you've chosen?" the doctor inquired.

"Yes. Bradley said the child was to be his father's namesake."

Dr. Hartzfeld chuckled. "Then I'd say it's a good thing you had

a boy. Can't imagine a little girl running around with that moni-
ker."

"Nor I," Jasmine agreed, returning his smile.

Kiara listened to the baby's lusty cry and felt awash in sadness.
Would she ever know the joy of such a moment? She backed away
from the scene, knowing she was imposing and no longer needed.

Bradley walked out of his Boston hotel and hailed a passing
carriage. The Associates had called a meeting, one that would be
held at the Beacon Hill home Nathan Appleton had recently constructed. Although Nathan had finally succumbed to his wife's
request for a home in the posh neighborhood, he'd not given in
to an elaborate edifice. In fact, the house was, by Beacon Hill standards, somewhat common. When he'd seen the return address on
the envelope, he thought perhaps the Appletons were hosting an
open house to celebrate the move into their new home. Instead,
the contents had been a rather ominous-sounding notification that
all members were expected to be present for the meeting in order
to discuss several critical issues.

The message had given him brief concern, but he soon
decided there might be talk of further expansion. If so, those
favoring such action would want a quorum present in the event
the matter could be taken to a vote. Expansion was a fine idea—
they'd need more cotton to operate additional mills. He leaned
back and rested his head against the supple leather of the carriage
seat. Between Jasmine and Kiara, his life had grown increasingly
complicated and unsatisfying. He'd been unable to accomplish
work of any consequence since the day Kiara had moved into his
wife's room to care for her. From his observations, they were
becoming much too friendly, and the possibility of Kiara revealing
the details of his secret visits to her attic bedroom loomed large in
his mind. Instead of concentrating on his work, he obsessed over
the prospect—not wanting to admit fear now consumed him.

As a stern-faced servant took Bradley's coat and hat, he noticed
that the Appleton residence was brimming with members who

were making their way from the dining room into the library. It was obvious he had been intentionally excluded. He hadn't misread the meeting notice; the words had been far too ill-omened. Since there were no other members presently arriving, he wondered if he had been the only member banned from the dinner party. The prospect was disquieting, but he attempted to remain calm.

Intentionally, Bradley wended his way through the gathering and approached Nathan. "Good evening, Nathan. I trust you've had an enjoyable dinner."

"Indeed we have," Nathan replied. "If you'll excuse me, I must speak to Matthew before commencing the meeting." Without explanation, he turned and walked away.

Bradley searched the room for a friendly face. Either his paranoia was taking root, or those in attendance were intentionally avoiding his company. There seemed to be no one interested in making contact with him. He spotted Robert Woolsey near the fireplace and advanced.

"Robert! Good to see you," Bradley said, forcing a smile and clapping him on the shoulder.

"Good evening, Bradley." Robert moved back a step, his discomfort obvious as he inched away. "I was hoping to have a word with Josiah, if you'll excuse me."

"That's fine. I'd like to visit with Josiah also," Bradley said, unwilling to permit his captive's escape. Robert had always been an ally, and right now Bradley needed the support of a comrade. At this point in time he cared little whether the patronage was zealous or reluctant. He would accept any modicum of alliance. "Was the dinner to your liking?"

"Quite enjoyable."

"I must have misread my notice. I didn't recall reading about dinner preceding the meeting."

"That's too bad," Robert said as he drew near to Josiah. "Josiah, I was wondering if I could have a word with you in private."

Josiah gave Bradley a sidelong glance and then turned his

attention to Robert. "Of course. I doubt whether Nathan would mind if we stepped into his office for a few moments. Excuse us, Bradley."

Bradley watched as the two men walked out of the room. There was little doubt they had intentionally escaped his presence. Each time he approached a group of members, they stepped aside. His walk through the room resembled Moses parting the Red Sea.

When the meeting was called to order, Bradley found himself sitting alone. Although he was surrounded by empty chairs, several men stood in the back of the room rather than take a seat beside him. It was abundantly clear that he had committed an offense. When Nathan took charge of the meeting, Bradley knew his behavior would be the topic of this evening's meeting. Matthew never handled matters dealing directly with an individual Associate.

"We need to have some important questions answered this evening—questions that are affecting the business and our profits. I believe you're the person to give us the answers we need, Bradley."

Bradley's muscles tightened into a knot. He gave what he hoped was a nonchalant nod.

"Cotton deliveries have diminished considerably. You've given no explanation for the reduction, though you surely must have realized this decrease would be of grave concern to all of us. I am at a loss as to why you've not brought this matter to someone's attention." Nathan paused for a moment. "Would you care to explain?"

The hairs on the back of Bradley's neck stiffened as the members directed their attention to him. He needed time to formulate an answer. He didn't even realize shipments had decreased. Why hadn't Malcolm notified him if there was a problem? His mind was racing. He thought of the letters that lay unopened on his desk, letters from his father-in-law that he'd pushed aside because his thoughts were centered upon Jasmine and Kiara—not upon business. Jasmine! *She* would be his explanation.

"I don't know if you are aware, but my wife has experienced

great difficulty with her health over the last several months. She's been confined to her bed, and my time has been devoted to her care. Although I've had hired help with her, it's me whom she desires by her bedside. And what husband can turn away from his wife in her time of need? I pray your indulgence, gentlemen. If you had come to me previously, I would have forced myself back to work. I didn't realize the shipments had slowed and will check my latest correspondence for any answer I can find from our Southern growers."

"You can hardly fault a man for taking time to care for his ill wife," Henry Thorne said. "Bradley is correct that none of us spoke to him. We had an obligation to call this matter to his attention before it spiraled into such a severe decline. Communication is the key, gentlemen, and it must go both directions."

Bradley wanted to jump up from his chair and shout his thanks to Henry. Instead, he was the model of restraint and self-deprecation. "Thank you, Henry, but even with the heartrending circumstances that have created a pall of sadness over my household, I should have been alert to my business obligations. What I've done is inexcusable, and I can't expect your forgiveness when my ineffectiveness has adversely impacted the business."

"None of us is immune from such events occurring in our own lives," another member agreed. "I can't fault a man for unbearable worry over his wife and unborn child."

Since the winds were blowing favorably in Bradley's direction, he decided it might bode well for him to add a few morsels of information in order to redirect the conversation away from himself. "I can share that shortly before my wife was forced to take to her bed, my father-in-law had reported many of the plantations were beginning to experience difficulties with their slaves due to the increasing abolition movement. However, he thought the problem would soon be under control."

"We must hold fast to our beliefs, gentlemen," another member admonished. "We can quietly assume a position against the expansion of slavery into other states, but we must be careful not to alienate our Southern suppliers. We need their cotton, and if it takes slave labor to meet our needs, so be it."

The men argued the issues of tariffs, slaves, and strikes within the mills while Bradley's mind skittered back to the unopened letters from Malcolm Wainwright. He wondered if those letters would reveal the answers his fellow Associates were seeking. After several hours had passed, he could abide the suspense no longer.

When a brief pause in the discussion occurred, he stood. "If I could be so bold as to beg your indulgence one more time, gentlemen, I have several matters of business that I wish to complete this evening. If I am able to do so, I will return to Lowell tomorrow morning to be at my wife's bedside."

"Of course, Bradley," Nathan responded. The remainder of the assembled group murmured their assent, while several men offered words of encouragement for his wife's speedy recovery as he was making his way out of the room. He took a deep breath of fresh air, momentarily marveling he'd been able to survive the meeting without receiving threats of an ouster from his position within the prestigious group. No doubt he would have to set matters aright in short order. He hurried back to the hotel. Malcolm's letters were in his satchel of business papers and would likely shed light on the decreased shipments.

"Bradley!"

Scanning the hotel foyer, Bradley saw his brother striding toward him. "Nolan. How are you?" he asked, continuing to move toward the hotel staircase.

"I'm fine. What an unexpected surprise to see you. Come join me for a glass of port."

"I'd like to, but I've several matters needing my immediate attention. Perhaps some other time."

"Is Jasmine faring any better? I'm hoping to visit within the week. From the tone of her last letter, she seemed to be enjoying the little Irish girl's company."

Bradley stopped in his tracks and turned to face his brother. "Jasmine has written you?"

"We correspond on occasion. Why does that surprise you? After all, I spent a great deal of time with Jasmine and

Mrs. Wainwright when we journeyed to Mississippi. Jasmine even sends me an occasional poetic offering for evaluation. At the same time, she usually informs me of what's happening in Lowell and adds a bit of personal information regarding the two of you. Why, if I had to depend upon you, I wouldn't even know of the impending birth of your child."

"You know I've never been one to discuss personal matters."

Nolan laughed and slapped his brother on the shoulder. "I don't think you'd be considered too much the gossipmonger if you revealed to your own brother that he was going to become an uncle. With your consuming desire for an heir, I didn't expect there would be anything that could entice you away from Lowell until after the baby's birth."

Bradley continued edging toward the stairway. "Urgent meeting of the Associates. I have some matters to conclude yet this evening, then I'll be returning to Lowell first thing in the morning—which is exactly why I cannot join you for a glass of port and further conversation."

"Of course. I don't want to detain you. Give my regards to Jasmine and tell her I hope to see her soon."

"Yes, of course," he said, taking the steps two at a time. He slipped his key in the lock, and by the flickering light of an oil lamp, slit open the first of two letters from Malcolm. Thumbing through the pages, he scanned the letter until his gaze settled upon words that sent a chill rippling down his spine. He began to read aloud: "We have received devastating rains in this part of Mississippi, and they could not have come at a worse time. Just as we were preparing to begin our first harvest, the rains came. Consequently we are suffering from boll rot, and our shipments will be reduced throughout the next month. Please advise how we may assist you with this problem. The possibility exists to seek help from other growers in Louisiana and Alabama, as their crops did not suffer from the heavy rains. We anticipate our crop will return to normal for our later shipments, as the remainder of our crop was planted at a later date."

Bradley threw aside the missive and opened the second. His

breath caught in his throat. When he thought the news could be no worse, he read Malcolm's final paragraph: "I will be in Lowell for a visit and hope to lend assistance wherever needed and of whatever nature upon my arrival."

Bradley read the paragraph more slowly and began mentally calculating the length of Malcolm's voyage. His father-in-law would arrive within the week, and it appeared he was planning a somewhat extended visit. This unexpected intrusion was yet another vexing tribulation he must resolve. Not that Bradley feared his ability to handle his father-in-law, but he preferred such matters be on his own terms. However, Malcolm had taken matters into his own hands, and now Bradley had little time to prepare.

He folded the letter and placed it in his satchel. "You may be coming for a visit, Malcolm, but you'll be returning home quickly," he muttered.

CHAPTER · 26

JASMINE HEARD the heavy footsteps on the stairway and knew Bradley had returned home. His eyes burned with expectation as he searched her face for a clue. She hadn't seen him appear so excited since their vows had been sealed. "Our son has arrived!" Her voice bubbled with delight as she expectantly awaited his reaction.

"A boy!" Bradley exclaimed. "But of course I knew I would have a son."

"Of course. The wee babe would be feared of comin' into the world any other way," Kiara muttered.

"Did you say something, Kiara?" Jasmine inquired.

"Just commentin' on the beauty of the child, ma'am. Lucky he is to be lookin' like you."

Bradley shot a glowering look in Kiara's direction. "Bring my son to me."

Kiara did as she was ordered and lifted the infant from where he slept. Bradley formed his arm into a large semicircle to receive the child. She looked heavenward and shook her head back and forth. "Push yar arm in. The babe will fall to the floor if ya keep yar arm spread open like that." She pushed Bradley's arm closer to his body, forcing it into a cradling position before settling the baby into his arm.

Bradley stared down at the child and then looked back and forth between the two women in the room. "His name is Spencer, and I believe he looks like me." His gaze settled on Kiara. "I'm certain Jasmine no longer needs your continued assistance. I'll have your cot removed from her room later today."

"I don't believe that's a good idea just yet," Alice said as she entered the bedroom. "Jasmine remains quite weak, and it won't hurt to have Kiara close at hand to help with the baby."

"Grandmother Wainwright. I didn't know you had arrived," Bradley said.

"I wouldn't have missed this event for anything. I left home only moments after the doctor arrived to deliver the baby and haven't departed since. I'm sorry you couldn't be here for the birth, Bradley. It would have been comforting to Jasmine had you been home for the birth of your first child."

Bradley handed the infant back to Kiara and turned his attention toward his wife. "The baby was not expected for another two weeks, and Jasmine completely understands the rigors of my business. I hurried home as quickly as I could. You understand, don't you, my dear?" Without waiting for an answer, he continued. "I have a bit of good news to share with both of you, one you will both be pleased to receive. Malcolm will be arriving within the week, and I'm certain he'll be surprised to learn of his grandson's birth."

"Really? How wonderful! When did you learn of Father's arrival? He didn't mention it when he last wrote—of course, that's been some time ago."

"I must admit he wrote some time ago and I mislaid the letter. Thankfully, I found it in my desk at the shipping office while I was in Boston, or his arrival would have taken us all by surprise."

His laugh sounded hollow, and Jasmine thought she had noted a strain in Bradley's voice when he announced her father was arriving. But perhaps it was the excitement of the baby's early arrival. She wanted this to be a time of happiness and healing. A time when they could come together and form a closer union—if not for themselves, then for the baby.

She smiled up at her husband. "Having Father here to see the baby will be joyous. I only wish Mother could make the voyage."

Alice patted Jasmine's arm and smiled. "Be thankful for at least this much, dear. I'm certain Bradley will be anxious to take you and the baby to Mississippi once Spencer is a little older."

Jasmine clapped her hands. "Oh, Bradley, do you think we might do that? The baby might be just the thing to bring Mother out of her sad reverie."

"I think it will take more than seeing a baby to bring your mother back to a state of reality," Bradley absently replied.

"That was uncalled for, Bradley," voiced Alice. "Your wife is recuperating from childbirth, and she needs your encouragement, not a callous rejoinder."

"We'll consider a visit when Spencer is older." He leaned down and brushed a kiss upon Jasmine's cheek. "I must go downstairs and attend to business matters. I'll come back up to see you later in the day."

"Of course. I don't expect you to spend all your time sitting here with us. I understand you must tend to business."

The three women were silent until Bradley's footsteps could be heard crossing the downstairs foyer. Alice closed the bedroom door and sat down beside Jasmine's bed. "It appears your father saw the seriousness of matters and is finally going to make an appearance. I couldn't be more pleased. His visit will be doubly blessed when he sees little Spencer."

Jasmine smiled and squeezed her grandmother's vein-lined hand. "You don't think Father will make mention that you've written and requested he visit?"

"No, I warned him Bradley must not know we've interfered. And your father obviously has concerns of his own. I don't think the plantation owners have been receiving prompt payments for their cotton."

Kiara moved closer to Jasmine's bedside and pointed back and forth between the two women. "Ya wrote to Mr. Wainwright and told 'im to come here to question Mr. Houston?"

Jasmine observed the disbelief—or was it fear?—in Kiara's eyes. "Don't worry. Having Father visit will be a good thing. Bradley has been terribly overworked throughout our marriage, and the stress appears to be taking its toll on him. Grandmother and I thought Father might be able to advise Bradley on how to relieve himself of some of his duties."

"I do na think yar husband will be pleased if he should find out ya've interfered. He's a proud man."

"Don't look so worried, Kiara. Father will be discreet in handling Bradley."

"I hope so, ma'am. I do na want to see anyone suffer should Mr. Houston lose his temper."

Alice gave Kiara an endearing smile. "You worry overly, my dear. I think what you need is some time to relax and enjoy yourself. You've been in this room around the clock for weeks. Why don't you go and visit your friend Bregetta and—"

"Bridgett," Jasmine corrected.

"Oh yes. Why don't you visit your friend Bridgett, and I'll look after Jasmine?"

Kiara checked the time. "She gets off work a little earlier on Saturdays." There was a hesitation in her voice.

"She should be home soon. If you leave now, the two of you could arrive at the Acre around the same time. Do go and have a time of relaxation," Jasmine encouraged. "You've been with me constantly, and you need to get outside. A change of scenery will do you good."

"I do na think Mr. Houston will be pleased should he find out I've gone."

"No need for us to tell him. If he comes to the room, I'll tell him I've sent you on an errand." Alice pulled several coins from her reticule. "Please stop by Paxton's and pick up some additional thread. I don't want you to have any excuse to quit making your lace."

Kiara smiled and took the coins. "Ya're also not wantin' to tell a lie."

Alice returned the smile. "That's true. Now off with you and have a good time."

———

Kiara peeked over the railing before tiptoeing down the stairs and could see the illumination of light beneath Bradley's library door. She flattened herself against the wall and edged down the side of the hallway where the floorboards didn't creak. Without a sound, she made her way into the kitchen.

Before Sarah could offer a greeting, Kiara placed a finger to her lips and shook her head. She made her way to the table and whispered, "I do na want Mr. Houston to know I'm leavin'. Mrs. Houston and Mrs. Wainwright gave me permission to go into town, but 'tis better if he does na know."

Sarah smiled. "Have a nice time," she whispered back. "What should I tell Paddy if he comes looking for you?"

"Tell him I'll come to the barn later but to say nothin' to Mr. Houston."

Kiara slipped out the door and was thankful for the cover of darkness. She half walked, half ran into town, deciding to stop at Paxton's before going to the Acre. The final bell hadn't rung and Bridgett wouldn't yet be home. Besides, stopping now would save time on her return. She hastened down the aisle, picked up a bobbin, and walked to the counter at the front of the store.

"I hear tell the Houstons have a fine baby boy."

"Aye, that they do," Kiara replied. "Both mother and babe doin' fine." The clanging of the final bell could be heard, announcing the day's end for the mill workers.

Mrs. Paxton greeted two customers as they entered the store, taking time to tell them of the store's latest arrival of bonnets and gloves. Kiara wished she would hurry, for Bridgett would be home any minute.

The customers stopped at a nearby display case, gazing down at an assortment of hatpins and jewelry. "I'm surprised Bradley Houston isn't at home this evening. I thought he'd be spending time with Jasmine and the baby when he finally arrived home."

Kiara listened while keeping her eyes forward. "Mrs. Hartzfeld mentioned he was out of town when the baby was born, but men have their business matters that require attention. You can't fault him for being dedicated to his work."

"I suppose not, but it's not as though he doesn't have servants who could take care of his errands."

"Oh, look at that locket. I believe I may have to purchase it. Mrs. Paxton, could you show me this locket when you finish there?"

"Of course," the store owner replied. She handed Kiara her change and the bobbin of thread.

Kiara clutched the bobbin in her hand, now afraid to leave the store. If what those women said was correct, Bradley Houston was somewhere nearby. What if he saw her?

"Was there something else you needed, Kiara?" Mrs. Paxton inquired.

"What? Oh no. I'm just leavin'. Thank ya." She had no choice but to depart.

Her hand trembled as she opened the door. She longed to silence the jingling bell, which announced to all nearby that someone was either entering or exiting the business. She prayed Bradley was nowhere in the vicinity, for surely the light from the store would illuminate her as she left the building. She looked down the street and saw only a small boy running with his dog and a number of carriages. Kiara bent her head, pulling her shawl around her face.

Nearing the Acre, she sighed in relief. She'd heard no footsteps and seen no carriage following her. Apparently she'd been overworking her imagination. Bradley had likely returned home. "I will na allow him to ruin my time in the Acre," she murmured before knocking on the door of Granna Murphy's hovel.

"Kiara! Come in. What a lovely surprise it is ta see ya." Bridgett's eyes sparkled as she pulled Kiara inside. "How did ya manage to get away from the house?"

By the time she'd explained the latest events of the Houston household, Granna Murphy was standing beside her with a wooden spoon in her hand. "I'm expectin' ya to stay for supper, lass, and I'll na be takin' kindly to the thought of ya walkin' out the door without first sittin' down to the table with us."

Kiara hesitated. "I do na . . ."

Before she could complete her refusal, Rogan burst through the door like the sunshine on a dreary day. "Good evenin' to ya," he said, his gaze circling the room and then resting upon Kiara's face. "What've we here? A lovely visitor from the other side o' town? Pleased we are to be havin' such a fine lady in our midst." He bowed from the waist and swept his cap in front of him in a grand gesture. "I see ya're joinin' us for supper," he said, pointing toward the extra plate Granna Murphy had just placed on the table.

Kiara gave him an embarrassed grin. "Aye. I thought 'twould be good for me to have the taste of cabbage and potatoes on me lips again."

He gave her a hearty laugh. "Sure and we'd be pleased to oblige ya. I'm thinkin' ya must get mighty tired of that fancy food they serve in that fine house where ya're livin'." They all sat down to partake of the meager fare. Rogan issued a quick prayer of thanks and then turned his attention back to Kiara. "And what's this I hear but that it's Kiara O'Neill we have to be thankin' for discoverin' what was makin' the mill workers sick?"

Bridgett nodded in agreement. "Dr. Hartzfeld's been tellin' everyone 'twas you who figured out the elixir was makin' the girls sick. Folks here in the Acre are callin' ya a hero."

"I'm no hero, but glad I am that folks will no longer be takin' that mixture and makin' themselves sick."

Although Kiara attempted to help clear the table and wash dishes, Granna pushed her off to the other room to visit with Bridgett and Rogan. Bridgett excused herself to go and retrieve her mending, and Kiara turned her attention to Rogan. "So what of yar family, Rogan? Are any of them living in this country?"

"My family's all gone to be with the Lord. I'm the only Sheehan to survive the famine. I worked hard, hopin' to supply them with fare for their passage, but 'twas too little, too late. Starvation took them afore I could earn enough money to help. When they went home to be with the Lord, I vowed that so long as there was breath in me body and trust in God, no one I loved would ever go hungry again. I'm thankful God gave me the chance to help Bridgett with her passage, fer it took some of the pain away being able to help her get here."

"So ya *still* trust in God?" Kiara meekly questioned.

"Aye. O' *course* I do. We can na be turnin' our back on God just because an ill wind blows our way."

"But when bad things keep happenin', how do ya trust? God hasn't done much for me and Paddy. Miss Jasmine explained all about Job, and we read the Bible each day. Knowing that a godly man such as Job suffered in his lifetime has helped some, but I'm still wonderin' why things happen the way they do. Ya know . . . why do some of the cruelest people seem to be blessed while good folks are abused? Seems as though God has turned away from those that love 'im."

"Ah, lass, ya can na be thinkin' that way. Just because bad things happen, it does na mean that the Almighty has quit carin'. It's not Him that's caused the grief in this world, but man with his devilish nature. Besides, lass, God has seen fit to give you a great house to live in and food on the table. Ya may be indentured, but ya're not livin' in squalor like most of us here in the Acre. Ya should be on yar knees thankin' God for the safety and security ya have in that big house, while the rest of us face trouble at every turn in this place where we're livin'."

"Safety and security?" she blurted out. "Is that what ya think? I'm hardly safe and secure. What I live is a life of torture and misery. Ya do na have any idea what I'm forced to endure."

His eyes widened at her reply, and she immediately put her hand to her mouth, realizing she'd said too much. Jumping up from the chair, she ran from the house.

"Kiara!" Rogan called.

She could hear his footsteps behind her and then felt his fingers circle her arm. He pulled her to a halt. "Tell me what ya meant back there. Is someone hurtin' ya?"

She looked up into his eyes and realized it would matter little if she told him the truth. She was already defiled. No decent man would ever want her now. It would be easier to tell Rogan the truth than continue living a lie. And so there on the muddy street, feeling as filthy as the trash on the ground around them, she told him of Bradley's visits to her attic room. Never once through the telling did she meet his gaze. When finished with her wretched tale, she turned and walked away, ready to retreat to the home she'd grown to detest.

"Wait, lass," Rogan said, once again at her side. "Do na run off from me. Ya need ta know I understand ya have been forced into a terrible situation. It was harsh of me to assume ya had an easier life than the rest of us. I beg ya to fergive me."

His gentle words of kindness were her undoing. Tears streamed down her cheeks, and he gathered her into his arms. "Do na cry, lass. Life is too short for all these tears. Ya can be certain that what ya have told me has na changed my feelings fer ya, lass."

Kiara leaned against his broad chest. Even if only for a brief moment, she wanted to feel loved and cherished. She leaned back and looked up into his eyes. "I was wonderin' if ya could explain what feelin's ya been havin' fer me."

Rogan gave her a wink and smiled. "I think ya're knowin' exactly what feelin's I'm talkin' about, lass. Come along now. I'll walk ya back to yar house."

The comments she'd overheard in Paxton's Mercantile fleetingly crossed her mind. Surely Bradley would have long since returned home. "I'd be pleased to have yar company," she replied.

CHAPTER · 27

JASMINE WAS delighted when the doctor pronounced her recovery, at least among the genteel women of Lowell, to be one of the swiftest in his career. She'd been anxious to be up and about, and Dr. Hartzfeld had not discouraged her. Of course, he was one of the few doctors supporting short confinements for women after the birthing process, but he had begun advocating such practice after seeing how well the women in the Acre, as well as the Yankee farmwives, seemed to thrive when required to immediately return to the duties of caring for their families after childbirth. Of course, those women had no choice.

"I can't believe you're out of bed," her father exclaimed upon his arrival. "And here I thought I'd already be in Lowell when you gave birth. However, I'm delighted the rigors of childbirth are behind you. You look radiant. Motherhood becomes you, my dear. And your mother will be delighted to hear she has a grandson."

"Do sit down with me in the parlor. I want to hear all about Mother and, of course, my brothers—and Mammy. I've asked Bradley if we can journey to The Willows when Spencer is a little older. I do want Mother to see her new grandson." She looked lovingly at the baby in her arms. "Tell me, how is she faring,

Father? I've had no correspondence for months, and her last letter made little sense to me."

Jasmine's father wagged his head back and forth. "She has little interest in life. I force her out into the garden from time to time, but she much prefers to sit in her darkened bedroom."

"Instruct Mammy to force her outdoors every day," she suggested. "The sunlight will help cheer her spirits. Shortly after Bradley and I were married, I heard a renowned speaker discuss the effects of sunlight upon patients suffering from melancholy. He said sunlight and exercise were of great benefit. Perhaps you could have McKinley take her on a stroll after he's completed his bookwork each morning. I doubt Mammy would be up to any strenuous exercise."

"No harm in trying," he agreed, "although you know your mother can be difficult to persuade. She borders on hysteria when forced to do anything against her will. I fear she's slowly slipping away from me. Dr. Borden thinks your mother has already reached the point of insanity. However, I heartily disagree."

"No! She merely grows sad over the rigors of daily life. She's always suffered from this malady, Father. Don't let Dr. Borden convince you otherwise. Next he'll be suggesting you place Mother in an asylum. Promise me you'll never consent to such a thing! Such a commitment would certainly mean an end to her life."

"You know I'd never send your mother to an asylum, dear. Now quit worrying yourself. It's not good for you. I'll pass your suggestions along to Mammy. She said to send her love and best wishes. She sent along this little white bonnet she crocheted," he said, handing her a small package. "I like the idea of having you visit. Perhaps it would help your mother. I'll urge Bradley to make good on his promise to you."

Jasmine examined the bonnet and smiled. "I'll pen a letter of thanks to Mammy, and you can take it back when you return. Have Mother read it to her. Perhaps it will startle her out of her reverie for a few moments."

"I'll be glad to take your letter. And how have you been faring, dear? The letter from your grandmother concerned me, and I must say that Bradley has somewhat disappointed me with his business acumen. I had thought him quite astute. However, his lack of attention over these past months has me greatly disturbed."

Jasmine studied her father's frowning features. "You know I was sorely disappointed when you chose Bradley as my husband."

Her father's expression took on a look of worry. "Yes, but I hoped that in time you would learn to love him, just as your mother and I learned to love each other and my parents before that. Perhaps I was as wrong about that as I was his competency in business."

"Bradley is a very difficult man to love, Father. He is moody and can be hurtful. I've attempted to make the best of my situation, but I must admit there are times when it has been quite distressing. I'm depending upon the Lord to see me through, and I'm hopeful this child is going to build a bridge in our relationship."

"You've grown up," her father said softly.

Jasmine smiled, realizing the truth of his words. "When I was still at home, I thought there was no better place to be. The Willows was a haven of love and strength to me."

"But not now?"

Jasmine heard the sorrow in his voice. "Papa, so many things have come to my attention, and I am afraid that I am not the naïve little girl who left over a year ago. Even so, The Willows will always remain dear to me. It will always be home in my memories." She sighed. "I cannot say that this place is home. It doesn't feel that way at all. In fact, Grandmother's house feels more like home than this house.

"I also cannot say that I am happy being wed to Bradley, but I am trying, as I said. I know that God is my protector and strength. I have to trust that He will see me through. Spencer will help, no doubt. At least that is my hope."

"I hope so too, my dear. Frankly, my concerns over Bradley's business behavior are disconcerting enough that I've made arrangement for a few private appointments."

"Truly? With whom?" Jasmine inquired.

"I'm going to Boston the day after tomorrow for a meeting with the Associates."

"What's this I hear?" Bradley asked as he strode into the room. "I didn't know there was to be a meeting of the Associates this week."

Jasmine turned toward the doorway. Her husband appeared pale and gaunt, and she wondered if he were ill. Even though her father's visit had been secretly arranged, she felt somewhat vindicated when she looked at her husband now. Bradley definitely needed time to relax and refresh himself. Having someone else assist with the cotton shipments would surely provide the relief he desperately needed to restore his physical health and allow him time with his family. Sending the letter had been the proper thing to do.

Jasmine's father turned as Bradley entered the room. "Good to see you, my boy. Thought perhaps you had gone into hibernation," he said with a chuckle.

"You mentioned a meeting of the Associates," Bradley persisted.

"Oh, nothing you need concern yourself with. Before my departure from Mississippi, I requested a private meeting with several of the members. This is not a gathering of the general membership."

"May I be so bold as to inquire what you need to discuss with the Associates that you haven't discussed with me?" Bradley asked. Jasmine startled at her husband's tone. His eyes had narrowed and taken on a menacing glare. He was angry.

"Excuse me, ma'am," Kiara interrupted. "I was goin' to take the wee babe to the nursery unless ya prefer he stay with you."

"Thank you, Kiara. I'd appreciate that," Jasmine replied.

"Incidentally, Malcolm, I've been meaning to discuss the possibility of having you take one of my indentured servants back to The Willows with you."

Jasmine lifted the infant toward Kiara, whose eyes were fastened upon Bradley in an icy stare of loathing and disgust. "He should sleep for at least an hour," Jasmine said.

"The boy's been working in the stables, but he hasn't been meeting my expectations. I really need an older man who has more experience handling horses."

Jasmine's father appeared perplexed but suggested, "We can talk about it when I return from Boston."

"I'll remain in the nursery with him, ma'am," Kiara said as she exited the room.

Jasmine could feel the tension escalate. Bradley was obviously goading Kiara, and Kiara apparently could not hide her hatred for Bradley. They exchanged glares that were charged with conflict. Jasmine knew Kiara would be upset over any suggestion that Paddy leave Lowell, but surely Bradley's offhand remark could not cause such immediate signs of loathing. There was something more at the root of this, and she intended to find out exactly what was going on in her household.

Kiara sat in the nursery watching the baby sleep and contemplating her situation. She had no choice but to get Paddy away from the Houston household before Malcolm Wainwright's return from Boston. She wasn't certain why Bradley was once again threatening to send Paddy away, but he was obviously enjoying the pain and discomfort caused by his latest threats. Had he seen her with Rogan? Surely not! More likely it was that she was sleeping in the nursery with the baby.

There had been little doubt of Bradley's anger over the situation. With Jasmine's quick recovery from her confinement, he had been livid when Alice suggested Kiara move into the nursery with Spencer. "Think of the added comfort and rest you'll be granting your wife," Alice had argued.

Kiara knew he wanted to mount an offensive, but such a move would have met with questioning disapproval. After all, he should want only the best care for the mother of his infant son. And so he had acquiesced. Although she'd been thankful for Alice's plan, Kiara had not been the one who had broached the subject. Surely he could not hold that chain of events against her.

Later that night after Spencer was asleep in his cradle, she pulled out the leather pouch containing her coins. "Pitiful," she murmured. "This isn't enough to rent a room and support us in Boston until I can find work." It was abundantly obvious her lace-making would not yet provide the two of them with a sufficient living. And even if she remained with the Houstons and gave Paddy all of the money she had saved, how would he fend for himself in a city the size of Boston?

She momentarily thought of sending him to the Acre, but Bradley would certainly find him there. Perhaps Rogan would have an idea. She'd have to find a way to slip away. Perhaps Jasmine would give her permission to visit the Acre when Bradley was away from the house.

Placing the coins back in her pouch, she tucked it into the dresser drawer and snuggled under the covers. The sound of Spencer's even, quiet breathing lulled her to sleep without further thought of the Acre.

A hand clasped around her arm, shaking her. She was half awake, not certain what she'd been dreaming, when her eyes fluttered open and she realized Bradley's face was directly above her own. He licked his thin lips, like an animal ready to devour his prey. "Go upstairs," he commanded.

"Nay! I will na go anywhere with ya. I want ya to leave me alone. Ya've done nothin' but threaten and harm me since the day ya laid eyes on me. I've done nothin' to deserve such treatment. I love Jasmine, and I will na permit ya to continue hurtin' her in this way. She's given you a beautiful son, and she's a gracious lady. Better than ya deserve! I'll na be part of this any longer."

"I ought to flog you for your insolent behavior. You'll do as you're told! You need not put on a pretense of virtue; I saw you in the Acre hanging on to the neck of that filthy Irishman. I know you enjoy being with men," he hissed, leaning close to her ear. His utterance spewed at her like venom from a poisonous snake.

Suddenly she understood why his threats had resurfaced. He had followed her the night she'd gone to the Acre, seen her with Rogan, and now planned to punish her by sending Paddy to Mississippi. This was her fault. If only she'd remained at home that evening.

He yanked on her arm. "I said get upstairs."

"I will na go," she shot back. Before she could argue any further, Spencer began to whimper and then burst forth with a lusty cry. "It's time for the babe to eat. If I do na take him to the mistress, she'll come to fetch him."

Bradley stalked to the door and then turned back to face her. His eyes were filled with a mixture of lust and hatred. "Don't think this matter's been concluded," he warned before leaving the room.

Kiara hurried to the door and turned the key before tending to the crying infant. "There, there," she cooed. "Just let me change yar wet nappie and I'll take ya to yar mother." The baby quickly settled, and once he was dry, she wrapped him in a warm blanket. "Thar ya are. Snug as a bug," she whispered. "Now let's go see yar mother."

Jasmine met her in the doorway that joined her bedroom and the nursery. "I'm sorry ya had to get out of yar bed, ma'am. It took me a wee bit longer to change his nappie."

"No need to apologize, Kiara. You've done nothing wrong." She reached for the infant. "Go back to bed. I'll keep Spencer with me after he's finished nursing," she said. "I'm sure you need some sleep. I can rest tomorrow while Father and Bradley are gone to Boston."

"The gentlemen are off on a short trip, are they?"

"Only for the day. Father told me this evening he's going to have Bradley join him, but say nothing, as Bradley doesn't know yet."

Kiara nodded her head. "A surprise, is it? Well, ya can trust me not to be sayin' anything to Mr. Houston." She returned to her room, her heart dancing with delight. She'd try to get word to Rogan tomorrow.

———

Bradley joined Malcolm at the breakfast table and signaled Sarah to pour his coffee. "I see no reason for you to travel to

Boston, Malcolm. I'm certain I can handle any matters needing attention if you'll merely take me into your confidence."

"I've already made arrangements for the meeting. No need to change them now."

"But it seems a shame to cut into the little time you have with Jasmine in order to conduct business outside of Lowell."

Malcolm forked a piece of sausage onto his plate and helped himself to a steaming bowl of scrambled eggs. "No grits?" he asked, looking in Sarah's direction.

"No, sir. Would you care for some fried potatoes instead?"

"If that's my only choice," he replied, helping himself. "You Northerners should begin serving grits. I'm surprised neither Jasmine nor Alice has begun the practice."

Sarah smiled at Malcolm. "They tell me they're not fond of grits."

"Hurrumph! They never told *me* such a thing."

Bradley found Malcolm's preoccupation annoying. Who really cared what was served for breakfast so long as there was good strong coffee? "Getting back to the topic at hand, Malcolm, wouldn't you prefer to spend your time with Jasmine?"

Malcolm looked up from his plate. "Why don't you come with me? Jasmine doesn't mind in the least that I'm going to be gone to Boston. She learned long ago that men require time to conduct their business if they are going to properly support their families. We'd have time to visit on the train, and you can give me a tour of your shipping business."

Bradley didn't want to show Malcolm his shipping business or anything else for that matter, but if he was going to find out what this meeting was about, he had little alternative. He needed to retain control. Of course, the best way to do that was to keep Malcolm in Lowell, but since that wasn't going to be possible, he'd attend the meeting and hope to bypass a visit to the shipping office. Hopefully Malcolm would decide to make an early departure for Mississippi.

"Thank you, Malcolm. If you insist on attending the meeting, I'd be pleased to accompany you."

Kiara watched from an upstairs window until the carriage pulled away from the house before entering Jasmine's room. "Sarah was needin' some things from town, ma'am. Would ya be mindin' if I took care of that burden fer her?"

"That would be fine. Grandmother's here to help me. Besides, you need to get away from the house more frequently. Be sure you go early in the day so you're home before the men return. I expect them on the last train this evening."

"I'll be goin' this mornin' and will be back afore noon." She dashed down the stairs, retrieved the list from Sarah, and scurried down the road. When she reached the mercantile, she approached Mrs. Paxton. "I have another errand to attend to. Would ya mind if I left my list to be filled and picked it up in a short while?"

"That's fine, Kiara. I'll have it ready when you return."

She ran down the street with her skirt flying in the breeze and her pounding shoes leaving tiny clouds of dust in her wake. She knocked on the door and waited, dancing from foot to foot. "Where is she? Where is she?" she muttered into the morning air. Finally she heard footsteps nearing the door. "Granna Murphy!" she exclaimed when the door opened. "Can I come in?"

The old woman gave her a cordial smile. "You need na ask, lass. Ya're always welcome in our home. What brings ya out at this time o' day? There's no one to visit but your old Granna Murphy."

"I need ya to give Rogan a message."

"Sure, and what would yar message be?" she asked with a crooked grin.

"It's urgent I speak to him. Could ya tell him to come to the Houstons' house and wait at the front of the house near the big tree at eight o'clock? He'll know which one I mean. Tell him to be sure and stay hidden until I call to him. Please do na ferget, Granna. It's important."

"How could I ferget? I'll tell him the moment he walks through that door."

Kiara leaned down and placed a kiss on the weathered old

cheek. "I wish I could stay and visit, but I must be gettin' back to the house. Don't ferget to give him me message."

"Off with ya, lass. I'll na be fergetting, so set yar mind to ease."

———————

Bradley forced himself to remain amicable, smiling and nodding at the proper occasions while his level of irritation swelled. Before they departed from Lowell, Malcolm said they would discuss business on the train. However, it now seemed he was more content discussing his sons and their capable management techniques at The Willows. "I'm proud of every one of them. They've taken hold, and all three are excited about remaining in the cotton business."

"Even Samuel? I don't recall him having strong leadership qualities. Has he made some improvement?"

Malcolm bristled at the remark. "There was never anything wrong with Samuel's abilities. You wanted him to whip the slaves into producing more cotton, but he didn't feel that was an appropriate measure—nor did I, for that matter. Our success hasn't depended upon such tactics. In fact, Samuel's duties will be expanding, and David will be taking over his previous duties."

Bradley said no more. He'd once again offended Malcolm Wainwright with his attempts to discredit his eldest son. The remainder of their journey was in silence. Once they arrived in Boston, Bradley hailed a carriage.

"Brackman Hotel on Beacon Street," Malcolm told the driver.

"You're meeting at the Brackman?"

"Yes. Nathan told me he'd arrange for us to use a small meeting room at the hotel since I don't plan to remain overnight."

"You're meeting with Nathan?"

"Nathan, Josiah Baines, Henry Thorne, and several others. I believe Matthew Cheever was going to come in from Lowell. Shame about Tracy Jackson. I didn't realize he'd passed away until Nathan mentioned it in his latest missive."

"Yes. Jackson's passing is a huge loss to the Associates. I didn't realize you and Nathan were on such an intimate basis."

310

"We've only recently corresponded. I find him an engaging man. Quite knowledgeable and an astute businessman."

Bradley could feel beads of perspiration beginning to form along his upper lip. What was going on? Why had Malcolm begun corresponding with Nathan Appleton? And more importantly, *what* were they corresponding about?

Nathan greeted them in the hotel foyer. "I'm surprised to see you, Bradley. Malcolm didn't tell me you'd be attending the meeting."

Bradley watched the two men exchange glances.

"I thought it might be best if Bradley was present. I find it more difficult hearing things after the fact. Secondhand explanations seem to lose something in the translation."

Nathan nodded. "Whatever makes you most comfortable, Malcolm."

Bradley watched Nathan pat his father-in-law on the back as though they were old friends as they entered the meeting room. Something had gone amiss. He didn't know what, but he was certain he was not going to like the tenor of this meeting.

"Why don't you take over the helm, Malcolm? After all, it was you who suggested this gathering," Nathan said.

"Of course. I'm certain you gentlemen have read my letter and are aware of my growing concerns, both for my cotton shipments as well as my son-in-law's health and well-being."

Bradley stiffened. *My health? My well-being?* What was happening here?

Malcolm continued. "As I told you in my letter, I want to present my proposal for using my son Samuel as the new buyer of cotton from Southern plantation owners. Samuel already has a working relationship with many of the cotton growers that you hope to entice into contracts. I believe you would see positive results from this. Samuel would take over those duties from Bradley, giving him more time for other duties with the Corporation. My hope is that you can assign Bradley to duties in Lowell to allow him to spend more time with his wife and new son."

Bradley barely stifled his rage. He shifted in his chair and reached for Malcolm's elbow. "What are you doing?" he asked between clenched teeth. "I don't want to be released from my duties as buyer for the Corporation," he whispered forcefully.

Malcolm ignored the plea and maintained his focus upon the other men gathered in the room. "With Samuel in Mississippi, I envision his role as a buyer who can travel among the plantations, keep track of inventory, arrange for shipments, and handle any other unforeseen circumstances that may occur with the growers. Additionally, as I stated earlier, with our many contacts in the South, I feel certain Samuel can further expand the number of suppliers as needed. You must realize Southerners are notoriously cautious where Yankees are concerned."

The men chuckled as if completely understanding his point. But Bradley felt like screaming. He was losing control and that was something he didn't brook well.

Malcolm spoke again. "And, of course, should the need arise for someone to accompany a shipment for any reason, I have two other sons who could make themselves available for such an assignment. Overall, I believe this will be a much improved method."

"I couldn't agree more," Nathan replied.

"Nor I," concurred Josiah while the other members murmured their assent. "To be honest, we've been very concerned. I don't know if Nathan informed you, but there have been grave concerns of late regarding the cotton shipments. I, for one, feel much more confident knowing there will be someone in charge who can follow the process and give it his complete devotion. No offense, Bradley, but you've certainly not been yourself recently, and by your own admission you feel the need to be closer to home."

"If I could have a moment alone with you, Malcolm," Bradley urged. If he didn't say something soon, he would explode.

"We can talk during our return to Lowell," Malcolm replied. "Well, gentlemen, if we're all in agreement, I'll have Samuel begin his duties as soon as I return to Mississippi."

The meeting was adjourned before Bradley had time to drink his second glass of port. He walked out of the hotel in stunned silence, and it wasn't until they were settled on the train that he once again voiced his objection to his father-in-law.

"If you had a problem with me, I wish you would have brought it to my attention. I truly do not understand why you think this change is necessary. It's not as though Samuel doesn't have many duties to perform on the plantation already."

"This has nothing to do with the plantation, Bradley. This has to do with the proper handling of the cotton shipments and payments. There needs to be a line of communication between buyers and sellers, an awareness of potential problems or delays. You've not handled matters well, my boy. You didn't even inform your business partners I had written to explain our first harvest would be smaller due to excessive rains and subsequent boll rot.

"After talking with Jasmine and my mother, I'm aware you are suffering under a burden of undue stress. Believe me, you need not feel inadequate. There are few men who could have coped with the magnitude of details and duties you were attempting to handle."

Bradley rubbed his forehead, certain he'd heard incorrectly. "Jasmine and Grandmother Wainwright told you I've been unable to cope with my business interests? They spoke against me?"

"They spoke no ill word against you at all. However, they were gravely concerned about you, my boy. I applaud their efforts on your behalf, and I'm certain that once you've begun your new duties in Lowell, you'll be delighted they took your best interests to heart."

Bradley seethed. How dare those two interfering women go over his head and contact Malcolm? Because of them, he was going to lose all of the income he'd come to depend upon. With Samuel managing the shipments and books, there would be no opportunity for Bradley to underhandedly increase his income. Worse yet, Malcolm was going to find out the percentages were higher than what Bradley had previously divulged. His anger neared a boiling rage, yet he knew he must remain calm.

"When are you planning to return to The Willows?" he inquired.

Malcolm appeared puzzled. "I've booked passage for the end of the week, which means we've much to accomplish prior to my departure."

Bradley arched his eyebrows. "Such as?"

"We'll need at least two to three days to go over the book-work. I'll want to take the ledgers and accounts with me as well as the contracts and any other papers relating to each buyer's position. I want Samuel to have opportunity to review all of the paper work so he'll have a firm footing to begin his new duties. In fact, I gave serious consideration to bringing him with me, but I wasn't positive the Associates would agree to this change."

Bradley grimaced at the thought of Samuel being present for this embarrassment and was thankful Malcolm had thought better of the idea. "Perhaps it would be best if you spent the remainder of your time visiting with Jasmine. I can have the paper work shipped to you."

"I will certainly visit with my daughter, but I want to go over the ledgers with you in order to gain a better understanding of the methods you've utilized so that I can explain them to Samuel. Besides, if I have questions, you can immediately answer them instead of my waiting for weeks to hear from you by mail—and you're not the best correspondent," Malcolm added.

Bradley turned his attention away from Malcolm and stared out the window. A sick feeling churned in the pit of his stomach. In the short time remaining, how could he possibly rework the ledgers before revealing them to Malcolm?

Kiara listened at the top of the stairway as the two men returned home later that night. Bradley stormed into the house and went directly to his library, although Kiara thought Mr. Wainwright appeared to be in a rather pleasant mood. She'd need to keep her distance from Bradley. She wanted nothing to interfere with her meeting this evening.

The baby was fast asleep, and Jasmine and Grandmother Wainwright were busy with their sewing as Kiara entered the room. "I was wonderin' if I might go for a little walk, ma'am. I won't be outside fer long. I'd just like a breath o' fresh air."

"I was thinking about taking a walk myself," Jasmine replied. "Perhaps I'll join you."

Before Kiara could object, Alice came to the rescue. "There's a chill in the air, dear. It could affect your milk. I think it would be best to remain indoors. Midafternoon would be a better time of day for you to take a walk."

"Perhaps you'd join me tomorrow afternoon, Kiara?"

"Certainly, ma'am. I'd be pleased ta go walkin' with ya on the morrow. But ya do na mind if I go tonight, do ya?"

Jasmine gave her blessing, and Kiara made her way down the stairway, careful to avoid Bradley. She didn't know where he might be lurking, but she didn't want to encounter him this evening. The kitchen was dark, and she managed to slip out the door and around the house without being noticed.

"Rogan, are ya here?"

"Aye, I'm here. How could I stay away with such a message as ya left with Granna? It sounds as though it's a matter of life and death."

"That it is," Kiara replied, tears of anger and fear welling in her eyes.

"Ah, it can na be as bad as that, lass," he said, pulling her into an embrace. "Come on now and dry yar eyes and tell me yar problem. We'll get it solved one way or the other."

"Mr. Houston is goin' to send Paddy to Mississippi, where he'll be forced to work on the Wainwrights' cotton plantation. He can na survive such a life, Rogan. And I can na survive without me brother. We're goin' ta be just like those slave families Miss Jasmine told me about. We'll be separated and never see each other again."

"Ya know I'll do whatever I can ta help ya, lass."

"I want ya to take Paddy and hide him. Mr. Houston will come lookin' in the Acre, so ya'll have to hide him in a place where he won't think of lookin'."

"I do na think yar idea is sound. Thar's strict penalties when ya break the servitude laws, Kiara."

Kiara backed away from him. She could not believe what she'd heard. "Ya're more concerned about my indenturin' papers than Paddy being sent off to some cotton plantation that might as well be on the other side of the world away from me?"

"I do na want ya endin' up in more trouble than either of us can handle. What good would ya be doin' Paddy if ya end up in jail, lass? And do na think they wouldn't put ya there. If this Mr. Houston's as mean as ya say, he'll have ya placed on public display before ya're hauled off to jail."

"Do ya not understand what I'm saying, Rogan Sheehan? Mr. Wainwright is leavin' the end of the week, and I've little doubt Paddy will be goin' with him."

"Let me talk to me boss, Liam Donohue. He'll surely be able to give us some sound ideas. He's smart and knows all the right people."

"There isn't time for talkin', Rogan. We need ta be doin' somethin' now."

"If you'll put a little faith in me and a lot of faith in God, we'll somehow find a way to get this whole thing settled. What ya need to do is take yarself inside and get down on yar knees. Pray fer God's intercession to look after Paddy. Will ya do that, lass? Give me but a day. We've got that much time."

"I'll give ya a day, and I'll pray, but I don't believe God cares enough ta do anything. He's given me little hope that He's ever heard one of my prayers."

Rogan gave her a wink and smiled. "You pray, and I'll take care of the believin' for the both of us."

CHAPTER · 28

JASMINE GREETED her father and Bradley as they entered the parlor. Bradley bid her good evening before hastily adding, "I'm exhausted. I'll be retiring for the night."

Jasmine watched from the parlor as her husband made his way up the stairs without so much as a good-night kiss.

"How was your evening, my dear?" her father inquired.

"Quite fine, Papa. Bradley appeared distraught. Was your dinner meeting unproductive?" she ventured.

He nodded. "I'm certain he found our time together extremely disappointing. I thought he planned to discuss the shift of his duties to Samuel, but I was incorrect. In fact, he wanted me to change my decision. He was amicable and repentant when we began dinner, but when he realized I would not be dissuaded, his mood changed dramatically."

Jasmine looked at him in understanding. "I'm not surprised. Bradley isn't accustomed to being refused."

"Well, I'm certain that given time, he'll come to appreciate that this is best for his family. His behavior this evening revealed characteristics I've never observed previously—angry conduct I fear you've been subjected to throughout your marriage, and it grieves me to know I placed you in this situation. I plan to have a long talk with your husband before I depart, but I do wish there were something I could do right now that would help ease your circumstances."

"There is one thing, Papa."

"Anything! You just tell me what you want, and I'll see to it."

"Please don't take Paddy back to The Willows with you. If Paddy leaves here, it will be Kiara's undoing, and she has been a true blessing to me. I don't know how I would have endured my marriage without her support and friendship. Bradley has been angry with Paddy ever since he accidentally forgot to lock one of the stalls and Bradley's favorite horse escaped for a short time. The horse suffered a small cut on his leg, but it healed long ago and no harm was done. The horse was retrieved before Bradley even returned home. It is pure foolishness that he continues to hold a grudge against the child. Paddy is an excellent worker, and everyone speaks highly of his abilities, especially given his tender years."

Her father rubbed his balding head and stared thoughtfully at some distant object. "Bradley seemed insistent. He said the boy is a troublemaker and consistently difficult to manage."

"You should speak with the stable master. Ask what *he* thinks of Paddy. He has told me the boy is a natural with horseflesh and works exceedingly well with the animals. He even mentioned he'd like to hire him on permanently once his servitude ends."

"I don't need to visit with the stable master, Jasmine. I can certainly take the word of my daughter. I'll tell Bradley I won't take the boy with me, but if Bradley feels strongly about this matter, he'll likely try to rid himself of the boy in some other manner, and should that happen, you'll have no control."

Thoughts tumbled through Jasmine's mind as she digested her father's words. He was correct. Bradley would undoubtedly sell Paddy to someone else. *Sell Paddy.* That was the answer.

She clapped her hands together. "I know, Papa. Tell Bradley you want to purchase Paddy's contract—that you wouldn't want to take him into your possession unless you had papers showing you were actually his owner. Then you can sign over his freedom, and he can live with Grandmother and work part time at the stables in town to support himself. He could still see Kiara, yet he'd be out of Bradley's control. What do you think?"

"Sounds like a workable idea, so long as your grandmother agrees."

Jasmine giggled. "She'll agree. Grandmother has developed a penchant for Kiara's lace, and this arrangement will give her ample opportunity to nag the poor girl about her handiwork."

"Sounds like an arrangement your grandmother would relish. She always did enjoy having the upper hand. Now, if you'll excuse me, dear, I think I'll go up to bed. Shouldn't you be doing the same? Spencer will be awake before long, and you'll wish you'd gotten some rest."

She smiled up at her father. "I'll just finish this last row of stitching, and then I'll be up."

Malcolm leaned down and kissed her cheek. "Good night, my dear."

"Good night, Papa. And thank you for your willingness to help Paddy."

He smiled and nodded, his eyes still reflecting some of the sadness she'd noticed earlier in their conversation.

Bradley paced in his bedroom as he waited to hear the sound of footsteps in the hallway. When over an hour had passed, his mild frustration was replaced by acute irritation. Finally he heard someone climbing the stairway. Malcolm must be retiring for the night, as there was no sound in Jasmine's adjoining bedroom. Why had Jasmine remained in the parlor? He had much to accomplish this night, but he dared not return downstairs until everyone was in bed. Had Kiara not been in the nursery, he would have awakened Spencer in order to force his wife upstairs.

Willing to wait no longer, he called her upstairs, feigning he'd heard the baby crying. Jasmine hurried up the stairs and met him in the hallway. "I couldn't enter the nursery," he told her. "Kiara has the door locked, but I'm certain I heard Spencer crying."

"I'm surprised. Kiara is always quick to awaken when he cries.

Go back to bed, Bradley. I know you're exhausted. I'll see you in the morning."

Bradley retreated to his room, glad they were still in separate rooms despite the baby's birth. He leaned against the door, listening. He heard Jasmine speak to Kiara and Kiara deny that the baby was awake. Jasmine then informed the girl she was going to prepare for bed. Bradley hastily made his exit out of the room and downstairs to his study. If he was to present his records and ledgers to Malcolm the following day, he must adjust the accounts tonight.

He had given consideration to taking the books and going into seclusion in Concord or some other small city where Malcolm wouldn't find him. But that would likely send alarm signals to both Malcolm and the Associates. Besides, he needed to meet with his father-in-law regarding Paddy. If he accomplished nothing else, he'd be certain Kiara knew who was in charge of this household and that he was a man of his word.

It would take all night to transfer the figures, but he had little choice. Pulling the books from his desk, Bradley began the tedious task of calculating and reentering figures into a new ledger book that he would present to Malcolm the next day. A ledger that would reflect figures matching those Malcolm believed the Associates were paying for his cotton. It would take little to alter the contract figures. But his thoughts were jumbled, and he'd not yet reconciled how he would explain the higher price he'd negotiated with the Associates. Malcolm, however, had never seen the contract, and Bradley would be safe so long as no one ever mentioned the higher figure. Bradley still maintained hope he might be able to convince the Associates he was to remain the payee on the later contract he'd negotiated for an additional percentage.

The entries were rushed and sloppy, smudged, and hopelessly illegible in places. Although he was exhausted and overwhelmed, Bradley completed the task just before sunrise. He checked his last entries, doubting Malcolm would be able to decipher the final pages of figures.

"He can recalculate for himself," Bradley murmured, looking for a fresh piece of blotting paper.

Finding the last of his blotting paper spent, Bradley spread the open ledger upon his desktop to dry, tucked the old ledgers into a drawer, which he carefully locked, and after turning down the wick of his lamp, shuffled up the stairs. He hoped for at least an hour of sleep before revisiting the ledger books with Malcolm.

———

Jasmine returned the baby to his cradle and heard Bradley's door opening. Then the bed creaked, followed almost instantaneously by her husband's snores.

Something was amiss. She wondered what Bradley could have been doing downstairs at this hour. Returning to her room, Jasmine was overcome by an irresistible curiosity. Candle in hand, she slipped into her robe, crept down the stairs, and entered her husband's study. She touched the lamp's glass globe and found it still warm. So he had been working in his study, she surmised.

She sat down in his large chair and looked at the ledger that lay open on the desk in front of her. This wasn't the ledger Bradley normally used when figuring the accounts. She held the candle closer, looking at the barely legible figures that were so unlike Bradley. Could he possibly be altering the books? Dare he be stealing from her family? She attempted to open the desk drawers. They were locked. If Bradley was stealing, there was no way she could prove her statements without the original ledger. Yet why would he be entering figures from two months ago if he weren't falsifying the books? Her husband was always careful to complete his records and present them to the Associates, for one thing Bradley always expected was immediate payment.

Bradley's sloppy entries left several blotches of ink on the page that had not yet dried. If she closed the books, the pages would smear against one another—proof the entries had all been made at one time. Without a second thought, she closed the book, pressed it tightly together, and left the room.

———

Bradley awakened with a start. A column of sunlight was

streaming through his bedroom window, cutting a wide path across the room. "It must be at least ten o'clock," he muttered while pouring water from a china pitcher into the matching bowl. Thankfully he'd slept in his clothes. He splashed his face with water, quickly finger-combed his hair, and straightened his tie before exiting the room.

It seemed breakfast was long over, although a plate remained on the table at his place. Sarah appeared from the kitchen and offered him coffee. "I'll heat your breakfast," she offered. "It won't take long."

"Just coffee, Sarah. I'm not hungry. Do I hear voices coming from the library?"

"Oh yes, sir. Mr. Cheever and Mr. Wainwright asked if they might take the liberty of using the room for their meeting."

"Matthew Cheever? What meeting? How long has he been here?"

Sarah furrowed her brow. "Forty-five minutes—maybe an hour."

"And no one awakened me?" He pushed aside the cup of coffee and hurried off.

Matthew Cheever was exiting the library as Bradley entered the hallway. "Matthew! I was just coming to join you and Malcolm."

"Good morning, Bradley. No need to hurry. We've already completed our conversation, and I must get back to the mills." Matthew retrieved his hat from the hallway and without further discussion took his leave.

Bradley hurried back to the library, where Malcolm was placing a folded paper in his breast pocket. "Why the early morning meeting with Matthew Cheever?"

"Oh, it was nothing of importance, Bradley. Jasmine informed me you had been up until the wee hours, and I certainly didn't want to disturb your sleep. You obviously needed your rest. Perhaps we should get started on the ledgers."

Bradley breathed a bit easier. Apparently the meeting with Matthew didn't impact him, and the ledgers had been completed last night. Everything would be fine if he kept his wits about him. "The ledger is in my study, Malcolm. I'll just go and retrieve it."

The sound of chatter caused him to look into the hallway, where Jasmine and Paddy were making their way toward the door. "Come in here, Paddy," he ordered. "Jasmine, would you retrieve the ledger from the top of my desk, please? Your father and I need to go over some accounts."

Jasmine nodded and walked away while Paddy entered the room. "This is the boy I mentioned, Malcolm," Bradley began, "the one I want you to take to Mississippi. His name is Padraig O'Neill."

"If I'm to have charge of him," Malcolm said, "I'll want to buy out his indenture contract. I'll not take him with you still holding his papers in your name."

"If you want to buy the papers, I won't object. I was merely offering him to you free of cost, but if such an arrangement makes you uncomfortable, I'm willing to take your money." Bradley flashed a look of self-satisfaction toward Paddy. "I'll get his papers after we've gone over the ledgers."

Paddy's shoulders slumped, and he hunkered down near the door. "Ya can na be doin' this to me, sir. I love takin' care of yar horses. Why are ya sendin' me away?"

"Nooo!" Kiara cried, dashing into the room and clinging to Bradley's arm. "Please. I'm beggin' you, do just this one thing for me. Do na send him away. I'll do anything. I promise I'll make it up to you." She met his hardened gaze with pleading tear-filled eyes.

Just when he thought he could take no more of Kiara's whining, Jasmine entered the library with his ledger tucked under her arm.

"Kiara, what's wrong?" She hurried to the girl and wrapped her in an embrace while handing the ledger to Bradley.

"Malcolm and I are attempting to conduct business. All of you need to leave the library," Bradley ordered.

Kiara ran from the room with Jasmine close on her heels, calling her name. Obviously unable to comprehend the situation,

Paddy remained in place, staring after the two women.

"Get on with you!" Bradley shouted. "Get back to the barn." Startled, Paddy darted from the room like a fox being chased by hounds.

"How much did you want for the boy's contract?" Malcolm inquired.

"I want to be fair," Bradley replied, producing Lord Palmerston's original paper work.

Malcolm examined the papers and said, "I'll give you an extra fifty dollars for the room and board you've provided since his arrival."

"Of course, he did receive excellent training in handling horseflesh," Bradley submitted.

"An additional seventy-five."

"Agreed." Bradley felt a sense of smug satisfaction at the arrangement. Malcolm wasn't such a shrewd businessman. Bradley would have taken nothing for the boy. It appeared matters of business were improving. "Now, then, shall we begin working on the ledgers?"

———

Jasmine couldn't keep pace with Kiara, and by the time she rounded the house, the girl was nowhere to be seen. Her cries for Kiara went unanswered even though she called out that there was a solution for Paddy's predicament.

Realizing Kiara likely didn't believe her, Jasmine continued searching and calling until her voice became hoarse. Frustrated by her failed attempts, Jasmine finally made her way to the stable, where she found Paddy huddled in a corner. She pulled him into a warm embrace and carefully explained that he would not be sent to The Willows.

"My father has purchased your papers and will send you to live with Grandmother. You'll be able to see Kiara and, if you like, I know Grandmother will permit you to work at the stables in Lowell. I'm certain they'd be delighted to have you."

"And do ya think they'd be payin' me?" he asked with a glimmer in his eyes.

"Of course they would," Jasmine replied.

"Then I'll save up me coins until I can buy Kiara's papers from Mr. Bradley," he vowed.

"As soon as you see Kiara, explain to her there's no need to worry and it's safe to come back to the house. Will you do that?"

"Yes, ma'am, and thank ya fer yar kindness."

For several hours, Bradley and Malcolm were hunched over the ledgers. They had gone over each entry, discussing the accounting procedures and computations.

"I think I'll go upstairs and get a cigar from my room, if you don't mind. I need to stretch my legs after all this sitting," Malcolm said.

"Not at all," Bradley replied. He leaned back in his chair. The explanations had gone well. There was only one final ledger page remaining, and it appeared Malcolm had detected nothing out of the ordinary. Bradley was pleased—especially since he'd already spent the funds he had stolen from his father-in-law.

Considering its unpleasant beginning, this day was now exceeding all expectations. He'd managed to make extra money from the sale of Paddy's contract, and he could now use the leverage with Kiara that if she wanted her brother back, she'd have to grant him favors. The only sour note remaining was the fact that he was going to miss out on the additional funds he'd previously been skimming from Malcolm. He had Jasmine to blame for that loss. If she and her grandmother would have kept their noses out of his business matters, this would have never occurred.

"Interfering women," he muttered contemptuously.

He sat forward and began to turn the final page. It was stuck. Horrified by the discovery, he took his letter opener and carefully pried the corner of the pages. Gently, he loosened the sheets until they finally separated. He stared down at the pages, with his disbelieving gaze focused upon the entries that had been smudged and transferred onto the opposite page. He could hear Malcolm's approaching footsteps and closed the book with a resounding crack.

"I'm ready for dinner. Why don't we take a break from this drudgery for a while? I'm sure working with these numbers is hard on your eyes."

"Nonsense, Bradley. We're nearly done. We can surely wait another half hour to have our dinner."

Bradley pushed away from the desk, his face forming a scowl. "This is my home, Malcolm, and I think I should be the one who decides when we will take our meals. And we are going to eat dinner now."

Malcolm stared at him as though he were a lunatic. "If you're that determined, go right ahead. I'll stay here and complete the ledger work on my own."

"Absolutely not! We'll resume when I say we will." He jumped up from his chair and stormed from the room, the book tucked securely beneath his arm.

CHAPTER · 29

BRADLEY RACED up the steps two at a time and retreated to the sanctuary of his bedroom, uncertain how he would handle this sudden glitch in his plans. Pulling a small case from beneath his bed, he unlocked the clasp and placed the ledger inside before retrieving a piece of stationery from his maple writing desk.

He thought for a moment and then dipped his pen and spoke aloud as he wrote. "'Dear Jasmine, I have been called away' . . . no, that's not good," he muttered, quickly taking out a new sheet of paper. "'Urgent business has developed. I must be away for several days,'" he wrote, nodding his head. That sounded much better. He continued scrawling the note, adding an apology to Malcolm for his hasty departure and giving his regrets that he would not be available to accompany his father-in-law to the docks in Boston. In a hasty postscript, he thanked Malcolm for his willingness to take Paddy to The Willows and wished him well in his endeavor to teach the boy a proper work ethic.

He gave the letter a cursory reading, folded it, and placed it atop his bed. Uncertain of Jasmine's whereabouts, he knew he dare not take the letter to her room and risk the likelihood of facing her. Without time for thoughtful consideration, he quickly packed a few belongings in a satchel and crept down the back stairway and out to the stables.

A dappled gray mare had been saddled in readiness for her daily exercise routine, and Bradley's spirits buoyed at his good fortune. Tying his bag to the back of the saddle, Bradley gave a self-satisfied grunt. His luck had obviously changed for the better. He untied the horse and was lifting his foot toward the stirrup when a hand clasped his arm in a tight grip.

"Mr. Houston, I'm beggin' ya, please do na send Paddy away. You should na be punishin' the boy and takin' yar anger out on him when 'tis *me* ya're angry with."

Lustrous black hair fell around Kiara's face in soft wispy curls, highlighting the beauty of her creamy white complexion. Bradley could not resist. With a rough jerk, he pulled her into his arms. "So now you finally realize the power I hold over you," he snarled, his lips coming down hard and crushing her mouth in a brutal kiss. She struggled against his assault, but her resistance caused him to desire her all the more.

He attempted to capture her lips in another cruel kiss, but she pushed hard against his chest, freeing her mouth. His anger intensified as she bent her head forward and positioned it against his chest in an effort to fend him off.

"Stop! Ya have no right ta hurt me!" she hollered while twisting against his hold.

He heard a rustling sound but didn't have time to turn around before a shocking pain jolted through his skull. His eyes grew wide as the tremor of pain sped throughout his entire body. He stumbled and fell backward.

"Paddy!" Kiara screamed over the neighing of the spooked mare.

Bradley grasped his head, momentarily dazed but quickly regaining his senses. Crawling toward Paddy, he reached for the boy's shirt, missing it, but finally gained enough strength to get on his feet. His arms flailed as dizziness overtook him and he stumbled backward.

"Look out for the mare!" Paddy hollered as Bradley fell beneath the horse.

Kiara screamed and pulled Paddy to her side. "Oh, Paddy, what are we gonna do?" She stared down at Bradley. He lay on the hay-strewn floor with blood pouring from the wound on his face where the horse had kicked him. "He's dead. Of that there is no doubt," she hoarsely whispered.

"We did na do anything wrong, Kiara. He was attackin' ya, and I hit him with the shovel, but 'twas the horse what killed him."

"They'll never believe us, Paddy," she cried. "I fear they'll accuse ya of murder after all the mean things Mr. Houston said about ya. He told Mr. Wainwright what a bad little feller ya are and that ya're hard to manage. No doubt they'll believe the worst."

A rustling caused Kiara to turn toward the stable door, where Jasmine Wainwright stood with a pistol in her hand. "Oh, Miss Jasmine! Please don' kill 'im," she screamed, pushing Paddy behind her skirts.

Jasmine's eyes grew wide and she arched her brows. *"Kill him?"* She lay the weapon down and walked to Kiara and Paddy. "I was outside the stable. I heard and saw everything that went on in here. I know what's been happening, Kiara. I haven't known long, but I know how Bradley has been tormenting you. Since the day I discovered what he was doing, I prayed that God would release you from this misery. I believe this accident is God's way of interceding."

"Why do ya have that gun?" Paddy asked.

"I didn't want Bradley to leave. I wanted him to come in and talk to my father and me. But I thought the only way he'd consent was if I threatened him," she admitted. "Bradley has been making many people miserable with his behavior, and I've prayed God would change him and soften his heart. I did not love him, but I wanted him to become a better man."

"Aye, 'twould have been easier for all of us had he been a better man," Kiara agreed. "I believe there are those what would argue Paddy's blow with the shovel is what caused yar husband's death. I do na think this will be so simple as you think. 'Twould be best for Paddy to run from here."

"No need," Malcolm declared as he walked into the barn. "Nothing but an accident. Pure and simple."

"That's right," Jasmine agreed. "Nothing but an accident."

CHAPTER · *30*

FEW TEARS were shed at Bradley Houston's funeral. It was, by Lowell standards, a small gathering. Alice was in attendance, Nolan came from Boston, and Malcolm delayed his return to Mississippi in order to lend his support to Jasmine. A few of the Boston Associates made their appearance, along with a smattering of Lowell residents. Most came to offer Jasmine support rather than to honor Bradley—she knew this well enough. Jasmine cried briefly as the service got underway. For the first time in her life she mourned the fact that someone did not know the Lord and cared nothing for God's truth.

Jasmine had not been exceedingly strong in her faith prior to her marriage, but now it seemed to be the only means of holding her life together. It comforted her to know that God's hand was upon her—that He truly cared for her just as He had cared for Job. She thought of a verse from the thirteenth chapter of Job, remembering it in part. "Though he slay me, yet will I trust in him." *And I will,* Jasmine thought. She would go on trusting the Lord, come what may.

The preacher offered a brief sermon, talking of the resurrection of Jesus and how all those who put their trust in Him would rise again. But Jasmine knew her husband had not come to know

God during his lifetime. Her heart ached with the knowledge that she had failed to guide Bradley into God's saving grace. Bradley had known the truth, but he had chosen to reject God's plan for redemption. And now he would pay the ultimate price—throughout eternity.

———

Kiara tugged on the sheet and tucked the corner under the thin mattress that lined her cot. Several days had passed since the funeral, and life had returned to a calm ebb and flow. Pleasant—much like the days when Bradley had been gone to Boston on business. From all appearances, Jasmine's words had been true. Nothing was going to happen to Paddy. Bradley was dead and buried, and no one had come forward asking any questions about his death. Mr. Wainwright had returned home to Mississippi, leaving Paddy to continue working in the Houston stables. And although Nolan remained in Lowell, he seemed more concerned about Jasmine and the baby than his brother's death.

Straightening the blanket with her open palm, Kiara gave one final pat to the bed. She owed Jasmine Houston a great deal, yet she'd not offered her mistress so much as a word of thanks.

"It's high time ya got in there," she chided herself. After tapping on Jasmine's bedroom door, she hesitated a moment and then peeked around the corner. "May I come in, ma'am?"

"Of course, Kiara. I'm always pleased to have you visit me. It's been too long since we've had a chat."

"I've come ta offer me thanks for what ya did for me and Paddy. I've never said it, but I hope ya know how much it means ta me that ya didn't hold the boy responsible for yar husband's death."

"Of course I know. There's no doubt you love your brother as much as I love Spencer, and I know how I would feel if someone threatened to take him away from me."

"Thank ya for understandin'. Now can I ask ya how ya happened to be outside the stables that day?"

"Several nights before Bradley's death, I was awakened by the sound of voices in the nursery. I went to the door and heard Bradley threatening you. I listened, not wanting to believe what I was hearing. I finally understood what had been happening right under my nose all these months."

Tears trickled down Kiara's cheeks. "I promise ya, ma'am, I never acted unseemly or encouraged him. I did na want his sinful advances," she sobbed.

Jasmine pulled her into a comforting embrace. "I believe you, Kiara. Please don't cry. I know you were trying to protect Paddy. I heard Bradley making arrangements to sell Paddy to my father and took matters into my own hands. I asked my father to buy Paddy's papers and then turn him over to Grandmother. We were going to have him work at the stables in town and live with Grandmother so you would still be able to visit with him."

Across the room, Spencer whimpered, and Kiara hurried to the cradle and lifted him into her arms. "Is he hungry?"

Jasmine nodded and took the baby, gently putting him to her breast. "You know, Paddy had several people looking out for his welfare. Papa related that Matthew Cheever had approached him, offering to buy Paddy's papers on behalf of a dear friend. At quite a profit, I might add," she said with a smile. "Once my father explained the final arrangements he was making with Grandmother, Mr. Cheever acknowledged the boy would be safe with her and he did not pursue the matter further."

" 'Twas Rogan at the heart of that," Kiara whispered, her love for him doubling as she grasped the depth of his kindness.

"Rogan?"

Kiara's cheeks grew hot with embarrassment. "Rogan Sheehan, Bridgett's cousin from the Acre. He works for Liam Donohue. He knew of my plight and said he would be helpin' find a way to save Paddy. He told me to pray, but I grew angry and told him I did na trust him or God to take care of Paddy. Rogan said Mr. Donohue was a friend of Mr. Cheever and he might help, but I did na think anyone would help. But I was wrong. Look how many people were tryin' to help me and Paddy. It seems God does care about us after all."

Jasmine smiled at her friend. "You know, Kiara, God has always cared about you and Paddy. If you'd only stop being afraid to believe others love you, you might find yourself truly blessed and even happy."

Kiara gave her a lopsided grin. "You're likely right, Missus—maybe that's already true." Kiara gave her a thoughtful glance. "But I still do na understand how ya happened to be in the barn that day."

"Early that morning, I went into Bradley's study, and what I saw made me believe he'd been up late into the night transferring figures. He had a new ledger, not the one I'd seen him use in the past, and the ink was still wet on the last page. That in itself might not have persuaded me, but the entries were for the months prior—all obviously entered that evening. I knew he was to have a meeting with my father to go over the accounts later that morning. I feared he was stealing money from my father and the other cotton producers in Mississippi and Louisiana. But I knew I wouldn't be able to prove what Bradley had done because I didn't have the original ledger book, so I closed the new book, knowing the pages would smudge and stick together."

Kiara looked unconvinced. "He could have told yar father he fergot to blot the pages and that would have been the end of it. I do na understand."

"If the pages were smudged in several places, it showed he had entered the figures all at one time rather than a few entries at a time, as would be normal."

Kiara's eyes sparkled and she nodded her head. "Oh, I see! Ya're quite the clever one, ain't ya?"

"I'm not pleased I had to resort to such tactics, but I knew something must be done to make Bradley come to his senses. I went to my father and explained Bradley was making false entries in the ledger. We agreed it was time for Bradley to admit what he'd been doing. My father was willing to work with him to resolve any misappropriation of money, still wanting to believe Bradley was merely under stress from being overworked. They met as planned, and my father slipped away for a cigar, knowing Bradley would discover the final pages were smeared and stuck together."

"So yar father was off to get a cigar, knowin' Mr. Houston would have to make a decision as to how he was going to handle his lyin' and stealin.'"

"Exactly. However, we thought he would beg Papa's forgiveness and ask to pay back the money he'd stolen. When he stormed from the room without showing my father the final pages, we knew he'd sneak from the house at the first possible opportunity. Papa immediately went to the barn to hide and wait for Bradley."

"And you, ma'am, where did *you* go?"

"I feared Bradley might grow violent when my father confronted him. So I went upstairs to get Bradley's pistol."

"I think I know the rest," Kiara said. "I'm truly sorry for all that's happened. My guilt is deep. Had I never come to this place, yar babe would still have a father and ya'd not be a widow, but I want ya to believe I never wanted nothin' bad to come yar way. I tried to stop him, but I could na. I'm beggin' yar forgiveness, fer ya have been nothin' but good to me."

"Oh, Kiara, you owe me no apology," Jasmine said, pulling the girl into an embrace. "If it will make you feel better to hear me say I forgive you, then know that for any perceived wrong you believe you've done, I give you my forgiveness. However, I know you were an innocent victim, and I believe you would never intentionally hurt me."

Kiara pulled a handkerchief from her pocket and wiped her eyes. Jasmine's forgiveness lifted her burden of guilt, yet she knew that it was God's forgiveness she truly wanted and needed—not for the things Bradley had done to her, for those reprehensible acts were not of her making. The visits he had made to her bed were his sin, not hers, and she knew she'd not face God's retribution for Bradley Houston's ugly deeds.

But she had hardened her heart against God. Even when Jasmine had read Bible verses to her, she'd turned away, not wanting to hear the truth of what God would tell her.

"Please don't cry, Kiara. All is forgiven and you're going to be fine," Jasmine said, obviously confused that Kiara's tears had not yet subsided.

"I'm thinkin' I'd like to be askin' God's forgiveness fer turning away from Him. Would ya be willin' to pray with me?"

Jasmine grasped Kiara's hands firmly in her own. "Nothing would please me more, dear friend."

———

"Kiara, could you come to the parlor? I need some help with Spencer," Jasmine called.

Kiara hurried down the hallway while wiping her hands on the tail of her worn cotton apron, wondering what possible help Jasmine might need with the wee babe. She stopped short when she reached the parlor doorway. Rogan and Paddy were seated side by side on the settee, and Alice Wainwright was settled in the sewing rocker. Jasmine was holding Spencer, while Nolan Houston sat opposite her.

Seeing all of them gathered together caused her to clutch the hem of her apron all the more tightly. "What's all this about?" Her voice warbled unrecognizably in her own ears.

"I sent Paddy to fetch Rogan. I thought he should be here for this gathering," Jasmine replied. "Come sit down and join us." She patted the cushion of a nearby chair.

Kiara's gaze darted from person to person as she made her way to the chair. They all smiled at her, yet she wasn't completely sure she could trust their smiles. There was an ominous feel to such an odd grouping of people. "And why are we all here?" she asked.

Jasmine handed the baby to Alice and retrieved several sheets of paper from the mahogany side table. "This is your contract of servitude," she said, showing it to Kiara.

"Aye. That it is."

"And this is Paddy's, given to me by my father," Jasmine added.

"I see," Kiara said, but in truth she did not.

Jasmine walked to the fireplace and threw the papers into the crackling fire. Kiara watched in awe as the flames licked up around the white pages, charring them as black as night. The fire snapped and ebbed as the burnt paper quickly turned to an ashy residue.

"You're free to go wherever you choose. Nobody owns you; nobody can hold you against your will ever again," Jasmine said. "But I want you to know that it's my hope that you and Paddy will stay here with me for a time. Grandmother has agreed to move in with me, but if you and Paddy are of a mind to make a decent wage, we could certainly use your help."

Kiara stared at Jasmine, unable to say a word. The woman's kindness had rendered her completely speechless.

"Can we stay, Kiara? Can we?" Paddy asked excitedly as he jumped up from the settee and danced about in front of her as though he'd been attacked by a colony of red ants. "Ya know I do na want to leave the horses. Ya do know that, don't ya?"

"I can na even think with you hoppin' from foot to foot in front of me, Padraig. Sit yarself down. I do na know how to thank ya for what ya're doing fer us, ma'am. As fer stayin' and helpin' ya . . ."

Rogan got up and stood before Kiara. "Before ya go makin' any rash decisions, lass, I've got somethin' to say in this matter. Ya know I'm in love with ya, lass, and I'm wantin' ta make ya my wife. Will ya marry me, Kiara O'Neill?"

Tears rolled freely down Kiara's cheeks as she nodded her head vigorously.

Rogan lifted her hand to his lips. "I do na have a ring ta give ya just yet, but I hope ya know my heart is full of love fer ya," he said. "I hope ya're not angry with me, Mrs. Houston."

Jasmine gave him a broad smile. "I had Paddy bring you here because I knew of your feelings for Kiara. I would never deny her the joy of finding true love. I've no doubt you make a fine wage working for Liam Donohue, but it's still my hope that Kiara and Paddy will make their home with me until you wed. I was even thinking that perhaps the three of you might be comfortable in the small caretaker's house until you decide where you might want to eventually settle."

Paddy moved close to Rogan's side. "I told her ya loved Kiara and wanted to buy a big farm out West when ya saved enough money."

Rogan tousled the boy's mop of black curls. "Aye, 'tis true enough."

"If we stayed here, I could help with the housework and the babe while we saved our money to buy a farm," Kiara said. "Do ya think that would work?" She searched Rogan's eyes for any sign of objection.

"I think ya may have a good idea, lass. One that would work well for all of us."

"And I want you to keep making your lace, Kiara," Alice said, holding up a piece of handwork from Kiara's basket. "There are plenty of women who are willing to pay a good price for it."

"I think we've got a plan, but perhaps it should be sealed with a kiss," Rogan said, pulling Kiara to her feet. "If ya will excuse us, I think we'll step outside fer a wee bit."

Paddy hurried to join them, but Alice quickly interceded. "I'm going to take Spencer up to the nursery for his mother. Why don't you come along and help me, Paddy? Do you remember an Irish song you could sing to Spencer while I rock him to sleep?"

"Aye, that I do. Before the famine, me mum and Kiara sang all the time. I'll sing him the lullaby Kiara used to sing to me."

"And I'm certain he'll enjoy every note," Alice said while lifting the baby out of Jasmine's arms. Paddy tagged along at her heels like a duckling following in parade formation.

"Thank ya," Kiara whispered to the older woman.

Alice winked and smiled. "Go on, now, before Rogan decides you're not interested."

The fire burned low. Only Jasmine and Nolan remained in the room. "I understand you've been seeing Velma Buthorne. She's a lovely young lady," Jasmine observed.

"Yes. She enjoys literature, and we have many acquaintances in common. I'm not certain she shares my strong abolition beliefs, but at least she voices a distaste for slavery."

"Her father is a member of the Associates, is he not?"

"I understand he recently invested quite heavily in order to become a member of the group. Prior to that, he owned a small group of mills in New Hampshire, along with a small shipping business. He controlled much of his own operation. I would assume he grew weary of shouldering the entire burden and viewed an investment with the Associates as a way of remaining in a business he knew while increasing his stature and wealth."

"Similar to Bradley," she mused. "Of course, Bradley was primarily enamored with the power he hoped would come his way once he became aligned with the Associates."

Resting his elbow on the arm of the chair, Nolan cupped his chin on one hand and looked at Jasmine. "I'm truly sorry for all the unhappiness you experienced in your marriage to Bradley."

"Yet had it not been for my marriage to Bradley, I wouldn't have Spencer, nor would I have developed a closer relationship to God. And my father and I have also learned some difficult lessons—he about his priorities and I about forgiveness. So, you see, there is good that can come out of even the most difficult situations," she said. "Of course, I must admit that while I was going through my trying circumstances, I didn't see anything but the desperation of my situation. It took God's strength to help me through each day, and now I can say I know I've become a better person because of all that's occurred in my life."

Nolan's eyes shone with admiration. "You're an amazing woman, Jasmine. I'm hoping that once Spencer is a little older and your life has settled, you'll give consideration to joining those of us who are growing bolder in our stand against slavery. I know your ability to work with the movement was thwarted by your marriage to Bradley as well as Spencer's impending birth, but I also know when we visited Mississippi, your heart was heavy when you saw the conditions on your father's plantation. And, as I told you, most plantations are even worse than The Willows."

"I don't know how much I'll be able to help, but you know you can count on my support wherever and however I can be used, Nolan. Grandmother has remained active in the antislavery movement here in Lowell, and now I'll be able to attend meetings with her once again. I've been told there's an even stronger movement here in Lowell than I had thought, and that pleases me."

"True. We've received both financial and verbal support, but it's dedicated workers who are willing to accept the risk and actually help more of our brothers and sisters find their way to freedom that make us truly blessed."

Jasmine nodded. "Placing yourself or others in peril is always a difficult choice. Now that I have a son, I can certainly understand the dilemma. I would give little thought to placing myself in jeopardy, while I would give grave consideration to such a notion should Spencer become endangered."

Nolan pulled his chair closer. "I know this may be an awkward time, but there is another matter on which we must speak."

Jasmine raised a brow. "Pray speak of it, then."

Nolan took a deep breath. "It has come to my attention through our family solicitor that Bradley has left his holdings to me."

Jasmine inhaled sharply. "I . . . what does this mean?" She knew that if she were left penniless her grandmother and father would see to her and Spencer's welfare, but that wasn't the way she wanted it.

"I don't want you to worry," Nolan said, his expression revealing deep concern. "I've already spoken to the solicitor and transferred everything to you, including this property. I do not want Bradley's holdings, neither do I wish to deny his wife and child their rightful inheritance. I have no understanding of why my brother did this. Perhaps he honestly never thought to change his will. Perhaps he did. But it doesn't matter at this point. Quite frankly, I'm surprised he left anything to me at all. The only thing he ever gave me in our adult life was his disapproval. But no matter—I've made it right."

Jasmine felt a deep tenderness for Nolan, for his gesture went beyond expectations. No one would have faulted the man had he maintained the inheritance left to him by his brother. After all, the shipping company had been in their family for many years. "I'm deeply touched you would do this," Jasmine said, lowering her face. She felt tears form in her eyes and willed them not to fall. "You have shown me nothing but honor and kindness throughout my marriage—even before that. Thank you for this."

"You needn't thank me for doing what should never have needed to be done. I do want to add that I have arranged for a man of good repute to handle the business affairs on your behalf. He will send you a monthly report and I myself will review his bookkeeping on a quarterly basis. I have directed him to deposit your funds here in Lowell when he comes to bring you the accounting of your affairs."

"I trust that you know best, Nolan. I have no reason to doubt you have seen to things in the very best of ways." She wiped at her eyes and looked up to meet his smiling face.

"I'm glad we've had opportunity for this chat. As you know, I must be leaving in the morning, but I want you to remember I am at your bidding—you need only send word. I want to be of assistance however I'm needed. Most importantly, I want to spend time with my nephew."

"And that is my desire also. I'm thankful for the time you've been able to spend with us, but I know you have matters needing your attention in Boston."

"What's this I hear?" Alice asked as she fluttered into the room. "You're leaving us?"

"I'm afraid so, but I've told Jasmine I'll be returning soon. I leave her in your capable hands," he said.

Jasmine's grandmother gave him a sly grin. "I think she'd be much better off in your warm embrace than my capable hands."

"Grandmother!" Jasmine felt her cheeks flush. "Nolan is courting Velma Buthorne. He doesn't need you playing the matchmaker. And you need remember I'm in mourning for his brother."

"Oh, pshaw! More likely you and Nolan are mourning the fact that Bradley didn't turn from his malevolent ways before his death. I know society has its code of etiquette and we're expected to hold fast to those rules, but—"

Jasmine held up her hand and silenced her grandmother.

"Enough of this talk. I believe we all need to get some rest. Nolan has an early departure in the morning."

"You will come back for Christmas, won't you, Mr. Houston?" Jasmine looked first to her grandmother and then to Nolan. "Please say you will," she encouraged.

"I would be honored. You are, after all, my only family. I will return with gifts and food and we shall have a festive time, despite Bradley and his passing."

"He was your brother; I do not expect you to forgo mourning his death," Jasmine said softly. She looked to Nolan, hoping he understood that she wanted very much to celebrate the Lord's birth but would put it aside for the sake of Nolan's feelings.

"I will mourn Bradley's passing in my own way," Nolan admitted, "but I will not forsake Christmas in order to do so. What say I come back the Saturday before? We'll go to church together— you too, Mrs. Wainwright. Then we'll have the whole week to make merry and decorate and find a tree. Would you like that?" He looked to Jasmine, his expression hopeful.

Jasmine nodded, knowing in her heart that nothing would please her more, unless it would be having the rest of her family with her for the occasion.

Nolan grinned. "Then it's settled. I'll be here."

CHAPTER · 31

JASMINE FOUND that as Christmas neared, she could hardly wait for Nolan's return. Grandmother said it was because Jasmine's feelings for Nolan were stronger and more important than she gave them credit for, but Jasmine said it was because of the holidays.

She had never looked at Christmas in the way she did this year. Before it had always been a happy celebration of family and friends, gifts and food. This year, however, with the birth of Spencer, she found herself caught up in the Christmas story. How wondrous that God would send His Son to earth as a babe. So tiny and helpless, just like Spencer. Jasmine thought of Mary and how hard it must have been to know the truth of the situation. Her son would also be her Savior. The very thought was marvelous and overwhelming to Jasmine.

When Saturday arrived and Nolan's appearance became reality, Jasmine knew there had been some truth in Grandmother's words. She was happy to see Nolan again; he made her feel safe and content . . . and there was much to be had in those feelings.

"I'm so glad the snow didn't stop you," Jasmine exclaimed as Nolan gave his coat and hat to Sarah.

"I do not think anything could stop those monstrous

contraptions of iron," he declared. "The locomotive is truly an amazing beast."

"Smelly and loud, if you ask me," Grandmother said, eyeing Nolan. "Have you eaten lately? You look half starved."

"I will admit that a meal would suit me fine just now."

Jasmine smiled. "Then it is a good thing we are nearly ready to sit to supper. Would you like to wash up?"

"Thank you, I would."

"I've got the bags," Paddy announced proudly as he came struggling through the front door.

"And so I see," Nolan replied as he took the largest of the three. "If you know the way to my room, why don't you lead me on?" He leaned down conspiratorially and added, "I'm supposed to wash up."

Paddy scowled. "The lasses are always makin' us wash up."

Nolan's face grew serious as he nodded. "'Tis the truth of it, my good man. 'Tis the truth."

Jasmine giggled as the men made their way upstairs. She and Grandmother exchanged a humored look and headed into the parlor to wait.

"You seem quite pleased to have him here," her grandmother said with a knowing nod.

"Stop trying to match us," Jasmine protested, but only half-heartedly. Nolan's absence and her reaction to it had given her much to ponder. "He has great virtues, but I'll not shame my family by acting the disrespectful widow."

"Pshaw! You never loved Bradley. You were forced from the start to marry him. If tongues wag because you take up with his brother, then they will have to wag. If you let true love get away from you, you'll always regret it."

Jasmine sobered. "But I don't know that it is true love. I may simply be longing for that which I've never known. I would like to give it time, Grandmother. Please honor my wishes. Nolan is a fine man. I wouldn't want to hurt him."

Grandmother sat by Jasmine and took hold of her hands. "I promise to mind my ways. I just want to see you happy. I feel I had a part in your misery with Bradley, in that I didn't try hard enough to intercede on your behalf. For that I'm truly sorry."

"And you are forgiven," Jasmine said with a grin. "For you have blessed me far more than any harm you perceive done. I thank God for you."

"And I for you, my sweet Jasmine."

Christmas week was delightful for all in the Houston household. Throughout the week they attended parties, and on Thursday, Nolan went deep into the woods and brought back the most perfect of trees.

"I think this is simply the most marvelous of traditions," Jasmine declared. "It makes the entire house smell wonderful. And I love the snow. This is only my second Christmas with snow."

"Come February you'll tire of it quickly enough," Nolan declared. He positioned the tree in the corner of the parlor and stood back to observe. "There. That should serve us quite nicely."

"Grandmother and I have made the decorations," Jasmine announced. "And we have the most marvelous candles to attach to the boughs. It's going to be beautiful."

Nolan smiled, his gaze never leaving her. "I have no doubt."

She smiled in return, knowing in her heart that this time next Christmas, things might be very different between her and Nolan. He'd not even hinted at his feelings, but she could see in his eyes— his expression—that he was feeling much the same as she.

On Christmas morning Jasmine awoke to a wondrous stillness. Spencer was sleeping soundly in the cradle by her bed. She'd had Kiara move him here because she enjoyed tending him herself. Kiara completely understood and because there was no longer anything to fear from Bradley, she relished the idea of going back to her own room.

Rolling to her side, Jasmine watched her son as he slept. From time to time he would suck at the air, his little lips pursing and relaxing in rhythm. It wouldn't be long before he awoke, demanding his breakfast.

Jasmine yawned and threw back the covers. The room was quite warm in spite of the chilly weather outside. Kiara was always good to slip in early and stir up the fire. Jasmine didn't know how the girl managed to do it so quietly, but she never disturbed Jasmine's sleep.

A quick look out the window revealed it was snowing. It seemed rather perfect for the day. Jasmine pulled on her robe and for the strangest reason thought of Bradley. She almost expected him to come bounding into the room demanding his son.

"His son," she mused. "As if I had no part in his existence."

She took up her Bible and, as had become her practice, settled into reading and praying. Still the thoughts of Bradley would not leave her.

"What is it I need to ponder, Lord? Is there something here about Bradley that I yet need to know?" Anger edged her tone, surprising Jasmine. "He's dead. Dead and buried and gone from my life. I need never think of him again."

But she knew that wasn't true. Spencer was proof of that. She would always have some part of Bradley in her life. The thought chilled her. Surprised by her reaction, Jasmine got up and began to pace. Still clinging to the Bible, she tried to sort through her scattered thoughts.

He was a cruel man. He demanded so much of us and nothing of himself. He stole my father's money and my innocence—as well as Kiara's. With each thought, Jasmine felt her anger mount.

He lied and cheated and wounded people just for sport. I'm glad he's dead. I'm glad he's gone. I don't want Spencer to ever know him. I don't want Spencer tainted by his father's blood.

She paused long enough to look down on her child. Bradley's child. He even looked somewhat like his father, only Jasmine comforted herself by believing he looked more like Bradley's mother and Nolan. She drew a ragged breath and suddenly realized she was crying.

"I don't want you to be like him," she whispered. "Please, God, don't let Spencer grow up to be like Bradley."

You must forgive Bradley.

The thought was startling. Jasmine stepped back and shook her head. "I don't want to forgive him. He didn't ask for forgiveness. He didn't believe himself guilty of anything. Why should I forgive him?"

Jasmine tried to steady her breathing and calm her anger. "Forgiveness—that's asking an awful lot, Lord."

She went to her rocking chair and sat back down. Shaking her head, Jasmine opened the Bible again, but she couldn't see the words for all of her tears. A knock sounded on the door and before she could acknowledge it, Kiara peeked in.

"Are ya all right?" she asked, then stopped. "No, for sure I can see that ya are na all right." She came into the room unbidden. "Now, what would be causin' ya such grief on the day of the Lord's birth?"

Jasmine lowered her face and shook her head again. "I don't wish to discuss it."

Kiara surprised her by kneeling beside the rocker. "My heart is breakin' for ya. Please let me share yar burden."

"It's Bradley," Jasmine said finally. She looked up and met Kiara's stunned look.

"And how would that man be causin' ya problems today?"

"I don't know. I just started thinking about him and I got so angry. All I wanted to do was shout and scream, and if Spencer hadn't been sleeping right here, I probably would have." Jasmine tried to push down her rage, but it resurfaced. "That man hurt so many people. People I love and care about. He hurt my father and mother—my brothers. He hurt my uncles and their families and you. Oh, I can't even bear to think about the pain he caused you." Jasmine buried her face in her hands, but Kiara reached up and drew them down.

"Miss Jasmine, ya can na go on like this. For sure, Bradley Houston caused a lot of hurt and sufferin', but he's gone. He can na hurt anyone ever again. Ya must forgive 'im and make a new life."

Jasmine gasped. "What did you say?"

Kiara looked confused. "I said ya must forgive 'im and make a new life."

Jasmine closed her eyes and leaned back in the rocker. "That's exactly what God told me. At least the forgiving part. But how can you say that? Can you forgive him for what he did? He stole your innocence. He threatened you. He hurt Paddy and—"

"Stop!" Kiara said, holding up her hand. "There's nothin' to be gained by such talk. Ya'll only hurt yarself—and Spencer."

"I don't understand."

"I know 'tis hard, but forgiveness truly frees the one who does the forgivin' as much as it frees the one forgiven. I will not go on through life holdin' Mr. Bradley a grudge. He's gone and my grudges can only hurt me—not him. For sure he stole what wasn't his to take, but God has restored me. Rogan doesn't care. He knows 'twas not my fault."

"He's a good man."

Kiara smiled. "Aye, he is. And ya're a good woman, and God is callin' ya to forgive yar husband. He can na hurt ya anymore, unless 'tis in this manner. If ya go on like this, then Bradley Houston's wounds will go on as well. Make yar peace, Miss Jasmine. Forgive him for what he's done. If ya don't, ya'll end up holding yar son a grudge because he's the only part of Bradley Houston that's left alive to blame."

Spencer began to fuss and Jasmine looked across the room to her son. Blaming her son for Bradley's mistakes . . . the insight of Kiara's words made her heart ache.

"Why don't I take him to the nursery and change him for ya?" Kiara suggested. "Then ya can nurse him."

"Thank you." She watched Kiara lovingly lift the baby in her arms. She spoke calmly as she crossed the room with the boy. Jasmine looked to the ornately molded ceiling and sighed.

"Oh, Father, I see the truth. I see what you've been trying to show me since Bradley died—maybe even before that. It's hard to forgive him, but I want to, Lord. I'm asking you to help me forgive him. I don't know what caused his heart to be so black, for surely he must have been tender and good at some time in his life."

She thought of Spencer and how Bradley might have been very much like him as an infant. No doubt his parents had been quite proud and joyous over his birth.

"Help me, Father. I want to forgive and forget the past. I want to forgive Bradley for all that he did against me, for I never want any of it to come between Spencer and me."

"Here he is," Kiara called as she returned with the baby. "He's mighty hungry and ready for his Christmas breakfast."

Jasmine laughed and took her son in her arms. "Come, my little one." She nuzzled him to her and smiled down into his open eyes. "My precious little one."

———

The Christmas revelry did much to lift her spirits. Jasmine was quite pleased to receive a lovely ruby brooch from her grandmother, an heirloom that had once belonged to her great-grandmother on her father's side. She was also deeply touched by a gift of lace from Kiara and a red ribbon for her hair from Paddy.

"Why, Paddy, it's absolutely perfect and it goes very well with my new brooch." The boy beamed.

"I picked it out meself," he said proudly.

"Aye, I can be vouchin' for that," Rogan said. "He took nearly an hour doin' so."

Jasmine laughed. She was so glad that Kiara and Paddy, along with Rogan, had agreed to spend part of their Christmas with them.

"And here's my gift," Nolan said, reaching behind the couch to pull out a large parcel wrapped in cloth. "I hope you like it."

Jasmine tilted her head to one side, trying to ascertain what Nolan had brought her. As she reached to take the package, Nolan waved her off. "I'd best hold it while you untie the string. It's quite heavy."

Jasmine worked to unfasten the bindings. When she'd managed this, she pushed back the cloth and gasped. "Oh!"

"It's my family," Nolan explained. "A family portrait when I was five."

She looked into the faces of the Houston family. Bradley's parents sat regally, while a very young Nolan and a smiling Bradley, fifteen years Nolan's senior, stood on either side.

"I know it might seem a strange painting, but I wanted you to believe and know that Bradley was not always a bad person. When I was young he was a loving and nurturing older brother. All who knew him were impressed with his manners and gentle nature. At times he seemed more like a father than a brother."

Jasmine looked to Kiara and then her grandmother. "What happened to change him?" For the first time she honestly cared to know the truth.

"He would never admit it, but I believe the mantle of responsibility made him old before his time. He was very close to our father, and he longed only to impress him. Little by little it consumed his life—he soon gave up everything that was important to him, even a young woman whom he cared for very much. They had been friends from a young age. They were to be married, but the business distanced Bradley from her and by the time he realized what he had lost, she had married another."

"How very sad," Jasmine said, feeling genuine sorrow for her husband.

"I wanted you to have this portrait of our family because it was made at a time when we were all very close and very happy."

"Thank you, Nolan. This will be a special gift for Spencer. I will prominently display it that he might take pride in his heritage." She met Kiara's gaze across the room. The girl smiled broadly.

The forgiving had begun.

That night in her bedroom, Jasmine sat nursing her son. Spencer grew more sleepy by the minute, his eyelids lifting heavily, then closing again. She almost hated for him to fall asleep. With Spencer awake and nursing, Jasmine didn't feel quite so alone.

"Oh, Spencer. You'll never know your father firsthand, and in some ways I think that a better way. Yet you are the best of him.

You are the love that he should have known." The baby finally stopped nursing, closing his eyes in sleep.

Jasmine put him to her shoulder and patted him gently on the back. "He loved you—there's no doubt of that. I think he honestly loved you more than anyone. You actually made him smile."

She thought of her dead husband and the past and knew there was nothing there for her. Nothing but sad memories of a hopeless relationship that could never be put straight. Kiara was right: forgiveness was the better path.

Still, her son was without a father now. She thought of Nolan's kindness and generous spirit and had to admit that those qualities had always attracted her. She had no desire to be untrue to her vows; she was simply sad that she had never seen those qualities in her husband.

But there was hope. With God, there was always hope.

Putting Spencer in his cradle, Jasmine knelt down and smiled. "We are in His hands, Spencer, and there's no other place I'd rather be. We're going to be fine—you'll see. For God has already seen our tomorrows and has smoothed the path before us. He has woven our lives as a tapestry of hope. Hope in His love. Hope for all of our tomorrows."

BESTSELLING
HISTORICAL FICTION
For Every Reader!

The Acadian Saga Continues...

History comes to life in this captivating new story of an American woman in the Court of St. James, formed by the new writing team of T. Davis Bunn and his wife, Isabella.

With the War of 1812 raging, Erica Langston is left to deal with creditors circling her family business. Her only recourse is to travel to England to collect on outstanding debts, but her arrival leads her into the most unexpected predicaments and encounters.

The Solitary Envoy
by T. Davis and Isabella Bunn

Bestselling Author Tracie Peterson's Unforgettable New Saga

From her own Big Sky home, Tracie Peterson paints a one-of-a-kind portrait of 1860s Montana and the strong, spirited men and women who dared to call it home.

Dianne Chadwick is one of those homesteaders, but she has no idea what to expect—or even if she'll make it through the arduous wagon ride west. Protecting her is Cole Selby, a guide who acts as though his heart is as hard as the mountains. Can Dianne prove otherwise?

Land of My Heart by Tracie Peterson

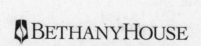